House of Rejects

DEVIN HOBBES

This is a work of fiction. All characters appearing in this work are fictitious. Any resemblance to real persons, living or dead, is purely coincidental. Organizations and events portrayed in this novel are either products of the author's imagination or are used fictitiously

ISBN: 0983754004
ISBN-13:9780983754008

Kidneymountain Publishing
facebook.com/HobbesDevin
Devinhobbes.blogspot.com

This is for Liza

ACKNOWLEDGMENTS

I'd like to thank Liza Lopez for supporting, encouraging, and pushing me to write. I'm also grateful to Mario, Edith, Christine, Tommy, Roger, and Lucky Joy for allowing me to turn their story into a novel.

CHAPTER ONE
Thursday, September 6, 1990

Roger frowned. His nervousness grew as he entered the school through the front doors into the space that served as both the gym and the cafeteria. Having heard the bell a block away he knew he was late. He had hoped, however, that things would begin at least a bit later on the first day. Roger hated being late. All his father's fault. "Wait for me, I'll take you," he'd said. Unable to wait any longer, Roger went by himself.

Since his class was in room 201, he made a left turn after the abandoned security guard's desk, walking toward the nearby staircase. Just as Roger opened the door leading to the stairs, a firm hand grabbed and spun him around. Startled, he looked up at a red, glowering face. He attempted to cringe, but the giant held him up.

"You're late!" A foul gust of air hit Roger's face. Although he wore a white button down shirt, a tie, and blue slacks, the piggish man reminded Roger of a drill sergeant from one of those war movies his dad liked to watch. He had no idea who this man was. He must have been new, or Roger was quite fortunate not to have run into him the past three years.

"Well? What have you got to say for yourself?"

Roger avoided the man's bloodshot blue eyes by looking at the beads of sweat collecting in the wrinkles on his forehead. He hoped none of them would fall on him. Roger didn't know what to say, so he kept quiet. He wasn't even sure his mouth would open.

"Alright wise guy. What's your name?"

"R-r-r-r—"

"Come on, spit it out." The man took out a pad. He removed a pen from his shirt pocket and violently clicked it, readying it for use.

"R-r-oger Wha-w-w-wharton." It finally came out. One of the hardest words for Roger to say was his own name. A trick he had discovered, while watching a PBS documentary about an MIT graduate student who stuttered, was to think of his last name before trying to say his first name. It often helped. Not so much this time.

"Well, Roger Wharton, you're late," the man said, writing. He ignored the commotion behind him as two older students ran into the building. Roger recognized the two loudmouths that sometimes bothered him in previous years. Brian and Craig were their names. Brian was definitely a fifth grader. Craig might've been younger. A few seconds later, the door burst open again, and one of Roger's classmates, Clyde Lee, hopped in on one foot after them. Brian carried a sneaker, holding it as a running back holds a football.

"Hey, give it back!" Clyde sobbed, bouncing toward Brian. Craig caught the sneaker and ran toward the basketball hoop on the opposite side of the cavernous room. He passed it back to Brian, who did a layup. The sneaker got stuck in the net with a swoosh. Clyde had no chance of reaching it with his jumps, but that didn't stop him from trying. Brian and Craig walked toward the staircase on the far right, and disappeared through the door.

The man finished filling out the form, detached it from his pad, and thrust it at Roger. "Report to the Principal's Office. Give them that," he pinned the form to Roger's chest with his index finger, "or you will be in more trouble." The man turned around and walked to Clyde. "Hey you! Where's your hall pass? You're late and it's against school policy to not have footwear on. What is your name?" Clyde started crying.

As Roger walked toward the staircase to the far right, which had a sign next to it with an arrow: "Principal's Office," another boy entered the school. He rolled on a skateboard past the man and sobbing Clyde, noisily flipped the board up to catch it in his hands, and went into the bathroom. The man paid him no attention. Instead, he told Roger to stop running. He wasn't. "I'll be watching you, Wharton," he called.

An inauspicious start to the third grade.

* * *

3

Ahead of Roger were the narrow stairs leading up to a landing where one had to turn right. The walls were painted green, and in some places gray. They had indentations, perhaps windows that had been painted over. Murky glass panels reflected the dim light at the top of the landing. Somewhere beyond them, one looking from below would be able to see the silhouettes of little children walking up or down the stairs. To the right were stairs leading down into the basement. They were sealed off by a chain-link fence, which had a sign with three black triangles on a yellow background with the words "fallout shelter" written above. Mysterious mechanical noises that usually intrigued Roger clanked down below. Other than the fresh coat of red paint on the railings, the staircase looked the same to Roger as it did two months before, albeit a tad smaller.

Roger pressed his teeth together and began walking up the stairs. Although he already knew how many steps were between each flight, he counted them to calm himself. To his nervousness of being late was added the dread of visiting the Principal's Office. Such thoughts, and the effort to keep from having a bowel movement, kept him from registering the muffled sounds of laughter and struggle above. Rounding the corner, Roger came upon Brian and Craig about halfway up the second flight of stairs, blocking the path to the second floor doorway. Craig held a round boy from behind, one hand covering the boy's mouth. Brian worked on the boy's stomach with his fists.

Anger swelled up in Roger. His nervousness suddenly gone, he found himself running up the stairs two at a time. He punched Brian on the right side of his face, below the eye. A startled Brian whimpered and ran up. He turned at the second floor landing, holding his face. His footsteps faded away as he quickly ran toward the third floor. Now outnumbered, Craig let go of his victim and bounded up after Brian.

"Thanks," huffed the victim. Roger looked at him, perplexed. The boy wore a winter hat, from which sprouted thick black curls. Large red cheeks framed a button nose. White mittens were attached to his puffy brown coat sleeves. His brown trousers bunched up at his purple boots. His school bag, also puffy and appearing to contain many heavy items, was buckled to his waist. Below and above the buckle, the coat swelled like a balloon about to burst. The school bag dangled like a tail, the straps having slipped off the boy's shoulders. He looked to Roger like a cartoon mouse. Roger understood why Brian and Craig decided to greet him.

"Are y-you okay?" Roger asked.

"Uh huh," the boy shook his head in a gesture that Roger took to mean no. He gave the boy a look. "Sorry," Mouse said. After a pause he nodded vigorously. "My dad says I have dysflexia."

5

"W-w-what's that?"

"It's when you opposite two things against each other."

A bit confused, Roger changed the subject. "It's l-like 80 degrees t-t-today. Why are you w-wearing..." he pointed at Mouse's outfit.

"My dad said it was hot, I mean cold. He tolded me to put on warm stuffs." After a moment, the Mouse said, "I'm lost. I went with my sister to her room find. I don't know where to go."

"D-d-d—who is your teacher? D-d-d," damn it why won't that word come out? "You know who y-your teacher is?"

"Noppers," Mouse blinked and his cheeks puffed up. They weren't as red as before.

"D-d-d—w-what's your class? You know? The office can tell y-y-you w-w-w-where it is." He suddenly remembered that was his destination. The butterflies resumed their dance in his stomach.

"Three A," the boy replied, following Roger up to the second floor landing and crashing into him when Roger stopped.

"My class," Roger said after a pause. He skipped the word "that's" because it wouldn't come out. He took out the letter informing his parents about his class and room number, and looked at it for the millionth time. "Room two-oh-one. It w-will b-be around the k-corner and on the other side of the b-building."

"Thanks," the round boy said when they exited the staircase and the door closed behind them.

The Office was across the hall. "I have to go in there now," Roger said. Cold sweat gathered under his armpits. He gritted his teeth and turned the knob.

No one paid attention to him at the Principal's Office. All the old ladies were either on the phone or using their typewriters. Roger had never been sent there before, so he didn't know what to expect. He figured someone would yell at him, maybe call his parents. Roger thought he might have an interview with the Principal. This was worse. He didn't like interacting one on one with adults. These people had power over him, and getting on their bad side was never a good thing. He was also concerned about being late to class—becoming a spectacle when he came in. He wanted to be unnoticed. He would bother no one and no one would bother him. It was a great, if not real, arrangement that worked for him since kindergarten.

But now he would make a fashionably late entrance on the first day. Everyone would look at him, and he would have to explain himself. Roger dreaded public speaking more than almost anything. By now the class was seated and Mrs. Dixon was probably giving out coat hanger assignments.

Someone noticed him. Finally. A lady with gold rimmed glasses looked up from her typewriter. "Can I help you, sweetheart?"

"I um—I, I, s-sent he-he-here..." Roger hated his stuttering. In his mind the words came quickly and smoothly. Out of his mouth, it was a mush of awkward noises.

The lady saw the pink sheet in Roger's hand. "Oh, I see. I'll take that. Run along to class now, sweetheart."

That's it? That was it? What was the point of that? I'm not *that* late. I get sent to the Principal's Office. So now I *am* really *that* late. And they just take the sheet of paper from me and that's it? Instead of relief Roger felt anger. The stupidity! The bureaucrats!

Roger left the office with these thoughts. He assumed a brisk pace, taking out the letter once more to confirm the room number.

As he rounded the corner Roger came upon Mouse trying to break into a janitor's closet. He pulled on the handle with all his might, his red cheeks and green hat reminding Roger of Christmas. "Wa-What are you doing?"

"Trying   to   get   class   in.   I knocked...they...don't...let...in," Mouse said between pulls.

"Th-That's not our classroom...the janitor's closet."

Mouse turned to face Roger. "But you said room 201."

"Yeah, b-but you're trying to get into room 210."

"Oh."

Roger walked to class and Mouse followed. He felt some relief that he would not enter the room by himself, but he was also a bit annoyed. This was his last chance to pass gas without anyone noticing, and this round faced boy had to be here.

With his large intestine throbbing, Roger let out a quick nervous breath and opened the door. A woman, about 40 years old with straight black hair kept in place by a light green band, stopped talking and looked at them. Feeling his classmates' gaze, Roger summoned the courage to explain himself.

"You're Thomas and Roger?" the teacher asked. The boys replied that they were in unison. "Take your seats. Roger, you're over there," Mrs. Dixon pointed, "and you sit right here, Thomas."

That was surprisingly painless. The boys took their seats with relief. A moment later, Mrs. Dixon asked them where their late passes were.

* * *

Lunch was Roger's favorite school activity. He loved the food and going outside to the yard. The hamburgers, heated in their foil wrappers, were delicious. The bun, where it touched the patty, was moist, and some of it would get stuck when one opened the burger to apply ketchup or mustard. Roger sniffed at his food. The smell always made him want more, so he took his time. He chewed slowly and sniffed at the burger after each bite. Every few bites he separated the bun and patty in his mouth, chewing on the bread first and swallowing it, before chewing on the patty long enough to almost liquefy it.

Although he didn't like milk, it was the only thing to drink. Something about the burger made even the milk taste better. And after the milk, the hamburger was heaven. It came with tater tots, pickles, and apple sauce. Roger ate these first. He saved the best for last.

The Mouse, Roger had forgotten his name, sat down next to him, dropping a paper bag onto the table. "I'm soooo hungry," he said. Mouse took out a sandwich wrapped in a paper towel. He reached back into the bag and took out a pomegranate, a fruit Roger saw only a couple of times in his life, and a one liter bottle of seltzer. He looked at Roger, holding out the seltzer bottle. "Can you open this for me?"

While Roger opened the seltzer bottle, putting it under his shirt to get better traction, Tommy took out a couple of paper cups and started unwrapping his sandwich. Roger slowly let the gas escape from the bottle, twisting it open and closed every couple of seconds. He learned about a year ago (about 12.5% of his age, Roger noted) how not to get drenched when opening club soda. Mouse's sandwich was weird. What looked like a chicken patty stuck out between two slices of strange colored bread. Green leaves that didn't look like any lettuce Roger knew, and ketchup that didn't look like ketchup sat atop the "chicken." Roger set the seltzer bottle next to Mouse, who ate his sandwich like it was the greatest thing in the world. Mouse smacked his lips loudly, puffing his cheeks. Perhaps he wasn't a mouse but a hamster.

"W-What is that, a ch-chicken sandwi-wich?"

"I'm vegetarian," the boy responded, taking another bite. "This is BBQ seitan with romaine lettuce."

"S-Satan?"

"Seitan is made from wheat gluten. My dad let me make it so good."

Roger figured he could look up "gluten" later. "What's wrong with your bread? And why couldn't you eat regular lettuce?"

"It's organic whole wheat bread. I like romaine lettuce."

"Org-g-ganic?"

"Uh-huh," the Mouse replied, his sandwich finished.

"B-b-but w-w-w-what is it?" Organs didn't seem vegetarian to Roger. "I d-don't l-like l-l-liver."

The Mouse looked thoughtful for several moments. "I don't know. I think it's healthy." He reached into his bag again and took out a salad in a plastic container, which he opened delicately. He poured himself seltzer into a paper cup. "You want some sparklies?"

"N-no, thank you." Roger didn't like soda of any kind. "And that," he pointed at the salad, "is that weird lettuce and organs too?"

"It's a jicama and kale salad with pumpkin seeds," the Mouse smacked his lips to show Roger how delicious it was. Roger felt like he heard a foreign language. He ate his burger, looking askance at the Hamster and the salad.

The teachers' aides left their posts by the windows, strolling toward the staircase doors. Roger inferred that they would open the doors to the yard to let them out. He wasn't sure exactly, because it was his first time eating in the big kids' lunchroom.

In the K through 2nd lunchroom/auditorium some distance away, he had figured out all the patterns and almost always was able to guess what the adults would do next. Here, on the other hand, everything was new to him. It must have been new for Hamster as well, since Roger never saw him before.

"Are you new here?"

"Yuppers," the Hamster replied. Then after a pause he said, "Do you want to be my friend?"

The directness of the question took Roger aback. No one had ever asked him before. He blushed with the flattery. "Sh-sure," he replied.

"My name is Tommy," the Hamster said ebulliently, extending his left hand.

Roger shook Tommy's hand, finding it sweaty and sticky. "I'm R-r-ra-oger."

The aides did indeed open the doors to the yard. Roger glanced at the clock on the wall behind its cage. It looked about 12:25. Children began filing out of the building. Roger was about to get up to throw away his Styrofoam tray when someone large stood over them. Roger knew who it was when he saw the white shirt and red tie.

"What have we here?" the man boomed. "Soda is a prohibited item on school grounds. Whose is this?" The man picked up the plastic bottle.

"Hey, that's mine!" Tommy protested.

"Not anymore," the man glowered. "It is being confiscated."

"No fairs. Sparklies are good for my tummy."

"That's it wise guy, report to the Principal's Office."

"I know don't where it is." Tommy looked up at the man with wide eyes and puffed cheeks.

The man stopped filling out the form on his pad and looked at Tommy. "What's your name you troublemaker?"

"I'm not a troublemaker."

"Talking back gets you extra detention and it goes on your permanent record," the man warned. "What's your name?"

"Roger. I mean Tommy," the round cheeks turned red. His lower lip hid in his mouth.

Roger sat there fuming at the injustice, but he didn't know what to do.

"Come with me, wise guy. Let's see how you like the Principal's Office." The man dragged Tommy toward the stairs, awkwardly swinging his pad and the seltzer bottle with his left hand.

Roger sat there for a moment, shaking with anger. Who was this ruffian? Where did he come from? As if reading his thoughts, Clyde, seated opposite from him said, "I don't like that guy." Roger saw that Clyde's lips were still as chapped as they were last year. They were shinier though. His parents discovered petroleum jelly. Clyde adjusted his glasses and resumed reading his Hardy Boys book.

Roger wasn't sure what to do. He threw out his tray and decided to put what remained of Tommy's lunch back in the paper bag. Some of the dressing from the salad went on his fingers when he fumbled with the container. It took him some time. With the salad finally closed and in the bag with the pomegranate, Roger crumpled the top in an effort to close it. He was somewhat successful. He tasted the dressing on his fingers without thinking. It wasn't like anything he had before, but he didn't dislike it.

Michael Ramirez, the class clown, came up to Roger. He held a tennis ball. "You guys wanna play Suicide?"

Roger nodded.

Clyde looked up from his reading.

"Hurry up already!" Michael ran outside.

Roger followed him, grabbing Tommy's bag. He loved Suicide. Together with Boxball it was his favorite game. Suey, as they called it for short, required a ball that bounced, preferably a tennis or (to make things slightly harder and more painful) a blue rubber ball, a wall, concrete, and at least two players. Next to a wall of the school in the yard was the perfect place to play. Plenty of players were usually available. Some of the boys from each grade always had a game going.

The object of the game differed from day to day, but was generally to be the last person remaining by getting others "out" or by avoiding being out oneself. More frequently, and the way Roger and his classmates played, the goal wasn't being the first person out three times. This unfortunate player would stand with his face to the wall, his arms covering his head, while the other players lined up a dozen feet behind him, throwing the ball at him three times each.

Peter, a clumsy boy, was the first victim today. He said "ow!" even when Michael's throw missed him. Some boys, Dan for example, threw as fast as they could. The entire objective of the game was, after all, to get to this point: to hurt another player while he stood defenseless. "Just wait! I'll get you for this!" Peter screamed while the others laughed. A secondary objective was revenge.

With the mock execution over, the player (Peter) would be reset to zero outs, and the game would continue, until someone else (Peter), reached three outs.

Most of Suicide's rules and variations were announced mid-game by different players as situations requiring them arose. Such announcements were usually accompanied by calls of "no fair," "cheater!" and "that's not how we did it last year," but by the end of the first couple of games of the year, the rules were settled. Occasionally an upperclassman or oblivious outside party was called in to settle a dispute presented in a narrowly defined way: "so Mike throwed the ball and it hit the wall and it hit Mary, who's not playing, and it didn't bounce and then Dan caught it and hit Peter. Is Peter out?"

"Um..." said Jennifer, a fourth grader. "Who's Peter?" She looked the chubby red haired boy over. "He's out."

"No fair!"

Such a judge's decisions were final. The decision having been rendered, Clyde announced the general principle of the case: "when the ball hits the wall with no bounces and hits someone not playing and you catched it, it's the same when you catched it when it just hits the wall."

"Or someone who's playing," Roger added. Everyone agreed but Peter. Since he was in the minority, he got a second out. One more and he would be back at the wall. If a similar situation arose later among the same group of players, or enough of them, this case would be a precedent, and it would generally be decided the same way, without outside arbitration. New players who joined in the weeks and months following were given some leeway until they were familiar with what was expected of them, probably a fairer arrangement than most.

The whistles blew. Peter rubbed his butt next to the wall. Roger and Clyde didn't get to throw at him in this second execution. Roger went to the wall and grabbed Tommy's bag. He walked briskly to where his class lined up in size order in two lines, one for boys and one for girls. Before he reached his class two older boys intercepted him. He recognized the one about his size as Harry, a fourth grader. The other, a giant he never saw before, must have been left back a couple of times.

No way could someone be that big and not be in junior high.

"Brian says he'll see you after school," Harry said. The other boy, the muscle, stood there silently. He stared into empty space with vacant eyes. With the message delivered, Harry turned to go. "Come on, Alex," he called after his companion. The large boy turned around and followed him. Apparently he was a fourth grader, or at least that is where Roger saw him line up. Roger went to his own line, jostling in front of Michael and behind Gregory after comparing heights with them. Same as last year.

Mrs. Dixon came down with Tommy in tow. He pouted as the teacher inserted him into the line. He was toward the front, between Charlie and Clyde. After assembling, the classes left the yard in waves.

As they waited to start moving, Michael flicked Roger's ears. Roger stood there patiently, but Michael didn't stop. Roger turned around and was about to get Michael back when Mrs. Dixon called, "Roger face front. The time for games is over." Michael snickered. Roger rolled his eyes. Another year of having Michael behind him. Why couldn't he have grown a bit more during the summer? Theodore, the tallest kid in the class didn't bother anyone, ever. Why couldn't he stand behind Roger? He vaguely understood the lining up in size order thing, probably better than most of the teachers, but its advantages didn't seem worth the trouble. Mrs. Dixon was of the opposite opinion. She moved a few of the girls around several times, unsatisfied with her arrangement of that morning. Roger wondered how long it would take her to figure out that some of the girls switched shoes for lunch. Probably as long as it would take him to figure out why they did it.

Michael flicked Roger's ear again. Roger turned around, this time to tell him to stop. "Roger, stop bothering Michael," Mrs. Dixon said. Roger turned back to face front and Michael snickered some more. Michael started blowing in Roger's hair, between stifled laughs. With Mrs. Dixon's line arranging completed for the time being, the class started moving. Mrs. Dixon went around the corner and up the stairs with the front of the class.

When Roger, Michael, and Theodore were the only ones left outside, Roger stopped and waited for Michael to get closer. He knew Michael would try to punch him. "Dead arm," they called it. It didn't hurt much, but it was difficult to move one's arm for a while after the punch. Hence the name. Sure enough, Roger saw Michael form a fist. Theodore stopped. He followed the rules to the letter. Even though they delayed him, he didn't go around them. He was last in line, no matter what. As Michael stepped forward, his fist ready and his tongue out the side of his mouth in concentration, Roger stomped on his foot as hard as he could.

"Ow! Sunnofa!" Michael said under his breath. Roger ran up the stairs after Gregory. He didn't have to run fast. Greg had something wrong with his right leg, and walked up slowly, pulling himself up only with the left. Michael followed the grinning Roger, ascending the stairs almost like Gregory, but with a theatrical display of effort. He drew his breath in through his teeth, making a sort of hissing sound, "sssssssssssss." He reminded Roger of David Hasselhoff's panting on *Knight Rider*, when Michael Knight chased criminals. He thought briefly whether this Michael got the sound from that show.

When they arrived at the second floor, Mrs. Dixon waited for them with her hands on her hips. She glanced at Gregory dragging his foot. Then she saw Michael huffing and puffing, dragging his own foot. "Michael Ramirez," she scolded, "stop that at once. Gregory's condition is not funny."

Roger saw Gregory's neck redden at the mention of his malady. He felt bad for him, and it put a damper on his triumph.

Once the class settled down, they had their first science lesson. Mrs. Dixon was a biology teacher by training, and Roger remembered her visiting his second grade class to show them a calf's heart. At the time he was intrigued. Mrs. Dixon told the class, responding to a question, that the heart was grown and picked on a farm, just like any plant. Roger thought it strange, but fascinating, that plants had hearts. It seemed reasonable, as he heard of artichoke hearts and hearts of palm. He found out over the summer and much to his shock, however, that the heart came from a baby cow. It died to display its organs to the students of PS 49.

The lesson was about the human circulatory system. Roger reminded himself that Mrs. Dixon's information in this area, and probably every other, was suspect. Her credibility was in question after that heart incident. So he tried to take what he heard and copied from the board not as true, but as needing verification. They hadn't visited the library much now that his mom was sick, but he might persuade his dad to take him during the weekend.

Mrs. Dixon started the lesson by explaining that they had blood vessels all over their bodies, and the heart, a muscle, kept blood moving in them. She took out the heart he saw last year, in its jar full of foul smelling liquid. She went around to all the table groups, showing it to six children at a time. His classmates, most of them his classmates last year, looked in the jar with wonder. It was as if they never saw it before.

Tommy started crying when the jar passed close to him. Roger wondered if it had something to do with being sent to the Principal's Office.

When the heart made its way to his table group (Michael, Dan, Charles, Aeshlie, and Meg had desks connected to his), Meg and Aeshlie, who sat opposite him on either side of Charles, covered their eyes and said "gross!" as if it were expected of them. Roger saw that most of the girls in the class had done so. Michael and Dan, sitting on either side of Roger, on the other hand, gave the organ a good look over. Dan asked if he could touch the heart, and Michael asked if he could eat it. "Gross!" Meg yelled, and Michael smiled sheepishly.

Mrs. Dixon continued talking about the heart, with its ventricles and atria, pointing with a yard stick to what she had neatly written on the board. Then she explained why veins looked blue in the skin. "Oxygen—Michael stop fussing—oxygen makes blood red. Blood coming out of the lungs is full of oxygen, which comes from air. So it is nice and red. Blood that returns to the lungs does not have oxygen because it gets used up by your cells. That blood is blue. The veins that you see in your arms," all the kids looked at their veins (except Roger—veins freaked him out), "have blood that does not have much oxygen, so it is blue."

Charles, who had been poking his veins with a pencil eraser, raised his hand.

"Yes, Charles?"

"How come when it bloods out, the blood's red?"

"Good question, Charles. The answer is that the blood turns red, because it hits the oxygen that is in the air." This sounded reasonable to Roger, but he planned to find out for sure by looking it up.

Mrs. Dixon continued, "Rich people are called blue bloods sometimes. That is because they have less oxygen in their blood. It is also why they do not live above 90th Street in Manhattan. They say the air is too thin for them there."

Roger found this interesting. He didn't know that Manhattan had areas where oxygen concentration varied. He also puzzled over how money affected blood oxygen levels. He thought it might make a good science project to investigate this if they had to do one later in the year and he wasn't feeling lazy.

* * *

Roger became more anxious as 3 PM drew near. He shared his classmates' excitement because it was the end of the school day, and, moreover, the school week. They had Friday off for some reason. A three day weekend was in store. But Roger was also worried about Brian and Craig meeting him outside the building. His fears abated, however, when he remembered that his dad promised to pick him up.

Mrs. Dixon spent the remaining minutes reminding the antsy children to cover their textbooks over the weekend. It was imperative that they do so, and that they return all of the books back to class, to store in their desks and to take home only when homework was assigned requiring their use. Roger knew the drill. In his last two years, it seemed as though homework was assigned from every book, and he would have to lug all of them back and forth every day.

Before the bell rang, everyone put their chairs, upside down, on top of their desks. The teacher shut off the lights and everyone lined up at the door. In size order, of course. Michael fidgeted but didn't bother Roger. Charles looked at the clock on the wall. "Three-two-one—" he whispered. "Lift off!" A few seconds later the bell rang. The class followed the teacher out the door and down the hallway to the stairs leading to the schoolyard. There they stopped to wait for another class making its way down from the third floor. "Come on, already!" Michael whispered. "No talking," Mrs. Dixon called.

When they finally got out into the yard, Roger saw his dad off in the distance waiting for him. He looked around and saw Tommy running, his puffy coat in his arm, toward a big girl he had never seen before. She got out of the auditorium door. Roger's class used that exit the previous three years. Having met up with the girl, big enough to be a fifth grader, Tommy went off with her to 79th Street to the left of the building. They got into the back of a dilapidated station wagon, which clunked away as they closed their doors.

Roger almost reached his father, who now saw him. He wasn't quite close enough to notice that his father didn't shave that day. "Hey you!" Someone called behind him. Roger guessed it was Brian. He continued walking, pretending not to hear it, or at least that the call wasn't directed toward him. "Hey you!" the voice said closer. "Roger!" Sneakers creaked on the concrete. More than one pair of legs, by the sound of it. He kept walking as if he were unaware, but the change in his gait gave him away.

Two boys got in front of him and blocked his way. He turned around as Brian and Craig came up to him. He had his back to Harry and Alex.

"Why'd you punch me for?" Brian demanded.

Roger looked at him defiantly. He hoped his fear didn't show. "You were bothering my friend."

"So?"

Roger didn't know how to respond to that. "Don't bother my friends, and I won't bother you," he said at last.

Brian looked at Roger, unsure. "What," Harry instigated, "you're gonna to take that from him?"

"No!" Brian said. "I ain't afraid of you!" he turned to Roger.

"Fight, fight, fight, fight," chanted the other boys. Curious onlookers joined in.

25

Brian kicked Roger in the ankle. It didn't hurt, but it got his pants dirty. Roger stood there, motionless. Blood rushed from his limbs, adrenaline made him shake slightly. He blushed at being the center of attention. Brian tried to jump on top of him and get him into a headlock. Roger stood there, the same way as before, only now with his head being pulled down.

"What are you waiting for?" his father's voice rang out. "Hit him back!"

And so Roger did. He punched Brian in the belly, and when the boy let him go and slouched over, Roger clipped him on the forehead. He was no longer aware of anyone around them. All he saw was Brian. He placed his right leg behind Brian's and shoved, like he saw on TV over the summer. Brian fell on his butt. He sat there for a moment, confused. Then he got up and ran away, crying. "Let's get out of here!" one of the other boys said, and they all ran after Brian. Nothing interesting happening anymore, the small crowd that had gathered for the spectacle dispersed. Roger's scuffed pants, throbbing ears, and adrenaline induced spasms were the only evidence that anything happened. He picked up his heavy bag, only then realizing that he dropped it on the ground earlier. Roger walked toward his dad, who said, "why didn't you hit him sooner?"

"I dunno."

"What is it with you? Everything I ever ask you, all you say is 'I don't know.' When are you going to grow up?"

"I dunno."

"How was your first day of school?"

"Okay."

"So you know something. Now we're getting somewhere."

"I guess."

"Did you meet any nice pretty girls?"

"*Dad!*"

"What? What did I say?" He lit a cigarette. "Are there any pretty girls in your class?"

"How would I know?"

His father made an exasperated grunt. "So you're telling me there's not one pretty girl in your class?" He was always like this when he'd been drinking—something he did more frequently since he got laid off.

Roger looked down at the ground, his hair covering his eyes from his father. They crossed 80th Street and waited for the light to cross Juniper Boulevard South. Roger asked his dad if he would take him to get some school supplies and to visit the library that weekend.

"We'll have to ask your mother what her plans are."

His mother hadn't been feeling well enough to get out of bed for several weeks now. Roger looked up in surprise, trying to suppress his hope to prevent future disappointment. "Is she feeling better?" His voice contradicted his projected stoicism.

"Yeah, I think so. She's been up and about all day. She said she's tired of lying around in bed."

Roger smiled and quickened his pace. The books in his heavy backpack and his father's questions no longer weighed him down.

CHAPTER TWO
Monday, September 10, 1990

Roger left for school a few minutes before 8 AM, trudging in the fog under a gray sky. He was determined to arrive before the 8:30 bell. The books seemed heavier than they did on Thursday. Roger's stomach ached, as it always did before school. His uncovered books didn't help matters.

The straps of his backpack dug into his shoulders. Roger rolled his eyes. He didn't see the point of lugging these things back and forth: the reading textbook, 2.3 pounds, the math textbook, 2.6 pounds, the science textbook, 2.2 pounds, the social studies textbook, 2.4 pounds, the ten composition notebooks (one each for reading, writing, math, science, and geography, and one for homework for each subject), the geography textbook, 2 pounds, and the writing workbook, 0.5 pounds. He weighed the books on Sunday, writing the figures in a notebook he reserved for such things, comparing them to last year. On average, he found, the textbooks were 10% heavier than the previous year. Roger hypothesized that the trend would continue. By the time he got to college, the number of pounds per book would be in the double digits.

From his past experience, Roger knew they would go through maybe a quarter of each book at most. For what was all the other stuff? Were the books made for smarter people? Or were they, he speculated after his father joked, picking up Roger's bag, sold by the pound? The point of carrying the books back and forth everyday (well, not all of them, but enough) eluded Roger. What were they teaching him, preparing him for, in forcing him to transport his reading, math, science, writing, and several composition books to and from school five days a week? That was carrying about 10 pounds, at the least, back and forth every day. One sixth of his weight!

Roger wiped rain drops and sweat off his brow. He hated hot and humid days, the usual New York weather at this time of year. And why were the books supposed to be covered? That must have been swell for the book covering industry. Was it their conspiracy? Roger imagined a group of craggy men in gray suits, sitting in the shadows around a dark boardroom table, thinking up ways to increase profits. Someone thought, hey, let's make them carry the books back and forth all day. Then we can sell them something to offer meager protection from the inevitable wear and tear. That man must have been promoted. The man who figured out how to convince schools to transform their students into book transporters became the boss, who then fired a bunch of workers like Roger's dad to save money. He adjusted the straps slightly. His shoulders felt tender.

Roger crossed Juniper Boulevard North. He turned in the direction of 80th Street. It struck him as odd as far back as he could remember that the street, the same as any other two lane, two way traffic road, was called a boulevard. Woodhaven Boulevard and Queens Boulevard had eight and twelve lanes, not counting where cars parked. They were big, wide roads—major thoroughfares. Juniper Boulevard North, and its sibling bounding the south side of the park, was no different from 80th Street in dimensions. In fact, the boulevard turned into 63rd Avenue where it intersected Dry Harbor Road, on the park's eastern flank. People had funny names for things. Roger often thought about who had planned and named the grid of streets in the not too distant past.

He had seen old photos of the school from the 1930s. A dirt road cut through the rolling fields that surrounded it. It used to be all farms and swamps. Now there was a manicured park surrounded by houses. Everything from the 1800s to the 1950s seemed black and white to Roger. He knew, of course, that the past was colored. Chuckling to himself at the pun, he pondered why that didn't stop him from seeing in his mind's eye stark, super-annuated images of men moving awkwardly in funny hats and ties when someone mentioned the past or "the olden days."

* * *

Roger's belly ached as the class ascended the stairs on Mrs. Dixon's heels. It started after the Pledge of Allegiance and the Principal's announcements. Roger really had to go to the bathroom. He had sufficiently relieved himself at home, but his body refused to acknowledge what his mind knew. Roger took deep breaths to calm himself, but it didn't seem to work. The problem, he knew, was caused by his mind. He was nervous because Mrs. Dixon would find out that he hadn't done the one homework assignment she gave for the long weekend, to cover his books. If the mind could agitate the body so, why could it not calm it in the same way? Roger walked up the stairs, huffing and puffing, trying desperately not to soil himself. He concentrated so hard he didn't notice Michael's attempts at persiflage.

Roger unpacked his books, and quickly threw them into his desk. He hung up his wet and now empty backpack on his assigned hook in the closet. After a curt "hi" to Tommy, he sat in his chair, straining with his legs stretched out in front of him. His face shook with effort. Sweat rolled down into his eyes, causing them to water and burn. The rest of the class was now seated and Mrs. Dixon was saying something. His concentration didn't wane, and, as if to reward him, his body gave him a reprieve. With his guts settled for the moment, he tried to catch up with the rest of his classmates in the first lesson of the day. They were learning cursive writing. Capital and lowercase letters a, b, and c were their objects of study. Because the writing workbook didn't have to be covered, Roger wasn't as anxious when Mrs. Dixon stood behind him as he practiced his B's. It was unnerving to have her stand over him, but it would have been more so if this were during a science lesson.

That would be after lunch, Roger saw. The day's schedule was on display in the front, to the side of the board, opposite the American flag. The schedule, a big rectangle with removable time and subject slots, hung from a hook on the bulletin board. Science was after lunch from 1:10 to 1:55. His current activity, writing, was to end at 9:30. Math, which required a covered textbook, was from 9:30 to 10:15. The butterflies in Roger's belly awoke with a fury, resuming their riotous party. Again he shook with effort, but it didn't help. He felt the need to stand up.

"Sit down, Roger." Mrs. Dixon looked at him from across the room. This wouldn't work, then. What was that terrible smell? Roger hadn't noticed it previously, but got a good whiff when he sat down. Meg wrinkled her nose. She must have smelled it too. Roger thought it might be him.

Maybe he stepped on something, or, worse still, maybe he hadn't held everything in. This made him so nervous, his stomach let out a whine. He looked around, startled. It didn't appear that anyone else heard it. Roger put his hand on his stomach, slipping it under his belt. Placing his hand that way, like Al Bundy did on TV, sometimes made him feel better. Not today. Roger thought he would soon explode.

He was always reluctant to go to the bathroom. Except in dire emergencies, he preferred to hold it until he got home. His current situation qualified as an emergency. Fighting against his instincts not to stand out, he raised his hand. Of course *now* she didn't notice him. When he stood up, she sat him down right away. The fatigue in his arm briefly took his mind off of the bathroom situation. He was about to put it down when Mrs. Dixon said, "Yes, Roger?"

"M-m-may I go to the bathroom?"

She thought it over. Mrs. Dixon was notorious for not letting her students go. A number of her third graders the previous year were rumored to have been sent home with dirty underpants. "Yes," she said finally, holding out the hall pass, "but don't dilly dally." Roger grabbed the pass and went out the door. The last thing on his mind was dawdling.

He ran down the hall so fast he skidded past the restroom. Roger laid out bathroom tissue as fast as he could on the toilet seat. This early in the day it wasn't yet drenched in urine. The stalls had no doors, but privacy wasn't a pressing concern at the moment. It only became one when he finally sat down and someone entered the bathroom. Craig went past him, whistling toward the urinals.

The whistling and purposeful sneaker screeching stopped. Craig's head came into view on the right side of Roger's stall. First the hair, then the forehead, and then a vertical pair of eyes. The head disappeared for a moment. Then Craig, in his entirety, appeared in front of Roger. He pointed at Roger and laughed. "You farted!" he exclaimed.

This wasn't true (and so what if it had been?), but Roger felt embarrassed and ashamed anyway. Despite its apparent need to relieve itself, his body refused. Roger pulled up his pants and left the bathroom. Craig's laughter echoed in the halls behind him.

* * *

Roger excelled at most things that didn't require much manual or social dexterity. Math was one of these. As the rest of the class sat learning multiplication tables, he did his best to hold his body together and to avoid Mrs. Dixon seeing his uncovered book. It was fairly easy, actually. Since it was open, it was hard to tell whether the book was covered. Just in case, he positioned his body between the book and the teacher, and adjusted the location of his math notebook, to cover the teacher's view of his textbook as she walked around the room.

By the end of the lesson, Roger's nervousness had abated. He was even able to notice the several errors the teacher made on the board. She clearly just copied the answers from the teacher's edition, but skipped over a problem by accident. Such things amused him to no end. Another type of error troubled him, however. Often, what a teacher said in class directly contradicted the textbook. The issue of truth didn't concern Roger much, as he could always find some reliable source to tell him which facts were accepted. The problem was what he should write as an answer on his tests. Should it be what the teacher or book said? It was sometimes hard to tell if the teacher made the question up or if she copied it from her manual. As a result, Roger got questions wrong on tests through no fault of his own—not a big deal in itself, but his dad yelled at him.

Roger continued getting whiffs of the terrible smell. He sniffed at himself surreptitiously when he thought no one saw, but he couldn't determine its source. He examined the soles of his sneakers, a few times, but found nothing out of the ordinary on them. He knew others smelled it too, from their wrinkled noses. It was a sort of acidic, rotting smell. Roger worried it was him, that his body had betrayed him. A bit irrational, he noted to himself, as he didn't remember smelling it on the way to and from the bathroom. It was clearly something in the room, near him. But these calming thoughts didn't prevent the rush of agitating ones. First, he was in no condition to notice the smell on his way to the bathroom. He might have reeked of it, but he was too concerned with making it to his destination. Second, he moved, most likely leaving the stink behind him. Third, on his way back, Craig had been on his mind. Again, he might've been too distracted to notice. Fourth, he was moving. Again, that probably left the smell behind him as he walked. And the smell that lingered from his previous trip had by then dissipated. Roger covertly sniffed at his armpit. Sometimes he hated his mind.

With the math lesson over, a teacher's aide came in to keep an eye on the class while Mrs. Dixon switched with Mr. Gorton, the other third grade teacher. Mrs. Dixon would teach the other class math and science and Mr. Gorton would teach them reading and social studies. Roger already knew Mr. Gorton from the after school program, which his parents placed him in the last two years. Together with Mr. Para, one of the two Special Education teachers at PS 49, Mr. Gorton organized Wiffle ball games and ping pong tournaments, and supervised the children as they played pool, table soccer, and various board games. Mr. Gorton, or

"Mr. G" as he liked to be called, had a sense of humor, which put Roger at ease. He wasn't worried about having his book uncovered.

Mr. Gorton came in their room, wheeling a cart full of paperbacks in front of him. "Hi guys," he said with a grunt, straightening himself. "I'm here to read with you. Are you excited?" He looked to Roger the same as last year. He had dark puffy hair with touches of gray near the sideburns. His face looked like one of those gag disguises: big bushy eyebrows, large frame glasses, and a big nose, from which sprouted a mustache that became a full beard. He wore a short sleeve button-down maroon shirt, a dark colored tie, and brown corduroy pants. Mr. Gorton examined Mrs. Dixon's math problems on the board, perplexed, before erasing them. He gave out copies of the first book the class would read. As book cards were filled out and collected, Mr. Gorton mentioned that he would give extra credit to those students who wore attire that supported the troops in Iraq.

* * *

The rain kept them indoors during lunch. Roger enjoyed a Salisbury steak with mashed potatoes and green beans. Many of the kids threw their green beans out because they looked disgusting, but Roger liked them. They were salty and squishy, wet inside and yet somehow crunchy. They went well with the mashed potatoes and the steak. Roger ate his green beans first, then the potatoes, saving the meat for last. He drank his milk first, to get it out of the way. Only with hamburgers was it any good. Chocolate milk, on the other hand, was awesome. But they rarely got that. He wished they would get juice or Kool Aid instead, but that never happened.

Tommy sat next to him, munching on a salad that contained what looked from a distance like Rice Krispies Treats. Tommy explained that the light brown colored cubes weren't sweet, but earthy. He said they were called tempeh, in a citrus vinaigrette.

"Y-your mom makes you w-weird food," Roger observed.

"My only mom makes spaghettis and Italian stuffs," Tommy replied through a full mouth. "And onlys sometimes. My dad cooks more." Tommy stuffed his cheeks like a hamster. "I made this," he said proudly. He drank from a thermos and made a face.

"W-what's wrong?"

"The bubbles are gone." Tommy swung his arms down to his sides, exhaled, and pursed his lips. He looked at Roger with his wide, sad eyes floating above his fluffy cheeks.

"You have seltzer in there?"

"Yuppers. I don't want it anymore without the bubblies."

Roger figured that Tommy came up with the thermos idea after he got in trouble for bringing a seltzer bottle to school.

"S-so what happened to you on Th-Th-The— last week?"

Tommy looked at him blankly.

"W-w-w-what th-that man took you to the p-p-princip-p-pal."

Tommy's confusion left his face. "They yelleded at me," he complained. "They are so mean."

Clyde, who sat across from them, looked up from his *Hardy Boys*, a different one from last time. That Franklin W. Dixon wrote a lot of books, Roger thought. Clyde moved his glasses, which had dandruff on the lenses, up the bridge of his nose saying, "yeah, I hate that guy." All three boys looked around, to make sure the man wasn't lurking nearby. Clyde went back to his reading, picking absentmindedly at his scalp and licking his chapped lips. He was engrossed in his book, oblivious to the noise of around 170 babbling and excited children. Clyde's real name, as Roger thought of it—the name teachers called him on the first day before he insisted on being called Clyde, was Ming Lang. Roger wondered how that translated into Clyde.

They finished eating with about 40 minutes left before they had to go upstairs. Roger threw out his tray. Tommy yawned and stretched. "I'm sleepy all of the sudden," he told Roger. Then he asked, "do you want to have a slumber party?"

Roger looked around, making sure no one heard. He studied Clyde's face for any hints of snickering. If Michael were within earshot, and not making fun of George with Dan, he would definitely have repeated what Tommy just said.

Roger put his right index finger on his lips. "D-d-don't say stuff like that," he fumed.

"Why not?" Tommy was hurt. "You don't want to be my friend?" He looked about ready to cry.

"N-no. S-s-s—those things are w-what girls d-do. Boys d-don't h-h-have s-s-s—parties. W-we h-h-h-ave sleepovers."

"Oh," Tommy lightened up.

"I'll h-h-have t-to a-a-ask m-m-m p-parents," Roger almost couldn't get that out. His stuttering was particularly bad today.

"Okay," Tommy replied happily, putting his head down on his arms.

"W-w-when?" By the time Roger managed to get the question out, Tommy was asleep.

* * *

Roger turned for home once they came down to the yard. His dad had to fix the car, or something like that, so he wouldn't get picked up. The rain had stopped, but the sky was still overcast and the air felt heavy. The bag on his back was heavy too. He decided to try to cover his books that night. He would ask his parents for money, and would try to go to the stationery store to buy the covers. These thoughts were interrupted by Tommy.

"Hey wait up!" the little boy said behind him. When Roger turned, Tommy said, "My mom had to go do stuff with my dad today. Can my sister and me walk with you?"

"Sh-sh-u-okay. A-are you g-going th—same way?"

Tommy hadn't thought of that. "I know don't," he said blinking.

"W-w-where d-do you l-live?"

"I don't know."

Roger looked at him incredulously. He doesn't know where he lives but has to walk home by himself? He was about to ask the question aloud, but Tommy tried to clarify.

"I know where, but I don't know," Tommy explained. "You know?"

Roger looked at him skeptically. Then a big, husky dark skinned girl with curly black hair bumped into Roger. She addressed Tommy: "Can we go now you lazy bastard? I'm missing wrestling."

"Okay, let's go," Tommy said to everyone. He took a few steps, then turned around. "This is my sister. Her name's Christine." Tommy introduced them.

Christine looked at Roger with suspicion. She narrowed her eyes. "Do you have any candy," she asked.

"N-No."

"Then you're useless," she said, facing forward. She ignored him the rest of the time.

Roger walked beside Tommy. They exited the schoolyard at the same place that Roger entered it that morning, walking down wet concrete steps. They crossed Juniper Boulevard South. Roger wanted to remark on the inappropriate naming of street but decided against it for now. The three walked next to the large section of the park, passing a group of old men playing shuffleboard.

Roger and Tommy discussed their favorite cartoons. They both liked the *Teenage Mutant Ninja Turtles*, it turned out. Tommy told Roger about *The Simpsons*, a new show that Roger didn't know. As they talked, Christine, seemingly oblivious to the world, would somehow get between them. So Roger would walk around, to Tommy's other side. A minute later, Christine would again be between them. Roger didn't know how to politely inquire as to why this was happening.

They crossed 80th Street, turning onto Juniper Boulevard North, walking across the street from the small park. They made a left turn onto 81st

Street. There the three halted to a stop. A vicious dog snarled at them. Roger didn't know what kind of dog it was, but it was big. It had no fur, like a Grey Hound, was big like a German Shepherd, and had a face like a Bull Dog. The dog had no leash. Roger looked frantically for the owner, but they were the only ones on the street. While his body was paralyzed, his mind raced. Maybe they should walk backwards slowly the way they came. Or maybe cross the street. Roger hoped dogs didn't cross streets. Saliva dripped from the dog's razor sharp teeth. It looked ready to attack.

"Three elementary school students mauled by a dog." Roger thought that might be a headline in the next issue of the *Juniper Berry*. Christine covered her eyes with her large palms, leaving an obvious hole through which she peeked. Tommy did the unthinkable. He approached the beast. Christine cowered behind Roger. Tommy put out his fist, next to the growling dog's snout. Roger closed his eyes. He couldn't bear to watch what would unfold.

The growling stopped. Roger opened his eyes a sliver to get a glimpse of what was happening. Tommy patted the dog's head with his palm, in a way a toddler might. "You're so beautiful," Tommy told the dog, which now yawned and licked its chops. It closed its eyes when Tommy's fingers got too close to them. "Come on guys, let's go,"

Tommy said. They followed. The dog did too. Roger was amazed.

When they got to 62nd Avenue, a man's voice called and whistled from behind, "here boy!" They all turned around and watched the dog trot to its owner, its short tail straight up in the air. "Don't worry, guys," he said. "He's friendly. Panzer hasn't bit no one for a week now." Great, Roger thought, a whole week.

They crossed the street. Tommy appeared to share Roger's opinion. "That dog should have a leash," Tommy said. Or maybe not: "He might get hurt by a car if he tries to cross the street by himself." Roger thought the dog was a greater danger to the cars than the cars were to it.

Roger followed Tommy and Christine to Eliot Avenue. As they waited for the light, Roger pointed up the street. "I l-live over in that d-d-d-ir—way," he said. "I g-guess I'll s-see you t-t-t-tom-morrow."

Tommy made a panicked face.

"D-do y-you know where you're going?"

"Noppers. I was following you," Tommy said and blinked. Roger looked at Christine. She rubbed her palms together, mumbling to herself.

Roger repeated his question to Christine. She looked at him for a moment, rubbing her hands together. Then she said, in a matter of fact tone, "I am missing wrestling."

"Your shoes untied," Tommy told his sister. He bent down to tie her laces. His shirt rolled up and his pants slid down, revealing a butt crack. Roger hastily turned away.

"D-d-do you know your address?" Roger asked them.

Christine looked away. Tommy replied, "noppers."

"How could you not know your address?" Roger was shocked.

"I dunno," Tommy shrugged.

Roger puzzled over what to do. For some reason he felt responsible for the two. He decided the best course of action would be to take them home. From there they could call Tommy's house, or the school, to find out where they lived. Roger crossed the street and Tommy and Christine followed. His mom would probably be in bed, Roger thought. His dad would be out. His parents usually got angry about unexpected guests, because they always liked to clean everything up before someone came over. Roger didn't think his house was messy, but his parents felt it was imperative to present an immaculate residence to company. If everything worked out, his parents wouldn't even know they had guests.

Roger opened the front door and let them in. So far the coast was clear. He went up the stairs about halfway, and peered at his parents' bedroom.

The door was closed, a sign that his mother was sleeping. He went back down to find out if Tommy knew his phone number. Christine made herself comfortable on the couch, fumbling with the TV remote. When Tommy saw Roger, he started bouncing up and down with his legs crossed.

"What's wrong with you?" Roger asked him.

"I haf-ta-pee haf-ta-pee haf-ta-pee haf-ta-pee haf-ta-pee haf-ta-pee," Tommy whispered.

"Bathroom is upstairs, first door straight ahead," Roger advised him. It looked like their visit was going to take longer than he expected. Roger checked the window for any sign of his father's imminent return. So far so good, but for how long?

Ten minutes passed, and Tommy had still not emerged from the bathroom. Roger became concerned. He had tried to ask Christine for her phone number, but her replies were to complain that he didn't have cable, or ESPN, where at that moment a "very important" wrestling match was being aired. Roger couldn't wait any longer. After a quick peek out the window, he went upstairs to check on Tommy. The bathroom door was ajar, and the room was empty. A thin stream of water issued from the faucet. All the drawers and the medicine cabinet behind the mirror were open. Irritated, Roger closed everything, and turned off the water. He flushed the toilet, something Tommy forgot to do.

After washing his hands, Roger stepped out of the bathroom and walked down the hall to his room, from which noises issued. "What are you doing?" Roger asked Tommy angrily.

"Stop yelling at me," Tommy said defensively.

"What are you doing in my room?" Roger was outraged. He grabbed Tommy by the hand and dragged him toward the stairs.

"Why are you being so mean?" Tommy was on the verge of tears.

Roger's anger waned a bit. "What were you doing looking through everything?"

"I curious was," Tommy said. "I'm sorry." Tommy looked at him sheepishly. "Am I still in trouble?"

Rather than answering him, Roger asked, "What's your phone number?"

"I dunno," Tommy said.

Roger sighed and went to the kitchen to find the school's number, posted near the light switch along with a list of dates the school would be closed or have half days. He hated using the phone. It made him nervous for some reason (what didn't?), more nervous than usual, and made his stutter worse. Roger didn't like interacting with people in person, but it was preferable to having a phone conversation. Too bad written communication couldn't be delivered and replied to instantly. That would be Roger's ideal way of talking with the outside world. He found the school's number. "You want to call them to find out where you live?"

Tommy shook his head no, sucking on his lower lip. Roger sighed again, this time nervously. He took a deep breath and dialed the number, flicking the cord that connected the phone's base to the handset. He waited, but no one answered after 10 rings. Roger hung up, looking at his watch. It was 3:40. The school, or at least the office, was closed. Roger was stumped. What would he do with them? "Do you know your last name," he asked Tommy. Maybe he could find them in the phone book.

"Yuppers."

Roger tried to think of where he had last seen the phone book. It would make sense to keep it near the phone, but he couldn't see it. He saw all sorts of magazines and catalogs, but nothing useful.

"What are you looking for?" his mom asked him.

"The phone book," Roger replied before he registered that his mother had just come up from the basement holding a laundry basket. Roger froze like a deer in traffic.

"Whatever do you need that for? Oh hello there," Roger's mom noticed Tommy and Christine. "Who are your friends?"

"Tommy and his sister," Roger said.

"Sorry about the mess," Roger's mom said, quickly arranging some things. "Are you hungry?" she asked.

"Yuppers," Tommy answered, rubbing his belly.

Roger's mom smiled at Tommy. "How about some pizza?" Tommy nodded enthusiastically. "What do you want on it, some pepperoni?"

"We're vegetarians," Tommy said.

Roger's mom thought a bit. "I'm not sure they have chicken or fish there, maybe fried calamari or anchovies?"

"Ewww!" Tommy made a face. "We eat don't meat," he said.

"Chicken isn't meat, it's a bird. Fish..."

"We love animals. We don't eat them."

"Okay..." Roger's mom looked at Tommy like he was an alien. "How about mushrooms then?"

"Awesomo!"

While they waited for the pizza, Christine watched TV with Tommy. Roger told his mother about why his schoolmates were there. He finally found the phone book, but Tommy's family wasn't listed. Roger figured it was because they had moved to the area over the summer. Roger was at a loss as to what to do to help them go home. He also wondered what his dad would say when he came back.

He sat down to watch the last few minutes of *Transformers*, a cartoon about robots that transformed into various land, water, and air vehicles. The good robots, commanded by Optimus Prime, who transformed into a truck, after a few setbacks, were saving the world from the bad robots once again. The last few minutes of almost every show were about them setting the world right, tidying up the mess that the bad robots created.

Roger rolled his eyes. He usually rooted for the bad guys in all the cartoons that he watched. They were the underdogs, misunderstood beings with understandable, even if not very nice, ambitions. The mediocre hero always foiled their well thought out plans at the last minute, often via some deus ex machina device. It was only at the end of the first of a two part episode that the bad guys had their day. The bad guys were usually smart, had a charm about them, and a certain pathos that Roger found endearing. The heroes, on the other hand, were usually dumb, arrogant, pompous, and entirely foreign to him. He was often bewildered how anyone could like the heroes, those one dimensional muscle-bound morons. Not that robots had muscles. Roger was therefore surprised when he heard Tommy whisper to himself, "poor Megatron." Megatron was, of course, the leader of the bad robots.

The pizza came. Roger's mother had everyone sit around the dining room table, where she arranged some glasses of lemonade. "So, what do your parents do?" she asked, searching for the garlic powder, the grated cheese shaker, and the Italian seasoning.

"My mom has a cleaning company," Tommy munched. "My dad is a student graduate."

"Oh, where?"

"Columbia."

"In what? What's he studying?"

Roger didn't really pay attention to what they said. He watched Christine eat. She was on her third slice. Bite after huge bite disappeared in her mouth. She gulped down her tall glass of lemonade, and poured herself some more. Her hands were like paws, or gigantic shovels, Roger thought. Christine took the crust from Tommy's plate and ate it when her slice was done. Then she picked up a fourth from the box. She was on her fifth slice by the time Tommy started to answer.

"Psy-psy-psy," his eyes turned up trying to remember the word. "Psyconotry," he said finally.

"You mean psychiatry?" Roger's mom asked.

"I think so," Tommy said happily. Roger had hardly eaten any of his slice, so enthralled was he in watching Christine. She took the last slice out of the box, folded it, and stuffed about half of it in her mouth. She swallowed with minimal chewing.

52

Christine's lemonade disappeared down her throat, and the other half of the pizza slice followed a moment later.

"Oh, that sounds interesting." Roger's mom sat down next to him. "Oh dear," she said, looking at the empty pizza box. "You guys must have been hungry." She put down the garlic powder, seasoning, and grated Parmesan. "It looks like we don't need these anymore."

Christine poured the rest of the lemonade into her glass, and funneled it down her mouth. She had a happy look on her face as she rubbed her palms together. Roger imagined her as a villain planning a great heist. In reality, he suspected, she probably just thought about dinner.

Roger's ruminations were interrupted by Tommy's questioning his mom whether Roger could sleep over on Friday. "Sure," Roger's mom said pleasantly, "that's if we find out where you live."

Once again they considered what to do with Tommy and his sister.

"Do you guys know what street you live on?" Roger asked them. Maybe they could walk around the area and see if a house looked familiar.

"I dunno," said Tommy. Christine looked into space, rubbing her paws together. Tommy said, "My address in is my notebook. I think the street might be listed there also." He rummaged through his schoolbag. Roger exhaled and rolled his eyes. Really? He had the address the whole time?

"Why didn't you say you had it written down before?" Roger was a bit angry.

"I dunno," Tommy said, taking out his note-book. Roger noticed that Tommy's books weren't covered. "You never askeded me."

"But I——." Roger couldn't go on. His mother patted him on the head to calm him down.

"87th Street," Tommy said. That seemed awful far. Roger looked at the page.

"78th Street," he said.

"Yuppers," Tommy said. "Sorries," he said mournfully. "I'm dysflexic."

Roger's mom suggested that she and Roger escort the two home. It turned out that Tommy lived only four blocks away.

CHAPTER THREE
Friday, September 14, 1990

When they settled into their seats after hanging up their coats, Mrs. Dixon announced to the class that they would have an observer that morning. They were to be on their best behavior while the Principal visited.

Roger's already upset stomach issued a complaint. He hated class observers. It always felt like they watched him specifically. His every breath an infraction. His every swallow a capital offense.

Something inside his belly stabbed him. Today was far worse. The Principal was visiting! The highest rank in the school! Worse still, Roger looked at Michael's empty seat, he knew exactly where she would sit. Next to him. Roger sighed. Of all the days to be absent. He should have been absent today instead of Michael. Then the Principal would sit next to him. But of course that didn't happen.

Roger didn't pay attention to the science lesson. He copied Mrs. Dixon's notes from the board. In his dread he failed to scrutinize, as he usually would, the strange assertion that the earth was flat until Columbus decided that it was not. Instead, Roger continually looked at the door for any sign of the Principal. After an hour, he began to calm. Maybe she wasn't coming after all. Maybe she was making the rounds and decided to stay in another class, or thought the whole endeavor was silly and went back to her office.

What did she do anyway? The teachers handled the children. The secretaries in the office typed and answered phones. The janitor cleaned stuff. The aides helped at lunch. The cafeteria workers made and gave out the food. What did the Principal do? Yeah, she was in charge, but she wasn't there to give out orders. Roger often came to school at the same time as the teachers. They waited for their class just as he waited for his. They left at the same time he did, most of them. So when did they receive their orders? And what would the orders be, anyway?

There was a knock on the door as soon as Roger relaxed. An old lady walked in, her cane out in front of her. Principal Santos wore a long navy blue skirt and a frilly white blouse with pictures of flowers on it. Her thick glasses hung from her neck. Her orange lipstick, crookedly applied, matched her short, thinning hair. Old ladies always had weird colored hair.

"Good Morning, Principal Santos," Mrs. Dixon said. "Class, what do we say?"

"Good morning Principal Santos," everyone said in unison. School is a great place to get everyone to do the same thing at the same time.

"There is an empty seat next to Roger. Raise your hand, Roger," Mrs. Dixon said. Of course.

The eighty year old woman trekked from the door to the seat on Roger's right. Roger continued to face the board, his back to the Principal. He could feel her eyes boring holes in the back of his head. Roger feigned scratching his shoulders, hoping he didn't have any dandruff. He hated sitting next to authority figures. His breathing became shallow. Roger tried to make as few movements as possible, and to be as quiet as a ninja.

Mrs. Dixon continued with her lesson. He copied from the board mechanically. Roger felt a tap on his shoulder. He was about to turn around and hiss at Michael to quit it when he remembered the boy was absent. Roger turned slowly. Principal Santos looked at him. He waited for a couple of seconds. Nothing happened. Maybe in his nervousness he imagined it? Roger turned back to the board and resumed copying. A few sentences later, he felt another tap. He didn't imagine it this time. Roger spun around just in time to see her withdraw her withered, veined hand. The Principal stared past him, at the board. What did she want? Why did she ignore him now? Was he imagining it? No. He saw her. Then what? Was Michael's seat haunted? Was the Principal playing tricks on him?

Roger turned to face the board. He waited, his body tense. He looked straight ahead but his eyes saw nothing. All his focus was on his shoulders. It seemed like an eternity, but nothing happened. Roger relaxed a bit. Tap tap tap. He swiveled around, almost saying "aha! Caught you!"

The Principal's face was directly in front of his. Her green eyes looked huge behind her glasses. Dark mascara covered the skin under them. Her mouth twitched. Roger noticed a long black hair on the side of her mouth. What the hell did she want?

The Principal whispered to him, "what does that say about Columbus?" Roger didn't know. He hadn't been paying attention. He didn't know how to respond. His mouth opened, "—"

"Shush! Who's talking back there?" came Mrs. Dixon's voice from the front of the room. "Roger! Turn around and pay attention!"

He did as he was told. He continued writing. There was the tap again. Roger exhaled. He turned to face the Principal. Now what?

"I don't understand what she means about Columbus," whispered the old lady. "Does she usually present material of this sort?"

"Shush! Roger, for the last time! Face the board and pay attention."

Roger turned around and the Principal tugged on his shoulder. What was he supposed to do with these conflicting orders? The Principal whispered again.

"Roger! I've had just about enough of this. You're normally a good boy. I don't know what's gotten into you. Go out into the hall and think about what you've done."

Roger went to the door. He was too confused to notice that all attention was on him. "Next time," Mrs. Dixon said as he opened the door, "I will send you to the Principal's Office. Now stand out there and think about what you've done."

* * *

Friday at 3 PM was Roger's favorite time of the week. The entire weekend was ahead and school was as far away as it could be without there being a vacation. He stepped out into the sunny yard. The warm wind swept his hair up. Roger felt free. He was also a bit nervous because he was going to Tommy's house. He had seen the outside, a red brick standalone house with a small attic porthole and wind chimes on the upstairs windows, when he and his mom accompanied Tommy and Christine, but what lay inside was a mystery.

Roger, Tommy, and Christine took a similar route as they did on Monday. They walked on 80th Street alongside the larger part of the park. High school students shouted in the distance as they played basketball. Christine, in her own world, sang a Queen song softly to herself. Roger and Tommy talked about the merits of playing for fun versus playing to win. The impetus for their discussion was their Boxball match during lunchtime. Boxball, Roger's other favorite game, was like table tennis, except that the area of play was two (or four, if there were four players or if the two opponents were athletic enough) adjacent concrete blocks instead of a table. A blue rubber ball was used, and the object of the game was to hit the ball into the opponent's concrete box, trying to make him miss it. Each time a player hit the ball into his own box (except during a serve, where this was required), missed the opponent's box in a return volley, or missed a return volley, his opponent received a point. Game was usually 11, sometimes 21.

"It's not about points," Tommy said.

"Then what's the *point* of the game?" Roger retorted.

"To hit the ball back for fun."

"What's the point of hitting the ball back? Isn't it to score points?"

"Yuppers."

"There! See! You agree with me!" Roger felt like a lawyer at a critical juncture in a very important case. He was Matlock and Perry Mason, getting a witness to admit on the stand that he was the culprit.

"I meant no!" Tommy's ideal Boxball match would have involved, first, volleying the ball in such a way as to afford one's opponent (Tommy said "teamer") an easy opportunity to hit it back.

Second, no points were to be tabulated. Playing in any other way was "mean."

"No take-backsies," Roger exclaimed.

"No fairs! Your honor, your honor, Roger is cheating!"

"Court finds in favor of Roger," Roger said.

"No fairs!"

"Do you wish to appeal this verdict?"

"Yeah!"

"Appeal has been denied. I'm sorry, but you have lost the case. The Supreme Court refuses to hear it."

"No fairs! How come you're the judge?"

"Because I am. Do you wish to appeal the fact that I am the judge?"

"Yeah!"

"Appeal denied."

"No fairs!" Tommy stomped his feet in protest. "I want to be the judge too."

"Sorry, only one judge. It's not fair, but that's life." They walked in silence for a few minutes. Tommy turned his head up when Roger looked at him. "We can play your wussball next time if you want," Roger said. "Sorry, Tommyball."

"Really?"

"Yeah."

"And you won't ball the hit really fast on purposes?"

"'Yuppers.'" And they were friends again. A thought occurred to Roger. "Hey, do your parents know I'm sleeping over?"

"Noppers."

"You haven't asked them?"

"I forgot. Don't worry." But Roger was worried.

They crossed Eliot Avenue, passing two stationery stores on each corner. They walked downhill through the Metfood parking lot, and made a left on Caldwell Avenue. Besides these stores and a real estate office, the only other businesses in the area were the dozen or so hair dressers. Roger thought it funny that he had to lead the way to Tommy's house. About ten minutes later (Roger would have gotten there faster by himself—Tommy blamed his slow walking on his short legs) they climbed up the four steps to Tommy's front door.

Christine pushed ahead of them with her keys dangling in her hand. Standing behind Tommy on the porch, Roger looked at the Welcome sign on the glass and gray metal storm door. The mat on the porch floor also said Welcome. To the right of the door was a small black mailbox with an envelope sticking out. To the right of the mailbox, jutting out was a half octagonal protrusion that Roger guessed was an alcove inside. One window faced the porch at an angle. Two windows, side by side, faced the street, and another window at an angle on the other side faced the porch of the house next door. All the windows had black bars.

Scrutinizing the facade, Roger realized that he got the wrong impression in his brief look on Monday. It wasn't made of brick as he previously thought. Rather, a rough, red cardboard-like material with thick black lines separating it into grids ("bricks") was stapled to what Roger supposed was wood. Some of the "bricks" were peeling in places. Rust decorated the ceiling where ornate black metal posts supported the porch roof.

Christine opened the red wooden door that was behind the storm door. The doors looked flimsy to Roger as he closed them behind himself. This didn't seem to go with the bars on the windows. Past the red door, which had a gold colored handle, was a small space, the size of a closet. Ahead was another door, this one with a window in the upper half and wood in the lower. On either side of this small space were stacks of things. Christine opened the third door and Roger followed Tommy through it.

Past the doors was a long dark hall that ended with stairs leading up to the second floor. To the right of the stairs was a doorway. Roger closed the last door behind him. The door handle fell on the floor, startling him. "I'll pick it up later," Tommy said ahead of him. "Watch out for the poopsies."

Poop? Sure enough, Roger saw Tommy step around an area where a dog had gone to the bathroom. And here came the guilty party. A small dog emerged from the doorway ahead, barking fiercely. Its fur was orange and white. It looked like a miniature fox. Roger was afraid of dogs, but this angry guy didn't scare him for some reason. Christine bent down and petted the snarling dog under his muzzle. "Hello you little bastard," she said. After a few moments Christine went up the stairs, rubbing her face. The dog continued yapping, spinning quickly on his hind legs. He looked up at Tommy and Roger.

"This is Lucky Joy," Tommy said. The dog barked and followed them into a cluttered space that looked to Roger like the dining room. "Be careful. He bites," Tommy said petting Lucky Joy. "Hello, Lucky Joy. How are you?"

A man came in the room from Roger's left. A stove could be seen in the distance. Roger deduced that was the kitchen. That meant that the opening to his right was the living room. "Hi daddy," Tommy greeted the man.

"Hey, how's it going?" the man replied. He had long white hair that was tied in a ponytail and a pair of reading glasses on the tip of his nose. A shirt collar protruded from under his buttoned cardigan. Under his right arm he held a magazine, which looked to Roger like *Foreign Affairs*. He had never read it, but it was familiar to him because he sometimes saw it at the bigger bookstores. Tommy's dad wore blue slacks and flip flops. This last part of his ensemble made sense to Roger, who wore shorts all week. It was hot. The rest of the man's outfit didn't seem a good adaptation to the weather.

Tommy's dad walked past Roger to the living room. He opened the drapes slightly to peek into the street. "You weren't followed, were you?" he asked.

"I don't think so," Tommy said.

"Good. You can never be too careful." He stepped away from the window and looked at Roger for a moment.

"This is Roger, my friend from school," Tommy said.

"Hi Roger, I'm Mario. Very nice to meet you" the man said, shaking Roger's hand.

Mario went off to the kitchen. Tommy sat down on the couch, and Roger followed suit. Tommy turned on the television for the usual cartoons. This gave Roger an opportunity to inspect his surroundings in more detail. Two loveseats, both overflowing with books, stood next to the angled windows. Between the loveseats was a small table, on which a few more stacks of books rested between potted plants. Behind the couch was a large bookcase, also filled with books, stretching from floor to ceiling. It was as wide as the couch.

Roger skimmed through the titles, impressed with the number of books. Many were about cooking and dieting. Others looked like novels and what Roger thought of as social studies books. Umberto Eco was one of the authors at eye level. Next to it was *Being and Nothingness* by someone called Jean-Paul Sartre. Roger noted that the books weren't arranged in any kind of readily perceptible order. In front of some of the books were figurines, of Indian gods, probably, and photographs of monks dressed in orange.

Between the couch and the television opposite it was Lucky Joy and a coffee table. Mounds of papers hid the table's surface from view. Under the table were a rug and a small basket containing soft blankets. Lucky Joy, quiet for a moment, sat panting next to the basket. The pot marked floor was an ugly greenish brown color. Roger couldn't tell from what it was made, but he guessed wood. Dusty shelves stacked with video tapes, various remotes, a cable box, VCR, and a CD changer supported the TV. To the right and left of the television were speakers, now emitting the voices of the Ninja Turtles.

The ceiling, in the living and dining rooms, had white square tiles each about a foot in length. Roger didn't have to guess what they were made out of because the ones near the chandelier in the dining room, which had several nonworking bulbs, were peeling off and on the verge of collapse. They looked like heavy cardboard. Underneath the chandelier was a large table with various things on top of it. A cursory glance revealed papers, books, and what might have been a hula hoop. Roger had trouble discerning all the things in the piles, but he was almost certain he saw tennis rackets and a guitar in the clutter. The chairs surrounding the table also had various things on them.

The couch Roger sat on was large. His legs dangled as he comfortably melted into its softness. His couch at home, in contrast, ended somewhere under his hamstrings when he sat on it. It was also not nearly as soft. The cartoon went to commercial break. Lucky Joy yapped at Roger again. Roger looked down at him. Lucky placed his paws on a dirty white sock, barked, made a full turn, pivoting on his hind legs, and barked again. His tail wagged furiously. With every bark his front legs lifted slightly off the ground, as if his barks were shells recoiling him, an artillery gun, backward with every shot.

"He wants you to play with the sock," Tommy said.

"The sock?" Roger looked more closely at the filthy thing. It had gray patches of dirt on the sole and yellow sweat stains on the toes. The rest of it was off-white in color leading to a red, white, and blue cuff ribbing. "What am I supposed to do?"

"You grab the sock, do war of tug, and throw it to him."

"He won't bite?" asked Roger as Lucky Joy snarled when he reached for the sock.

"I don't think so."

Roger squeamishly tried to pick up the sock, and Lucky Joy pulled it away from him, dropping it to the floor. He barked at Roger, as if to say, "come on, you can do better than that." Lucky Joy smiled. Roger grabbed the sock more firmly, and Lucky Joy pulled on it with unexpected strength. His fangs showed as he snarled and his eyes bulged, revealing large brown irises and yellowish sclerae. Lucky Joy dropped the sock and ran to the living room. Roger threw it to him. Lucky Joy grabbed it from the floor, growled, shook the sock violently, and brought it back to Roger. This went on for about five minutes. Lucky Joy didn't return the sock unless it was thrown directly to him. Roger had to get up several times to retrieve it. Lucky laughed. After a while, and this only occurred to Roger later, the dog began to drop the sock on the floor further and further from the couch. Roger moved more than the dog.

Lucky Joy eventually got tired of having Roger fetch. He trotted off to the kitchen. Roger sat back down in the center of the couch, looking after Lucky. The dog had a funny way of walking. His body was angled in such a way that it was almost like he walked sideways, with his hind legs parallel with his front.

Lucky Joy ran back from the kitchen, stopping twice to sneeze. He settled down on his rug under the coffee table, panting and looking at them.

"What kind of dog is he?"

"Pomeranian," Tommy said.

A loud succession of booms announced Christine's presence. She flopped down on Roger's left, with her back to the armrest.

"What happened," Tommy, sitting on Roger's right, inquired.

"The stupid remote upstairs is out of batteries. I told my stupid mom to get more, but she's useless." Christine sat Indian style, looking at Roger. "Can we watch wrestling?"

"Sure," Tommy replied. "What channel is it?"

"ESPN," Christine said.

Roger had never watched wrestling before. He didn't have cable at home, and besides, his parents wouldn't let him. Tommy switched the channel. Muscular men in Speedos filled the screen. One guy hit the other and stomped his foot with every jab. That seemed weird. Then the man that got hit (why couldn't he just step away or block the hits?) snapped out of his daze and grabbed the first man's hand. He pulled and then pushed the first man into the wrestling ring's ropes. The first man turned to bounce off the ropes with his back and in a deft motion ran at the second man, who had one of his arms outstretched perpendicular to his body. The first man crashed into the arm (why would he do that?) and fell to the mat. He held his throat and made a choking face.

"That's so fake!" Roger exclaimed.

"You don't get it," Christine said. "It's funny."

"I think it's real," Tommy said.

"Doof!" Christine grunted and clapped in excitement as one of the men, Roger lost track of who was who, slammed the other onto the mat. The announcer on TV narrated with excitement.

Roger felt something strange under his butt, wiggling. Turning to Christine, he realized it was her toes. While he was thinking about the stupidity of wrestling, she had thrust her toes under him. "Hey! What the hell?"

"Oh, sorry about that," Christine said, withdrawing her feet by bringing her knees up closer to her body.

"My sister is a bit special," Tommy whispered to him. Roger had noticed.

The match was over, and Christine started rubbing her palms together and grunting. Her body still faced Roger. Roger didn't understand how sitting like that could be more comfortable than facing the television. After a few commercials, the next match started. This one had two masked opponents. The crowd cheered for one called the Patriot. The other, the Anti-Patriot, was showered with jeers and boos when he entered the arena. Except for the colors of their getups, the two looked exactly the same to Roger. Both had masks with skull faces. The Patriot, of course, had a red, white, and blue mask and pants. His nemesis wore gray. Roger rolled his eyes. Christine cheered. "Get him, get him!" she grunted.

The Patriot was in trouble. His opponent must have cheated or something, because the Patriot stood in the middle of the ring (why was it called a ring and not a square?) as if in a trance. The Anti-Patriot climbed up one of the posts to a loud chorus of boos. Roger wondered if members of the audience thought what was happening was real, or if the audience was fake too, provided for the immersion of the television audience. Christine was completely absorbed. Tommy was too. He bit his nails, staring at the screen.

The bad guy finished climbing and turned around to face his stupefied, wobbling enemy. The commentator announced that the Anti-Patriot was getting ready to do his special move, "the Scud Missile."

"Oh no!" Christine shouted. Toes wiggled under Roger again.

"Hey!"

"Oh, sorry about that." The toes were withdrawn.

The Anti-Patriot lunged forward off the post, twisting in midair. His arms were out in front of him. He landed near The Patriot, gently tapping him. The Patriot collapsed. The camera panned over the slack jawed faces of the stunned audience. Even the commentator was quiet. The Anti-Patriot went to pin the man down to seal his victory. The referee counted, "One! Two!" And here comes the miracle, Roger thought. Sure enough, the Anti-Patriot was thrown off just as the ref's hand swung down to tap the mat a third and final time. The Patriot got up, grabbed his opponent by the top of his head and threw him against the ropes. The Anti-Patriot bounced off of them and ran back. A fist stopped his head but his legs kept running. He fell on his back with a thud that was somehow louder than the audience and excited commentator. The Patriot once again lifted the Anti-Patriot by the head, and, with feet stomping, delivered a series of jabs. Then he grabbed the Anti-Patriot by the pants. The Patriot fell backward and the Anti-Patriot jumped. The Anti-Patriot was briefly airborne, landing with another loud thud. The commentator called it a "suplex."

"Vertical suplex!" Christine corrected, rubbing her palms together furiously. Toes wiggled under Roger.

"Come on already!"

"Sorry about that."

"When you say sorry it's a promise not to do it again, or else you're not really sorry!"

"Sorry about that. I'm really sorry."

"Your toes are still under me!"

"Sorry about that, buddy."

"She's a bit slow," Tommy whispered in Roger's right ear.

The Patriot climbed up on a post and faced the audience, raising his arms in triumph and basking in their adoration. The Anti-Patriot, meanwhile, waited in the ring's center. The Patriot turned around. The crowd chanted "Do it! Do it! Do it!" The commentator explained that "the Patriot Missile" was coming up.

"Get him!" Christine yelled and clapped. She turned to face the television, putting her feet up on the coffee table. She shook her legs in excitement. "Get him!" she grunted. A paper fell off the table and drifted down to Lucky Joy, who dragged it to his nest and began eating it. The Patriot jumped in exactly the same way as the Anti-Patriot. Roger glanced at the digital clock on the VCR. It was 4:26. He knew that the referee would get to count to three without any additional drama. "Yeah!" Christine shouted when the show cut to commercials. "That was awesome!"

"It's so fake! They have a script!"

"No." Christine and Tommy said.

73

"Sometimes they bleed and everything," Christine said.

"So what? They bleed in movies and plays too."

"That's different," Christine replied.

"What about them bouncing off the ropes and stomping when they throw wussy punches?"

"That's the rules," Christine said.

"Yeah," Tommy said.

Roger sighed. He was getting nowhere. Tommy went off to the kitchen to get some juice. Christine rubbed her face. She got up and raced off up the stairs. Her sudden motion startled Lucky Joy. Bark-bark-bark howl, bark-bark-bark howl. His front paws rose off the floor with every bark. The Pomeranian was within Roger's reach, so he bent down to pet him. Lucky Joy snapped at his fingers and growled. Roger barely had time to retract his hand. His pulse quickened at the sudden attack. Lucky Joy sneezed, made a circle and ran to the dining room.

He came back, dragging a teddy bear with his mouth. The toy was slightly bigger than the dog, who growled when it wouldn't move behind him. He dragged it past his rug to between the coffee table and the loveseats. He flopped down, his front paws almost hugging the bear, biting it. He looked to Roger like a crocodile. Lucky Joy growled, the sound muffled by the bear, when Tommy came into the dining room, carrying two books. "Christine!" Tommy yelled up the stairs. "My dad wants you to read something."

No answer.

"Yeesh," Tommy said, putting the books down on the couch to Roger's left and reaching for the phone that was on a stand between the couch and dining room archway.

As soon as Tommy picked up the handset, Lucky Joy sprang up and ran at him. He barked furiously, making circles every four barks or so. Tommy dialed. A phone rang upstairs. There were footsteps above. "Hello?" a man said loudly. Roger heard him both from the receiver and the ceiling. The phone had a slight delay.

"Can I talk to Christine?" Tommy asked.

"Hold on," said the ceiling and phone. Roger heard steps, then muffled talking. Someone thudded their way across the ceiling.

"Hello?" Christine said from the ceiling and phone.

"Come down here, buttwipe. My dad wants you to read something." Tommy put down the handset. Lucky Joy let out a final growl and settled by his teddy bear, sneezing.

Christine emerged after a series of thuds down the stairs. "What does that idiot want from me now?"

"My dad says for you to read chapter four and three and write reflext-tions about it."

"I'll do it tomorrow," Christine said.

"My dad says due it's today," Tommy said.

"Why is my dad always taking classes and messing up my Friday?" Christine asked and marched up the stairs, mumbling to herself. Roger could only make out "idiot."

Tommy flopped down next to Roger. "My dad has homeworksies," he said. "I have to read this now." He opened a book.

"What is it?" Roger asked.

"Foucault," Tommy answered, flipping the pages.

"The guy with the pendulum?" Roger asked.

"I think so."

"What's it called?"

"Punish and Discipling."

The work was unfamiliar to Roger. "You're going to read now?" he asked.

"Yuppers."

"Are you gonna turn the TV off?"

"Noppers. Read at commercials."

Roger reached behind and brought his school-bag in front of himself, setting it down on his knees. As he unzipped it a thought struck him. "Wait a minute. You're doing your dad's psychiatry homework?"

"Yuppers," Tommy replied, flipping through the pages, as if this assignment was perfectly normal.

Roger thought it was weird. "Why can't your dad do it?"

"He's busy," Tommy said. "He has a yoga class."

Roger raised his eyebrows and looked through his bag. He might as well take this time to finish his own homework. The math, a few addition, subtraction, and multiplication problems, was easy. Roger could do them all in his head for two years now. He found it stupid and tedious that he had to copy the problems into his notebook instead of just writing the answers, which would save time, pencil lead (why was it called lead if it was made of graphite?), and notebook space.

He put his math textbook and homework notebook away, taking out his science textbook and homework notebook. They were supposed to read a chapter and answer questions. Roger had a different method. He read the questions first, copying them into the notebook, leaving a space between each for his answers. What a waste of time, the copying. Sometimes the answer required more room than he allowed for, so he wrote in the margins. This elicited question marks from his teachers. They would ask, in their red ink, why he wrote in the margin instead of continuing in the regular fashion, that is, writing on the next line. Roger tried to solve this problem by copying all the questions down first, with each subsequent question directly below the preceding one, and then writing the answers, with numbers corresponding to the question numbers, below them. Teachers found it unsatisfactory for some reason, even though his answers were correct. So Roger just took to giving himself extra space under each copied question. He also adjusted the size of his letters as he ran out of room.

After copying the questions, Roger skimmed the chapter text looking for the keywords that were mentioned in the question. He copied the text into his answer spaces. Question six was labeled "Critical Thinking" in bold letters. Roger hated these because the answer wasn't found in the text directly. Instead, one had to connect different parts of the text. What a waste of time. Question six said, "Why is the ocean blue?"

Roger was confused. The chapter, from what he gleaned from the other questions and his answers, was about reflections and colors. The answer the book wanted, he deduced, was that the ocean is blue because the sky is blue, and that the ocean reflects the sky. But that weekend in the library he had read in an encyclopedia that water, the chemical H_2O, is blue by itself. He thought it correct because he had seen pictures of lakes on cloudy days, and the water looked blue. He had also been at the beach when the sky was overcast, and the water looked blue. It was darker, but still blue. So the answer to the question, "why is the ocean blue?" was that water is blue. He thought about this for a moment. The question didn't specify as to the weather. That surely meant the book wasn't looking for the sky reflection answer, because the ocean wouldn't be reflecting the blue sky on a cloudy day. So he wrote down, "Because water is blue by itself and the ocean is made up mostly of water. Water reflects the blue spectrum of light."

He closed the book and looked at the VCR clock. A half hour wasted. His fingers and palms had newspaper ink on them. Unable to buy covers that week, he had taken a few newspaper pages from the dining room table in his house to cover his books. He felt like an outcast because of it, and still hid his books when using them in class. Everyone else around him had covers that gleamed in the light with university logos. Meg had Brown University written on hers, Dan had Harvard. Were the Ivy Universities the ones pushing book covers? Roger spent some time thinking about that as he tried to fall asleep on Thursday night.

Tommy watched the television as if hypnotized. One of his fingers was in the Foucault book, now closed, keeping his place like a bookmark. The title said *Discipline and Punish,* and the author was a bald guy called Michel Foucault. That didn't seem like the pendulum guy, but Roger couldn't remember the name. He had trouble with names. "How were you able to call upstairs?" he asked Tommy. This began troubling him as soon as Tommy hung up.

"We have two line phones." Tommy stared at the TV.

Another thing occurred to Roger. "You dialed from memory. How come before you said you didn't know your number?"

"I know the upstairs number, but only my uncle uses it."

"But we could have used it to call your house that time you didn't know your address."

"Oh. I didn't think of that. You're a genius!"

That last remark quashed Roger's annoyance. He resolved to ask Tommy more specific questions in the future.

Tommy's trance broke. He yawned. "I'm sleepy all of the sudden," he said groggily. "I think I'm gonna take a nap." Tommy's head dropped in the direction of the window. He was probably sleeping already. Roger looked at his watch. It was four minutes faster than the VCR clock. He wondered what made digital watches desynchronize, assuming they were set correctly at the beginning. His science book from school would probably not answer such a question. He thought he might try to look it up in the library.

The five o'clock news was on, but Roger couldn't find the remote. Tommy might have been sleeping on it. Roger tried to get up to check. As he moved his legs they bumped into something. Lucky Joy, who had been sleeping next to his feet, yelped and jumped away. A startled Roger sat down. How and when had the dog gotten there? Lucky Joy flopped down on his rug and looked at him, licking his nose sporadically. His tongue darted in and out of his mouth like a snake's. Roger tried to get up, to find the remote or change the channel manually.

The five o'clock news was always the same. The first thing they talked about was how someone got mugged, stabbed, or murdered. A story about some sort of scandal, like a government worker taking pens home from work led into a segment about a new product and how good it was. A summary of the day's sporting events followed, and finally the weather.

Lucky Joy growled. Roger sat back down. Lucky Joy became silent, looking up at him, licking his nose. Roger moved to get up again. Lucky Joy growled. It seemed as though he wasn't allowed to leave the couch. He sat back down, turning to reach for his schoolbag. His homework was finished. Too bad Mrs. Dixon didn't give out assignments in advance. Roger's second grade teacher did that, and Roger was a month ahead of the class the entire year. It would help if Mrs. Dixon assigned things in order, but they seemed to be going over the material haphazardly, and, unfortunately, too unpredictably for him to do the homework in advance.

Roger looked at the bookshelf behind the couch. A title caught his eye. *Different Seasons* by Stephen King. Roger climbed onto the couch with his knees, reaching for the book. Lucky Joy started to growl but cut himself off when he saw that Roger wasn't attempting an escape. The boy retrieved the book and sank back down. Why was this so familiar to him? His fingers traced the lettering on the cover. It looked as though the book was new. This was a treat. Roger was used to books with yellowed and bent pages, sometimes missing or falling out, from the library.

Stephen King must have been a popular author because his name was in a larger font than the title. Roger examined the cover for a couple of minutes, tracing his fingers over the letters and pictures. He opened the book to the table of contents. It had four separate stories, the subtitles of which made Roger chuckle: "Hope Springs Eternal," "Summer of Corruption," "Fall From Innocence," and "A Winter's Tale." Springs, Summer, Fall, Winter's. Roger liked that. It was clever.

Roger flipped through the pages, starting from the back. He passed an afterword, thinking he would read that first. Words flew past his eyes. He wished he had Number 5's ability to read books quickly, just flipping the pages from end to front. "More input!" Roger said inside his head, moving his lips, mimicking his favorite movie robot. Channel 11 showed *Short Circuit* often, and Roger never tired of watching the movie about an escaped military robot that developed sentience.

Roger passed the start of "The Breathing Method," and flipped from the end of "The Body," which seemed familiar for some reason. Certain names caught his attention: Gordie, Vern, and Chris Chambers. Castle Rock also sounded so familiar. But why? Roger's eyes widened. He figured it out. He turned to Tommy to tell him his discovery, but the boy was snoring. Tommy faced him now, his mouth slightly open, drooling on his shoulder and the couch's soft white-gray back. Roger debated waking him, but decided against it. Tommy looked so peaceful and happy.

Roger saw a movie on channel 11 just before school started that must have been based on this story. It was his favorite movie of all time. It was called *Stand by Me*. It centered on four boys from the town of Castle Rock who went in search of a body in the woods. It was the greatest, most awesome adventure movie he ever saw. And it was this Stephen King, apparently, who had written it. Screw the afterword. He was reading "The Body" first. It didn't matter that he already knew what it was about and what would happen. The story was so good, at least the movie was, that it had to be read.

A few pages in, Roger was still excited. He knew from the first page that it would be good, even better than the movie. For one thing, there was cursing! Roger had never read a book before that had curse words in it. For another, the writing was awesome. He thought that he could read this all day. But by the end of the fourth page, he found himself rereading the same sentence, understanding but being unable to process it. He was too tired to read more, he realized. Stupid homework, wasting his time and energy. He closed the book on his lap, and rested his head on the back of the couch. He stared up at the ceiling, looking at the cardboard squares. He couldn't wait to tell Tommy about the book he found. Did Tommy ever see the movie? He would ask him that too. Roger grouped the squares on the ceiling first into fives, then into fours. He made shapes with them, one square being in the middle and four surrounding it on its edges.

Roger pretended his mind was a series of chess pieces. First he was a knight, jumping around the tiles in L shaped moves. Then he was a rook, going from side to side. He was a bishop, moving diagonally across the ceiling, bumping into the surrounding walls, bouncing off wrestling style, and coming back to his original spot.

He was a king for a short time. That wasn't much fun. So if chess was based upon feudal or monarchical society, with its knights, bishops, kings and queens (rooks were shaped like castle towers, and the pawns were, well, pawns—the peasants) how come the king was so crappy? Sure, he could move in whichever direction he wanted, but one space at a time. Was it a snide comment on monarchy? That the queen could do whatever she wanted but the king, the most important piece, was an invalid? Who would know about this sort of thing? It was in a book somewhere, he was sure.

The king's powerlessness in chess was starkly different from the video games he knew about. All the bad guys in video games had a whole set of minions at their disposal. Once these were dead, the player would face the boss of the level. These were always much harder to beat than the minions. The final boss was especially hard. Roger angled his head, pursing his lips. What about the good kings? If there ever were any, the player had to do everything for them. They were invalids requiring help from others all the time. Return to them the princess, the crown, the precious jewels, even the kingdom. Why should someone like that even have a kingdom?

These ruminations were cut short by Tommy, who sat straight up and announced, "I'm awake." Tommy turned to him, his eyes closed and hidden by his cheeks. "Stop laughing. Sometimes they don't want to listen to me. It's not funny."

Lucky Joy yawned and raised the back of his body. He kept his front on the rug, looking like a check mark as he stretched his back. He got up, chewing something in his mouth, and with his tail wagging, walked over to Tommy. Lucky Joy appeared to enjoy his petting thoroughly. Roger watched, fascinated. He had never observed a dog this close for so long. Now the Pomeranian looked like a lion. His golden, orange, and white hairs reminded Roger of a mane. Lucky turned this way and that, making sure Tommy didn't miss any area of his back or head.

The dog yawned again and moved closer to Roger, bumping into his leg. "He wants you to pet him," Tommy explained.

"I don't know. He tried to bite me before."

"That's 'cause he didn't want to be petted then."

"He's the boss?" Roger reached down carefully.

"Yuppers."

The dog made no attempt to bite him this time. Lucky Joy sat on Roger's feet while the boy massaged his back. He had never petted a dog before. He didn't expect the animal to be so soft and warm. Roger's hand got tired. As soon as he withdrew it, the dog started growling.

"He's not done with the petting," Tommy said.

Roger continued with his other hand and the dog quieted. Twenty minutes later, just when Roger couldn't go on any longer, Lucky Joy got up off Roger's feet and trotted to the dining room. He sniffed at a chair leg, moving his body in a wave from side to side. It was as if he was attached to the chair by his nose. His body flapped almost like an eel swimming. After a few moments the dog stopped with his side to the chair, lifted his hind leg, and urinated.

Roger was flabbergasted. "Aren't dogs supposed to go to the bathroom outside?"

"Lucky Joy only pees inside," Tommy said. "He holds it until we get home."

"Why?"

"That's the way he is."

Lucky Joy stood before them. He looked up and barked. Every couple of barks he made a counterclockwise circle.

"Now what?" Roger asked.

"He wants food."

The dog's bark struck a demanding tone.

"So there's pee all over the floor?" Roger asked as Tommy got up.

"My uncle cleans it up."

Roger wrinkled his nose and followed Tommy and Lucky Joy to the kitchen. He saw pots and pans everywhere. In the sink directly ahead under a window, the faucet stuck out like a twig from under and between piles of dirty dishes, utensils, and soapy water. To the right of the doorway (there was no door, however) hovered a couch crammed with all sorts of books. Mario sat like a sardine between them, reading *Foreign Affairs*. On the windowsill to the right of the couch was a small boom box. Roger's mom was a classical music buff, so he knew right away that he heard the third concerto of Vivaldi's *Four Seasons*.

Tommy went to the right of the sink to a little counter. He took some bread out of the fridge, which stood near the door to the backyard to the right of the counter. From the fruit stand opposite the couch, he took a couple of bananas. They looked spoiled to Roger, no longer yellow, but a light brown with lots of black spots.

"Are you hungry?" Tommy asked.

"I can eat," said Roger.

Lucky Joy barked, running around in wide circles. The nails on his paws made wet sort of sounds, as if it were raining. His hind legs lost their footing at times, making his rear slide on the tiled floor.

"Want an almond butter and banana sandwich?"

"What's that?" Roger asked.

"It's like peanut butter but deliciouser."

"Okay," Roger said skeptically. They got peanut butter and jelly sandwiches on school trips. That was probably the only school lunch meal Roger didn't like. The bread was too dry. The jelly was too sweet. The peanut butter was too salty, and it stuck to the roof of his mouth. And it wasn't even filling. Now almond butter, he never had. Nor had Roger ever eaten a sandwich with a banana in it.

Tommy took six slices of gray-brown bread out of a plastic bag, and laid them out on a cutting board that was about as big as the upper part of his body. He took two bananas from the fruit stand and put them next to the bread.

"Aren't those spoiled?" Roger asked.

"No. They're just right—ripe."

Roger wasn't sure about that. Green bananas tasted funny, but as soon as they turned yellow, it was the time to eat them. When they became brown with black spots, it was time to give them to his dad, who hated to throw out food.

Tommy went to the fridge again, taking out a jar containing a brown substance. "Oh, sorry Lucky Joy," Tommy said, having almost tripped on the excited dog. Roger turned his gaze back on Tommy, who held a giant, razor sharp knife. He stretched up on his toes, slicing the fruit. His eyes were level with the counter. Roger was at once impressed with Tommy's dexterity and worried that he might hurt himself. Roger looked at Mario to

89

see what he thought of the situation. Tommy's dad was busily reading his magazine. He probably didn't even know they were there. But all went well and the sandwiches were assembled.

Before they could eat, Tommy tore pieces off one of the sandwiches and put them in Lucky Joy's mouth. Lucky chewed on them like they were the best thing in the world. After three or four bites, he took what was given to him and ran with it to the living room. A few seconds later he returned for another bite. The entire sandwich was gone in a couple of minutes.

"Here you go," Tommy handed Roger a sandwich.

"Thanks. Uh, can I have a plate?"

"Oh. Sorry." Tommy gave Roger one of the plates from the sink. He got himself one too, and they went to the living room.

Lucky Joy relaxed on his rug, parts of his sandwich disassembled before him. He was licking the almond butter off of the bread. The banana slices were already eaten. The chunks of bread that had most of the nut butter licked off were deposited next to Lucky Joy's teddy bear.

Roger took a bite out of his sandwich, holding it above his dirty plate. He decided to use it as a crumb catcher, determined not to let his sandwich touch the weird green stuff. He watched the dog lazily play with its food. Tommy flipped through the channels, looking for something to watch.

The bread was delicious. It had a sweetness to it, was perfectly soft, and was neither too moist nor too dry. The almond butter was smooth and grainy at the same time. It didn't get stuck on the roof of his mouth, and had just the right amount of salt. The bananas, despite their spoiled appearance, were quite good. They added a cool creaminess that reminded Roger of butter. And they counterbalanced the saltiness of the almonds with a prominent, but not overpowering, sweetness. Roger had a new favorite sweet sandwich, relegating the honey and butter sandwich that he asked his mom to make after reading Tolkien to the number two spot. It wasn't his favorite sandwich of all time, however. That one was his mom's salami, American cheese, mayo, lettuce, and tomato on wonder bread.

"What kind of bread is this," Roger asked. He had never tasted wonder bread like it.

"Organic wheat whole grain seven bread," Tommy said.

Roger had never heard of it. "Can I have another one?"

"Yuppers," said Tommy happily.

"What's this green stuff on my plate?"

Tommy turned to look closely at the plate in Roger's hands. "Um," he said, taking a finger and scraping it with his nail. He put it in his mouth. "Um. I think it's avocado."

"Avocado?"

"It's a vegbatle."

"Never heard of it."

"It's got old people wrinklies green dark outside, inside creamy green and yellow, with big pit. It's so good." Tommy smacked his lips to show Roger how good it was.

"Big seed? Then it's a fruit."

"Noppers. Fruits are sweet. Avocados are vegbatles."

"I suppose you'll tell me next that tomatoes are vegetables too."

"They are."

"No. Tomatoes are fruits. The definition of a fruit is the stuff that has the seeds."

"No, tomatoes aren't sweet. Fruits are sweet."

"So are sweet potatoes fruit then?" Roger asked.

Tommy ruminated, tapping his chin with his index finger.

"See," said Roger, "sweetness has nothing to do with whether something's a fruit. Lemons are fruits, but they're sour."

"All it know," Tommy rolled his eyes.

Roger followed Tommy into the kitchen. "So you agree that these avocado things are fruits?"

"Nope." Tommy said defiantly.

Roger tried to think of another way to persuade Tommy. Before he could, Mario asked his son how the reading was going.

"Almost done," Tommy said.

"Okay. Remember those reflections are due at 8."

"Yuppers."

They sat down in the living room with their second sandwiches. Lucky Joy snored by their feet.

"So how come you have to do your dad's homework?"

"He has to go to yoga class."

"But he's in the kitchen reading a magazine. Why can't he read his homework?"

"'Cause he's waiting for my mom to pick him up."

That didn't make sense to Roger, but he didn't know what else to say. He changed the subject. "How old is Lucky Joy?" The dog looked like it was having a dream about running. His legs walked in the air.

Tommy counted on his fingers. "He was born on Christmas when I was one. I think he's..."

"Seven?"

"Yuppers. He was the grunt of the litter. If my dad didn't get him, he'd die."

"So he's kind of a reject then?"

"Yeah," Tommy said lovingly at Lucky Joy.

When he finished eating, Tommy picked up his book and began to read again. His lips moved with his index finger as it went from word to word. Roger decided to continue reading the Stephen King book. He had not expected, when Tommy asked him over, that he'd be reading. He thought maybe they would play video games or do stuff outside. But that was alright, since he liked to read.

About half an hour later, Tommy took a pile of stuff off a chair near the dining room window, making room to sit. He uncovered a typewriter, sending up a cloud of dust. Tommy loaded a sheet of paper into it and began hitting the keys with his index fingers. Roger watched and listened to him for a while, the sounds reminding him of his office visit on the first day of school. Whatever happened to that guy that sent him to the Principal? Roger hoped he got fired.

The typing stopped. Tommy jumped off the chair and disappeared in the doorway. Roger listened to his feet pound up the stairs. Talking accompanied footsteps. He tried to figure out how many feet he heard, but gave up when Tommy sped down the stairs. Tommy emerged from the hall with a loose leaf sheet. He sat down at the typewriter again and began typing what was written on the loose leaf.

A car honked its horn outside. Roger saw the car's headlights. "Dad! Mom's here!" Tommy shouted without stopping his typing. He pulled the sheet out of the typewriter, jumped off the chair, and ran to the kitchen. After some muffled talking, Tommy came back to the living room. He jumped down onto the couch proclaiming, "I'm done!" He rubbed his belly. "My tummy hurts," he said. Then he turned to Roger. "So what do you want to do now?"

"I dunno. What's there to do?"

It was decided that they would play Super Mario Brothers on the Nintendo. It was Roger's first time ever holding the controller. He was excited. Although he heard many of his classmates talking about having it, his parents refused to get one for him. It was too expensive, they said. He had seen a sample version at the local electronics store on Queens Boulevard, but someone else always used it.

They had been playing for at least half an hour when Mario came out of the kitchen and went upstairs to change for yoga. His steps reverberated everywhere, shaking the floor. Was he stomping on purpose? It took lots of energy to ascend the stairs that way. The station wagon outside honked a few more times in between. The honks were a gentle reminder each time, no louder or longer than their first iteration. Roger thought that if he were waiting in the car, he would keep honking until Mario came out. Maybe he would even bang on the door.

They were up to world 4-2 when Mario came back down the stairs. Roger's character died twice, but he collected enough coins to make up for the losses and net a life. Tommy was an expert and had not died yet. There were secret passages to skip levels, he said, but he wanted Roger to see everything in the game. It was Tommy's turn now. His body moved with Super Mario. He jumped from his seat every time he avoided the ducks and their shells. He swayed from side to side, sometimes bumping into Roger, when he avoided the sewer plants' fireballs, the flying hammers, and various other dangers. With his tongue in the corner of his mouth, Tommy expertly flicked his fingers over the controls.

"Ciao!" called Mario from the door.

"Bye daddy!" shouted Tommy. He nudged Roger with his elbow.

"Wha—bye," Roger said.

* * *

They played until 10, when Tommy announced again that he was sleepy. Roger was somewhat tired too, accustomed to going to bed around 9. Sometimes he stayed up later on Fridays because he didn't have to wake up early for school the next day.

"So where am I sleeping?" Roger assumed it was going to be in Tommy's room. He hadn't seen it yet. His trip upstairs to the bathroom involved walking through a dark hall bounded by several doors, all closed and with dim light filtering out from under them. The bathroom had a cabinet above the toilet, containing yet more books, but also various perfumes and organic soaps.

"In my room," Tommy said, leading him to the kitchen. Lucky Joy looked up at them for a moment, but was too lazy to give chase.

"We're eating again?" If food was offered, Roger felt that he could eat.

"I'm so full," Tommy said. "And my tummy hurts," he rubbed his belly.

Knowing Tommy, that might mean that they were eating again. The "I'm so full" might actually have meant "I'm so hungry" on account of his "dysflexia." But it didn't appear as though Tommy would prepare food. Instead, he opened the closet door to the left of the kitchen doorway, next to Lucky Joy's water bowl. It looked to Roger to be directly under the second floor landing.

"Follow me," Tommy said, bending down.

"You live in the closet?" Roger was shocked. Unless Tommy slept standing up, Roger didn't see how he could fit in there. And the two of them? Roger imagined himself standing the whole night crammed next to Tommy. No wonder the boy was always saying that he was sleepy. "That's okay. I'll just sleep on the couch," Roger suggested.

"My mom sleeps on the couch," Tommy said.

"She doesn't sleep with your dad?"

"Noppers. Dad says she snores too loud."

And Roger thought his own family was weird. "I can sleep on this couch, maybe," he said, looking for a place to put all the stuff on it.

"If you want," Tommy said. "Or you could go down here with me," his voice trailed off and was accompanied by descending footsteps.

Roger turned to the closet. Where the floor had been a few seconds ago was now a hole. Off to the side was the trapdoor Tommy had lifted. Roger looked down and saw stairs, at the end of which was a nightlight. The stairs creaked under Roger's sneakers as he started to descend carefully. When he was halfway down, the trapdoor slammed shut above him. Had he been taller, he would not be enjoying himself right now. Tommy's head peeked out from the dark to the left of the stairs.

"Sorry," Tommy said. "My mom hasn't fixed that yet."

When he reached the bottom, Roger saw that the nightlight was attached to a refrigerator. In the thin, dusty light coming from the kitchen he made out piles of stuff. For a moment it seemed like an eye peered out at him from the shadows. Roger blinked and it was gone. A light went on to his left. Tommy stood in a doorway. "This is my room," he said.

Roger came after him quickly, away from the darkness. He felt watched. The stale, damp air of the tenebrous basement, and the spider web he managed to walk into when he reached the bottom were fuel for the fear he felt creeping up in him. Roger didn't like dark places. His imagination was too fertile. Ghosts, demons, and boogeymen (whose existence in daylight hours Roger would be first to deny) lurked around every dark corner. Piles of whatever it was in the distance were all shaped by his mind into monsters.

He followed Tommy into the room, peeling the web off of his forehead. A fish tank on the stand to the left of the doorway partly blocked his way. It had hay and a little wooden house in it, along with a puffy white substance in the far corner. Tommy slid the door closed from left to right. It was a regular door, but without a handle or hinges. It was anchored to the top and bottom of the door frame, on which it slid. "That was my dad's idea," Tommy explained when he saw Roger examining it. Roger was starting to get an impression of the hierarchy in this household. The only question was whether the dog outranked the man.

Tommy's room was directly below the kitchen. On its far side was a small window with bars on it. That was probably a fire hazard, Roger thought. To the left of the window were small bookcases. In addition to books they had various stuffed animals, framed artwork, and clay bowls of different sizes. To the right of the doorway was a little table draped with a white cloth. Papers and assorted art supplies covered it. To the right of the window was the largest object in the room, a bunk bed. Roger guessed that he would be sleeping in one of the bunks.

"How come you have a bunk bed?" he asked.

"I always wanted one. Then it was on sale, so my parents got me it. I can't sleep on the top one 'cause I fall off." Tommy rubbed his shoulder, remembering a past injury. Tommy slipped off his sneakers and stepped in his socked feet onto the carpet. Roger followed suit.

"Am I sleeping in the top one?" Roger looked at the ladder.

"Yuppers." Tommy changed into his pajamas. He stripped to his underpants and undershirt, and then put on soft looking blue pants with large pictures of strawberries on them. Roger tried not to laugh but couldn't help it.

"What?" asked Tommy defensively.

"Nothing. You look like a Smurf."

"I like the Smurfs," Tommy said, climbing into his bunk. "Can you turn off the light? I forgot—"

"Where is it?"

"Next to the door," Tommy yawned.

Roger looked to where Tommy pointed and saw a group of four switches. He tried them all.

The first two turned something on, an exhaust fan probably, the third did nothing, and the fourth turned off the bare lamp hanging from the low ceiling in the middle of the room. Everything went dark. Roger inched toward where he thought the bed was.

"Ow!" He bumped into something. Tommy giggled behind him. Roger moved slowly in the opposite direction, closer to Tommy's giggles. He realized that he could see by the moonlight from the small window when he reached the bed and grabbed hold of the ladder. He climbed up the wobbly wooden ladder, almost bumping his head on the ceiling. He would have to be careful getting up in the morning.

Roger opened the covers and lay down. The mattress was soft and comfortable, unlike that of his bed at home. His parents preferred hard mattresses because they said it was good for the back. Roger thought that might be the reason why his neck and shoulders were sore when he woke up. His parents disagreed, telling him it was all in his head.

It had cooled down some, and the breeze coming from the window made it necessary to put the covers on. The bed shook and Roger heard Tommy rubbing his hands together. Roger stared at the ceiling, his hands behind his head. "You're cold?"

"Yuppers."

"How come you're always cold?"

"I dunno," came the groggy reply. "I feel so slumberful," Tommy said.

"This is my first sleepover," Roger told him.

"Mine too," Tommy said. "You're my best friend." He yawned again.

A loud, despondent moan came from the direction of the door. *Oooooaaaaoooww. Oooooaaaaoooww.* Was that a ghost? Adrenaline flooded Roger's body, causing him to shiver. "What's that?" he asked trying not to betray his fear.

"That's Mr. Smith," Tommy said.

"What's wrong with him?" Roger asked. Who was Mr. Smith? Why was he down here? Why was he moaning?

"Nothing. He does that before he goes potty."

Roger's puzzlement conquered his fear. "What do you mean?"

"When he has to go poopsies, he makes noises like that. And then he goes to his litter box."

Litter box? "Is Mr. Smith a cat?" That didn't sound like a cat to Roger.

"Yuppers."

"So you have a cat?" Roger remembered the eye he thought he saw.

"Yuppers."

"Does Lucky Joy fight with him?"

"Noppers. They're both scared of each other. Mr. Smith likes to live in the basement."

"I see."

"Said the blind man!"

"What?"

"Nothing." Tommy yawned. "I'm so sleepy."

"Where did you get the cat?"

"This old lady we knew had him. She died and no one wanted him 'cause he's old. So he lives here now."

"How old is he?"

"We got him when he was 11." Roger could hear Tommy's fingers counting below him. "He's," the bed creaked as Tommy reached for his toes, "13 or 14 now. He had a tough life. Someone took away his claws. That's why he's a cranky cat. But I love him. He's so beautiful."

"I see," Roger said.

The moaning stopped with an annoyed meow. Roger listened as Tommy's nose made soft *sss* sounds. He was asleep. A couple of minutes later, Tommy said, "...milk. He also likes the wet cat food. Lucky Joy eats that sometimes."

"What?"

"You asked me about what he likes to eat and I was telling you."

"No I didn't."

sss.

Roger felt himself drifting. It was a great day, he thought. Although he was a bit hungry and quite tired, he was happy. Roger dozed off. He was soon playing Mario Brothers. For some reason his character kept dying. He would press the button to jump, and Luigi would, but not high enough. He collided with the green and red ducks, the Nintendo played the annoying sound when you die, and he fell off the screen. It happened over and over. Roger woke up. He looked at his watch, pressing the light button. It was 11:20 PM. He closed his eyes and again played Super Mario Brothers in Tommy's living room.

CHAPTER FOUR
Saturday, September 15, 1990

Roger awoke from a dream. He had a fleeting recollection of his mom at the window in Tommy's backyard. She beckoned him to go with her, but the bars on the small window prevented him.

Roger rubbed the crust from the corners of his eyes. He looked at his watch. It was 7:44. Yawning, Roger couldn't remember the last Saturday that he was up this early. His body was damp with sweat, and his clothes clung to him uncomfortably. It was a bad idea to sleep in them. He turned his head toward the noises below. Tommy hopped on one foot, trying to get a pair of pants on. In his concentration he didn't see Roger watching him wobble.

Tommy fell over after somehow inserting both feet into one pant leg.

"Hey! That's not funny!" Tommy said. Roger thought it was and continued laughing. Tommy fell on the carpet with his legs in the air, trying to free himself from the pants. With his pajama top Tommy looked like a ladybug struggling to flip over. His cheeks were puffy and red with effort.

Roger got up to help him and hit his head on the ceiling. "Ow!" This wasn't going to be a good day. Tommy laughed. Roger gave him a look, rubbing his forehead vigorously. His mom taught him to rub any head injury really hard. That was supposed to prevent bumps. He wasn't sure if it worked, but he did it just in case. He carefully inched down the stairs in the gray morning light. From outside the window came the sound of small droplets of rain knocking yellowing leaves down to the ground.

"I laugh when I get nervous," Tommy apologized.

Roger pulled on Tommy's pants' leg, but it wouldn't budge. "How'd you get your legs in there?"

"I dunno. The blubbers make the pants too small." Tommy's stomach made a high pitched whining sound. "Stop complaining, tummy," he poked it and it jiggled. "I'll feed you soon enough."

"Okay, let's try again," Roger said. He pulled as hard as he could. He felt the pants give way bit by bit, but as soon as he stopped pulling, they retracted to where they had been. Tommy's face scrunched. He put his head back, panting.

"It's not working."

"We might have to cut you out."

"But I like these pants so much."

"You'll grow out of them eventually anyway."

Tommy was on the verge of tears. "Please don't make me cut my pants. I love them so."

"Okay, let's try again," Roger said and pulled. The pants once again slid down Tommy's legs and retracted as soon as Roger stopped pulling. What were these pants made out of, rubber bands? Roger looked for suspenders or anything else that might be holding the pants up.

"I wasn't ready that time," Tommy complained.

Roger started. "Are you pushing or pulling?"

"Yeah."

"Which one?"

"I don't know."

"What?"

"The first one."

"You're pushing?"

"I think so. Wait. I'm confused." Tommy tapped his chin with his right index finger, pontificating. After a few moments he said, "I don't know." The dimples in his round cheeks rolled as he spoke.

Roger had to go to the bathroom. He also realized that he forgot to call his parents last night like he promised. They were probably worried and angry with him. Annoyed now, "what do you mean you don't know? You either push or you pull. How hard is it to know which one you're doing?"

"Why are you yelling at me?"

"I'm not yelling!" Were his parents waiting up all night for him to call? Would they yell at him when he got home? He was getting nervous. "It's all your fault," he told Tommy.

Tommy looked up at him with quivering lips. "Why are you being so mean?"

Roger had enough of this. His bowels announced a movement. His parents were most likely upset with him. "I'm going home," he announced.

"Okay. Fine."

"Fine."

Roger slipped into his sneakers, opened the sliding door, and stormed past the big white cat that sat at the doorstep. It looked after him with its one eye, letting out an annoyed *waaa*, almost like a child. Roger grabbed hold of the banister, made a right turn and almost started running up the stairs. But they led to nowhere. The trapdoor was still closed. Roger walked up half way and pushed on the door. Nothing happened. It must have been locked somehow. He couldn't find a latch or anything of the sort.

Roger returned to Tommy's room. The boy was still on the floor, his curls spread out on the carpet. The big white cat lounged by his head. It looked up at Roger, opened its maw, and let out another cranky *waaa*. "I can't get out," Roger said sheepishly, avoiding eye contact with Tommy.

Tommy looked at him, still struggling with his pants.

"I'm sorry I was mean earlier and I left you here on the floor."

Tommy raised up his chin and looked away. "I'm not talking to you," he said.

"Okay...but I really have to go home now. Let me help you with your pants, and then I have to run."

Tommy made a show of looking away.

Roger sighed. Time to switch subjects. Tommy loved his animals. That was the place to get him to talk again. "How come you have a rat in that fish tank?"

"He's not a rat. He's a gerbil." Tommy realized that he spoke, and clamped both hands over his mouth. There came a muffled "ow!" as he smacked himself accidentally.

"What's the rat's—gerbil's name?"

Tommy pretended that he closed a zipper over his lips, locking it at the end and throwing away the key.

"What's wrong with the cat?" Roger asked.

Tommy was mum.

"The cat—Mr. Smith, what's wrong with his eye?"

"He only has one," Tommy replied.

"How come?"

"Something happened to him before we got him."

"I see."

"Said the blind man!"

"I thought you said you weren't going to talk to me."

"No fairs! You trickeded me."

"Friends?"

"Maybe," Tommy said defiantly.

"Oh come on."

"You won't be mean to be anymore?"

"I'll try."

"Pinky swear?"

"Okay."

"Okay. You promise?"

"Yeah. Let me help you with the pants then, and then you have to let me out. I gotta go home."

"Okay."

"Don't do anything this time while I pull."

"Okay."

Roger pulled on the cuff of the pant leg in which Tommy had his legs stuck. Roger really had to go to the bathroom. Being patient was out of the question. Nothing happened. He pulled again, feeling it give way, slightly. He pulled a final time. With a ripping sound the pants came down sufficiently for Tommy to be able to get his legs out himself. "Let me out, Tommy. I gotta go."

"Freedom!" Tommy shouted. He began to sing, "Power to the people/The people's power." Mr. Smith didn't like it and walked out the room annoyed, wobbling from side to side. He crashed headfirst into a box as he turned. He got up, shook his head, and walked off as if nothing happened, muttering something in cat language. He walked sort of like a robot, Roger thought. Like in that *Terminator* movie. Android, he corrected himself. No, cyborg. Why wasn't Tommy here to help him yet? The pressure was building.

"Tommy!"

"I'm coming, I'm coming," said the chubby boy, jumping into his pants. Roger didn't want to waste time informing him that his undershirt was sticking out of his zipper in the front while most of his back was exposed on the other side. He followed Tommy up the stairs. Tommy effortlessly opened the trapdoor and led the way through the dining room to the hall.

Lucky Joy chased them to the door, barking. Roger opened the door with the large window, then the main front door.

Damn it. "I forgot my bag," Roger turned.

"Where is it?"

Roger thought for a moment. "I think I left it on the couch," he said. Tommy went to get it while Roger waited at the door. Tommy had a giant hole in his pants.

Tommy came back empty handed. "My mom's sleeping on it," he said.

Roger really had to run now. "I'll come by for it later. Change your pants. Later!" He stepped out the door and started jogging. It never occurred to him that Tommy had a bathroom, which he could have used in such an emergency.

"Bye!" Tommy called after him.

* * *

Roger got home wet, cold, and out of breath. He went up the steps of his porch with trepidation. He also hoped he'd make it to the bathroom. He dropped his keys on the damp concrete and picked them up with a shaking hand. Were they waiting for him? Would they be angry?

Roger opened the front door and went inside. His dad sat awkwardly on the couch, looking distraught. He stared through Roger with swollen red eyes. Roger thought that maybe if he quickly took off his sneakers and ran up the stairs to the bathroom, he could better prepare himself for getting in trouble. His dad looked odd, though. It was not his angry look. Actually, he had never seen him like this before.

"Where've you been?" asked his dad.

"At Tommy's. I told you about that."

Silence.

Roger put on his slippers as fast as he could. He went for the stairs and started climbing them two at a time.

"Your mother passed away last night," his dad said.

"Okay," Roger called back, racing to the bathroom. He closed the door behind him, undid his pants, and sat down. Wait. What? What had his father just said? His mom passed away? No. That couldn't be. He must have misheard. Roger's heart rattled in his chest, like a bird stuck in a cage. His body prickled with heat. He misheard. She must have passed something, some test. That was a good thing, right? But why did his dad look so strange? Well, maybe he was up all night worrying about Roger. But why was there no screaming? Well, Roger must have caught him by surprise, running up the stairs so fast. But what did his father say? That his mom passed away? Surely he heard something wrong. That Tommy, with his "dysflexia." Maybe it was contagious. Maybe this was a dream? Was he still sleeping? Roger looked at the gray light in the small window above the bathtub. But she had been feeling better. She had been out of bed the whole week. That was progress, right? It couldn't lead to dying. His dad misspoke. He misheard. A combination of the two, maybe. But no, she wasn't dead. That didn't make any sense at all.

Roger washed his hands. He was afraid to exit the bathroom. He was afraid of what would happen next. Now was a good time to cry, he thought. This private place with the gray light. No one would see him. His eyes were watery, and it felt like something lodged in his throat. Roger knew that if he swallowed he would start sobbing. He didn't swallow, but a sob escaped anyway, convulsing his

113

small frame. Roger righted himself, grabbing the soap again. He scrubbed his hands furiously. It wasn't true. He misheard. His dad misspoke. His mom was in the other room, sleeping. He would see her as soon as he came out of the bathroom.

But he was afraid to leave. The prospect of being in trouble no longer frightened him. Indeed, he wished his parents were outside the bathroom door, or downstairs, waiting to yell at him. He would take any penalty they gave him with a smile. So long as his mom was okay.

Please God let her be okay. He would do anything. Go to church, pray all the time, not question the things the priest said. Anything. Just let her be alive and well. Whatever God wanted, Roger would do it. Just let her be okay. Just let it all be a misunderstanding. His father said something. Roger misheard him. Everything was fine in the world. God was supposed to be good, so why wouldn't his mom be okay? She was probably persuading his dad to be lenient with him. It was his first sleepover. It was the most fun he had had in some time. How could it be that while that was happening his mom lay dying? She was fine yesterday morning. She even made him pancakes for breakfast.

Roger had to go to the bathroom again. He surely misheard. Or his dad was kidding. Or his dad spoke figuratively. Yeah, his mom was so distraught over his not calling that she almost died

114

from worry. But she didn't. She was alive and mad at him. She would yell at him so good, levying upon him a mountain of chores and punishments. God, look at all the choices You have. Just please don't take her away. What kind of a universe would it be if his mom died while he was out having fun?

Roger flushed and scrubbed his hands again. God, he would do anything. Just let him hear her voice downstairs. Let him know that everything was fine. Everything would be okay. Please God. Roger never asked much. He never asked for anything, really. He celebrated Christmas and Easter. He didn't understand what the tree, bunnies, and eggs had to do with anything, but he did it. He would do more. Anything. Just make his mom okay. He turned off the faucet, cocking his head and listening. All quiet and still. Maybe they were waiting for him, stewing in their anger. Roger hoped it was so. Please God let it be so. Or his dad was downstairs, waiting angrily, while his mom slept in their bedroom, ready to get up and make pancakes. Roger would even eat cream of wheat, even lumpy cream of wheat. Just let her be alright. He wrinkled his nose. Roger would even eat oatmeal, that disgusting mush of gray stuff that made slimy sounds when you took it out of the bowl with your spoon. He would eat that with liver. He would do whatever it took. Just let her be sleeping in the other room.

He took a deep breath, taking extra time to dry his cold, sweaty hands on the towel. Roger opened the door, his heart pounding. Please God let everything be good. His dad spoke downstairs. Roger almost felt relief, standing at his parents' closed bedroom door. Let him be talking to her. He stood quietly, turning his head, trying to better hear what was said. Roger made out words that did not soothe him. They were bad words. Words that should not be uttered: casket, cremation, urn, wake.

Maybe someone else died? Someone from dad's work? But he didn't work anymore. Still, he had friends, right? Maybe one of their mothers died. Please God, let that be what happened. No. No, let everyone's mother be okay. Let everyone be okay. What kind of world was it that people's mothers died?

Roger turned the handle, opening the bedroom door. He hoped he would see his mother there, the covers gently rising and falling with her breathing. But he already knew that the room would be empty. The wind picked up then. Yellow and red leaves slammed into the window. Roger walked up to it and stood there for a while. He looked down at the backyard, where his mom hung the laundry on the days she felt well enough. The clothes hanger was empty now. Yellow, red, and green leaves littered the small lawn, their brightness a reminder of how gray it was. The wind deposited some in the fence.

Roger left the room, closing the door behind him. He went downstairs to sit with his father. He did not know what was supposed to happen next, but he knew he wouldn't like it.

CHAPTER FIVE

The days and weeks after his mother's death were mostly a blur for Roger. He did not go to school on the following Monday. That was the funeral. The dutiful Tommy brought Roger's bag to school and handed in his homework. When Roger returned, the lunch food didn't taste as good as it did before, and Roger didn't feel like playing tag, suicide, or Boxball. Tommy accompanied him on his silent walks around the schoolyard. Christine joined them sometimes, when she was allowed out. She had been getting into trouble for eating from her classmates' trays.

Tommy's face scrunched up almost into a ball, his cheeks, wet with tears, hiding his eyes when Roger told him his mother had died. "It's so sad," Tommy said in despair, holding his hands at his face. "What a cruel world." A teacher's aide took them to the Principal's Office, thinking Roger beat him up.

Tommy shed more tears over Roger's mother than Roger did. He could not bring himself to cry. He just felt cold. Nothing amused him anymore, not even when he got his sleepover homework back. Of course he got the critical thinking science question wrong. The right answer was that the ocean was blue because its water reflected the sky.

It said "5 out of 6 correct" in red ink at the top of the page in his science homework notebook. He didn't laugh, as he normally might, when he saw "92%" next to it. Not even the teacher's error in his favor made him feel better.

Roger continued doing his homework. It was ingrained. His on time arrivals in school, the completion of all his work, and his near perfect scores belied the fact that his dad took to going to a bar on Eliot Avenue instead of looking for work. When he was home, which became an increasingly seldom event, he was at the TV with a bottle or passed out on the couch. Roger spent more time at Tommy's house, where he ate delicious food with no appetite and played video games with no interest. And he felt safe and comforted in Tommy's company. He petted Mr. Smith's neck with one hand and massaged Lucky Joy's back with the other absently while Christine clapped excitedly next to him, watching her wrestling programs.

Roger had gotten lots of extra credit from Mr. Gorton because he frequently wore his support the troops "Desert Storm" shirt. His mother had bought it for him sometime after he mentioned the assignment to her. He had found it in her stuff. She never got a chance to give it to him. The shirt gradually became bigger on him. Roger did not eat breakfast. No food remained in the house, and at the start of the year his parents only paid the school for lunch meals, not breakfast. He ate his dinner at Tommy's house. Tommy cooked most of the food. In the rare event that his dad cooked, it was pasta.

One day Roger came home to find an eviction notice on the door. From the Office of the Sheriff, the note said at the top in bold lettering. The word EVICTION was in red. Roger took a moment to correct the spelling in the document with his pencil. He packed his clothes and tooth brush into a garbage bag, along with his mom's classical music tapes, and plodded to Tommy's house. He left his teddy bears and toys behind. He didn't think he needed them anymore.

Roger affixed a note for his dad, saying he'd be at Tommy's house. He asked Tommy if he could stay there. He didn't know where his dad was. Nor did he think he had any other family. Tommy said he always wanted a brother. Christine didn't share this sentiment. "You'll have to pay rent, Wharton," she said. Tommy suggested that they go find his "sociable security and passaport." Roger went back that afternoon. He didn't have a passport, but he found his birth certificate. Their family documents were all in a folder in a desk drawer in the spare bedroom. He stuffed it into his school bag while Tommy conversed with a couple of squirrels outside.

Roger did not know what Tommy's parents and uncle had been told about him staying at their house, but they all gave him presents for Christmas. Mario signed Roger's report card along with Tommy's and Christine's, saying "wow," when he saw all the excellents, and one good. Roger would have gotten into trouble with his dad for that one good in art, and even more so for the needs improvement in "plays well with others," but Tommy's parents were more accommodating. They congratulated their children affectionately for their good and satisfactory marks. Mario decided to go out to dinner to celebrate the occasion.

Sitting next to Christine during a meal was a challenge, Tommy warned him in advance. Like a piranha (although Roger thought this might be an exaggeration about the fish), Christine ate everything edible within her reach. It didn't matter where it was, whether hidden in the fridge or cupboard. Nor did it matter if it had someone's name affixed to it, or if Christine was told not to eat it and she promised the same. If food was within her grasp, it was grasped and eaten.

There were exceptions, naturally. Vegetables, onions in particular, were generally safe, though a danger always existed. More often than not, if she came across, say, a stir fry on the stove, Christine would pick out everything she found delicious, leaving the onions and sprouts. But the general rule was, if it had some sort of sauce on it, Christine would probably eat it.

If one wasn't vigilant, Christine would take food from one's plate. Tommy was watchful, but this didn't help him. He was a small boy. Christine used her heft to overpower him. So Tommy took to eating as fast as he could. It became a habit, and he ate fast even when Christine wasn't there to steal anything. Roger surmised that this was a reason for Tommy's daily refrain, "ow, my tummy hurts."

Some of Tommy's family's routines were familiar to Roger, but he quickly noticed the differences. His family went to libraries; Tommy's went to bookstores. His family shopped at large supermarkets where most of the products had "high fructose corn syrup" and "hydrogenated palm oil" in their ingredients; Mario shopped in small stores where food labels listed "agave nectar" and "expeller pressed grapeseed oil." The word "organic" was on almost everything. Instead of bored teenagers cracking gum bubbles, the cash registers at these places were manned by men with long beards and sandals. On one of their bookstore excursions, where they always went after having lunch or dinner at a vegetarian restaurant, Roger thumbed through an issue of the *Scientific American* with great interest. He was delighted, the following month, when a new issue arrived addressed to him.

He missed his mom, and thought about her almost daily. He missed his dad too, and was worried about him. Sometimes he almost broke down and cried, but he could never quite swallow the lump that formed in his throat. He couldn't bring himself to visit the house he grew up in to see who lived there now. He would think about it, occasionally, wondering about who now inhabited his room. How did they decorate the place? What did they do with the stuff he left behind? He hoped his toys found some use. Although these thoughts were always near the surface, their urgency gradually diminished.

Other things began occupying Roger's mind. He read a lot. At first it was almost all Stephen King. His favorite was *The Stand*, a tome about a government created flu virus that killed most of the world. He read every King book he got his hands on, and Tommy's family had quite the collection. Roger reread *Different Seasons* two or three times before he moved on to denser texts.

The gerbil in Tommy's room had been named Friedrich Nietzsche by Mario. When Roger saw a paperback authored by the Gerbil's namesake in a book pile, he felt compelled to examine it. Who would name a book "The Gay Science"? That seemed so odd. Why did gays have a different science from everyone else? What would Mrs. Dixon think of this gay science? Roger flipped through the book, looking at the short passages. They didn't make much sense to him, and science wasn't even mentioned. He expected charts, graphs, and equations of all sorts, as in the regular science books in the library. None here. He was about to put the book down forever when he came upon a section called "The Madman," in which a crazy guy yelled at people about how God was dead and how they killed him. Roger didn't understand it, but something about it resonated with him. He took the book with him to Tommy's room and put it under his pillow.

CHAPTER SIX
Sunday, August 18, 1991

The letters started coming in early August. Roger saw one of them on the first floor radiator in the hall by the stairs, where Christine routinely dumped all the incoming mail. This one was from the IRS. Roger wasn't exactly sure what was going on, but from conversations he overheard it seemed like Edith's business owed the government lots of money.

Christine was upset. "You fucking idiot!" she screamed. "How could you be so stupid?"

Roger's heart started beating fast. It looked for a moment like they were going to get into a fight, but Christine ran past him up the stairs, almost knocking him over. Mario and Edith talked in whispers in the kitchen and Lucky Joy barked at them.

Roger sat down next to a worried Tommy in the living room. "What's going on?" Roger asked him.

"I don't know," Tommy shrugged. He was petting Tigger, a kitten that sat in his lap. The other two were melting on the floor at his feet.

"Can I turn the fan up?" Roger asked.

"Yuppers." They were sweating. Roger wondered how hot the kittens felt with all their fur. The three additions to the household arrived that

May and June. A number of stray cats moved into the backyard during the winter, probably because of the concentration of birds and squirrels that came to eat from the bird feeder Tommy put up.

Tommy built the cats a shelter with Edith out of old rugs and plywood. He, or Lucian, his uncle, put food and water out for them every morning. One of the cats, a gray one that to Roger looked bewildered because of her always wide open eyes, started to get a big belly. At the beginning of May it had several kittens. Tommy was quite excited, and tried to steal glances at them whenever he could. "They're soooo cute," he would say.

At first the bewildered cat appeared to take good care of all of them, dragging them about by their scruffs from place to place, cleaning them with her tongue, and nursing them. But one day there came from the backyard a sound that Roger imagined was made by a pterodactyl. It was a loud, predatory shriek. They investigated, but saw nothing. Roger scanned the neighboring trees for signs of a gigantic bird. Tommy brooded over the kittens' safety, but these too were out of sight. The shrieking went on, almost continuously, for a week, but only when they were in the house. As soon as they went to try to find the bird, all was quiet.

Then in late May, Roger and Tommy found a little orange cat crawling in circles on the concrete next to the house. Its eyes were glazed over with green mucus. It couldn't see. Tommy recognized it as one of the kittens. The mystery of the gigantic bird was solved when it let out a powerful chirp. This little critter, who fit in Tommy's palm, was the one responsible for all the shrieking. Roger was surprised by the kitten's ability to make such a loud, dreadful noise. It was stronger than it looked, writhing on the ground blindly.

They took it to the vet immediately. Roger thought he learned more at the vet's office that day than he would have in school, but he still felt guilty for not attending. Several hours later, Edith drove them home with assorted creams to put on the kitten's eyes, a bottle with special milk, kitten food, and a $500 charge on Mario's credit card. The cat had a striped tail so Tommy named him Tigger. He slept in a blanket lined shoe box, cozy between sock wrapped bottles full of hot water, situated at Tommy's side in his bunk. Roger washed and blow dried the kitten when it soiled itself.

Christine was against bringing the cat into the house, and refused to help or even look at it. "First a gerbil, then a Wharton, and now a cat? We already have Mr. Smith. We have a cat. What are we, running a refugee camp? These things cost money." Christine rubbed her hands and kissed Mr. Smith on his head. After enjoying the attention, Mr. Smith, sensing the new arrival in the house, expressed his discontent by relieving himself outside the litter box.

Christine and Mr. Smith, just getting used to the idea of having another cat in the family, were upset once more when a few weeks later, in early June, two of Tigger's siblings were found abandoned in the bushes. The bewildered cat had moved on. Tommy grabbed Roger's shoulder and said some people weren't meant to be parents.

Tigger had an orange sister, who hid between piles of books and clothes if one let her go, and a black brother. He had a line of spiky gray hair along his back. Tommy said he looked like a punk rocker. To Roger and Christine he looked like a baby skunk. Tommy named the second orange cat Peek-a-boo, and the black one was called Shadow.

The vet and food bills piled up: initial examination fees, inoculation fees, neutering and spaying scheduling fees, neutering and spaying fees, de-worming fees, second de-worming fees after the first de-worming didn't work, prescription pill fees for pills the kittens refused to eat, and eye cream fees. These were on top of what they already spent for Lucky Joy's and Mr. Smith's regular checkups.

Tigger jumped down and started pawing at Shadow, who bounded away like a bunny. Peek-a-boo hid behind the couch. "They don't walk around like they have diapers anymore," Roger commented.

"Noppers. They were so cute."

"Do you think Lucky Joy will get used to them now that they're in the general population?"

"I hope so."

Tumbling sounds came from the stairs. Roger listened for activity. He was often worried that they would get hurt. And he was particularly concerned that someone would step or sit on them because they had a propensity for fall asleep everywhere.

At first Roger thought Edith was the chief danger. She was a huge woman, over six feet tall. Roger estimated she weighed at least 300 pounds. She probably wouldn't even know if a kitten slipped under one of her gigantic feet. But Roger changed his mind after observing the woman more closely. She was incredibly gentle. You could hardly hear her when she walked, and she was careful where she stepped. Tommy told him that all three kittens slept on her belly at night, rising up and down with her snores. Christine would probably grow up to be like her mom, in appearance at least. Edith didn't seem to have a temper. Roger never heard her raise her voice.

The chief danger was the thin Mario, who got even thinner since Roger first met him. He liked to make piles everywhere. These could fall on the kittens, Roger told Tommy. He told him that he should persuade his dad to be less negligent. Mario also flopped down without looking behind him and stomped with his feet when he walked. Roger didn't know whether the stomping was part of Mario's many religious rituals (he was currently fasting during the day and drinking only boiled milk after sundown) or if he simply walked that way. Mario complained about pain in his legs, one of the reasons Edith had to drive him everywhere.

Roger got up to check on the kittens, but Tigger bounded into the living room, sliding and almost crashing into the wall. Shadow was close behind him. Tommy left for the kitchen, presumably to find out what was going on while Roger watched TV and the cats. Lucky Joy ran back from the kitchen with a large piece of cheese. He sat down on his rug, eating it delicately.

Lucky was shocked when he first saw the cats a week ago. He barked at Tommy, demanding to know the meaning of this outrage. Then he appeared to accept their presence. Or rather, he pretended that they weren't there. When they slept next to him, he angled his body awkwardly to avoid them. He pretended to look past them when they walked by. "He's got social problems," Christine remarked a couple of days ago, laughing and clapping.

"We need lots of moneys," Tommy said when he returned.

"How much?"

"I don't know."

"I thought you went over there to find out."

"Don't yell at me," Tommy petted Shadow. Peek-a-boo was trying to pet Lucky Joy, who alternated between ignoring her and growling.

"So what happened then?"

"The RIS says mom has to pay lots of moneys."

"The IRS?"

"Yeah."

"How come?"

"I don't know. My dad says we might lose the house. But don't tell Chris because she'll freak out more," Tommy said. Christine paced upstairs, clapping.

Edith came through the dining room and into the hall. She left the house. Roger thought Mario and Edith had an argument.

"Noppers. My dad says to get dressed. We're going to the city." The station wagon hiccuped and sputtered outside.

"Why are we going?"

Mario had a plan to save the house, Tommy told him. They would discuss it when they went out to lunch to celebrate the arrival of his Master's diploma in psychology.

They piled into the car. The kittens stayed behind with Lucian. Lucky Joy ran back and forth over Roger, Tommy, and Christine, in the back. When Roger questioned Tommy about why they

131

were going east on the highway, Tommy explained that they were going food shopping first in Long Island, before heading in the opposite direction to Manhattan. When they got out of the car to go to the Price, a giant warehouse store, Roger had to remind Tommy to remind his parents to leave the windows open so Christine and Lucky Joy weren't roasted to death inside the hot car as they waited. Christine didn't like going to stores and always remained outside with the dog and her Gameboy for company. Roger never figured out why Christine didn't stay home.

After about an hour they trekked west to the most expensive and least tasty, in Roger's opinion, vegetarian restaurant in the city. He didn't like raw food. What was the point of going to a restaurant where they didn't even cook anything? They just mixed stuff together and served it to you cold. It was only healthy because you couldn't eat a lot of it, and nothing in small quantities can be bad for you. Roger picked at his cumin seasoned beets, envious of Christine, who had been bought a pizza before they entered Mets Crus Crut. Roger had to remind them again about the windows. "They have no sense of self preservation, do they?" he had asked Tommy outside the pizza place.

Tommy, on the other hand, seemed to really enjoy his kale salad with lime dressing. Roger thought kale should rank near the top, if not at the top, of the all time most disgusting vegetables list. When he cleared out his desk at the end of the school year, he had finally discovered the source of the terrible smell haunting the classroom. It was Tommy's kale salad. How anyone could eat that was beyond him.

Mario ordered a number of dishes, but didn't eat them because he was fasting. When the food arrived Mario revealed his grand plan. They would play the lottery more, giving them a better chance of winning the jackpot. Roger surveyed the family, looking like the kittens' mom. Tommy and Edith didn't seem to think anything was wrong with the plan to restore the fiscal health of the household. Had they been listening? Then Mario said, "I agree, it is a great plan," even though no one had said anything. "That cauliflower looks good. Edith, try some." And as for reducing spending, a few minutes later Mario said they had to "cut down on spending. It's getting out of control. From now on we will only go to restaurants to celebrate special occasions, and we will only make necessary purchases." Because Mario liked to celebrate every holiday listed on the calendar, in addition to such milestones as report card day, Roger doubted their restaurant trips would become less frequent.

As usual, after lunch they went to St. Mark's bookstore on 8th Street. Mario bought several magazines and a book on how to manage money.

133

Roger wondered if Mario had read any of the dozen books on the same subject that lay around at home. They left the store and followed Edith as she wobbled toward the car with half a hotdog in her hand. Roger decided to start thinking of his own plans to save the family.

"We have to make moneys," Tommy told him. "I have an idea how." Evidently he had similar concerns about Mario's plan.

"What's your idea?"

"We can sell lemonade. It's hot and people like lemonade in summer."

Roger didn't think they would make much money, but Tommy did make great lemonade. He had a whole bunch of weird ingredients in it, like agave and mint. The same sort of ingredients as he read on all their hippy food packages.

Christine, with tomato sauce in the corners of her mouth, thought it was a terrible idea. "When are you going to get a real job, you lazy bums?"

"When you learn how to tie your shoes," Roger said. Tommy's mouth dropped in shock. Roger apologized for the low blow. Christine laughed and rubbed her palms together, kissing Lucky Joy in between.

When they got home they found a large envelope taped to the door. Edith was being sued by the local union for uncollected dues. None of her workers were members, but the smell of blood was in the air and the vultures were circling. They unloaded the car with a sense of urgency. Edith then drove Tommy and Roger back to Long Island to pick up supplies for the lemonade business. On their way Tommy decided that they should sell cupcakes as well.

They got up early the next morning. Friedrich Nietzsche, unaccustomed to seeing them at that hour, stopped work on his tissue house and hid inside his wooden enclosure. He peeked out at them stealthily while they got dressed. Tommy had found the gerbil in the street on a pile of hay the day his family moved to Middle Village about a year ago.

Roger dabbed his sweat with a tissue after hauling up the last bag of lemons from the basement refrigerator. For once he was glad that it was hot outside. He hoped that the hotter the weather, the better their sales. The overcast sky, however, was troubling. They ate organic raisin bran with soy milk for breakfast while the rest of the house slept. Roger peeked into the living room. Only Shadow rose and fell with Edith's snoring. The other two troublemakers (they had been collapsing many of Mario's piles, and Christine complained about them breaking one of her games) were nowhere in sight.

The house's quiet was shattered by Tommy's use of a food processor and juicer. The kittens started hopping around almost immediately. They would have to be fed soon. Someone stirred upstairs. Roger washed gallon milk containers as best as he could.

It took them an hour to make three gallons. Lucian had come down almost as soon as they started. The prematurely aging man (or was he much older than his brother Mario? Roger would have to ask Tommy later) swept the floor with a dirty broom, spreading dust bunnies from corner to corner. Making the lemonade would have taken less time, but Lucian kept getting in the way.

Roger tried a teaspoon of the drink. The lemonade was delicious. It wasn't too sour, not too sweet, and perfectly refreshing. "Where are we going to sell it?" Roger asked.

Tommy pointed toward the living room.

"In front of the house?"

"Yuppers."

"Not that many people pass by here though."

"We'll sell it so good. You'll see."

"Okay. So how much are we charging for each one?"

"I don't know." Tommy looked perplexed.

Roger grabbed a sheet of paper and a pencil to do some calculations. "How much did the lemons cost?"

"$40."

"That seems like too round a number. How much was it really?"

"Hold on," Tommy said, shuffling through the garbage.

"What are you doing?"

"I'm looking for the receipts."

"But I told you to put them in a safe place."

"I forgot."

Roger sighed.

"Don't yell at me."

"I wasn't yelling."

"You were yelling at me with your eyes." More shuffling. "I founded it!" Tommy said jubilantly.

"Okay, so what's it say?"

"Lemons, $52.17."

Roger scribbled on his paper. "And the cups?"

"Um, $2.50."

"How many in a package, do you know?"

"100."

"The lemons are kind of expensive. How much were they again?"

"$25.17."

Roger crossed out what he wrote previously.

"How many cups in a gallon?"

"I dunno."

Roger maneuvered around Lucian and grabbed a composition book, Christine's, from the couch. Its cover indicated that it was used during the previous school term. These books usually had conversions in the back. For once that would be useful. "Okay, that's 16 cups per gallon," Roger said. He paused to look at Christine's doodles. He could not tell what they were of, if they were supposed to represent anything at all. If Jackson Pollock had worked in the medium of pen on composition book, his art might have looked like Christine's. Roger again looked at the cover. This was her math homework book. He flipped through the pages but found no math problems. There was nothing except Christine's name scrawled in chicken scratch at odd angles near the top of every page, and doodles, like chicken droppings, scattered throughout. Above the occasional doodle was neat handwriting in red ink. It said things like "very good," and "good job Christine." Mario's signature was at the bottom of a few pages. He looked at the conversion table on the inside back cover again. "So we got three gallons. That's 48 cups. How many lemons have we used?"

"I dunno. Half maybe."

"Yeah, I think it's half."

"So that's $12.59 for lemons. The cups are two and a half cents each. That's $1.20. How much was the mint and that agave stuff? We used half the mint, right?"

"Yuppers. Mint was $8. Agave $10.69."

"Two agave bottles, right?"

"Yeah."

"So $4 for the mint and, um, we used one agave bottle?"

"Yuppers."

"$5.35 per bottle. So let's see. $4 plus $5.35 plus $1.20 plus $12.59. That's $23.14 for the three gallons, 48 cups, we've made. Not counting the cooler and ice your mom bought for us. Why'd we have to get ice again? Why couldn't we make it in the freezer?"

"I dunno."

"So it cost us 48 cents per cup."

"Yuppers."

"So anything above that is profit."

"Awesomo!"

"I think we should charge a dollar."

Tommy furrowed his brow and pursed his lips. This was his new serious look. "I think that's too much," he said finally.

"We'll make about $25 in profit if we sell all three gallons at $1 per cup. And that's not counting how much the cooler was."

"$1 is too muchy much."

"Well, starting at 48 cents, we have to charge more than that. I think at least double, because we might not even be able to sell everything."

Tommy thought for a moment. "We should start with a smaller number," he said.

"How?"

"Let's make the lemonade cost 10 cents."

"But it cost us 48."

"But I want it to be 10."

Just then Mario came into the kitchen. He wore a winter hat on his head. "Oh wow, is that lemonade?"

"Yuppers, daddy."

Christine was in the doorway eying the drink. Tommy rushed to block her. "No, Chris! You have to pay for that!"

"How much you lazy bum?"

"One dollar per cup," Roger said.

"I'll be right back," Christine replied, heading to the living room. "Mom! Wake up you lazy! Mom!"

Mario whispered in Tommy's ear. Tommy said, "My dad says it's too much. We should charge 30 cents, he says."

Roger whispered in Tommy's ear, "but it costs us 48 cents to make. We'll be losing 18 cents on every cup."

Tommy relayed the message. Mario whispered into his ear again. "Making lemonade is not about money. It's about the, the, um..." Mario whispered again. "Oh yeah. It's about the pleasures of the work. And charging less gets us more steady customers." Roger finally understood why Edith's business was in the red.

"I thought we were doing this to make money," Roger said to Tommy when Mario left the room.

Christine came back with a $10 bill. "Ten cups please," she said.

Roger took the money. "No, Tommy. Let her use the same cup over again. We'll save a quarter."

Christine drank each cupful in one gulp. "Delicious," she said. Roger didn't think she really tasted anything. Everything she ate did not stay in her mouth long enough for that. The texture of the food, often only provisionally chewed (Roger knew this because of the many nasty surprises he encountered in the bathroom—Christine wasn't one for flushing), sliding down her esophagus must have been her chief gustatory pleasure. Roger shuddered.

"I'll be back," Christine said, leaving the room, possibly to ask Edith for more money.

Tommy placed two of the gallon containers into the fridge, making an effort to hide them with vegetables. It was sort of like a garlic defense against vampires. Lucian gave Tommy a dollar for a cup, and said it was very good lemonade.

They went downstairs to rest after putting the almost finished lemonade container in the fridge. "We made $11," Tommy said cheerfully from his bunk below Roger.

"No. Around $5.75." Roger thought about it, watching a spider crawl above him. Yeah, that sounded about right.

"Awesomo!"

"But it's your mom's and uncle's money."

sss.

"Tommy?"

sss.

Roger took out *The Gay Science* from under his pillow. He had made some headway. Reading the introduction by the translator made him understand the confusing title. The gay part meant happy or joyful—not what Michael had in mind when he sometimes screamed at lunchtime lineup that "Gregory is gay!" And the science part didn't have to do with formulas and equations, though maybe it did, but more like the science in political science and social science, or maybe just wisdom. Joyful Wisdom, Roger thought, would've been a better title. "The total character of the world," Roger began to read, "is in all eternity chaos." Roger smiled. Had Nietzsche lived with Tommy's family?

* * *

Around noon they filled the cooler with ice and put the remaining gallon of lemonade inside. While they napped, Christine, Edith, Lucian, Lucky Joy, and the kittens drank the remainder of the first gallon and discovered the two full ones, one of which they consumed. The discovery was Edith's fault. Unlike Christine, she wasn't deterred at the sight of vegetables. She gave Tommy $21 when they came up. Roger was concerned about the kittens when he learned that they drank some. He had read somewhere that citrus was poisonous for cats. But they appeared to be just fine, chasing each other past a hissing Mr. Smith.

They unfolded a table and dragged it outside. It started raining. Roger commented on the deserted street, but Tommy said it would be alright. They taped the "Organic Lemonade" sign that Tommy had made the previous night to the table's front. After dragging the cooler under the table and hiding several paper cups in a plastic bag, they were in business. They sat on the porch steps waiting for customers. Rain occasionally pelted them when the wind changed directions.

Only one person walked past, and by three o'clock Roger didn't think anyone would buy anything from them. They had about 12 cups left in their container, Roger and Tommy having drunk two each to quench their thirst as they waited for business to get going. "Ten more minutes," Tommy said, "and then I'm done. I think I have the sniffies."

"Nothing's gonna happen in ten minutes. Let's go in now," Roger told him. It was a terrible idea to sit in the rain. And it was a terrible place to try to sell anything. Roger took down the sign, giving it to a shivering and sniffling Tommy. Roger put the cooler up on the porch and started folding the table. "If we do this again, we should go to the park. Not Juniper, but the small one near the mall and next to all those bus stops on Woodhaven and Queens Boulevard."

"Okay," Tommy sniffled. "I think I'm going to be sick."

Roger believed him. Tommy had a cold at least once a month, and the flu several times a year. There was always something wrong with him, as if his immune system was unionized. They went inside and put the remaining lemonade in the refrigerator. Roger didn't think it would last long in there. Christine, who had been hovering about, took the container out of the fridge as soon as they put it in.

"Why didn't you just ask for it before Tommy put it in the fridge," Roger asked.

"I didn't think you'd notice me taking it," Christine responded.

"But we're standing right here!"

"Yeah, you got me." Christine drank straight from the container. After letting out a burp, she capped the now empty jug and crunched it back in the refrigerator. "I'll pay you back as soon as I get the money," Christine burped again, making "money" sound like it was uttered by a deep voiced man.

Roger shook his head and went down to the basement. His stomach grumbled. He wondered when Tommy would make those cupcakes he talked about.

CHAPTER EIGHT
Thursday August 22, 1991

Two days passed before the rain stopped. Roger, Tommy, and Christine spent the time watching television, playing board games, reading, and going out with Mario and Edith. The previous day Mario took them to a fancy restaurant to celebrate the success of the lemonade selling venture and that it was a Wednesday ("It's very important to be happy in the middle of the week," Mario said). The bright morning sun told them that it might be a good day to sell lemonade.

They made the lemonade in the same fashion as their first try. This time around Lucky Joy was there to supervise them. He barked and ran around the kitchen. Christine hovered around for a while, but decided that playing video games was more exciting. "Let me know when you're done so I can have some," she said. Roger replied that they would, secretly planning to get out of the house with all three gallons before Christine noticed. Video game sound effects came from the living room along with MIDI music. Christine clapped. "The Colombians!" she said in her voice-over voice and clapped some more. Roger wondered what game she was playing. "Lucky Joy is the devil. Come here you little bastard." Roger heard scampering feet and kissing. "The Colombians," Christine whispered loudly, making gun noises with her mouth.

When they finished, it was discovered that only two gallons fit in the cooler. The third was taken in a plastic bag. Tommy didn't feel well enough to bake cupcakes. That was left for another day. Roger looked for the hand truck he had seen a few days earlier in the basement. His search was fruitless. Tommy said it might have been left in one of the two storage areas the family rented. Edith offered them a ride, which they gladly accepted.

They got out of the car and Edith drove off to park. They set up their table right at the park entrance. People were everywhere. Kids their age ran screaming in the playground while their parents watched. Others played basketball. Off in the distance a softball game was in progress. Near where Roger and Tommy unfolded the table, people waited for the Q29 and Q38 buses. Some had shopping bags from the mall across Queens Boulevard to the north. Off in the distance, along the east boarder of the small park, people waited for the Q11 bus on Woodhaven Boulevard.

Roger had high hopes. Tommy was excited too. "Look at all the pigeons!" he said. "And there's a squirrel over there. Come on little one, come here." He hunched down, holding out a peanut. Roger rolled his eyes. Tommy was always on the lookout for animals to feed and pet. Roger was more concerned with finding paying customers.

"Don't pet it," Roger said.

"Why not?" The squirrel inched closer. It stopped every so often to stand on its hind legs with its paws tucked to its chest. It looked around for potential dangers, its ears straight up.

"Because it could have all sorts of diseases. And it's bad for business."

"Alright, alright. I won't pet the squirrel." Tommy whined. He threw the peanut to the rodent. "There you go, cutey."

Tommy taped the discolored "Organic Lemonade" sign to the front of the table. They unfolded their chairs and sat behind it with their backs to the fence. People glanced at them as they entered and exited the park, but none came up to buy a drink. Roger observed a number of them buying beverages from the hotdog man stationed at the corner by the subway entrance. So it wasn't like they weren't thirsty. What was wrong? He looked at the shoppers waiting for the bus. They cast suspicious glances at the sign. It looked like a boy their age wanted to go up to them, but his mother dragged him by his shirt collar back to her. Then she sent him to the hotdog man. He returned with a soda can.

Something was definitely wrong. He didn't think that they were overcharging. People didn't know how many cups were in a soda can, but they were willing to pay $1 for it. So why not a cup of organic lemonade? That's it!

"What are you doing?" asked Tommy.

"I'm ripping off the word organic from our sign," Roger said struggling with the cardboard.

"Why?"

"Because I think it's keeping people away."

Tommy looked unsure, but he didn't try to stop Roger.

People started coming up to them almost as soon as Roger finished. They sold a gallon in less than five minutes. After casting distrustful looks from the bus line, a man came over.

"So, um, is this lemonade organic?" he asked. The man had a cap on his head with no logo on it, glasses, and a goatee. The top of his blue t-shirt said "Bush is a murderer," with a portrait of the president below the words. Around the portrait was a red circle with a red diagonal bar going through it, like a no smoking sign. Roger thought that below the gray cargo shorts the man had sandals, but the table blocked his view. Had he seen him at one of the health food stores Mario was always taking them?

"Y-y-yeah," said Roger. What was this guy an idiot? He had seen the organic sign for some time, thanks to the terrible bus service. And he came over only after that part of the sign was torn off.

"How much?" asked the man, taking a chain wallet out of his back pocket. The chain was too short and he had to bend awkwardly to his right to open the wallet.

"30 ce—"

"Www-one d-dollar," Roger interrupted Tommy, tapping the sign.

"Here ya go. Okay, thanks. Remember boys, capitalism is wrong." The man walked away with a cup in his hand. It wasn't sandals he was wearing, but flip-flops. The man had to backtrack to get one of them as it fell off his foot. What was the point of wearing such uncomfortable footwear? Roger preferred sneakers. The flip-flop man tried to reenter the line where he left it, but the woman previously behind him prevented him. The flip-flop man went to the back of the line after the woman hit him on the head with her handbag. A young police officer stood near them, opposite Roger and Tommy at the park's entrance, laughing.

A Q38 arrived. It was so packed with people that a few were bunched up in the stairwell next to the driver. The bus stood there for a while. The backdoor swooshed open, a person practically flew out, and the bus left. The people in line had to wait for the next one, probably praying it would be less crowded.

"Big lines," Edith said. Roger was never sure to whom she spoke. It was always sort of a whisper directed at herself.

"Y-yeah," Roger replied. "Th-th-the l-last b-bus w-wa-was f-full."

"Oh wow," Edith said to herself.

"D-d-did y-you p-park near h-home?" Roger joked. It took her about that long to get there. Sure, she made a detour somewhere to buy that pizza slice, but it still took her a long time to park the car.

"Yeah," Edith said.

A few minutes later they were sold out. Business was good here. As long as they didn't have an "organic" sign, people were willing to buy it. Roger thought for a moment. "H-h-how m-much d-does one of those l-l-lemona-ades f-from th-the s-s-store c-cost? L-less th-th-th-than ours, r-right?

"Yuppers. $3.50 I think."

"L-l-let's b-buy those and s-sell th-th-them th-th-th—same way."

"Noppers. That's cheatseying."

"M-m-more p-profit."

"Noppers."

Edith left them to get the car. Roger didn't think the now only ice-filled cooler was too heavy for them, but Tommy thought it would be better if they stayed there and waited for her. As soon as Edith left (Roger thought later that the man had waited for Edith to leave to approach them) a parks officer came up to them.

"Do ya havf a perlit fo selling dem lemons?" the man asked. The name tag on his green and brown uniform identified him as "Col. Roberts."

Oh, Christ. Roger shook his head as fear crept up in him and the butterflies awoke from their summer slumber.

"Yuppers," said Tommy. He took out a laminated sheet of paper. Roger stared at him wide eyed. Where the hell did he get that?

Colonel Roberts took the paper, examining it closely. "Na, na, dis fo da city, yo. Ya need dif one fo parks."

"It's for city and parks," Tommy said. "It says right there," he pointed with a chubby finger.

"Na. Yo dis be expirationed."

"Noppers. It expires in 1992."

The police officer watched with a smirk. He moved closer to their questioner.

"Na. Yo. I'm a gonna havf arres ya."

"What for?" Tommy yelled. Roger was having trouble keeping up with what was happening.

"Fo invading parks wit illegal lemons."

The cop laughed so hard he had tears in his eyes.

"I tella ya what. Ya givea me yo cash an I let ya go."

"No fairs!"

Roger understood that. "O-o-fficer, this m-man is trying to r-r-rob us!"

The cop wiped the tears off of his cheeks. "Sorry kid. I go off duty in a couple of minutes. I ain't got time for paperwork."

"What the fuck!"

"Hey little man. Watch your language or I'll call the paddy wagon and take you away."

Roger was shocked.

"Where be da moneys?"

Tommy gave Colonel Roberts the cash.

"I takes dis table an coola too. Evidez." He dropped Tommy's papers at his feet. After loading the table and cooler into the back of his green pickup truck he drove into the park. The cop looked at his watch. Still laughing, he walked to his squad car, got in, and drove away.

Roger fumed, "We have to get our stuff back."

"Noppers. Let it go."

"What do you mean? How can you be so calm?" Roger shook.

"If he has to do that, his life isn't good. He already has a hard life to live."

"If my dad were here, he'd beat that guy up," Roger said. "Fuck you!" he yelled at the pickup, which was currently interrupting the softball game by driving through the field. People turned around to look at Roger. Then activity resumed as if nothing happened. Adults went back to their conversations. Kids went back to their play.

"But he's not here," Tommy replied. "He has a hard life too."

"Fuck him too," Roger said with tears in his eyes.

* * *

Edith had much the same attitude toward the theft as Tommy when she found out the parks department officer robbed them. The only thing she added was, "Mario doesn't like involving the government."

It seemed only Christine shared his view. "I'll kill him!" she shouted when she heard what happened. Tommy had to make her three sandwiches before she calmed down. She was still excited though, clapping more loudly than usual. She gobbled up her sandwiches, said they were delicious, and went to the living room to continue watching the news. Christine laughed. "Ha-ha-ha. Gorbachev was under house arrest for three days! Ha-ha-ha-ha!" In her excitement her spit went down the wrong pipe, making her cough between laughs. A politician's plight always tickled Christine's funny bone. She forgot all about the theft.

Roger couldn't sleep that night. He was at turns angry and despondent. He thought up various revenge schemes as he tried to get to sleep. He would slash the guy's tires. He would get firecrackers, and collect Lucky Joy's and the cats' poop for a while. He'd put it in a bag. Then he'd place the bag in the pickup, light the firecrackers, and drop them inside. Then close the door and watch the shit splatter all over the inside of the cabin. Let's see how Colonel Roberts likes that. Or, if the doors were locked, Roger would smear the poop under the door handles so the thief would get it all over his hands when he tried to open the door.

Maybe that was too scatological. The tire slashing idea wasn't. Roger could make sure the truck was closed and put something in the key slot so Roberts couldn't get in. Roger could also throw something through the windows or spray paint "thief" all over the truck. He didn't know exactly what, but he would have his revenge on Colonel Roberts. With these thoughts Roger drifted off to sleep. He dreamed of government goons chasing him for a crime he did not commit.

CHAPTER NINE
Friday September 13, 1991

It had been about a week since school started. Roger was still upset about the lemonade debacle, but his thoughts of revenge gradually diminished. He was preoccupied with other things. The bills, he noticed, had been piling up. Mario and Edith talked about them in the kitchen in hushed tones. Tommy did not know how much was owed, or to whom, other than the government. His only answer to Roger's queries was "we need lots of moneys."

Christine was getting nervous. She came into Tommy's room almost daily, asking "are we going to lose the house?" Tommy grew pale and complained about his stomach more often than usual. Christine, Mario, and Edith all yelled at each other above Roger as he lay in his bunk reading.

He didn't know the extent of their debt, but he saw envelopes from the IRS, the New York tax authority, and various collections agencies all over the house. Notices from the bank regarding late mortgage payments also lay around. Lucky Joy used some of them to fortify his nest. The City of New York demanded compensation for unpaid parking tickets and several unions stated their intentions to file suit. What had started as a trickle of mail became a torrent. Everyone blamed Edith.

Roger was glad, then, that their fourth grade teacher was Mr. Gorton. He knew what to expect from the man. School had added to his worries over the summer. There had been rumors at the end of the prior term that Miss Child, a weird old woman that fed the pigeons in the morning and screamed at the children in the afternoon, might be their teacher. The news regarding Mr. G was therefore a great comfort.

Roger's other worry, a more important one, was resolved on the same day that they found out Mr. Gorton would be their teacher. He didn't know who, if anyone, now lived in his house, but the letters the school sent there might have been returned. He imagined there would be a note attached: "no Roger lives here," or worse.

Once it was found out that he did not live there, school officials might start asking questions. "Where did you live now? With who?" Roger feared that he might get passed into foster care. Maybe Tommy's family, from whom he would definitely be separated, would be charged with kidnapping. And then there were Mario's tales of the government conducting medical experiments on children in foster care. Roger wanted to stay with Tommy's family.

During the middle of their summer break, then, Roger asked Tommy to type up a letter to the school. He thought a typed letter would conceal the author's true identity. Only the signature would be handwritten, and no one could tell from that. A typed letter also had a certain air of formality about it that would assuage any doubts its reader might entertain. Roger breathed two sighs of relief when about a week before school started a letter from the school came to Tommy's house addressed to Roger's dad. The letter contained information about the upcoming school year, including the name of their teacher.

It only occurred to Roger later on that he and Tommy were now listed at the same address in the school's records. It was a good thing that their last names were far apart on the alphabetical list, or someone might get curious. Most people, Roger came to know, are dull, uninterested creatures when it comes to almost everything. But when it comes to other people's business, they become as curious as the kittens roving Tommy's house, poking at everything and leaving no stone unturned. Roger smiled, remembering how Tigger got his whiskers cropped by the fan and how Tommy later explained to an incredulous vet that Tigger must have lost his baby whiskers and new, adult ones were growing. People were like the kittens when it came to gossip. They rummaged where they shouldn't, with no thought as to the potential consequences.

* * *

Roger liked Mr. Gorton. Books didn't have to be covered, and oral presentations didn't have to be given. Best of all, at least once a week, if last year's reading lessons were any indication, Mr. Gorton would roll a television and VCR into the room and show them a movie.

Finished early as usual, Roger watched his classmates compose letters to Saddam Hussein. Their assignment was to urge the leader of Iraq to reform his ways. Tommy sat to Roger's right. His tongue was out in the corner of his mouth, his brow tensed. His curls had gotten long, and often went into his eyes. He blew them out of the way in sudden bursts. At home this always made the kittens stop what they were doing and look up. At school the girls did that. Tommy finished his letter too. He now drew peace signs and what looked like puffy clouds and rainbows. Roger wondered if the letters would really be sent to Saddam Hussein.

He checked the time. He had to go to the bathroom, but thought he might hold it until lunch, about 40 minutes away. They were supposed to write their letters until then. The blue sky showing in the window meant that they would get to go outside. Roger checked in his desk for the handball he had brought that day. Tommy was excited about Boxball and Edith bought them a pack of balls.

He knew he had brought it and put it in his desk, but he checked whether it was still there throughout the morning. Roger felt over his books, pencils, pens, and loose sheets of paper. Terror struck him, as it did every time, when he couldn't find it. Where could it be? How did he lose it? Wasn't it there just a minute ago? He rummaged some more. His hands didn't touch the ball.

This wouldn't be happening, he thought, if his desk were clean. Roger dismissed the thought as soon as it came, for here was another cool thing about having Mr. G as their teacher. He made no mention of desk cleaning and didn't seem to care in the least about inspecting them. Mrs. Dixon would have already made the rounds a couple of times. Roger flushed with the memory of Tommy's salad stinking up the room last year. Good thing he wasn't caught.

Roger doubted he could hold it in much longer. Half an hour now until lunch. Tommy looked up from his letter (were those Care Bears?) as Roger got out of his seat. Roger walked up to Mr. G's desk, grabbed the hall pass, and went to the door. Mr. G stopped stroking his beard, glanced at his wristwatch, and resumed reading his newspaper. That was another cool thing about having him for a teacher. No one had to ask for the pass. If you had to go to the bathroom, Mr. G said, just get the pass and go. That was less of a distraction for the class. And Roger didn't feel self conscious about having to ask and feel the class' eyes upon him. Mrs. Dixon could've learned a lot from Mr. G, Roger thought. A lump pressed into his thigh as he walked. Ah. There was the ball. He remembered now that he had put it in his pocket so as not to forget to bring it down.

The bathroom on the third floor had a design similar to that of the second, though it might have been a bit bigger. Roger walked past the stalls to the urinals. He pivoted to avoid a puddle, trying not to think about what it might be. In the process he cast a glance inside the last stall. He nearly jumped from seeing Craig sitting there.

Roger got to the urinal. As he relieved himself, a thought occurred to him. Had he just been presented with an opportunity for revenge? Was Craig sitting there, completely defenseless, trying to take a dump? Would Craig remember? Would he understand if Roger stood there in front of him, pointing and laughing? Maybe he should do something extra, Roger thought, washing his hands. Water splashed on the rust around the drain in the trough. Craig was the school bully, the highest on the food chain now that Brian somehow managed to graduate.

Roger turned to the exit and paused outside Craig's stall. "What?" Craig sneered at him. "Whatchyou starin' at?"

Roger was taken aback for a second. This is not what he expected.

"Well? Whatchyou want gay boy?"

It was decided then. Roger pointed and laughed. "You farted!" he said, and laughed some more. At first the laugh was fake. It became genuine when Craig started to whimper "stop." Roger could barely contain himself when Craig started crying. He went back to the trough. Roger hit one of the faucets and cupped his hands below it. He went back to crying Craig and threw the water at the boy. Most of it missed, but the boy cried harder.

Roger felt a pang of conscience. "Y-y-you r-remember all the s-stuff you d-did to me l-last year?"

The boy, looking much younger with his red eyes and snotty nose, squinted at him and shook his head. "I ain't never seen you before."

Never seen me before, huh? "L-l-laughed in b-bathr-room, p-p-punched m-m-m-me, t-t-ook my l-lunch, m-made f-f-fun of m-mmme, s-s-s-sp-sp-spitballs..."

The boy shook his head, sniffling. So he did all these things to him and didn't even remember? That set Roger off. Craig deserved it. Roger ripped the toilet paper roll from the two metal handles holding it up. He went back to the sink and wet it. Roger came back to face the bully. Craig sat on the can, looking up at him. Roger tore off a wet glob and hurled it at the boy. He missed, but the wet mass bounced off the wall and hit Craig on top of the head. "Ewww," Craig whimpered, on the verge of tears again.

"You crybaby!" Roger said with disdain. How do you like it now? You feel all big and powerful now? Craig? Like Colonel Roberts? He hurled another chunk of wet toilet paper. It splashed between Craig's defending hands, striking him in the face. The boy started crying. Roger couldn't help himself now. "You know why it's wet? I pissed on it," he lied. Craig cried harder, almost falling off the toilet. Roger was giddy with pleasure, heaving chunk after wet chunk. It was like giant spitballs.

When he ran out of ammo, Roger took out his handball. He squeezed it, positioning himself to throw it. Where could he aim that would be most painful? Craig covered his face, his body moving back and forth, as if pumping out his tears. Roger stopped himself. Too much. It was time to go back to class. He pocketed the ball. "Have fun wiping your ass with your hands, moron crybaby." Roger basked in his victory, looking down at Craig. He left the bathroom. His heart didn't stop its thudding until it was time for lunch.

* * *

In the lunchroom, Roger told Tommy about what happened in the bathroom with so much zest that he didn't notice Tommy's reaction. "Wasn't that so great?" Roger asked.

"Noppers." Tommy was horrified. "Why were you so mean?"

"What—what? How was I mean? I just got revenge."

"You did bad stuff to him on purpose. And you likeded it. That's super mean."

"But were you not listening when I told you about how he did the same thing to me?"

"That doesn't matter. Just because someone does it to you, doesn't mean you can do it to them. It's just not right." Tommy looked at him. "You're being a Hippocrates."

"Whatever," Roger rolled his eyes. Stupid Tommy was making him feel guilty. "By the way, it's 'hypocrite,' not Hippocrates."

Tommy gave him a dirty look.

"What, we're not friends now?"

"I'm mad at you," Tommy averted his eyes.

"But I just did back to him what he did to me!" More or less.

"What a cruel world. Someone who gets bothered gets a bit of power and what does he do? He bothers too. I don't like this world. I'm mad at you."

"Oh come on."

Tommy turned away.

"Craig bothered you too."

"So? That doesn't make it right."

Roger took a bite of the tofu sandwich Tommy had made him that morning. "But can't you see that he deserved it?"

"Noppers. People don't deserve bad stuff. You do bad stuff, you're just like everybody else."

"But he gave you wedgies and called you names and punched you and stuff."

Tommy made the motion of zippering and locking his lips.

"Oh, so you're not talking anymore."

Tommy shook his head.

"Are we still playing Boxball?"

Tommy shook his head.

"Your loss."

Tommy shrugged.

"So how are you going to eat your sandwich with your lips sealed?" Roger smiled.

Tommy looked at him with narrowed eyes and raised cheeks.

"I got you there, huh?"

Tommy got up and moved to the other side of the table, where Peter sat.

"Whatever," Roger said to himself.

What would Nietzsche say about revenge? Roger fumbled in his jacket pocket, where he kept the book on school days in anticipation of stretches of time during which he had nothing to do. He flipped through the index of the small paperback.

Section 69, it said. A cursory look suggested that Nietzsche sided with him.

Roger got up and walked to Tommy's end of the table. He put the open book in front of Tommy, tapping the relevant section with his finger. "See, Nietzsche says I'm right."

"You don't understand the greatness that is Neeché," Tommy said without looking at the text. "Fighting monsters shouldn't become a monster toopers!"

"What? Anyway, look right here," Roger said bringing the book up to his face in preparation to read aloud.

A firm hand grabbed Roger by the shoulder, spinning him around. He looked up at a fuming red face he hadn't seen since the previous year.

"What's this, a book? *The Gay Science*? Friedrich Ni-Ni-N—Come with me," the man said, dragging Roger by the crook of his elbow.

Oh boy. Roger prepared himself for explaining what the book was about—how it didn't have anything to do with gays. "It's n-n-not wh-what y-y-y-y-y-you—"

"Silence!" The man dragged Roger up the stairs. They were going to the Principal's Office then. Having met the Principal the previous year, Roger wasn't much worried about an encounter with the old lady. The whole permanent record business was scary, though. Mr. G never threatened anyone with it, but his teachers in the prior years did. Especially Mrs. Dixon. Not a day went by where she didn't say that such and such infraction would "go into your permanent record." Roger remembered how that late slip this big ape gave him on the first day of school last year was probably in his permanent record. It would stay with him forever. That was what permanent meant. And now this. He would get another black mark unless they gave him an opportunity to explain.

The pit of Roger's belly burned. His eyes widened as it dawned on him. If this offense was serious, his parents might be called. He hoped no one at Tommy's house would pick up. They never did. So all they had to do was not pick up this time. Let the school leave a message. Hopefully that would be the end of it.

His unease persisted. What if they wanted to have a meeting? What then? Going up the last flight of stairs, Roger thought maybe another typed letter from Tommy might do the trick. But what if it didn't? Would Mario and Edith pretend to be his parents? He had already been a burden to them, he thought. This wouldn't be good. And last year, weren't they always going to the school to talk with someone about getting Christine out of Special Ed and into a normal class? Wouldn't somebody remember that? Would Lucian pretend to be his dad? Or would Roger be taken away into the system, to be tortured and experimented on and all those things Mario said happened to orphans and foster kids?

The Office was full of children. Roger was pushed down into the only remaining chair. The ladies were at their usual posts, typing away and making phone calls. The door to the office where the Principal had her desk was closed with the blind down. One of the typists looked up as Roger sat. "Another one, Mr. Leslie?" she asked.

The man who had brought Roger there grunted an affirmative. So his name was Mr. Leslie. Wasn't that a girl's name? Is that why he was so mean? Roger scanned the faces of the other children. He had seen them before, but they were in other classes and he did not know their names. All but one of them. Craig sat three seats away, sobbing with bathroom tissue in his hair.

Roger felt a new conflagration in his gut. Did Craig tell on him? Is that why Roger was here? But then why did Mr. Leslie take his book away? Roger knew what Tommy would say: karma. Roger hoped all the good karma he'd accumulated over the years would help him get off with no penalty.

The big ape sat down behind a desk. "You there," he pointed at a boy several seats over. "Get over here," he pointed down at a chair next to the desk. The frightened boy got up and walked to Mr. Leslie with his head down.

Roger watched Mr. Leslie yell at the boy. He couldn't make out any of the words, given the distance, the ringing phones, and clattering typewriters. Whatever Mr. Leslie said made the boy cry. After a few minutes the boy was sent out of the room. The next victim was called, and on it went. It looked as though they were being called in the order they came in, sort of like at a doctor's office where no one had an appointment.

Roger watched Craig carefully when it was his turn. He leaned forward, straining his eyes and ears. He thought he might have heard "bathroom" from the sobbing Craig, but he wasn't sure. Roger hoped that he wouldn't be mentioned. Cold sweat formed on his forehead and under his armpits. Liquid streamed down the sides of his body as if he were a snowman caught in a sudden warming.

Craig turned around. It looked like he pointed at Roger. Oh no! That's not good. Roger ducked awkwardly in his chair. An onlooker might have thought that Craig threw something at him. Then Craig turned back and Mr. Leslie continued talking. Roger's butt began to sweat. He hated that. He knew that when he got up there would be a line of moisture on the chair.

Craig was sent out, still crying. Mr. Leslie followed him. Roger heard him now. "Stop your crying. We'll get to the bottom of this." Mr. Leslie glanced at Roger. "You!" he pointed at Roger.

"What are you waiting for? Get over there!" He pointed at his desk and left the room.

Roger did as he was told. He was a dead man walking. His destination might as well have been the electric chair. He sat down heavily after a sudden weakness in his legs. He hoped that whatever trouble he was in, and this thing with Craig was now additional cause for worry, it wouldn't lead to questions being asked about where he lived. Mr. Leslie seemed just the type to go to the extra trouble of raising such questions.

"You okay, sweetheart?" asked one of the typists next to him. "You don't look so good." Roger smiled weakly at her. She turned to her colleague who had just put her phone down. "Leslie puts the pressure on everyone. It was sure better when he was sent to sensitivity training after he punched that boy last year."

"Umhmm," the phone lady nodded.

"I hope Mrs. Santos retires after me, girl, because having *him* as principal will not be good."

The other lady was about to reply, but Mr. Leslie returned. "Back to work, all of you!" he yelled.

Now Roger was terrified. His body felt like stone. Despite his fast beating heart, he was cold. The sweat kept running.

"So," Mr. Leslie said, adjusting the Assistant Principal sign on top of his desk. "So," he said again. Roger was confused. Was he supposed to re-spond in some way? "So." Yeah, what? You're the one who brought me here. "What's your name, boy?" Mr. Leslie took out a brand new manila folder.

Roger closed his eyes and took a deep breath. "R-r-r-roger W-w-wharton."

"So, 'R-r-roger,' how do you spell that? With two g's or one?"

"w-w-one."

The Assistant Principal wrote Roger's name on the folder. "This is your permanent record, 'R-r-ro-ger.'"

Didn't he already have one? From when he was late last year? Or what about all the other stuff that was supposed to be in there, like how he got in trouble for talking in the second grade and Miss Belchi said that was going into his permanent re-cord? It would make sense if they already had a big folder with his name on it—and a big folder for each of the school's other students. But here was Mr. Leslie making a new folder for him. And he spelled Roger with two g's.

"So," the man said yet again. He must have ex-hausted himself yelling at the other kids, Roger thought. Now he would talk about Craig.

Or maybe not. The man took out the Nietz-sche book, flipping through it. "So. Were you read-ing this?"

"Y-yuppers." Stupid Tommy. "Yes." Now he would have to explain about the whole gay thing. But that was kind of stupid in itself. Roger didn't understand what was so wrong with being gay anyway.

"You are admitting to me that you were reading a book during lunch time?"

"I g-g-guess s-so." Roger realized he had no idea about what was going on.

"You 'g-g-guess' so?" mocked the Assistant Principal.

Roger nodded and shrugged at the same time. His handball pressed into his hamstring. Playing Boxball with Tommy would have been so much better right now.

"Do you not realize that reading during lunch time is not permitted?"

"Um, no?"

"It is against the school's rules."

It was the first Roger heard of it. He sat there silently, waiting for his punishment. Roger looked around the office while Mr. Leslie filled out a form. The muffled sound of several whistles blowing in the schoolyard made its way from the window Roger faced. That meant class would resume in about ten minutes. Mr. Leslie must have heard the whistles too. He glanced at his wristwatch and continued writing.

"Alright," Mr. Leslie looked up. Roger hoped for a warning or something similar. Surely his infraction didn't merit anything more severe. The rule itself was most dubious. "Your parents are going to have to come in and see me, as this is a suspension," the Assistant Principal said. The butterflies in Roger's stomach, which had taken a break during the interrogation, rose up in full force. It was as if they were trying to stomp on Roger's guts like Mario stomped on the stairs (or the kitchen floor when he wanted Tommy to come up). Parents had to come? What? It took Roger several moments to grasp that he was being suspended. He didn't feel anger yet. That would come later. Right now he was like a bug on its back, struggling while some demented child burned him with a magnifying glass. Parents had to come? Suspended? Roger couldn't believe it.

As if reading his mind, Mr. Leslie said, "yeah, that's right. You're being suspended. Your parents have to come in due to the seriousness of what you've done. Suspension will be for a week, starting from the end of school today." Mr. Leslie gave him one of the forms he had filled out. "Give this to your parents. I will be expecting a call from them. And give this to your teacher." Roger took the papers with shaking hands. "Now out you go. You don't want to be late to class. That'll add to your punishment. Go on now, while I'm still in a good mood."

Roger went back to class. He arrived at the same time as everyone else. No one seemed to notice that he wasn't there for lineup. Tommy looked at Roger with worried eyes when they sat down at their desks. "I've been suspended," Roger mouthed to Tommy.

"What?" Tommy mouthed back.

"Suspended," Roger mouthed.

"Stop being mean," Tommy mouthed and pouted.

Roger rolled his eyes. He stuffed the paper he was supposed to give Mr. G into his desk, making crinkling sounds. He was so nervous he didn't notice their teacher pull down the window blinds with the long brown pole with a hook at the end. Roger usually liked to watch others perform this task, as he had been the window monitor in second grade. The pole was heavy and unwieldy. He almost broke a window on more than one occasion trying to close it. He also didn't notice that Mr. Gorton turned off the lights. The sound from the television, which Roger had walked past without seeing, startled him from his anxious stupor.

So they were going to see a movie. It was by Columbia Pictures. Roger liked to know what studio made what movie, and what their logos were. The title came on with no sound: *Close Encounters of the Third Kind.* And then rose dissonance from stringed instruments, gradually gaining in volume and intensifying Roger's nervousness. Roger watched a desert scene unfold. He kept one hand in his desk, fingering the paper he was supposed to give Mr. Gorton.

Did Roger really have to give him the paper? Couldn't he just go to school and pretend nothing happened? If he avoided Mr. Leslie, who would know? And what would Mr. G think of him when he found out about the suspension? Would he be disappointed? Roger remembered his father's disappointment when he got an 80 on a test. Suspension was many times worse.

Roger toyed with the paper some more. Richard Dreyfus drove a truck in the fog, looking at a bunch of maps in the dark. How could he see anything? Dreyfus waved to a car behind him, telling the driver to go around.

Roger thought that he might drop the sheet of paper on Mr. Gorton's desk when the teacher stepped out during the movie. He did this often. Presumably it was to go out for a smoke. So, Roger thought he would get up and put the paper on the teacher's desk when Mr. Gorton left.

And there Mr. G went, quietly slipping out the door. It amazed Roger how no one misbehaved or even seemed to notice that the teacher was gone. This wasn't the first time he had this thought. On the television, another car approached Dreyfus. He noticed its headlights and started waving for it to go around. But it wasn't a car! The lights started rising. It was a craft, a UFO! And it was going over Dreyfus' truck. The mailboxes by the side of the road shook.

Intrigued, Roger decided to watch the movie instead of placing the sheet of paper on the teacher's desk. He would do that at the end of the day when they were leaving. Yeah, that made better sense anyway. If he put that paper there now, Mr. Gorton might see it before they left. Roger didn't want that. He didn't want to face his teacher. Putting it there at the end of the day, however, would ensure that Mr. G would see it on Monday, when Roger wasn't there. Yeah, that was definitely the way to go. First problem almost solved. Roger watched the movie, calmer.

Tommy, on the other hand, was quite tense. He concentrated on the screen. He clasped his hands tightly on his desk. At the same time, it looked like Tommy was trying to pull them apart. It was as if they were stuck, or he was doing isometric exercise. Roger figured when they went home from school Tommy would say something like his "handsies hurt." He smacked them lightly. Tommy turned to him. "Sorry," Tommy said.

"Shhh!" Meg hissed at them.

Tommy turned back to the screen. They continued watching the movie.

* * *

They had just enough time to get their jackets and schoolbags out of the closet when the credits began to roll. Mr. Gorton unplugged the television and VCR and rolled the set to a corner while his students put up their chairs. Roger clutched at the paper as they lined up next to the board. Mr. Gorton turned off the lights and escorted the class out. Now was the time to leave the paper on the teacher's desk. The butterflies did their usual dance.

Roger turned toward the desk. He hesitated. "Come on, hurry up," Michael said behind him. Roger moved toward the desk. "Come on!" Michael said again. Roger stopped. "What's wrong with you? Go!" Roger crumpled the paper in his jacket pocket and ran out the door to catch up with Tommy. As they left the building, Michael called, "'step on a crack/ break your mother's back!'"

Roger looked at Tommy sadly as the boy walked gingerly around the various imperfections in the concrete tiles that made up the schoolyard. What was he going to do with the note? How was he going to do the meeting thing? He didn't want to be taken away from Tommy's house. Despite all the craziness he thought of it as home.

Better not think about it. It was a Friday, after all. He had two full days to figure it out.

"So what's up?" Roger asked Tommy. The little boy raised his cheeks and rubbed his hands near the thumbs.

"Ow, my handsies hurt," Tommy reported.

"My handsies hurt," Roger said at the same time.

The boys stopped and faced each other. They narrowed their eyes and took deep breaths. And then:

"Jinx!" they said in unison.

"Double jinx!"

"Triple jinx!"

"Quadruple jinx!"

"Quintuple jinx!"

"Sextuple jinx!"

"Septuple jinx!"

"Octuple jinx!"

"Nonuple jinx"

Roger ran out of breath.

Tommy said, "Dectuple jinx!"

The boys started walking again, breathing hard. "I win!" said Tommy, raising his hands in the air. His jacket went up, along with his shirt, revealing a plump belly.

"No," said Roger. He took a moment to inhale. "I won. You said 'septuple' instead of 'sextuple' before."

"No I didn't!"

"And anyway, you said 'dectuple' instead of 'decuple.'"

"So?"

"So you didn't win."

"Sore loser."

"I know you are, but what am I?"

Tommy squinted at Roger again. The boy was planning something. Indeed. Tommy tapped Roger with his hand and started running from him. "Tag, you're it!" he said.

Roger stretched his hand out and tagged Tommy back.

"No fairs!" Tommy said, chasing the laughing Roger.

They got to the house just as a short school bus let Christine out at the curb. She didn't like her new school, but appreciated the door to door transportation. "It's Friday, you lazy bums!" she yelled at them. "Now get out of my way, I'm about to miss wrestling," she stormed into the house after Tommy unlocked the front door. "Don't let the cats out," Christine said as she rounded the corner into the dining room.

Roger closed the door behind them. Tigger stuck his head out from the second floor landing, watching them. Roger walked carefully around one of Lucky Joy's deposits.

"What the hell?" Christine said from the living room over Lucky Joy's excited barks. "Shadow, where's the TV? Where's my Nintendo?"

Roger entered the living room. The things Christine mentioned weren't the only ones missing. The couch was gone. The area where it had been standing looked much cleaner than the surrounding floor.

"Oh my God! I'm missing wrestling!" Christine said.

"We've been robbed, and all you're worried about is wrestling?" Roger asked.

"It's a very important match. Oh my God. Oh my God." She rubbed her palms and coughed in the way that she did when she got excited. Then Christine laughed. "Where is mom going to sleep?"

Mario came out of the kitchen holding a book about the Kennedy assassination. "Did you see what they did?" he whispered loudly to Tommy.

"Yuppers," Tommy said in a sad tone.

"Did he call the police?" Roger whispered to Tommy.

"Daddy," Tommy said, "did you call the police?"

"Oh, what heavens for? They were such nice young boys. I gave them a tip."

"What does he mean a tip?" Roger whispered to Tommy.

"How come you gave the robbers a tip, daddy?"

"No, no. They weren't robbers. They were re-po-men. One of them gave me a receipt. Such a nice young man." Roger looked to see what Tommy thought as Mario stomped up the stairs with his book under his arm.

"No TV today, then." Tommy said.

"Ha ha, suckers!" Christine said, racing up the stairs. Lucky Joy barked in the hallway, telling her to slow down. No doubt she was going to make Lucian watch wrestling with her, assuming Lucian's television wasn't taken. "Those stupid Jews!" Roger looked up at the ceiling. The upstairs television had been used to service their debts too.

Roger went down to the basement. Mr. Smith greeted him crankily at the bottom of the stairs. Nothing appeared missing there, but who could tell? Edith searched for something in the piles of rubble along the narrow path that led to the laundry room. "You'll find what you're looking for in the last place you look," Roger remembered Tommy saying. A chuckle escaped his lips. At least none of the books were repossessed, he thought. The pit of his stomach burned briefly as a memory of what had transpired that day shot into his mind. He ignored it. He would deal with it later.

Tommy came into their room just as Roger finished changing into his lounging clothes. Roger asked him whether his mom was going to sleep with his dad that night, since the couch had been taken away.

"Noppers," said Tommy. They would put lots of blankets on the floor where the couch had been, and Edith would sleep there. Tomorrow they would go to a furniture store to buy two beds. Roger was confused. Tommy shrugged and announced he was sleepy.

"And your tummy hurts too, doesn't it?" Roger asked.

"How did you know?" Tommy was amazed.

"In spite of all the chaos you are quite consistent."

"See? And you said me and my family was all craziness."

"My family and I."

"My family and I."

"So why are they getting two beds? And where are they going to put them?" Roger asked.

Tommy replied with his slumbering nose, *sss*. The gerbil made the only other sound in the room, attempting to destroy his wheel. Roger bent down next to the bookshelves, looking for something new to read. Again he felt a pang of heat in his stomach as thoughts of his suspension resurfaced. He ignored it, moving a soft toy piglet out of the way to see the book titles. They took his *Gay Science*. Maybe *On the Genealogy of Morals* would cheer him up. Roger grabbed the book, climbed up on his bunk, and started reading.

CHAPTER TEN
Saturday September 14, 1991

It was another sunny day. Roger looked at the trees from the kitchen window as he waited for Tommy to cook breakfast. It wasn't really breakfast, or cooking, Roger thought. It was still warm outside, but some of the leaves started to yellow.

The sound of the blender drew Roger's attention back to Tommy. The boy had decided to become a "rawfarian." His first creation, after consulting the multitudes of detox books, was the concoction he currently worked on. Roger looked at the zaftig brunette on one of the book covers. "So, what's in that stuff?"

"Um, um, um," Tommy tapped at his chin with an index finger. "Spinach, beets, apple, ginger, lemon, Swiss chards, and garlic. And hemp powder for protein."

Roger grimaced. "And you can't cook the spinach with the ginger and garlic, and chards I guess, and then make like an apple lemonade and put the beets back in the fridge?" he asked, hopeful.

"Noppers. This is so healthy and gives you lots of energies."

"But what about—"

Christine walked in then. "What's for breakfast," she said, rubbing her shoulder.

"Green juice!" Tommy announced happily.

"What are we eating it with?" Christine asked, clapping her hands on her belly.

"That's the whole thing. It's raw," Tommy explained.

"They took our stove too?" Christine shouted.

"Noppers, it's here."

"Then why can't we have a normal breakfast?"

"Yeah," Roger agreed.

"Silly Billies. Try out it first. It's so good for you," Tommy gave Christine a glass. Roger already knew what opinion Christine would express. First of all, she was hungry. Second, her only gustatory faculty was the analysis of the texture of clumps of poorly chewed food going down her throat.

"Delicious!" Christine said, handing her glass back to Tommy for seconds. Of course, Roger thought.

"See, Chris likes it."

"Christine will eat anything," Roger replied, taking a cautious sip. Not terrible. Not bad, actually. "When she's hungry, she even eats onions."

Christine laughed, motioning to Tommy that she wanted a third glass. "We're going shopping for beds today, my dad said."

"Why two beds?" Roger wanted to know.

Christine gulped down her third glass. She wiped her mouth with her forearm. "Because my back is all sore from sleeping on the floor with mom last night."

"What?" That didn't explain anything. "Why did you sleep on the floor? Did they repo your bed?"

"Okay, Wharton. Let me explain this to you so your puny mind can understand it."

"Okay..." Roger prepared himself for the revelation.

"We're getting two beds because I don't want to have to share with my mom."

Roger waited for more. Christine finished her fourth glass. Tommy started making the concoction again, for the rest of the family. Lucky Joy wandered in to drink water. Roger wondered if the dog had to eat raw stuff now too. He looked back at Christine. She stared at him.

"Well?" Roger asked.

"Well what?" Christine answered.

"You were going to explain to me why they're going to buy two beds."

"I already did, you lazy Jew."

"You said you didn't want to share with your mom."

"Yeah."

"But that doesn't explain anything. And what's with all the Jew comments lately?"

"I don't know. Wharton, you ask too many questions." Christine went down to the basement, patting her bulging belly. "Mr. Smith!" she yelled. "How are you doing today?"

Mr. Smith replied with his usual cranky "maah!" Roger heard purring.

Roger finished his juice. He turned to Tommy. "Can we have that soy bacon stuff with something delicious now?"

"I want some too!" Christine shouted from downstairs.

* * *

They piled into the car in the usual way: Edith in the driver's seat, Mario in a big fluffy coat, gloves, two scarves, and a thick hat riding shotgun, Roger behind Edith, Christine to his right, and Tommy in the middle. Lucky Joy ran over them from window to window. The destination was IKEA in Long Island, but they went to Brooklyn first to eat falafel.

Traffic slowed on the Brooklyn Queens Expressway. This made a driver behind them angry. He honked his horn every few seconds for at least ten minutes now. Roger tried not to pay attention. Instead, he looked past Christine and her Gameboy at the cemetery just off the road. To him it looked like a replica of the Manhattan skyline. The view in his own window was of smokestacks, silos, and warehouses. Roger wondered what was made there. Or, in this recession, were these buildings abandoned? They looked abandoned. Was it as dirty inside those buildings as it was outside?

They slowly rolled over Kosciuszko Bridge, a short span over a murky canal. The honking car was now directly behind them. It looked like a Buick or Oldsmobile to Roger. He couldn't really tell the difference. The man behind the wheel seemed to shout. It sounded like, "come on already, go!" but maybe Roger imagined it. He didn't quite understand the man's honking. It clearly had no effect on the speed of the cars in front of him. What was the point?

Roger resumed thinking about the canal and surrounding buildings. Probably the canal was made for the warehouses in the area. He didn't see any ships, though. Maybe because it was the weekend and goods were delivered during the work week. Or maybe all these buildings were empty. Maybe only the mafia used them, like in the movies, to kill and torture people. Or maybe aliens had a base there, abducting people. Roger yawned. He hadn't slept well the night before. He dreamed about aliens chasing after him in their space ships, trying to suspend him from school. He woke up periodically, terrified. It was only by dawn that he was able to fall soundly asleep. The light always made things less scary.

Roger wondered to what body of water the canal connected, and whether it was the same canal that he saw when they drove to Manhattan on the Long Island Expressway. The East River maybe? Or the Long Island Sound? It would be cool if he had a map. Roger would have loved to study that. Were there fish in the canal? Or was the water too poisonous? Who made sure that nothing bad was dumped there? After the run in with Colonel Roberts and the policeman, Roger suspected no one did.

The driver behind them switched into the lane to their right. He honked and cursed alongside their station wagon. Christine paused her Gameboy to laugh at the man, who waved a cigarette out his window frantically. He really must be in a hurry, Roger thought. Past him, off in the distance, was the Citibank Building. It was a tall building, probably the tallest in New York City outside Manhattan. He had gone there once long ago with his parents for some sort of court hearing. He knew for certain that it was in Queens, which made him laugh, despite a pang of sadness, when during a school trip Mrs. Dixon called it the tallest building in Brooklyn.

They finally approached the source of the traffic. Drivers heading in the opposite direction were almost at a stop. They gawked at a truck in the shoulder next to the divider. The road ahead of them was empty. The truck's hood stood open and its operator, tiny in comparison, fiddled inside. Cars honked on both sides of the road now. The enraged Oldsmobile driver swerved left ahead of their Caprice, cutting them off. Edith honked and slammed on the brakes. The Oldsmobile driver stopped his car in the third lane and popped his head out the window. Apparently he wanted a closer look at what was wrong with the truck. Roger wondered why the man was no longer in a hurry.

Once they got around the Oldsmobile, the road was clear ahead of them all the way to the falafel shop.

"That's so stupid," Tommy remarked. "They caused all that traffic to look at a broken down truck. And, like, whenever they have a sign that says roadwork, or just a tow truck or something, everyone slows down for no reason!"

"What's falafel made out of?" Roger changed the subject.

"Chickpeas and stuff," Tommy replied. "It's soooo good," he smacked his lips and puffed his cheeks.

"Is it cooked?"

"Yuppers. It's fried or baked."

"Aren't you raw now?"

"Yuppers."

"But you're going to eat falafel."

"Shhh! It's a secret. I'm going to eat cooked food on the weekends."

"Okay," Roger said. He wondered from whom this information was a secret, as almost everyone that Tommy talked to was in the car. As Edith told Lucian everything, that left no one out.

They parked across the street from the Greek take-out place. Christine asked Edith for pizza money. Edith waited in the car with Lucky Joy while Mario, Tommy, and Roger went to the falafel shop and Christine entered the pizzeria next door.

Although it had been his idea to go there, Mario said he was not going to order anything for himself. He wasn't hungry. Tommy and Roger waited outside for their order. It took a while, Tommy explained, because everything was made fresh.

Christine came out of the pizzeria with an open pizza box. She devoured a slice in the few moments it took her to approach them. Her eating ability never ceased to amaze Roger.

"You should enter one of those competitions. Like that hotdog eating one."

Christine laughed and ate another slice. "I don't eat meat," she said, her laughter causing cheesy spittle to fly from her maw.

Roger stepped away as Christine edged closer. "What about like a pie eating contest or something?"

"I'll think about it," Christine was on her third slice. "So, Wharton, when are you getting a job?"

"You know how old I am, right?"

"So? Don't be lazy. You can work for the government and do nothing the whole day. You get paid for pretending to do work."

"I thought you said I shouldn't be lazy."

"*The Medellín Cartel*," Christine did her voice-over voice. She was back in her own world. Roger guessed she would be rubbing her palms together if she didn't hold the pizza box in one hand and her fourth slice in the other.

Christine had one slice left in her pizza box when they got back in the car. She gave the barking Lucky Joy a few bits and ate the rest herself. As the car pulled away from the curb, Christine asked where her falafel pita sandwich was.

"Wait! Stop the car!" Tommy shrieked. Edith obliged, and Tommy motioned for Roger to get out.

"Wha—?" Roger managed as he got out of the car. Tommy was quick to follow. "What's going on?" he asked, but Tommy ignored him. The little boy ran off in the direction of a small black fence bordering a grassy area next to an apartment building. Roger turned back to look at Christine, Mario, and Edith. They all sat in the car, waiting patiently. Christine ate her pita and Lucky Joy demanded some. Mario also ate a pita. Edith drummed on the steering wheel to music she heard in her head. It

192

was as if nothing at all out of the ordinary had just occurred. "What's going on, Christine?"

She turned to him, put the last of the pita into her mouth, and grabbed the dog. "Come here you little bastard!" she said affectionately, petting Lucky Joy. Then she looked at Roger. "What's wrong with you, Wharton? Close the car door before the dog escapes."

Roger did as he was told, more confused than ever. He turned back to the direction Tommy had run. The round boy was now on his way back. His light jacket was off and wrapped around something that he cradled in his arms. As he got closer, Roger saw that it was orange.

When they got back in the car, everyone looked at the kitten Tommy found. Everyone except Lucky Joy, that is. The dog growled for a second, and then pretended the cat wasn't there. Roger marveled at Tommy's preternatural ability to find helpless animals. He had a radar for such things. This one was quite energetic, clawing playfully at his shirt.

"Oh my God, Tommy. Another cat." Christine looked up from her Gameboy. "Are we running some kind of orphanage? Wharton here doesn't even have a job. How are we supposed to support all these animals?"

"So why don't you get a job, Chris?" Roger asked.

"I don't need a job," Christine said. "As soon as I turn 18 I'm going to bag me a rich man. Then I'll be on easy street."

"I suppose this man will be blind?" Roger said.

Christine let out a loud belch.

"And deaf!" Roger cried. Then, waving a hand before his nose, "and with anosmia!"

"Stop being mean to my sister," Tommy said. Christine laughed.

They continued talking in the same way all the way to IKEA. Roger ate and enjoyed his pita. The falafel was like meatballs, but with a different texture. Roger wondered whether Socrates ate falafel, or if it was invented at a later date. And was it Greek? Did chick peas grow in Greece?

As Tommy held the kitten, Roger had to hold Tommy's pita in front of him. Tommy took bites from it and chewed quickly. They were making a mess. Roger had to contend with the bumpy ride, the numerous turns Edith made, and Christine's attempts to snatch the sandwich away. One never noticed how much one was swayed by various physical forces in a moving vehicle until one sat on a seat that wasn't cushioned or tried to keep something steady in front of someone else. Roger cursed. He learned that pita bread had almost no structural integrity. Lettuce, humus, tomato slices, pieces of falafel, and crumbs rained down on the kitten. It reacted by hiding underneath Tommy's jacket. It looked out occasionally until it fell asleep. Tommy's face wasn't as fortunate. On his every bite, and sometimes in between, it collided with the sandwich, smothering more humus on him. Parts of the sandwich clung to his nose and forehead. He somehow managed to get some on his ears as well. By the time they stopped at a CheapPets to buy a bottle for the new cat (between bites Tommy explained that he forgot where he put the bottles they used to feed Tigger, Shadow, and Peek-a-boo) Tommy's face resembled that of a clown. Christine almost poked Tommy in the eye grabbing the crumbs from his face.

* * *

Mario bought two bookcases at IKEA. Although IKEA also sold beds, their original intended purchase, Mario decided to go to the Price for them. Everyone was tired when they finally drove up to the house, except for the kitten, who slept throughout the journey. Lucky Joy pooped and peed in the hallway when they entered the house. He must have been holding that in for a long time, Roger thought. Tommy looked for a shoe box and empty bottles to house the kitten at night. Christine scoured the fridge for something to eat. After a moment Edith joined her. She was hungry, as Mario ate her sandwich.

Then Mario told everyone to move Christine's bed out of her room and put it on the curb for garbage pickup. Mario went to his room to relax while Roger, Christine, and Edith struggled with the mattresses and bed frame down the stairs. Roger couldn't see what was wrong with the bed.

"So how come you couldn't sleep on it yesterday, tonight, tomorrow...?" Roger asked Christine.

"Because we got a new one."

"But that doesn't answer my question. Is there something wrong with it?"

"No, we got a new one," Christine said heading up the stairs to the front porch.

"But the garbage men don't come around until Tuesday morning. I don't get why you had to throw your bed out, especially since there's nothing wrong with it."

"Because we got a new one," Christine repeated. She seemed to think that the matter was settled. "Oh my God," she said. "I can't believe I have to sleep on the floor again tonight."

"But you could've slept on your bed! That's what I was asking!"

"How many times do I have to tell you? We got a new bed."

"So why don't you sleep on it tonight?"

"Because my stupid mom is too lazy to untie the mattresses from the roof and build everything. Because she's lazy I have to sleep on the floor."

Roger rolled his eyes and went to find Tommy.

CHAPTER ELEVEN
Sunday, September 15, 1991

Roger awoke to the commotion in the kitchen above him. Mario's heavy thuds, this close to the ceiling, made Roger think that at any second he might see a foot come through. Edith probably sat on the couch. Her rhythmic tapping provided the tempo for Christine's randomly timed jumps. It was always two quick jumps in succession, but when they would occur was a mystery. In his mind's eye Roger saw Christine bowing up and down and swinging her arms to and fro. Where she picked up those strange motions was also a mystery.

Tommy was up too. His bunk was empty. The kitten was in its box next to Tommy's bed. They had to put a weight on top of the cover to prevent the kitten from getting out. He was a strong little guy, older than the other three kittens when Tommy and Roger first rescued them. Roger looked back towards the noise coming from the ceiling. It was time to go up there and see what was happening.

When he came up the stairs, Roger heard Christine laughing and clapping her hands. She always clapped so arrhythmically. It was never continuous and came in random spurts. "Ha ha ha ha." Clap. "It probably cost," clap clap, "them more to

197

tow it away," clap "than it's worth." Clap clap clap clap.

Tommy sat on an overturned bucket next to the couch. He petted Mr. Smith, who overflowed from his lap. Lucky Joy ran around demanding food. This was the kitchen, after all. Roger bent down to say hi to the dog, who was completely oblivious to Mr. Smith's presence. Christine often remarked that Lucky Joy wouldn't let out a peep if robbers ever came to the house. Looking at the demanding Pomeranian now, Roger thought maybe the dog would lead the thieves to all the good stuff. Lucky ran off to Edith, who handed him a giant slice of cheese. Lucky trotted to the living room, his head bent by the cheese's weight.

"What's going on?" Roger asked Tommy.

"The repomans took away the car," the boy said glumly.

Roger thought for a moment. "Were the mattresses still on the roof?"

"Yuppers."

"So what's going to happen now?"

"They might have to borrow my aunt's car," Tommy replied. Roger knew the reason for his anxious tone. Everything from Tommy's aunt Hernia came with strings attached. Knots, actually. Gordian knots. Christine already had to shovel snow, rake leaves, and mow the lawn for Hernia for the next two years after Mario asked for two cups of sugar that summer. It's true, borrowing two cups of sugar wasn't exactly borrowing, as they would never be returned. But Roger wondered what price Hernia would set on lending out her car. He hoped it wouldn't involve him or Tommy. Her house was cold and scary, and once you entered Hernia didn't let you leave.

"Do we have to go back to the store today then?"

"I dunno. My dad's not feeling well. He accidentally closed a door on his head this morning."

"How did that happen?"

"I dunno."

"Tomorrow's Monday!" Christine belched. "I hate Mondays." Clap. Clap. Clap. "Roger, you should be a repoman. I guess they work on weekends, but it's a fun job." Clap. "Come on. You know you want to. Make little kids cry when you take their stuff away and say, 'you shouldn'ta bought all this stuff.'" Clap. Christine laughed. "I hate Mondays. Oh look, it's the black guy, Shadow!" Christine kissed the surprised kitten on the forehead.

Roger and Tommy spent most of the day playing with the new kitten. Roger suggested naming the cat Galen. Tommy agreed. But for some reason everyone else ended up calling the cat Leland.

* * *

It was late afternoon, normally the time when everyone took a nap. Everyone except Roger. Try as he might, he couldn't sleep during the day. And as far back as he could remember, he had trouble falling asleep at night. The only time when he had no trouble at all falling asleep was in the morning. So the next two hours were usually reserved for reading.

Christine's pacing, jumping, and clapping directly above him, however, made it difficult the last couple of days. Edith had no trouble sleeping on the floor, or at least she didn't complain. Christine, on the other hand, walked on Roger's head. Now she muttered between syncopated claps. It was a mash of noises, squeaks and mouth farts. Roger had trouble understanding most of it, but he heard one sentence clearly because Christine uttered it repeatedly every Sunday: "Tomorrow's Monday."

Roger's suspension had been in the back of his mind the entire weekend. But now it sprang to the front on a jet of adrenaline. What was he going to do? He debated pretending that nothing happened. He could just go to school tomorrow. He hadn't given Mr. G the suspension slip. That was still in his jacket pocket. But what about Mr. Leslie? Roger would have to avoid him. Plus, would that guy even remember? It seemed to Roger that Leslie always had a train of students that were in trouble. Would he remember Roger? It had been a couple of days.

The man didn't seem to remember Roger from last year. Sure, it had been a long time, but maybe the man's memory wasn't that good. Maybe most of the kids at school looked the same to him. But what about the whole meeting with the parents thing? Wouldn't he remember that? Roger tried to recall if he saw Leslie making a note of it anywhere. He did not think that he did. And if they had to call him to make an appointment, maybe he wouldn't remember at all. But what about the note in Roger's file? Did it say anything about having to meet with his parents? Roger didn't know.

Maybe it was time to get Tommy's perspective on the matter. Roger looked down over the side of his bunk. Tommy slept at a weird angle with his mouth open. The outline of his legs under the covers did not match his torso. They were bent one way, his body the other. A teddy bear was tucked under one of Tommy's arms. His nose made *sss* sounds, as usual, when he exhaled. "Hey Tommy," Roger whispered. Now louder, "psst! Tommy!"

The boy didn't even stir. His teddy bear looked up at Roger with small, shiny black eyes. It rose and fell with Tommy's breathing. Roger wondered where his teddy bears were now and who might be using them. "Psst! Tommy! I have to ask you something." No response.

Roger returned to his former position. He played chess with the little globs of paint and other imperfections in the ceiling for a few minutes. What would Mr. G think? Would he be disappointed with Roger? Suspension was a big deal. Short of expulsion, it was the worst punishment a student could receive. Roger thought about it some more. It actually wouldn't be so bad if Leslie didn't want a meeting with Roger's parents. It would be sort of like a week vacation. Come to think of it, that didn't sound like a punishment at all. But what about the parent thing? Roger noticed that he was clasping his hands together. He tried to relax. He burped and little pieces of his lunch burned their way into his mouth. He swallowed them back down painfully.

Roger turned back onto his stomach and looked over the edge of his bunk at Tommy. "Hey, are you sleeping?" Well, duh! Roger looked for something soft to throw at the boy. He checked his pockets and found a tissue. He tore off a small piece that didn't appear to have any buggers on it. Roger folded it into a small ball and flicked it at Tommy. It wasn't heavy enough. The tiny ball glided to the carpet. Roger thought a moment. Then he folded the entire tissue, like a snowball. This more massive projectile would hopefully reach its target.

Roger threw it and it hit its mark. Roger stifled a laugh and watched Tommy stir. The little boy opened his eyes and looked at his teddy bear.

"What's that Sweeney?" Tommy asked. "Yuppers, I'm sleepy too. Good night then." Tommy squeezed his bear and turned his body toward the wall. A moment later Roger heard soft snoring. He gave up and returned to his back. He picked up his book and began reading. He shifted slightly and the bed creaked, almost inaudibly.

"I'm awake!" Tommy announced. Roger heard him sit up and then felt and heard a thud under him as Tommy bumped his head. "Ow!" the boy said below him. Roger looked down at his bunk mate. Tommy rubbed the top of his head with one hand. With the other he unfurled the tissue Roger had thrown at him and blew his nose into it. Tommy looked up at him. "I'm awake," he yawned and smacked his lips.

"You were just sleeping so soundly. What happened?"

"I don't know. Something woke me up." Tommy's stomach made a rumbling noise. "Was that yours or mines?"

"Yours, I think," Roger replied to one of Tommy's standard questions.

"Why are you making so much noise, Tommy?" Tommy patted himself on the belly. "I fed you so good already."

"You call your stomach Tommy?" Roger asked.

"Yuppers. So what?"

"Nothing." He paused. Then, as Tommy rubbed the sleep from his eyes, Roger said, "I have to ask you something."

"About your suspension and for my mommy and daddy to go talk to the school for you?"

"Uh, yeah." Roger started. "How did you know?"

"We already talkeded about it."

"Pretty sure we haven't."

"Maybe I dreamed it."

"So what did we agree upon then?"

"I don't remember. I'm sorry, but I don't remember! Stop yelling at me!"

"What? I wasn't yelling."

"Your face was yelling at me. I'm sorry I forgot, okay?"

"As far as I know, we didn't have that conversation."

"Oh, okay. Maybe that's why I don't remember. What? Why are you rolling your eyes and sighing so?"

"No reason," Roger replied. "So what do you think I should do?"

"About what?"

"Mr. Leslie said I got suspended and my parents have to meet with him."

"Okay. So when are your parents going to meet him?"

Roger gave Tommy a look. "My mom's dead and I don't know where my dad is."

"That's so sad," Tommy said, tearing up. His right hand went up to his face in a solemn wave. This was his not so successful way of avoiding tears.

"I thought you knew all this."

"I do. Sorry, I forgot that I remembered."

"So, what do you think I should do? I'm not even sure that Mr. G will find out because I didn't give him a note I was supposed to. I thought maybe I could just go to school and pretend that nothing happened. Avoid Mr. Leslie for a week, and then all will be forgotten."

"That sounds like a good plan."

"But the whole meeting thing. I'm not sure if Mr. Leslie will forget about that."

"Yeah."

"So what do you think?" Roger asked.

"I don't know."

"Can you ask your parents if they could meet with Mr. Leslie?"

"I already did," Tommy replied.

"What? When?"

"Yesterday. They said 'okay.'"

"Really?"

"Yuppers."

"How come you didn't tell me?"

Tommy shrugged. "I dunno. I forgot I guess. By the way, who's Mr. Leslie?"

Roger sighed. This was going to be more difficult than he thought. "What do you mean 'who's Mr. Leslie'? He's the guy that suspended me and wants to meet with my parents."

"Oh. Okay. He's mean."

"So all this time when I kept mentioning Leslie you didn't know who I was talking about?"

"I dunno." Tommy shrugged. "Belly, I will feed you soon. I'm having a very important discussion with Roger right now," Tommy said and poked his belly. "Isn't that right, Mr. Sweeney?" Tommy made his teddy bear nod.

Roger began from the top, trying to figure out exactly what Tommy knew, what he told his parents, and what they said. They talked for another half hour. Just when Roger thought he figured everything out, Tommy said something that made his understanding crumble. It was built up and collapsed several times before Roger thought he was on firm ground. It was determined, finally, before they went upstairs to get food, that Tommy mentioned Roger's suspension to his parents the previous day. They thought it was stupid and unfair, and would help in any way they could. Mario let it be known that he was against the foster care system, his reasons being the various biological experiments he had read about. Edith indicated her support as well, by nodding. Christine, for some reason, wasn't to know about any of this. Mario's paranoia had something to do with it, Roger reckoned. Tommy's parents would meet with Leslie sometime during the week. Roger and Tommy could come with them if they liked.

"So all this was decided and you didn't tell me anything?" Roger asked when they entered the kitchen. Edith's snoring on the living room floor reverberated in the walls.

"I was going to, but I forgot. Please don't yell at me. I feel bad about it already. Oh hello Tigger! Who's my special little guy?" Tommy chased after the orange cat. "Boo! I caught you! Yes I did! Yes I did!"

"Focus," Roger implored.

"Oh, right." Tommy let the cat down. "What were we talking about?"

* * *

It was evening. Roger was on his bunk on his stomach. His book was open before him on the pillow, but he wasn't reading. Christine paced above him. As usual, her complaints about Monday filled the house. There came an isolated clap, followed by what sounded like rummaging in the fridge.

Roger still didn't know what to do. He could ask Tommy to put the note on Mr. G's desk. He could also go to school and pretend nothing happened. Although not having to go to school was any kid's dream, Roger felt apprehensive about it. What would his classmates think when they found out that he was suspended? What would Mr. Gorton think? Would he have a disappointed look on his face when Roger came back a week later, now a center of attention? Then there was the issue of being a week behind on his schoolwork. Not that it was hard or anything. But it would be like he was an outsider, having missed out on a week's worth of happenings. He had the flu in the second grade and missed two weeks of school. It was strange coming back. When you are involved in something, you do not notice how much happens. When you are away, it is as if everything is different when you come back. Everything that happened in those two weeks became an inside joke he wasn't privy to. He didn't want to repeat the experience, especially not with the stigma of being suspended. So he pondered.

Tommy had gone upstairs to "the temple" to consult his tarot cards in an effort to help him. Roger was confused but not exactly surprised. He had been wondering why Christine's bed and furniture were removed. She paced in the kitchen a lot more than usual. He should have guessed that she had been evicted from her room. Roger blamed his worries about school for his inability to figure it out earlier.

Roger wondered about what kind of temple Mario built in Christine's room. They celebrated every holiday on the calendar, and many that were not. Roger knew that they went to the nearby Hindu and Buddhist temples, most of which were just rooms in yoga instructors' studios. They had those pictures of various bald men in red and orange colored robes in the living room. And what about the large bowl with its various figurines and dollar bills that he saw Edith take out occasionally on Mario's prompting? Perhaps it was some weird conglomeration of religions. Tommy's tarot cards pointed in that direction. Roger ruminated. Tommy's calling it a temple probably meant Jesus was not involved. Maybe that was Lucian's area of expertise. He went to church every morning, except Saturdays when he went to the synagogue. Then again, Mario, when he was awake at that hour, liked to throw holy water at them when they left for school. It was definitely weird, Roger thought. He wondered if other people had temples in their houses.

Roger asked Tommy more than once why they celebrated everything. Tommy replied that it was for luck. They had a lot of money problems. Roger asked why, instead of all the rituals and costly celebrations, they could not instead focus on fixing their money woes. Indeed, the celebrations seemed to be part of the problem, if perhaps not as bad as all the donations they gave to monks, psychics, gurus, and other spiritual wanderers. At times it seemed to Roger that Tommy's family was financially supporting most of the world's religious itinerants. And probably an even larger percentage of stray cats, if the backyard was any indication. The neighbors, a nosy elderly couple, were threatening for weeks to call the police.

Tommy didn't have an answer for that question. And neither, it appeared, did he have any further advice for Roger regarding his current dilemma. "I dunno," Tommy said on his return. He brought with him a cloud of incense.

Roger sneezed. "What did your cards say?" he asked skeptically as Tommy reached in the aquarium to fish out his gerbil. Roger still thought it looked like a rat.

Tommy petted the furry creature and put him in a plastic blue ball. Friedrich rolled around after Tommy, as the little boy went to put away his cards. "I dunno. They said you'll be okay ways both."

"In other words, you don't know what I should do."

Tommy shrugged.

They stayed up past their usual bedtime playing Uno. Roger couldn't sleep because he was worried. Tommy was uncharacteristically awake. Roger asked him if his stomach hurt or something.

Tommy had to think about it for a while, petting the sleeping Galen who rested his chin on the little boy's leg. "I think I'm my usual 65%," he replied.

CHAPTER TWELVE
Monday, September 16, 1991

Roger awoke at the foot of Tommy's bunk. He peeled an Uno card off his face, looking over at Tommy. He was sleeping. *Sssss.* Roger couldn't see the clock on the bottom shelf of one of the bookcases, but judging from the faint light in the window, it was somewhere between five and six. He thought about climbing into his bunk to sleep some more. Then he remembered that it was Monday and that he still didn't know what he was going to do. That thought ensured that he would not get any more sleep that morning.

He felt clammy. Cold moisture clung to his body, collecting under his armpits and between his thighs. Roger decided to take advantage of the early hour with a quick a shower. Normally he had to wait for someone, despite two working bathrooms. Tommy's family had the uncanny propensity to beat him to it almost every time he had to go. No, he thought to himself as he looked around for his towel. That can't be the case. The real explanation was probably that he didn't remember those occasions when he had to go to the bathroom and it was unoccupied. On the other hand, it was memorable when it was in use. For it made him annoyed. When he had to go and they were in there, he would definitely remember that. It was like passing people in doorways or narrow paths, Roger reasoned. It always seemed that people got in his way in those places. But most likely he passed people all the time, and only noticed them crowding in doorways and narrow hallways because they got in his way. Roger nodded to himself. That made sense. He slung his towel over his shoulder and put on a pair of flip-flops.

Roger slid the door open and was greeted by Peek-a-boo. She looked at him with her big eyes and arched her back awkwardly. Tommy said the other day that the cat was autistic. He made a mental note to look that word up. He patted the cat on top of her head. Her purr sounded like she swallowed a toy engine. It was sort of like when the older kids put a plastic bottle between the body and rear wheel of their bicycles, but quieter. Peek-a-boo's eyes opened even wider and she ran off up the stairs, hissing and purring at the same time. Roger looked down at his feet to see Galen hopping around. He would feed him after he got out of the shower.

Roger walked around piles of stuff. What was it with Tommy's family and making narrow passages everywhere? Why couldn't they stack things in the corners? Better yet, why did they have to buy any of this stuff? Was it really necessary to get all those detox books? How many different ways were there to do an enema anyway? Why couldn't they move all this crap to that big open space right there?

He jumped when Mr. Smith let out a *waaa* right next to him. He had not seen the cat sitting atop of a stack of boxes. "Oh man, Mr. Smith, your breath smells horrible. Even worse than Christine's." Roger made a mental note to mention that to Christine when he saw her. Roger slid open the bathroom door and turned left to the shower.

Oh my God. He jumped out of the bathroom with his eyes shut and his hands pressing over them. Mario stood in the tub. Naked. Roger tried to erase the image from his mind. The more he tried, the longer it persisted. The water wasn't on. What the hell was he doing in there? And this early? And what was wrong with the bathroom upstairs? Mario started humming, "ommm."

Roger grumbled to himself and climbed the stairs. Hopefully that bathroom was free. He moved quietly through the dining room and into the hall, though stealth wasn't required. Edith and Christine snored so loudly it was doubtful that any noise he made could waken them. Lucky Joy snored too, and whimpered. Perhaps he had a nightmare. If he woke up and started barking, that might actually awaken the two giants. Roger crept faster. Up the stairs he went. Shadow ran past, almost tripping him. Tigger was close on his brother's tail. Soon Galen would be joining them. He was already climbing and tumbling down the stairs in the basement.

Oh, to be a cat in Tommy's house. To not have a care in the world. It was like a cruise. The food and water bowls were always out. It was all you could eat. Any time you wanted a massage, you just had to come up to someone or jump on them. Plenty of friends were around for play and exercise. And sleeping and lounging was so comfortable, one could do it on his back with his paws up in the air, enjoying the warmth from the always on radiators. Roger reached the landing jealously. The butterflies that lived in his belly were now working in full force. Good thing the bathroom was near. He realized that he had to go.

Just as Roger rounded the corner, however, Lucian emerged from his room and ran down the hall. He slammed the door to the bathroom. Really? Roger heard the lock click into place. "You see," Roger said to Tigger, who wanted him to rub his belly. "This always happens. It's like they know."

* * *

It was probably the first time in the fourth grade that Roger felt especially nervous about going to school. Perhaps it was because he wasn't supposed to be there. It felt like it would be a hot day, and Roger already sweated. He looked to his left, past Tommy. The scorching sun shimmered in the haze between yellowing tree branches. The cars that passed them on 80th Street all had their windows rolled down. Edith was supposed to get a replacement car today. That was the morning talk in the kitchen, anyway.

Roger took a deep breath, trying to calm himself. All he had to do, he told his tightening stomach, was avoid Mr. Leslie. He already had the weekend to forget all about it. Most likely he had forgotten the moment Roger left the office, and the whole thing would blow over. One could hope.

Something shuffled in Tommy's book bag. Roger watched with interest as the top zippers undid themselves. A small pinkish nose and white whiskers stuck out.

"Is there a cat in your schoolbag?"

"Yuppers," Tommy replied happily.

"It's trying to get out."

"Oh." Tommy removed one of his shoulder straps and gently whirled the bag around. "Go back in, little one." He nudged, and the cat collapsed down into the bag.

"Is that Galen?"

"Yeah, it's Leland."

"What are you doing bringing him to school?" Roger was worried.

"I thought he might want to come."

"You're not going to keep him in the bag all day?"

"Why not?"

"Because it's too hot."

"Oh."

"How about I take him home?"

"Noppers. It's okay. I think he'll like it. I'll out figure something." Now Roger was really worried. What the hell was Tommy thinking bringing the kitten?

They entered the school through one of the yard doors and went to stand under one of the basketball hoops where their class lined up. Isadora and Clyde were already there. Roger looked around while Tommy played with the kitten inside his bag. Craig made the rounds. He punched Clyde and gave him an Indian burn. He approached the occupied Tommy, intending to smack the back of his head, from the look of it. Roger stepped between them, glaring. Craig went off in the other direction, like a cat pretending that nothing happened. No sign of Mr. Leslie. So far so good. Students slowly trickled into the building, and by the 8:30 bell the space was as loud as it was at lunch.

After a series of whistles quieted everyone down, the Principal made several announcements. Or perhaps it was just a long one. Despite her use of a megaphone, Roger didn't quite hear anything she said. Mr. Leslie, who normally stood at her side

217

for this morning ritual, was nowhere to be seen. Roger hoped he was absent. It would be so cool if he got fired or transferred.

Tommy was in front of him. His schoolbag emitted strange sounds and bulged in its sides as Galen poked around. No one else appeared to notice. They recited the Pledge of Allegiance. It was a cacophonous affair. Most of the children made up their own words. Roger tried to decipher what Tommy jubilantly chanted at the top of his lungs, ignoring Michael's tapping on his shoulder. "I pledgeabaleegence to the flag and the understands of America. And the republic which it stands on nation under God, invisible, with libraries and justice for all." That made Roger smile.

Michael was still tapping his shoulder. He turned around. Michael pretended to look elsewhere while his arm flicked down to his side. Roger thought about telling him he was a one trick pony, but he didn't want to encourage any innovation. He turned to face forward as the class started to follow Mr. G to the staircase. There came the tap again.

"Seriously! You got nothing better—" Roger started to say. He found himself face to face with Mr. Leslie. Beady eyes stared at him from the deranged pink face. He looked far scarier than Roger remembered.

"You!" the man said. "You're not supposed to be here." He pulled Roger to the front door by the top strap of his bag, lifting him. Roger followed along with his toes barely touching the shiny floor. "Do you understand that you're suspended, you stupid kid? God, I hate my job."

Roger said nothing. He felt like it was all a dream. Maybe it was. Tommy wasn't silly enough to bring a cat to school, was he? No, that did seem like him. "Don't let me see you here again for a week, or you're trespassing," Leslie said and slammed the door. Roger stood on the steps for a bit. He debated about going back in and trying to evade the Assistant Principal. But what was the point? He was suspended. What the hell was he thinking coming to school in the first place?

Relief suddenly washed over him. Roger's gait became more springy, excited almost. His serious and anxious mien gave way to one of frivolity. Someone observing him from a distance might have mistaken him for Tommy. Fuck Mr. Leslie. He was on vacation.

Deciding to enjoy his day as best as he could, Roger strolled to the park. Except for a couple of dog walkers and a few old men playing bocce ball, the park was deserted. Even the squirrels and birds that typically ran all over the place were nowhere to be seen. Roger thought they might be preparing for the coming heat. Animals were smart like that. Tommy said so, anyway.

Roger dropped his schoolbag on the playground's black rubbery mat and flopped down on a swing. He gripped the almost too hot chains that kept it aloft, twisting his seat counterclockwise. The chains clinked together every time he made a rotation, and his seat rose higher. He rotated until his toes barely touched the ground. Then he let his feet go and the chains slowly unraveled, spinning him clockwise at an accelerating rate. The world past the tips of his feet became a blur as trees, the baseball field, swings, tennis courts, and the playground spun around him. Roger felt himself pulled by an unseen force in the direction of his feet. It occurred to him then that the earth's centrifugal force, generated by its rotation, must be weaker than its gravitational force. Or was it centripetal force? He could never quite remember. Would he weigh more if the earth stopped rotating?

He missed going to the library. The answers to that and other questions were sometimes to be found there. It was maybe half an hour's walk from the park. Maybe he'd go there next. Roger was swinging in the regular fashion now, dizzy from the earlier twists. It was a tall swing, so he was able to achieve a good height at the apex of his back and forward swings. The playground was situated on a hill above a massive tree lined field. It included four giant baseball fields, with plenty of room in the middle for soccer or football. Beyond the park, ahead of him and seemingly at the same level, was Manhattan. To the left were the Twin Towers, two ugly gray rectangles. He had gone there on a school trip in the first grade, but couldn't really remember anything of note. That he felt nauseated on the school bus was his only memory. Almost in the center of his vision was the Empire State Building. He went there with his mother once. The glass in the observation deck was so dirty he couldn't see anything. The Chrysler Building, which he sometimes confused with the Empire State Building, was over a bit to the right. And to the right of that was his favorite building that could be seen from this vantage point, the Citicorp Center. He liked it because its roof was angled at 45 degrees. Nothing else was special about the building, but that roof made it unique. Roger chuckled. Supposedly it was built that way so they could install solar panels. But they didn't realize when they designed it that sunlight wouldn't ever hit the solar panels directly. A loss for the building owner and a gain for the electric company.

Roger watched the city bob up and down as warm air pushed his hair back and forward. He probably needed a haircut. It was starting to get in his eyes. It looked like a cemetery, the city. He had the same thought every time he saw it. A long skyline of tombstones winking in the sun.

When he swung back, Roger turned his head left to glimpse his school through the trees. He wondered what Tommy was doing now. He hoped the cat wasn't stuck in his friend's schoolbag in the closet. That might kill it. But where would Tommy put it? Underneath his shirt? In his desk? Would it fit in there? Where would it go to the bathroom? What would it eat? Roger worried about the cat. Despite his good intentions, Tommy probably didn't think of any of these things. They always had to be pointed out to him. "That's not true! I'm very thoughtful!" Roger heard Tommy pouting in his head.

He stopped moving his legs back and forth. He was lower with each swing, until his outstretched legs dragged on the ground and he dismounted. Roger decided to go to the library. So far, it was a fine start to his vacation. It occurred to him that he should treat himself to something. He did have that $5 bill that Edith gave each of them that morning before they left for school. Roger exited the play-ground and started walking toward the little deli on the corner of Juniper Boulevard North and Dry Harbor Road, at the edge of the small park. He took out the bill to make sure it wasn't a United States note, as Mario said these were worth more than $5.

A few minutes later, he crossed Dry Harbor Road, recalling that this was where the boulevard turned into an avenue. Who was responsible for naming and classifying streets anyway? A bell by the door rang as he went in. It was a small shop, with two aisles and two refrigerated sections on the side walls. Up ahead was the register and lotto machine. A middle aged Korean man looked at him with suspicion. Roger figured the man's wife had the later shift today. Behind the man was a large selection of cigarettes, cigars, and dirty magazines.

Roger went to the chip section. Three high schoolers shuffled next to the fridge containing beer. One of them glanced at him in the same way the proprietor did, before turning back to his friends and snickering nervously at something another of them said. Chips were one of Roger's favorite foods. Fried corn or potato with salt and various other flavors was so awesome. His favorite was BBQ Flavored Dipsy Doodles. They were the only BBQ flavored corn chip product he was aware of, and they were magnificent. They were spicy, just the right amount of salty and sweet, and had a smoky smell. Roger would lick his fingers clean, as well as the bag. Then he would smell his fingers the rest of the day, relishing the smokiness.

He scanned the shelves, spotting the regular Dipsy Doodles. They were tasty and crisp, although a tad salty for him. His target must have been around there somewhere. He couldn't find them, however. He felt the man's eyes on him and became self conscious. What was he going to do? He felt uncomfortable leaving with nothing, but what he wanted wasn't there. He spotted the Cheese Doodles. These were good too. Not as good as BBQ Flavored Dipsy Doodles, mind you, but quite good. He kept scanning for them, but they were nowhere to be found. Oh well. He grabbed two packs of the Doodles. Tommy liked those, he knew. One pack would be for him. Roger thought about Christine. He reached for a third pack, but decided against it. He felt cheap all of the sudden. She was fat, and wouldn't enjoy it anyway. She *would* enjoy it, but in the way she enjoyed anything —just textures down her throat. He pulled his hand away and almost dropped the two packs he held. He remembered how he asked his mom for cheese doodles once. She came back from the store with cheese puffs. He didn't like those. They sucked, in fact. Roger remembered explaining to his mom the difference. The Doodles were thin and crunchy. The puffs were bloated. They looked like pieces of foam, and tasted the same.

Wiping his teary eyes with his forearm, Roger trudged to the cash register. The high schoolers beat him to it, putting two six packs of Budweiser on the counter. Roger fumbled in his pocket for his money while the man at the register asked the students for ID.

"I forgot it at home," said one, affecting a deep voice. Roger had to keep himself from laughing out loud.

"Yeah," said one of the other two. "I forgot mine too. My wife, she, um, yeah, my wife put it away somewhere when she did the laundry."

"Uh-huh," chuckled the proprietor. "What your excuse?" he asked the third one.

"What you talking about, Mr. Miagee?" he said with fake confidence. "I got it right here," he put something down on the counter.

"My name not Mr. Miagee," the man said, picking up the proffered ID. "What your name?"

"Bill—um, Jamal Jenkins."

"Uh-huh. And when you born 'Jamal'?"

"Uh, 1972. January 12th."

"What sign you?"

"Aquarius?" One of the teen's friends hit him. "Capricorn?"

"I think you not Jamal," the man said over the counter, shaking his head sadly.

"Wha—why not?"

The man looked at him for a moment. Then he turned the ID so that it faced his customer. He said, tapping on the picture with his finger, "Jamal black. You white kid with blond hair and blue eyes." He got him there, Roger thought.

"See, told you it wouldn't work!" said the kid whose wife did laundry.

"Shut up!" said his friend.

"And," the man interrupted, "even if you Jamal, have Michael Jackson operation, it say you not 21."

"Oh man," the married one whined. "We got ripped off!"

"You put back beer. You buy soda. Be good boys, okay? Maybe go to school study math better."

Roger barely heard the bell ring behind him as the door to the shop opened and closed. The teens in front of him were grudgingly reaching to take the six packs off the counter.

"Wha dis? Ya be sellin' alcoha ta minors?" said an oddly familiar voice behind Roger. He was pushed out of the way by green and tan sleeves. Roger looked up to see Colonel Roberts. "Sellin' al-coha ta childrens be illegal," the parks officer said.

"I no sell anything," the Korean man said. "Who you? What you want?"

"Damn boy. You gotta tick axtent. I ain't un-derstand nuthin you sayin'. I'ma confiscate dese beers from ya as evidents. An I tella ya what. Ya givea me yo cash an I let ya go, yo."

"What? I no understand what you says," the man said over the counter.

Roger's body prickled with heat. His face was probably red. "He-he-he i-is t-t-trying t-to r-rob you!" he managed to say.

Colonel Roberts bent down to Roger. He pulled his shades to the bridge of his nose, revealing two vacant, rapacious eyes, which Roger would forever associate with government employees. They stared at him, not a hint of intelligence behind them. Roger stared back, defiant.

"Why ya not in skoo, lil' cracka?"

"Suspended."

"Ain't tha righ'?"

Roger continued staring. Roberts straightened up and looked back at the proprietor when the man said, "I call police. You leave store now!"

"I is police, son."

"N-n-no he isn't!"

"Quiet boy!"

The Korean made his way around the counter, knocking down some candy with his white apron. He grabbed a baseball bat. "You get out of store now!" he shouted.

"Hol' on now, son. Yo hol' on," Roberts backed away, pushing Roger into one of the shelves, which started wobbling. The teenagers must have thought this was a good time to leave. One of them put a bill on the counter and hastily grabbed the six packs. "Come on, let's go!" The bell rang as they fled.

"Get out of store!" yelled the proprietor. "I call the police."

"Taket easy man," Colonel Roberts backed away. He slid around Roger, placing him between himself and the proprietor.

Roger stepped out of the way. He rooted for the store owner as the man slowly drove Roberts toward the door.

The bell rang and in stepped a police officer. The Korean jumped for joy. Looking at the man's vacant eyes, Roger thought this was premature. "Put down the bat!" the cop shouted, one hand on the butt of his gun in its holster, the other extended in front of him. The blue uniformed man edged toward the shopkeeper. Roger's heart galloped now, but he couldn't help thinking, of course, it can never be as simple as walking into a deli and buying BBQ Flavored Dipsy Doodles. They don't even have it, and I can't buy the Cheese Doodles either. "Put down the bat!" shouted the nervous cop a second time.

"He robbing my store! Arrest him!" the proprietor yelled back.

"Put down the bat!" the cop said more forcefully, drawing his sidearm. Shocked to have a cop pull a gun on him in his own store, the Korean did as he was told. The cop made him get on his knees with his hands up. Then he, with Colonel Roberts' help, cuffed the man.

The Korean protested. "He robbing me! Arrest him! Arrest him!"

"So what's going on here?" the cop said to Roberts. Roger had a feeling that he should leave. He put his chips down as quietly as he could on the shelf before him, next to varieties of roasted nuts and sunflower seeds. He always felt bad about putting things back in the wrong place at a store, but he thought under the circumstances the owner would understand. He inched toward the counter, figuring he would quietly make his way down the adjoining aisle. Then he would be out the door as quickly and quietly as possible.

"Da yella man wer sellin' alcoha ta lil man ova der," Roberts pointed at Roger, who froze in his tracks and gulped. Of course. Of course he would say that. Roger didn't really understand everything uttered from that illiterate mouth, but he understood enough. The two innocent parties in the store were getting the shaft.

"I no sell anything! I no sell anything! He robber!" the Korean man protested.

"What's this man saying? I don't understand a thing. We need a gook interpreter. You!" the cop said. Roger didn't see him, but he knew he was being pointed at. "Turn around!" the cop instructed. Roger did as the cop said something unintelligible into his radio. Colonel Roberts tried to look important too, talking into his own radio. Roger was scared, but his anger displaced his fear. He wondered what these two apes, fiddling with technology they would never understand, were going to do next. "Get over here," the cop said to Roger over the radio chatter and static.

Roger complied. He didn't like where this was going.

"What's your name, son?"

"R-r-roger Wh-w-wharton."

"Shouldn't you be in school, Roger?" The cop gave him a stern look.

"I'm s-suspended," Roger explained.

"Suspended, huh? Trying to buy beer will get you suspended."

"I w-w-was t-trying t-to b-b-b-buy ch-ch-chips."

"Yeah, lots of people like having beer with their chips. But you're too young, son."

"I w-wasn't t-t-t-b-buying b-beer!"

"It's no use trying to deny it. You're already in a lot of trouble."

The cop asked Roberts whether he was going to press charges. Colonel Roberts held up a finger, indicating that he was busy conversing with someone on the radio and couldn't be disturbed at the present time. "Yeah girl. Ya knows I is."

When the officer's backup arrived, remarkably fast, Roger thought, he said to the boy, "Where do you go to school?"

"P-p-p-S f-f-forty nine."

"Oh, that's right here. Why are you playing hooky so close to your school? Come on, I'll take you there." Roger was led out the door to the officer's cruiser. "Watch your head, Roger," the cop said, opening the door. Roger sat in the back seat, looking around. He had never been in a cop car before. It smelled like the boy's bathroom. A metal net separated the front from the back. It had dents in it. Roger imagined someone kicking it. The doors had no handles on the inside. That was smart, Roger thought. He wondered if the windows were made of something that would prevent them from shattering if someone kicked them.

The officer started the modified Caprice, revved the engine, and drove to the light. He didn't have to unpark because he had left the car in the middle of the street. Despite the light being red, the cop made a left turn onto Juniper Boulevard North. He made a left again at 80th Street, also against the light. This time he bleeped his siren a couple of times to stop the cars that had the right of way. All the time there came static and unintelligible chatter from the radio. A couple of times the cop answered, saying a combination of numbers and names. Roger wondered how anyone could understand any of that. And did they? Maybe they just made noises the whole time, and no one understood. But everyone pretended to understand because they didn't want to look stupid. Roger imagined himself as a cop saying, "What? What? I don't understand you dispatch. Can you say again?"

The car made a right, with the light this time, onto Penelope Avenue and stopped at the school's front entrance. The cop got out and opened the door on Roger's right. Roger slid over the seat, hoping he wouldn't get anything smelly stuck on him, and got out. "Now listen here, son," the cop looked down at him. "Look at me. I said look at me." He patted him on the shoulder. "I know it's a confusing time for you. I've been there. But going to school is important. Don't drink beer until you're old enough. And no more playing hooky. I'm giving you a big break here." He paused, looking around. Then he looked back at Roger. He made a face like what he was about to say would be really important. It sounded rehearsed: "School is where you learn things. It's what makes you smart. I went to school, and look at me now. Sure you might not get good grades—I've been there—but you gotta keep going and trying. Most of the things you learn there, you can't use in real life. Like how to love a woman, drive a car, or stop a robbery. But it's important to go to school because they teach you things that you have to know. It helps you in real life." He surveyed the street around them again. "Do you understand what I'm telling you, son?"

Roger didn't, but he nodded.

"Okay. Off you go." The cop gently pushed Roger toward the stairs and tussled his hair. "Stay out of trouble, you hear?"

Roger went up the stairs and opened the heavy brown door. A few steps led to the pink doors ahead. The security guard's desk lay behind them. A couple of fluorescent lights flickered from the gym's ceiling through the doors' windows. Roger wondered what he should do. The cop might still be out there, so it wasn't a good idea to go out yet. Maybe he could cut through the school and exit in the yard? Then make a run for it? It was either that or wait here for a while, to make certain the cop left. Why had he been in the deli anyway? To buy something, right? So he probably still wanted to buy it. He was probably already on his way. But Roger didn't want to risk peeking out. It was a shame the heavy outer doors didn't have windows.

What if someone came in while he waited? How would he explain what he was doing here? Roger determined that exiting through the yard was the better choice. What about the security guard? The answer flashed in Roger's head. He could open the door quietly and then crawl by the desk. The woman wouldn't see him. Then he could tiptoe to a column and use it as a barrier until he got to the door. And whatever happened, he could just run. The old lady wouldn't catch him. That was the plan then.

Roger went as quietly as he could up the stairs to the pink doors. There must have been something sticky here or on the floor of the cop's car because Roger's sneakers were hard to lift. And when he lifted them, they made weird sounds, sort of like when you peeled Velcro. Roger pulled one of the pink doors toward himself, making a louder noise than he wanted. It wouldn't budge. He tried the other. Same thing. "Have they installed locks?" he thought.

He realized then that he had to push. What an idiot. He'd done it hundreds of times by now. It was different when you didn't think about it. Thinking always makes doing things more difficult.

He pushed the door as gently as he could. It opened slowly. So far, so good. After making a small crack, it opened no further. Roger pushed harder. The door creaked loudly. He stopped. His heart thumped in his ears. He hoped the guard didn't hear it. Stupid janitor. Wasn't he supposed to keep the hinges oiled? Roger opened the door another smidgen. It creaked again. Oh who was he kidding? That sound could have raised the dead. It reverberated in the large space. What the hell? Roger pushed harder and stepped through the door.

The security guard was at her desk. She stared directly at him. Roger froze. The plan was to run, but his legs wouldn't move. The guard kept looking at him, but nothing else happened. Something should have happened. It suddenly occurred to him, was the guard dead? He waved at her. She didn't respond. He made faces. She didn't tell him to stop. Was she really dead? Roger held his breath, looking at the old lady intently for signs of life. It was a while before he saw her chest move. He let out a breath of relief. She was just sleeping with her eyes open. A bit strange, but at least she wasn't dead.

Roger closed the door behind him gently. He winced as it creaked and slammed, but the guard remained unperturbed. He tiptoed past her and almost fell over as his left sneaker got stuck to the floor. Someone was coming, probably from the auditorium. He tried to get his sneaker, but it wouldn't budge. Roger hopped on his right foot and hid behind the column opposite the guard's desk. The basketball hoop, hanging from the ceiling, was a few feet ahead of him. What if someone crashes into the column while playing basketball? Roger admonished himself, someone's coming, you don't have a shoe, and you're thinking about basketball safety? What's wrong with you? Roger shrugged. He shook his head, what the hell was he doing?

He leaned his back against the column's cool yellow-orange bricks. He listened, trying to filter out his heart beat. Keys jiggled. Not a good clue for deduction. Practically every adult in the school had a large set of keys. He could only guess that it was a man, because he hadn't seen any of the female teachers carrying a key ring. Where would they put it anyway? Their dresses didn't have belts. The whistling confirmed that it was the janitor. Was he trying to scoop up Roger's shoe?

Roger peered around the corner. Damn it! He was! Why did the old man have to work so hard? Roger groaned mentally as his shoe was unstuck and deposited in a large pocket in Mr. Flannery's overalls. This was turning out to be not such a good day. Think. Think! Hopping home on one foot was not acceptable. He had to get his sneaker back somehow. He could just ask for it, couldn't he?

Roger dismissed that option right away. Mr. Flannery was a nice man, by all accounts, but Roger didn't know what would happen. Would he be asked any questions? Probably, if he didn't have a pass. He might even be taken to the Assistant Principal by the janitor. And that wouldn't be good. He didn't want to be charged with trespassing. Roger was loath to meet that cop again. He could ask for his shoe, get it back, and run away. But that wasn't any good either, because Mr. Flannery would see him next week, and he might get in trouble at that time.

Roger thought some more as the janitor walked toward the bathroom. Roger moved around the column to keep it between himself and the janitor. If the security guard awoke now she would see him. He hoped that she would have pleasant dreams for a while longer.

The janitor didn't have his cart with him, or a mop, or anything like that. Nor was he carrying his toolbox. So what was he doing here? He came from the direction of the auditorium. Roger brought his wrist up to his face. Damn it. He forgot his watch. Or lost it. He hoped that he forgot it. Roger looked at the clock in the distance, but couldn't see what it said. He squinted and tried to make his eyes tear by yawning, which sometimes helped him see distant things better. No luck. Roger tried to estimate the time. Maybe it was about 11? Then the janitor was going to set up the lunch tables that were folded by the windows. That made sense.

In the times that he saw the janitor fold and unfold the tables, it looked like a hard job. Roger hoped that his sneaker would make it uncomfortable for Mr. Flannery. Hopefully he'd set it down somewhere. Roger could then sneak up and grab it. Not a bad plan, he thought. But where would this happen? He tried to remember which side the janitor started with. The far side he thought, and hoped, hopping in that direction before the janitor came out of the bathroom. The books in his schoolbag bounced up and down, pulling him backward with every jump forward. Roger heard a flush. Cursing the laws of motion, he hopped as fast as he could. Just as he slipped behind a column, he heard the dangling keys on the janitor's belt. Roger lifted his hands to his mouth to quiet his heavy breathing.

The janitor's footfalls stopped. "Who's huffing over there?"

Roger's eyes widened. He held his breath. His feet were starting to hurt, one from hopping and the other from being held up so long.

The footsteps and jingling keys commenced once again. "Who's there?" the janitor called again. It seemed to Roger that he was heading toward him. He peeked around the corner and saw he was right. "Tommy, if that's you, I didn't kill any spiders. I let them go outside." Roger put his head behind the column quickly, just before Mr. Flannery saw him. The janitor went around the column. Roger, holding his breath, went around too. The janitor saw nothing. He proceeded to the tables. "You're getting old and jumpy," he said, apparently to himself. It was a miracle, Roger thought, that he wasn't spotted.

Roger timed his exhale with the unfolding of the first table. He thought he was going to pass out. He heaved quietly, leaning against the column. The janitor moved on to the next table. He did not take the shoe out of his pocket. It was a stupid plan anyway. What now? Well, what did the janitor do with the things that he found all over the place? Roger pursed his lips. The janitor would either throw it out, or put it in the lost and found. Or he might keep it. That third option was the worst. But what would Mr. Flannery do with one shoe? Roger imagined him building a robot with one foot. Nah. He was left with the other two possibilities. Whichever one it was, he would have to tail the janitor to see. That was a daunting prospect. Roger groaned inside. This was supposed to be his day off.

The janitor finished assembling all of the tables. The kitchen staff rolled in their carts. The security guard finally woke up and started chatting with one of the old ladies with a black hairnet. Roger looked at the clock, closer to him now, and saw that it was noon. Soon all the students would come down to eat lunch. Roger thought he'd be able to blend in. He could even sit with his class. He only had to avoid the Assistant Principal and Mr. G.

What did the janitor do during lunch? Roger didn't remember seeing him in the cafeteria, except when someone vomited. That meant that he went somewhere. Then he came back after lunch to fold the tables and sweep up. So Roger had to follow him. Maybe he'd leave the sneaker some place and Roger could get it when Mr. Flannery cleared the cafeteria after lunch.

The janitor went past him toward the stairs. When the door closed behind him, Roger followed.

This hopping business was getting annoying. He didn't want to get "cooties," however, by touching the floor with his sock. He'd lost count of the number of times someone in his class, usually Peter, stepped in dog crap. Maybe these were exigent circumstances, but Roger thought he could manage on one foot for a bit longer.

It looked like the janitor was going up to the third floor. Roger swung up the stairs one at a time like a gymnast, bracing himself on the railings. He hopped down the hall after the janitor disappeared around the corner.

No sign of Mr. Flannery. That meant the janitor was close. But where? Roger hopped as quietly as he could up the hall. A voice, quiet but forceful, came into his hearing range. It had been there all along, but in his efforts to be quiet Roger hadn't noticed it. He paused, leaning his hand on the cool wall. Roger couldn't quite make out what was said. He hopped some more, now seeing a shadow on the wall opposite an open door, moving along with the words. A long shadowy finger, craggy and crooked as a witch's nose, stabbed at the air with each quiet, terse syllable: "You. Will. Pay."

Roger gulped as he edged closer, wincing at the squeak coming from his last hop.

"I don't have it," came Mr. Flannery's voice.

"You. Better." The finger stabbed. "Ain't my problem your son's a degenerate gambler."

Roger plastered himself against the wall as the shadow loomed larger, into a blob, and a man stormed out of the supply closet. He groped at his utility belt and turned his radio on. The policeman looked at Roger as he passed him with a crackle of static. Roger recognized the sneer almost instantly as that of the cop who laughed at him in the park.

Mr. Flannery exited the room a few moments later as Roger tried desperately to hop away. The janitor turned to him. It looked like he'd been rubbing his eyes. Now he re-affixed his glasses. Roger didn't know what to say.

"What can I do for you, young man?" the janitor said in a pleasant, but shaky voice.

Roger looked up at him, but nothing came out.

"Someone threw up somewhere and they sent you to get me?"

Roger shook his head. A short but awkward silence ensued. Then Mr. Flannery noticed Roger standing on one foot.

"Oh," he laughed. He pulled out Roger's shoe. "This must belong to you," he handed it to Roger and patted him on the head.

Roger wanted to say thank you, but nothing came out.

Mr. Flannery seemed to understand. "Go on now," he smiled. "You don't want to miss your lunch." The janitor walked away, his keys jiggling.

Roger leaned against the wall to put his shoe on. As he tied it, he thought he heard the clicking of footfalls to his left. He turned his head and almost fell over. The Assistant Principal, redder than usual, glowered at him. Mr. Leslie grabbed Roger by his upper arm and dragged him down the stairs. Roger, too surprised to be frightened, only had time to wonder whether Mr. Leslie's hand would now smell like armpit. Then he found himself back in the street. The door slamming behind him with the Assistant Principal murmuring, "stupid kids, can't get them to come to school, can't get them to leave."

* * *

As Roger approached the porch, he saw Tommy sitting on it. The round boy was petting a small orange cat curled up next to him. Tigger sat in the windowsill, trying to be petted as well.

"Ta ta ta ta ta, all we are is dust in the wind, ta ta ta," Tommy sang. He looked up at Roger. "I forget the rest. What's the rest? Oh come on, tell me how the rest goes. Please?" He continued singing, "ta ta ta ta ta, dust in the wind." He stopped. "Don't just stare at me like I'm some kind of weirdo. Don't laugh!"

Roger suppressed his smile. "What are you doing here so early?" he asked Tommy.

"I got suspendered," Tommy said sullenly.

"What?"

242

"Why can't you bring a cat to school! That's so stupid!"

"Oh. Mr. Leslie, huh?"

"Yuppers," Tommy pouted. Galen purred next to him. Tigger, inside the house, scratched at the insect guard through the open window and got his nail stuck. He looked worriedly at them, trying to get his paw out.

"Why are you sitting out here?"

Tommy was in the shade, but he wouldn't be for long as the sun descended toward the west. Tommy gently removed Tigger's paw from the net. The cat began scratching at it again. Lucky Joy heard their voices and started barking.

"I remembered my key."

"Huh? Then why are you sitting out here?"

"Oh you know what I meant!" Tommy complained. He wasn't having a good day either.

"No one's home?"

"Noppers."

"So how long you get suspended for?" Roger rummaged through his pockets for the keys.

"One week," Tommy said, following Roger inside the house. "And my parents have to come." Tommy crashed into Roger's back.

"What do you mean your parents have to come?" Roger turned around.

"'Standard procedures' the guy said."

"But they have to go for me, remember?"

"Oh yeah. What are we gonna do?" Tommy's eyes were wide. Lucky Joy ran into the hall barking. He saw Galen, who had been let down. The dog skidded to a halt, his hind legs sliding out in front of him. He sat there for a moment silently, as if in shock. Then he ran off barking.

Roger turned back to Tommy. "I don't know," he said.

"I'm thirsty," Tommy replied. "If you didn't come, I'd die of thirst."

"Don't you have your juice box in your bag?"

"I forgot about that. The noggin, it doesn't work sometimes," Tommy said tapping himself on the head. "Anyways, I want sparklies."

They headed to the kitchen. "You really like them, don't you?"

"Yuppers," Tommy replied. "Bubbles are the best. They pop so good. And if you're gentle you can squish them because they're squishy. And they can fly so good. What if we split them up? And they just pop so awesome."

Roger almost tripped over a couple of boxes that probably came in the mail. Panting on the dining room table was Mr. Smith. He looked at Roger with his one eye, his body stretched out. He was too hot to emit his usual greeting.

"Well? What do you think?" Tommy asked, moving the boxes out of the way, basically under the archway between the dining room and living room. Lucky Joy watched him curiously, tilting his head.

"Think about what?"

"My idea."

"What idea?" Roger asked.

"My idea from before."

Roger gave him a questioning look.

"What if my mom pretends to be with you, and my dad pretends to be with me?"

"Oh, that's pretty good. Or maybe Lucian can help?"

"Noppers. He does not like public school."

"Okay."

"So how come you didn't say you liked my idea right away?"

"It's the first I hear of it."

"But I said it before."

"I thought you were talking about bubbles."

"You have to pay attention better."

Roger rolled his eyes and strolled into the kitchen. He stopped and Tommy crashed into him again. For the second time that day Mario gave him a shock. At least he was wearing clothes this time. The man sat ensconced between the two piles on the couch, reading something. Shadow purred behind him.

"Hi daddy!" Tommy said.

"Oh hello son!" Mario looked up from his book. "Isn't it such a great day? Yes it is," he answered his own question, "it's warmer." He still wore a sweater and a scarf, however.

"You won't believe what happened today, daddy." Tommy took out a seltzer bottle from the fridge. He poured some into a cup.

"Tell me all about it," Mario said.

"Bah. It's flat," Tommy said. "Roger, can you drink this?"

Now that he thought about it, Roger was thirsty. He took the cup from Tommy and gulped it down. He didn't like seltzer. The bubbles burned his pallet and the water tasted funny. Like it had salt in it or something. The bubbles were gone, but it still had that weird flavor. Roger grimaced and put down the paper cup. Tommy handed him a new seltzer bottle. "No thanks," he said. "That was enough for me."

"No silly. Can you open it?"

"Oh."

As Roger tried to unscrew the cap, his fingers sliding along the little ridges, Tommy began to tell the story of his day. He started with how they left home in the morning and how Roger was cranky about something. Then Tommy saw a beautiful squirrel and Roger yelled at him about it.

Roger didn't remember that at all. "No I didn't," he said. He used his shirt now, trying to get a better grip.

Tommy continued about how Roger yelled at him for bringing Leland with him. "Oh, you brought Leland?" Mario asked. "What a great idea."

"Yeah," Tommy agreed. He said quickly in a voice that rose in pitch, "And then we got to school. And then we did the pledgeabalegence. And then we went up to class. And then Roger wasn't there no more. And then I thought he got in trouble. And then we did reading quiet."

Seltzer always leaked out when you opened it too fast. When Roger finally got the cap to turn, he started to slowly untwist it and then twist it closed as the liquid ran toward the top.

"No! You're letting all the bubblies excape!"

Roger gave Tommy the bottle, who unscrewed it quickly and wet his chest. "Oh man!" Tommy complained and Roger laughed.

Tommy resumed his story. He kept the kitten in his desk, among his books. Roger imagined Tommy keeping one hand in his desk, playing with the kitten while stealing the occasional glance at it with naughty eyes. Tommy said there wasn't much room in his desk, so he let the cat into Roger's. Roger didn't understand the logic in that since his desk was filled to capacity with garbage, thanks to Mr. Gorton's lenient policies. Then Tommy apologized, and Roger fumed, because Leland might have "left some poopsies" in Roger's desk.

Some time before noon (Roger gathered, because Tommy said they were doing their "geographies") Mr. Leslie came in for a surprise inspection. He was also there to implement a new program he was developing to make students think about their futures. The students were to go up to the front of the room, one at a time, and tell the class what they wanted to be when they grew up. Roger was suddenly glad he wasn't in class today.

Tommy had thought about his future profession for most of his life, so he was prepared. After a few future astronauts, firefighters, and homemakers, it was Tommy's turn at the board. He announced (quite jubilantly, Roger imagined) that he wanted to be a witch.

"You mean a warlock? Or wizard?" Roger interrupted.

"Noppers. I want to be a witch."

"But a witch is a girl," Roger said.

"No! It can be a boy too!"

"No it can't."

"Can too! Dad?"

"One is not born a man or woman, but becomes one," Mario said.

Tommy continued with his tale. Mr. Leslie didn't like it at all. Tommy was going to explain how he wanted to make healing potions and special herbal mixtures that helped people and animals and made everyone happy, but Mr. Leslie started yelling at him. Leland wanted to see what all the commotion was about. After tumbling down from the desk's storage compartment, the kitten found his guardian, perching himself on Tommy's shoe. To the Assistant Principal this was *prima facie* evidence of witchcraft. He sought to confiscate the cat and threatened to discard it most heinously.

Roger already knew what happened next. Ordinarily, Tommy was a happy go lucky boy. He tolerated various infractions against himself with nary a complaint (except if it was Roger, whose any remark with the hint of sternness was considered yelling), and often had the inability to say no. Christine and Mario (and Roger too, if he was going to be truthful) took advantage of Tommy's gentle and compliant nature. Roger often told Tommy that he was too kind for his own good. But when it came to his animals, or any animals really, it was as if Tommy grew into the Incredible Hulk. He would do anything to protect the world's helpless creatures, and his gentleness gave way to incredible anger and physical strength. In short, one didn't mess with animals when Tommy was around.

So when Mr. Leslie prepared to carry out his threat, Tommy stomped on the man's feet and punched him in the gut. "Oh wow," Mario said. "This reminds me, I wanted to take boxing lessons."

Tommy was then taken to the office. While nursing his wounds, the Assistant Principal gave Tommy a talk about how it was wrong to use physical violence against others. Roger imagined Tommy clutching the kitten protectively, staring at Leslie defiantly with a piercing anger reserved only for animal abusers. The Assistant Principal must have been uncomfortable, because Tommy was sent back to class, where the geography lesson had resumed. It was a few minutes later that Tommy received his punishment, via an office aide. They tried to call his house, apparently, but no one answered. He was sent home immediately.

Roger thought he understood now why the Assistant Principal swept him out of the building without any further punishment or threats. Shock did that to a man.

Roger went downstairs to relax while Tommy continued talking with his father. Roger never really talked much with his dad, and felt uncomfortable when he did. His dad had two sorts of questions for him: why did he not do better on his test and whether a girl in class was pretty. His dad yelled at his mom frequently, making her cry. But apparently he really loved her because he lost it after she was gone. Maybe people wouldn't think he was normal or whatever, but he didn't really miss his dad anymore. Roger felt a little jealous, though, at the easy way with which Tommy and Mario communicated. But that was all—really.

No doubt Tommy was making lunch now while Mario lectured him on some crazy theory or other. He had been reading a book on the JFK assassination. So that was probably what the excited voice upstairs was going on about. Some things Roger heard Mario say sounded true. Others seemed as crazy as official government explanations of various events. Like the JFK explanation, for instance. A single bullet really made all those course corrections and injuries and then wound up, undamaged, on a hospital stretcher? Really? Come on. People really would believe anything if it was official.

Tommy came downstairs. "The potatoes are boiling," he said.

"Cool," Roger replied. "I thought you said no one was home."

"Yuppers."

"But your dad was in the kitchen when we came in."

"Yuppers."

"So someone was home. Why didn't he let you in?"

"I dunno."

"And I wanted to take a shower really early and he was in there doing something weird," once Ro-

251

ger got to complaining he wanted to let it all out. "Why was he down here?"

"Oh. He has athlete's foot, so he doesn't want to make the upstairs bathroom dirty."

"But we use this one!" Roger was outraged.

Tommy shrugged. He was looking through his tape collection for something to play in the kitchen while he cooked. "Nirvana is gonna have a new album!" he said excitedly.

That didn't answer Roger's question about why Mario used their bathroom, or why he didn't let Tommy into the house, but Roger was interested. "Really?" He and Tommy listened to Tommy's *Bleach* tape so many times that it ripped and they had to ask Mario to get them a new one.

"Yuppers."

"How do you know?"

"Remember we went to St. Mark's?"

"Yeah."

"I saw it in a magazine. There's a baby swimming and it's called 'Mind Never.'"

"That's a cool title."

Tommy agreed.

"I hope it doesn't suck," Roger always knew to let his optimistic side show.

Tommy looked up. "Why would it suck?" They agreed that Kurt Cobain was a genius. They enjoyed his often pun-filled, sarcastic lyrics. And the words were screamed by the melancholic voice of a fellow stomach sufferer. Roger also liked all the guitar feedback. It sounded so awesome. Kurt Cobain made Roger want to learn how to play guitar, as Tommy well knew. So he was understandably confused.

"You saw an ad in a magazine. What was it, *Rolling Stone* or something?" They had gotten the *Bleach* tape at a second hand record shop because Tommy liked the cover and the band name, being a part-time Buddhist. It was a real effort to find a replacement copy. Mario had to put out a classified ad in the *Village Voice* for them.

"Yeah," Tommy replied not seeing what that had to do with anything.

"So how would Sub Pop records have enough money to advertise in a national magazine?"

"I dunno. They took out a mortgage?"

"Right. Either they borrowed a lot of money or Nirvana went to a big record company. Either way, whoever paid for the ads thinks it's gonna sell big. That means there's lots of radio friendly unit shifters on the record." Good bye feedback and screaming.

"I dunno. I think it'll be awesome. Kurt Cobain is Pisces you know. I'm Pisces too." Tommy said it like it was a religion or ethnicity. He got up from his crouch. "There's a Dream Theater tape in the *Bleach* box."

Roger didn't want to listen to Dream Theater. Tommy claimed to be impatient, and most indications pointed to him being so, but he sure liked to listen to a band that never got to the point. "You should check your walkman."

Tommy looked through his piles of clothing. "I can't find it."

Roger groaned. He wasn't prepared to listen to Dream Theater.

"Don't worry silly. We're not gonna listen to DT. I know you don't like them, even though they're awesome." He took something out of a Michael Jackson box. Roger looked at him skeptically until Tommy said, "How about the Dead Kennedys?"

"Cool," Roger said. "Let's go cook." Roger jumped out of his bunk and followed Tommy upstairs to the kitchen.

It had become Roger's job to cook the tofu ever since his experiments with Tommy yielded delicious results. The first step was to cut the fermented soy block into rectangles. Then Roger heated a good amount of canola oil in a medium pan. He dropped the tofu chunks in the pan as the oil started to smoke. Water leaked from the tofu and right away boiling particles of oil and water exploded in the pan. This always happened before things eventually settled down.

"So what did your dad lecture you about this time? He sounded really excited." Roger asked when Mario left the room.

"I don't remember," Tommy replied over "Macho Insecurity." "Watch out!" One of the stray oil projectiles ignited, causing a large flame to envelope the pan. This happened from time to time. Nothing to worry about. Christine hovered about them one time (she was always in the kitchen when someone cooked, like a vulture following an army) when something similar happened. Except that time the fire was bigger. Even Roger freaked out a bit. Christine ran as if the devil were after her. She later admonished Roger and Tommy for putting the fire out rather than running away like she did. "We have fire insurance, don't we?" she had asked. When Tommy asked her if she would rather lose the house than put the fire out, she said "damn straight" and clapped her hands. Roger then called her "a super wuss" and she laughed.

"But it just happened a few minutes ago."

"The noggin," Tommy said, "it doesn't work so good sometimes." He thought for the length of a couple of songs. Roger decided to check if it was time to flip the tofu chunks over. The wooden spoon wasn't working.

"Where are the tongs?" Roger asked. Lucian, who rarely cooked, loved to come down when no one was around and move things from where they usually were. Various kitchen utensils would go missing for months as a result, prompting Mario to spend more money on replacements. The missing tools would then reappear, and they would have more than anyone could ever want or need.

"I dunno," Tommy said looking in the drawers and cabinets.

"We have like four of them."

"Yuppers, I know. But what can you do?" Tommy shrugged. "Here, use this." He handed Roger a tiny salad tong. It was filthy. Trapped in the grease were cat and dog hairs, along with ancient clumps of food.

Roger washed it as best as he could. "It was about time travel," Tommy said over the cacophony of punk rock, sizzling tofu, and Roger's cleaning.

"What?" Roger replied. He had completely forgotten what they were talking about. What did dirty tongs have to do with time travel? How could someone just put them away without cleaning them, and how did all this extra stuff get stuck on them? Were the tongs dragged throughout the house by someone? Is that what Lucky Joy did at night when everyone slept and Roger heard him scampering above him?

"What daddy and I talked about."

"Oh. And what did he say?"

"I don't remember."

Roger frowned at him. He finished washing the tongs. Tommy gave him a dirty towel to dry them. Roger was so excited about finding out what Mario said about time travel that he didn't notice himself taking the towel and wiping the tongs. Ordinarily he would have stopped himself and "yelled" at Tommy. That towel was on the floor practically every time Roger saw it, incredibly close to one of Lucky Joy's pee spots.

Lucian came down then and started sweeping in the kitchen. The smell of food always drew him out of his room. He moved dust bunnies around from spot to spot as Roger again washed the tongs. "Did you ask him about the paradoxes of time travel?" Roger asked. Time travel was something he thought about a great deal. He was interested in hearing what Mario said on the subject, as one of Mario's doctorates was in physics. He had taught briefly at a university before being fired. It was rarely mentioned, but from what Roger gathered Mario had tried to patent some sort of a device. It was quickly classified by the government and Mario was forbidden from any further work in that area. Edith, a mathematician by training, was also threatened. Hence the family's move to New York, and Mario's paranoia. Tommy didn't remember much, but he recalled that "meanies" in dark suits visited his previous home several times.

"Paradoxes?" Tommy asked.

"Yeah. There are a bunch of them that should make time travel impossible."

"Like what?"

"You probably heard of the grandfather paradox. That's when a time traveler goes back in time to before his father was born. He kills his grandfather before his grandfather meets his grandmother. The paradox is, how can he do that? If he kills his grandfather, then his father and he, himself, wouldn't be born. Since he was born, he couldn't have gone back in time to kill his grandfather. And if he did kill his grandfather, he wouldn't be born. Get it?"

"I think so," said Tommy. He thought for a bit as Roger turned off the faucet, finally satisfied with the cleanliness of the tongs. Tommy offered him the dirty towel and Roger waved it away. "My dad doesn't believe in time," Tommy said finally.

"Is that why he's always late?" Roger asked. He turned a tofu chunk over. It wasn't starting to brown yet, but would soon he hoped. It was interesting, tofu. It took a long time to start browning, but once it started, one had to be diligent or else it would form a black crust quite quickly.

"I dunno. But he says that time is an illusion."

"What do you—ow! God damn it!" Water dripping from the tongs triggered a small explosion in the pan, shooting a jet of oil into Roger's eye.

"What happened?" Tommy asked, concerned.

"The freaking oil went into my eye," Roger said. It didn't hurt, but his vision was blurring. Roger was afraid he would be a Cyclops like Mr. Smith. Lucian was washing something in the sink now, of course. Roger wanted desperately to wash his eye. Mario's loud humming indicated that the downstairs bathroom was occupied. Of course. Off he raced to the second floor. The door was locked. What the hell? Was Edith back?

"Sorry," Tommy said from inside. "I had to pee."

"Hurry up, will you?" Roger alternated between cupping his palm over his eye to putting his hand at his side. He wasn't sure what the best course of action was in such a situation. Someone looking at him might have thought he was doing some sort of exercise or practicing a weird ritual. "What's taking so long?"

"My zipper got stuck."

"Oh for the love of—"

"Almost done!" Tommy shuffled around. Then a thud. "Ow!"

"Now what?"

"I hurt my head on something," Tommy moaned.

Roger let out a breath and stood by the door. Just as he resigned himself to being a Cyclops, Tommy emerged. Roger shoved past him and started putting water in his eye. It was probably one of the most difficult parts to wash, the eye. It was starting to hurt now. His vision was still blurry but he didn't know whether it was the oil or the water.

Tommy came back and handed him a plastic container. It had a few breadcrumbs, hairs, and onion skins stuck to what looked like an oily bottom. "My dad says you should use this."

"It's got a bunch of crap in it," Roger said, examining it with his good eye. The other one throbbed and Roger had trouble opening it. Maybe he washed it too much. "Thanks anyway," Roger gave the container back to Tommy.

Tommy followed him downstairs, where Lucky Joy was taking a dump. They returned to the kitchen. Mario was back in his crevice on the couch. A Tony Bennett song blasted out of the CD player. Roger hoped it wasn't on repeat. Someone had put the tongs away while they were upstairs. Tommy began to look for them, but it appeared to be a lost cause. When asked, Lucian didn't know what he did with them. Typical.

Tommy found real tongs this time around. Roger set about washing them as his eye burned and Tony Bennett hurt his ears. He wasn't certain yet if Mario had the song on repeat as he was wont to do. Roger wouldn't mind listening to Dream Theater at that moment.

Having washed the tongs, he again checked the tofu. Still not getting brown yet. What the hell?

Then he noticed that the flame was really low. Stupid Lucian. Roger turned it higher. With a pop in the pan a jet of oil shot Roger in the eye. Mario was using the sink. Keeping his eye closed, and without a word, Roger went through the dining room and up the stairs. The bathroom door was locked. Lucian was humming inside. Roger let out a breath and went to the basement. The door was closed and the light was on. Edith had come home.

Eventually Roger got access to the upstairs bathroom. Lighting a match only made it worse. Roger held his breath while washing out his eye. It stung from all the water. Whether it teared for the same reason or because of the smell was unknown. He hoped it would be okay. Roger imagined he was at some sort of chemical spill disaster, his Hazmat suit having been ripped by an unknown contaminant. Now he was racing against the clock to save his eye. Roger wasn't a sickly boy like Tommy, but he often thought he was. His mind made him feel symptoms that weren't caused by anything physical, earning him a title from Tommy: "hypochondriact." It was all in his mind, Roger told himself. His eye wouldn't fall out. He washed until he could hold his breath no more. He came out of the bathroom, his vision blurry in one eye from all the washing. Roger went down the stairs, slightly woozy, almost tripping on Tigger, who chased a bug up the stairs. Roger didn't see the bug,

261

but he assumed that was what was going on. A couple of weeks ago Shadow ate a moth and got sick. Mario spent several hundred dollars at the emergency vet's office figuring that out. Now that cat was all better, following after Tigger and possibly another meal ticket to the vet. "Geniuses! They are not very bright, these cats," Christine remarked that morning, clapping.

Roger grabbed the tongs carefully this time. He shielded his eyes with a glass saucepan cover and picked up a piece of tofu. After what seemed like 10 hours later, it was finally getting brown. After a couple of minutes, Roger flipped over all the chunks to let them brown on the other side. A few minutes later, after giving Tommy an admonishing look when the boy started singing along with Tony Bennett (it was still not determined whether it was the same song playing on repeat), Roger removed the tofu onto a paper towel on a plate.

Tommy proceeded to make a vegan gravy (the recipe of which cannot be revealed here owing to its top secret nature) while Roger mashed the potatoes. Mario said he was "very excited" about eating the food they had made. Then he announced that as soon as the boys were finished cooking, they were going out to a restaurant to celebrate Edith's buying of a new used car. Edith, who had silently come up the stairs from the basement, took that as orders to go sit in the car outside.

With the food ready, and Tommy and Roger famished, they went out to the car to sit with Edith. During their 20 minute wait for Mario, Tommy's and Roger's bellies had a contest as to which one could make the loudest cry for food. The new car was almost the same as the old car. It was the same model, a Caprice station wagon. The seats were a darker color and the smell inside was a bit more funky. Lucky Joy would have to wait to meet the new car. When Tommy asked him to come along, Lucky ran under his coffee table and growled. Only Christine knew how to get him out of there without getting bitten.

They drove to Christine's junior high and pulled her out of class early. "Is everything alright?" she kept asking, clapping and getting used to her new surroundings in the backseat. After being reassured multiple times, Christine said, "Thank God you pulled me out of there. We were learning about Thomas Edison."

"He electrocuted animals just for the hell of it," Roger remarked.

Tommy's mouth dropped. "What an evil man!"

"Yeah," Christine clapped. "No one ever talks about Tesla because he was the inventor of everything electrical."

"Yeah!" Tommy said. "They always want to suppress everything that is good in the world to make it mediocre and stupid."

This gave way to a lecture by Mario on mainstream science and grant money politics. Original work, he said, was often suppressed by the establishment, always the judges of such work, because it interfered with their grant money. Why allow technology to exist that would render one's work obsolete when you could simply say it didn't work and was foolish nonsense? Edith interjected a couple of times with verbal nods.

They went to Long Island, to buy beds again. Then they went to Manhattan to eat Korean food. Mario wanted to go food shopping in Staten Island, but everyone was tired and he was persuaded against it, though he was a bit miffed by their defiance. So they went back to Long Island to do that.

Everyone was hungry again when they finally got home, but it was discovered that Lucian ate all the food that Tommy and Roger made. Lucian said it wasn't his fault. He blamed Lucky Joy, who happily snored in the living room and could not defend himself from what he would surely characterize as a baseless accusation. Lucky Joy had a strained relationship with Lucian because Tommy's uncle liked to sweep up the various treats the dog hid for himself throughout the first floor. If you brought a broom or mop next to Lucky, even when he was sleeping, he would growl instantly.

After a brief break, Tommy and Roger assembled one of the beds where the couch used to be. Actually, it was Tommy who did the assembling. Roger stood there, handing him the parts and tools as the need for them arose and complaining in a hushed tone about their inefficient journey and expensive restaurant visit. He was glad they didn't go to Staten Island, though. Roger had never been, but Michael once mentioned that the whole place was just a garbage dump. It smelled like crap everywhere, his classmate had told him. Watching Shadow meticulously clean his paws in the litter box and listening to Mr. Smith make his moaning sounds (one day the neighbors might call the cops to investigate why a baby wailed in the house), Roger thought that they had enough Staten Island in their lives to merit not going there.

"I'm sleepy," Tommy yawned. No rest for him yet, however. He was the only one in the house capable of assembling anything. Roger couldn't make heads or tails out of the instructions and diagrams, no matter how plainly they were written. Mario would more likely break everything and hurt himself in the process if he tried. Lucian's only talent was sweeping, as far as Roger knew. Edith was great at mechanical things, and often disassembled items around the house to fix one of her vacuums (for instance, the lamp next to the bookshelf no longer worked because Edith removed something from it to replace a broken part in a floor buffer), but by the time she would get around to it, the beds would be lost. Tommy's house was a repository for lost things. Rumor had it that another couch was somewhere in the house. Like the story of Atlantis, it couldn't be verified, but every once in a while an expedition was organized in high hopes of finding evidence, only to run into difficulties and the eventual abandonment of the project.

Christine, who had not even been considered for the assembling task (for obvious reasons), seemed acutely aware of this phenomenon and often worried about one of the cats going missing. She came up to them now and asked, "Have you seen Shadow?"

"No."

"Oh my God, oh my God, oh my God. Where is he?" Christine wouldn't stop until they went to look with her. Christine did this every couple of days. The missing feline would always be found in the most obvious spot, sometimes in the middle of the floor. This didn't prevent Christine from worrying again as soon as one of the cats was out of her sight.

"He's right there, sis," Tommy said pointing.

"Oh there you are," Christine picked up the cat and kissed his belly. "You're a black guy, aren't you? Ha hahaha."

"If he understood you, he'd be mad," Roger said. Shadow purred in Christine's grasp.

"How's the job search going, Shadow?" Christine said, in her own world. "You are too lazy! You have to conform and work." The cat squinted in delight as Christine planted a fresh batch of kisses.

With the bed assembled, Christine was charged with putting the mattresses on it. It was revealed then that Christine would sleep there and it would be her bed. When they first began assembling the bed, Roger had asked Tommy about who was going to use it. Tommy didn't know. With the frame completed, he suddenly had the information. Was there some sort of telepathy at work? Roger often wondered this. All the time Mario magically communicated orders to his son, wife, and daughter without anyone else hearing.

"What about the other bed?" Roger asked. That was going to the basement, he found out shortly thereafter, dragging the box down the stairs with Tommy after briefly getting it stuck in the closet. After a grueling 10 minutes or so, the box and mattresses crashed to the basement floor. Sometime between their leaving the house and returning someone had cleared out just enough space for the bed to be assembled. Mr. Smith ventured down the stairs to supervise them. Roger hoped that the cat completed his bathroom going activities for the moment. The heat and various animal smells made him dizzy.

Speaking of animal smells, Christine came down. She walked around them, clapping. She asked if they were finished and demanded that they help her look for Peek-a-boo. After they said yes, she told them they both needed to get jobs. The house wasn't paying for itself. With a flash of heartburn, Roger expected Christine to start asking about whether they would lose the house, like she did with increasing frequency. She surprised him by saying, "my dad told me to tell you that the fat lady [this was how Christine referred to her mother when she was angry with her] and dad will meet with Mr. Leslie tomorrow." The pit of Roger's stomach started burning. Tommy yawned and began singing "Dust in the Wind."

So apparently Mario had been in touch with the Assistant Principal. Roger hoped Mario didn't call the school on behalf of both of them, instead making Edith represent Roger. He was a bit angry at being left out of the loop. But notice a day in advance was an uncharacteristic show of consideration for others by Mario. Tommy didn't seem to be worried, but Roger knew better. He would soon announce that his tummy hurt.

CHAPTER THIRTEEN
Tuesday, September 17, 1991

It was nearly fall, but temperature was again in the mid 90s. They piled into the station wagon. Christine was given a day off from school so she could sit with Lucky Joy in the car while the four of them went to the office. The logic of this bothered Roger, but he was too focused on the upcoming meeting to complain. He didn't have a comeback line to Christine's laughing at their predicament.

His belly hurt and his bowels threatened release, like a movie hostage taker with a grenade. But Roger knew he was empty, having gone to the bathroom three times already. Tommy was pale. He clasped his hands tightly. This car made creaking noises that the previous one didn't. Roger wondered where Edith got it and how much she paid as Lucky Joy panted at his window. Cold sweat streamed down Roger's arms. He shivered, despite the heat. He thought maybe Mario was perpetually nervous. Perhaps that was the reason for his always being cold. Mario's ensemble consisted of a winter hat, a ski parka and frighteningly bright green pants today. What would Mr. Leslie think?

They parked opposite the school on Penelope Avenue. Mario and Edith signed in at the sleeping security guard's desk automatically, having been there so often the previous year on account of Christine. Roger and Tommy followed behind Mario and Edith. The janitor swept the floor with a large broom, and Edith paused briefly to admire his work.

Roger gulped as they headed up the stairs. Roger and Edith were scheduled for 1:20, but were 10 minutes late because of Mario. Tommy and Mario were scheduled for 1:45. Roger wanted to ask Tommy if his legs felt heavy too. Looking at the boy's pale face he decided that they were. It sucked that Tommy got suspended too, but Roger was sort of glad. He wasn't here by himself, and his best friend would be there with him during his week off.

All four went into the office. Mario and Edith came up to the first old typist. After a few brief murmurs, Mario was motioned toward the seats and Edith and Roger were directed to Mr. Leslie's desk. There the man sat, with glasses on his nose and papers on his desk. His desk had been clear the last time. Were they all meant for him? Roger hoped not.

The Assistant Principal looked up. "Oh there you are," he said. "Mrs. Wharton?"

"Call me Edith," Edith said pleasantly. She wore a business blouse and skirt. Tommy had said she liked to dress up, but Roger didn't believe him. She hardly ever took a shower, and only did when Mario scolded her into it. She usually dressed like a hobo. Now Roger thought Edith might actually enjoy this sort of thing. She took a shower that morning, combed her hair, and dressed up fancy.

Mr. Leslie's hand seemed to shake the slightest bit as he extended it to Edith. Was he feeling nervous? "Candice," the Assistant Principal said to the nearest typist. "Can you get me a coffee, and, Mrs. Wharton, would you like something?"

"Oh sure, whatever you're having," said Edith. She wasn't one to pass up on free food or drink.

The secretary gave Mr. Leslie a look as if to say, "are you serious?" She rolled her eyes and went back to her typing.

"Excuse me one second," the Assistant Principal said, his skin redder than a moment ago. "I'll be right back with our coffee."

Roger sat there in the middle of the typing and telephone noises. Now that it was actually happening, he wasn't as nervous. His stomach stopped hurting and he no longer had to go to the bathroom.

Mr. Leslie came back, handing Edith a coffee cup. She took it delicately, making small sips.

"Would you like milk or sugar?" Mr. Leslie inquired.

"Oh no, thank you."

"Now to business. Your son here, Mrs. Wharton, Edith, sorry, he's in a serious bit of trouble."

Edith had an interesting way of communicating with people, Tommy once told Roger. She nodded and repeated everything they said to her. This made them think she listened and shared their concerns. In reality, however, no one really knew what was going on in her head. For example, most of the things that Mario told her were repeated back to him, but Edith rarely, if ever, actually did what he told her to do. Now Roger witnessed it firsthand. "Yeah, yeah, son...trouble," Edith nodded at Mr. Leslie, mimicking his serious expression.

"Oh, hold on a second. Are you *the* Edith Wharton? As in, Edith Wharton the writer?"

"Yeah, yeah," Edith continued to bob her head at the Assistant Principal. "...a writer."

"Oh my God. It is such an honor to meet you."

"Yeah, yeah, honor. Thank you."

"My favorite book, one that I read back in college, is *The House of Mirth*."

"Yeah, yeah, earth." Edith nodded.

"It's just a great book. You are one of my favorite writers."

Edith nodded, "thank you," taking credit for a book written over fifty years before her birth.

Mr. Leslie chuckled. "This is turning out to be a good day." He opened Roger's folder. "Now, getting back to the matter at hand. Your son here committed a very serious offense against the rules of the school code that I have begun developing here during my tenure as Assistant Principal."

"Matter at hand...son...rules...Principal."

"Right." Mr. Leslie was glad Edith was on the same page. "He was caught reading during the lunch hour, where students are to engage in eating and recreation...a flagrant violation."

"Oh yes, yes...eating," Edith nodded between sips of her coffee.

Roger watched the exchange in amazement. Was Mr. Leslie really that dense? More than once he had to stifle a giggle that threatened to become uncontrollable laughter. He pretended he had the hiccups.

"Now, I'm going to return the confiscated book. Young Roger here must not read during school hours."

"...no reading in school," Edith repeated, taking a copy of *Carrie* by Stephen King from the Assistant Principal's hand. Roger wondered who in the school besides him liked Stephen King. It might have been Clyde, to whom Roger recommended that particular work.

"Do you allow your son to read such books?" Mr. Leslie asked. "It is vile and satanic. In my opinion, Stephen King should be banned. Why can't that guy write good, wholesome work. Like those movies I saw recently on TV. Um, what was it? Oh yes, *The Shawshank Redemption* and *Stand By Me*.

Now those were good movies. Whoever wrote them is thousands of times better than Stephen King garbage."

"Garbage," Edith repeated.

Roger whispered to her.

"This is the wrong book," Edith said. "We had the Nietzsche." She gave *Carrie* back to Mr. Leslie.

"Oh dear. My apologies. We've had quite a bit of trouble lately with students reading."

Edith took *The Gay Science* from Mr. Leslie and handed it to Roger.

"Under normal circumstances I would also talk with you about Roger's grades and the concerns I have about their being substantially higher than his classmates'. We do not view this kind of thing favorably here. No one likes 'know it alls,' Mrs. Wharton, Edith. There is also an important funding issue. I'm sure you understand."

Edith continued nodding and repeating the Assistant Principal.

"But since you are such a celebrity, I will cut you and your boy a break."

"Yeah, ...break." Edith nodded and sipped her coffee. She delicately set down her cup, tiny in her gigantic hands, on Mr. Leslie's desk. "Thank you for your time," she said.

As they got up the Assistant Principal leaped from his chair to shake Edith's hand. "No, thank you," he said. "It's been a pleasure."

Edith nodded. "...a pleasure..." She and Roger walked toward the door.

That went much better than expected. Relieved, Roger gave Tommy a wink as they walked past him and Mario and out the door. Outside the office, Edith sat down on the bench and chuckled. "What an idiot that man is. I had a boss like him once," she said with a hint of nostalgia. "The coffee was good though."

"Thank you," Roger told her.

"No problem. He thinks I'm a writer. Who's Edith Wharton?"

"Beats me," Roger shrugged.

Mario's meeting with the Assistant Principal started then, as Mario's voice boomed through the door. He could get quite loud when he got excited. It was his lecture hall voice.

Although Mr. Leslie had called the meeting, Mario did all the talking. That's what Roger thought, at least, because there were no pauses. Mario kept on going and going. One would think that at some point he'd run out of breath, but that didn't happen. The Assistant Principal might have tried to say something, Roger supposed, but Mario probably talked right over him.

The first lecture topic was the indoctrination system of public schools, and schools in general, with some tangential remarks on the inculcation of stupidity. Tommy must have had his face in his palm the entire time, the poor boy.

"Why do you actively use all your resources—the money that is not siphoned off and pocketed—on making children stupid? Why do you recruit the least knowledgeable teachers? Why do you fire those teachers that actually teach the children something useful? Why is it that the smart children have to pretend that they are stupid so that the other children will not bother them and so their teachers will not hate them? Why is it that everyone must think the same thing all the time about everything?"

These must have been rhetorical questions because Mario didn't give his audience time to respond. After explaining and expanding his critique on the state of education, Mario moved on to the state of politics, a natural outgrowth of the decades of educational decay. This led to a discussion of the coming globalized society, which Mario argued would lead to a worse environment, greater poverty and stupidity among the masses, and more authoritarianism. "From our current kleptocracy will, after a series of wars and when the system collapses under its own weight—by design!—emerge a global government of the most repressive kind." The seeds were already sprouting, Mario said. First it was Tommy with a cat. What was wrong with bringing a cat to school? Nothing. Witchcraft? Just how stupid was Mr. Leslie, exactly? It would soon follow, Mario predicted, that children would be punished for bringing toy guns to school. Then they would be punished drawing guns. Then they would be arrested for bringing the wrong kind of marker. Eventually they would be incarcerated for thought crimes. That's where it was all going.

Then Mario talked about the Iran-Contra Affair (maybe to buttress his case), about how even though it was clear that criminal wrong doing reached the highest levels, no one important got charged, and the lackeys got pardoned.

It was a lot of material to fit in two hours. Roger was impressed. The classrooms had emptied out for the day already. The shouts and steps of children, free at last, faded from the yard a while ago too. Yet Mario kept talking. No one left the office. Roger figured that the secretaries got out at three like everyone else. That meant they stayed to listen. Tommy had once mentioned that Mario's classes were popular and always filled to capacity.

From the scraping noises and Mario's instructions, Roger gathered that Mario spotted a portable chalkboard in the room. It was now being positioned in front of him, maybe. He was going to write notes or draw diagrams. Roger was getting tired. He wondered how much longer it was going to take. Edith had fallen asleep beside him about half an hour ago. The bulletin board at her back vibrated with her snores.

Around six in the evening, Mario finally emerged triumphantly from the office. He wiped chalk dust on his pants. The secretaries filed out past him, some shaking his hand, others whispering in laudatory tones and patting him on the arm. A sleepy Tommy stood by his side.

"Oh my God!" Christine said. She and Lucky almost died, and it was all Wharton's fault for forgetting to remind them to leave the windows rolled down.

Edith pulled out of their parking spot. They were going to Manhattan to eat somewhere, to celebrate. Mario told Christine and Lucky Joy about his successful meeting while Christine laughed and clapped. Tommy slept next to Roger, who looked out the window. The way Mario described Mr. Leslie's reaction, Roger began to think that the meeting might actually have gone well.

Roger changed his mind the next day when Child Protective Services called to notify them of an upcoming surprise inspection. Roger understood then why Tommy's family picked up the phone so infrequently. It wasn't just Lucky Joy's hatred of it. Incoming calls rarely relayed good news. Usually it was debt collectors. Edith answered sometimes, putting the phone down for a second to find her checkbook.

CHAPTER FIFTEEN
Wednesday October 9, 1991

To say that Roger was pleasantly surprised when, at the be-ginning of the day, Mr. Gorton announced the special as-sembly wouldn't be entirely accurate. It was pleasant, as it meant that they didn't have to do any schoolwork for a couple of hours. And the announcement was somewhat surprising. But the latter was so only be-cause Roger didn't know exactly when the an-nouncement would come. He had been expecting it, however, for about a week.

Every year, around this time, two men came to speak to the students about raising money for the school by selling candy. Roger had some difficulty remembering faces and names, so the men who came each year might have been different people. But they all had the stereotypical sleazy used car salesman look, in Roger's opinion. All the business crooks that he saw on the five o'clock news' "shame on you" segment and on the cop television shows he sometimes watched with Tommy looked like these guys. He wouldn't be surprised if they were the guys on the news.

The class lined up at the front of the room. Mr. Gorton didn't care about size order. This meant that Roger could walk down the stairs behind Tommy, and usually not have Michael behind him.

Today wasn't the case, however. As Mr. Gorton rounded the corner and the class followed, Michael flicked Roger's ears. From the shuffling, huffing, and suppressed laughter behind him, Roger suspected that Michael did the bunny ears thing to him. This involved making a peace or Nixon victory sign with one's hand and waving it behind someone's head.

Ignoring Michael usually was enough to dissuade him from further buffoonery, but not today. Michael demanded his attention with the ear flicks. They didn't hurt, but they were annoying. Roger turned around. Michael, who had his hands up near Roger's ears put them down quickly, looked up at the ceiling, and pretended nothing happened. "Come on, hurry up," Theodore said at the back of the line. "Yeah, hurry up," someone, Peter maybe, agreed. Roger flicked Michael in the belly and rushed to catch up with Tommy, who entered the stairwell. Michael huffed something unintelligible. His sneakers squeaked as he ran after Roger. A quick glance back revealed Michael holding his belly as if he had just received a grave injury. He made his customary David Hasselhoff noises.

Roger went through the stairwell doorway, noticing Mr. Gorton standing on the landing to his right, out of view of the door. A fence there blocked the stairs leading to the roof. Roger often wondered what was up there. He was shaken out of his thoughts and almost fell down the stairs when Michael hit him with a karate chop. "Michael!" said Mr. Gorton behind him as he ran down after Tommy. Roger smiled. That was a point in his favor. But it meant that Michael would be vengeful. Roger would have to be vigilant during the assembly.

The class waited for Mr. G on the first floor in the space between the stairs and the gym. Roger and Tommy speculated about the big, metallic gray voting machines that were stacked against the wall. They were here early this year. Jim, the new assistant janitor, sprinkled sawdust on a puddle of vomit nearby. It must not have been a terribly good job, cleaning up after a couple of hundred kids. It was sort of the family business, Roger supposed, as Jim was the son of the white haired man who found his shoe. Jim wasn't as friendly as his father. In fact, he cast the children snide looks when he didn't stare at the ground. "Eww!" a couple of the girls said, covering their mouths with their palms. Roger, on the other hand, played mind chess on the otherwise shiny tiled floor. It was easier to play here than at Tommy's because the tiles were dark green and brown colored, almost like a real chessboard. Roger was a knight, skipping around the sawdust covered puke.

Mr. G went to the head of the class. "No more horseplay. You hear me Michael?"

"Yeah," Michael said. Then quietly to Roger, "I'll get you back you homo." Roger was almost positive Michael didn't even know to what he referred. It was, of course, when two men liked the same woman. Christine had told Roger that. He hadn't been to the library in a long time, so that wasn't verified yet. It seemed reasonable, though, and helped explain why homosexuals weren't allowed in the military. Imagine what would happen if two men who liked the same woman were trained to use deadly force and given weapons.

Jim left the vomit puddle unsupervised. He had probably gone to get a dust bin or mop or something. Or maybe it was to put away the sawdust container. Where did all that sawdust come from, anyway? Who was the genius that figured out that he could sell what was essentially his garbage to schools across the country? Was it the same guy that Mario sometimes ranted about? The one who figured out that he could bribe city water authorities to buy his industrial waste, taken from phosphate fertilizer smokestacks, and put it in the tap water as fluoride? That claim had also not been subject to verification, but Roger and Tommy weren't allowed to drink tap water in their home. Mario had purchased an expensive water filter earlier that year, but it was currently in storage. Instead, they drank bottled water, various juices not from concentrate, and organic nut milks. It always puzzled Roger, however, that Mario still cooked with tap water, like when he made pasta or bean soup.

As they walked past the vomit, Michael tried to push Roger into it. They were still about the same height, but Michael was heavier. He almost succeeded. It was thanks to Tommy that Roger's vomit collision was avoided. Tommy grabbed his arm and pulled him back just in time. In the process he inadvertently elbowed Michael in the stomach.

Michael doubled over and theatrically crossed his arms over his abdomen. He stumbled back and forth, bumping into Gregory and Meg. He moved forward saying, "That was the death blow." He stepped on the vomit, dragging wet sawdust on the floor in a pattern that was not unlike Roger's knight. The stumbling became more labored, and Michael bent lower. He bumped into the wall, bounced off wrestling style, fell to the floor, and died.

Jim came back with a broom and dustbin. He surveyed the mess, looking indignantly at Michael, his brown mustache quivering. "Michael! I told you no more horsing around. Get up and help Mr. Flannery clean up the mess you made!" Mr. G said. "The rest of you, follow me." Michael got up and panted toward the scowling janitor. Mr. Gorton led the class past the basketball hoops. They turned the corner, went past the kitchen, and entered the auditorium, where several classes were already seated. The noise level was much louder than was usual at lunch time. Special assemblies always put the children in a frenzy.

When all six classes were seated—two classes for each grade that was there, Roger figured the K through 2 students would have the assembly after lunch—the Assistant Principal got on stage. He screamed, "Settle down, people! We're not running a zoo here. If you want to eat your lunch and go outside later, you will be quiet!" The room became silent. "I said silence!" the man screamed from the stage anyway.

Everyone turned when the auditorium doors opened. Michael was pushed into the room by the janitor. He gulped audibly, looked around for their class, apparently did not find it, and tiptoed to the nearest chair. He sat next to Craig.

"Give me your attention!" said Mr. Leslie. Everyone turned back to him. "We have two very special guests today who will tell you how you can raise money for the school." Roger knew it.

The curtains opened, and all the students exhaled simultaneously in a collective "wow." It seemed as though no one noticed the armpit fart noises coming from Michael's direction. The last fart noise came to an abrupt end and Michael himself decided that what was on stage was more important than attention on him. "Holy moly," he said, "that's some great stuff!" He was shushed by multiple parties, all entranced by the display in front of them. Two used car salesman looking guys dressed in suits that Roger saw in mafia movies stood amid a collection of various toys, bicycles, and shiny plastic packaging. It looked like they brought their own lighting equipment. A spotlight danced between the various items on the stage to what sounded like Michael Jackson. Someone must have closed all the curtains while Assistant Principal Leslie yelled at them, because it was all dark in the room, except for the shimmering stage.

"Hello everybody!" said one of the enthusiastic men. To Roger it sounded like when annoying people talked to small animals or babies. He turned to Tommy to see what he thought. Tommy was entranced too. But Roger could tell that he wasn't listening to the two men. He just wanted the toys.

An hour into the presentation, quite an upgrade from last year, Roger longed to go back to class. The cold metal chair hurt his butt. It was like being forced to watch an infomercial. In fact, they were watching one. The screen had been pulled down from the ceiling, a projector was set up, and a movie about little Johnny, who raised his school so much money by selling candy that he won himself a trip to Disney World played for them. Any one of them, "at PS," the voice-over cut out and one of the men on stage said with an inadvertent cough "49," "could be just like Johnny."

The movie ended to thunderous applause. Roger did not clap, of course, and slapped Tommy's hands to make him stop. Tommy looked at him defiantly and started clapping harder. Roger couldn't tell if Tommy just liked clapping or if he really liked the presentation. The men continued talking then, explaining how "easy" it was to sell the candy. It basically sold itself, they said. Yeah, right. Then why were they here? Among the many awesome prizes, one could get a bicycle if one sold "only 700 chocolate bars." A brand new Walkman was 100 bars.

Roger stopped paying attention. His eyes hurt from rolling. Here was another excellent business model. On further thought, the candy did sell itself. The two guys, probably employed by some middle-man company, used children and their parents to buy and sell the candy. Their job was to do these presentations to get free labor. Well, it wasn't exactly free, as there were prizes (but who knows, maybe these were donated as advertisements by the prize manufacturers), but it was as close to free as it could get. They employed children and parents for sub-minimal wages and no regard to labor laws. Paying off a superintendent or two, or maybe just the schools' Chancellor, was probably the only real cost. Forget lemonade. Roger wanted to think of a way to make money like this too. He was reminded of something he once read about one of the Rockefellers, probably the one that started the oil business. That guy said something like he would rather earn 1% of a 100 people's labor rather than 100% of his own. Here it seemed like the students and their parents would contribute far more than 1%.

Before the assembly ended, the salesmen handed out glossy envelopes to all the students. These contained a brochure listing all the prizes for selling a certain quantity of candy, a candy brochure for their customers, and an order form. This last document, once filled out, would be sent, along with the money proceeds, to the administrators of this operation. Those students who sold the minimum quantity of candy to qualify for a prize filled out a prize form, dividing their candy points among those toys that they wished to receive. A couple of months later the candy would arrive in the mail. The student sales boys and girls then had to deliver the candy to their customers. Some time during the spring, usually long after the students completely forgot about them, the prizes came in the mail. Roger thought the idea was brilliant.

On the stairs, going back up to their classroom, Tommy turned around to face Roger. "I wanna get that bike," he said. "It's so cool!"

Roger sighed. "It's all a scam, you know."

"Yeah. No one will get to go to Disney. But I can win that bike. I can ask mom to buy some candy, and she can ask her workers and stuff."

"We're trying to save money, remember?"

"But I can ride a bike and stuff and that'll save moneys toopers."

"How would that save money?"

"Come on, hurry up!" Theodore yelled from the back of the line.

Tommy ran up the stairs to catch up with the class. Roger followed.

They continued their discussion during lunch. Roger looked up from the prize order form. "It's 700 'premium' chocolate bars for the bike. The 'premium' bars are $2 each. You have to sell $1,400 worth of crap to get the bike."

"I can do it," Tommy said confidently between bites of his tofu and broccoli stir fry.

"How?"

"I'll get mom to buy half. And we can sell the other half to peoples around the neighborhood and stuff."

"So your mom is gonna fork over $700?"

"Yuppers."

"That's a lot. A bike probably costs like $100 at most. Everyone will be better off if you just get a bike from the store."

"Noppers. That costs moneys. But if we sell the candy we get the bike for freesies."

"How do we get it for free?"

"Because we sell the candy for it."

"But you said your mom will have to buy $700 worth of candy."

"Yuppers."

"So how is that for free?"

Tommy said something Roger couldn't understand.

"What?"

Again. Tommy mumbled into his food. This was becoming a new habit for the boy.

"Finish chewing and then enunciate." Roger was annoyed.

Tommy did as asked. "I emunciated perfectly. I think we have to need to look at your ears."

Roger rolled his eyes. "What were you saying before? When I couldn't hear you?"

"I forgot."

"I asked you, how is it free if your mom is spending $700?"

"Oh. Because we get all the candy *and* the bike."

Roger sighed. "You can probably buy that candy in any store for way cheaper. And I'm sure it sucks anyway."

"Noppers, it's premium. That means it's super good. And with the profits we can pay off the house."

"What profits?"

"From the candy sales, silly."

Roger hoped Tommy would lose the order form like last year.

"Noppers," Tommy scolded Roger. "The turkey is a beautiful bird and peoples shouldn't eat it!" He had gotten worked up since Roger first teased him after they got out of school. Now opening the front door of the house Tommy was still going at it. "It has feelings. It feels pain. It wants to live a happy life with no one to bother it. It's not right to kill it. We don't have to eat the poor turkey. They did nothing to us."

"I know," Roger said rolling his eyes. "You already said that."

Thanksgiving was around the corner, and Mario left it up to Tommy to cook. Mario had given him a pen and notepad to write down the list of all the delicious food Tommy and Roger were going to make. Mario dictated the list and Tommy had to write it down. Roger supposed this was an improvement from prior lists. Tommy usually had to guess what his dad wanted. Mario made a big fuss the previous year because certain dishes were left off the menu.

Edith didn't pick them up with the car today, as she usually did when something didn't come up, because she had to take Mario food shopping for their Thanksgiving feast. After Thanksgiving there would be Hanukkah, Christmas, New Year's, Chinese New Year, and several Indian holidays whose names Roger couldn't remember. There was a special occasion every week, anyway. But Thanksgiving was a big one. Mario was especially into it. Roger thought it was a bit weird, with all of Mario's talk about the extermination of the Native Americans and denunciation of puritanical culture and values. Such contradictions didn't seem to bother anyone in the household, except Roger. No matter how much Nietzsche he read, he couldn't get past them. In an effort to calm him Tommy tried to explain about the so called "third" that logic always excluded, and how the world was itself contradictory and always "both and" instead of "either or," but Roger didn't get it.

A big Lucky Joy pile greeted them in the hall. Everyone was good at avoiding the dog's presents for them. Except Roger and Mario, the latter of whom sometimes dragged it all over the house. He went down to the basement far more than usual when he had dog poop on his shoes, Roger noticed. He cursed as he narrowly avoided the pile. "How come he doesn't go poop outside like a normal dog?" Roger asked.

"Because he's not a normal dog," Tommy petted Lucky. "He's our lord and master, Lucky Joy." The dog barked at the sound of his name.

"I knew it," Christine said from the living room. "Wharton is here. I knew I smelled something rotten." She was home earlier than usual. She lounged on her bed with all the cats around her, watching the new television. Edith couldn't survive long without TV. A new one was purchased on credit as soon as she scrounged up enough for the down payment.

"If you close your mouth for a second you'll find that the rotten smell will go away," Roger retorted.

"Shut up," said Christine and clapped. Mr. Smith complained that she was not petting him. He flopped down on her lap and hissed at the other cats, swinging at them with a soft white paw. "When's dinner?" Christine asked hopefully.

"I don't know," Tommy responded. "I'm not sure Wharton here and I are up to making it."

"Oh come on," replied his sister. "I only had three of those sandwiches you made me for lunch. Besides breakfast I didn't have anything to eat today. I'm starving!"

Roger made her another huge sandwich while Tommy fed the cats. Galen was getting big. He no longer hopped around. His legs now appeared too long for his body, like he was a miniature giraffe. The other kittens were much bigger too. Tigger and Peek-a-boo were getting fat. Shadow remained the runt. He had a cold. White snots accented his pitch black nose in recent days. Tommy worried, but Roger assured him the cat would be fine. He was just a bit of a wuss.

Roger made the sandwich out of a loaf of Italian bread. It had lettuce, tempeh, mustard, tomatoes, and a soy spread that reminded Roger of mayonnaise. He was going to cut it into three large pieces, which he knew would leave Tommy and himself full until the late evening. Before he could do so, however, Christine, who had been spying on his progress from the doorway, grabbed the entire thing. It was gone in seconds. It was Roger's fault, of course. He should have been more vigilant.

Someone knocked on the front door. Whoever was out there must have been there for a while, because people normally rang the bell first. The bell had never worked, however. Mario wanted it that way because nothing good ever came from coming to the door when strangers were about. Lucky Joy barked at the unexpected guest from his spot in the hall. Mr. Smith started wailing. He prepared to go to the bathroom. The guest was going to receive an interesting welcome.

Wiping her mouth with her forearm, Christine went to check. "It's some lady," she called from the hall over Lucky Joy's barks.

"Don't open it," Roger and Tommy said together.

"Jinx!" Roger said before Tommy, and Tommy pouted.

Their warning either came too late or went unheeded. Despite being told many times not to do so, Christine was the only member of the household to open the door to strangers. When he saw the lady's rapacious eyes, without a hint of humanity or intelligence, Roger knew who the uninvited guest was. "Child Protective Services," Roger whispered to Tommy.

"Where are your parents," the lady asked them. She wore a black trench coat and held a notepad and pen.

"They're out somewhere like usual," Christine said. "I'm starving," she patted her big belly.

"They don't feed you?" the lady asked, writing furiously.

"Shut up Chris," Tommy elbowed his sister.

She paid him no attention. "Hardly at all," she said to the lady.

"That's not true," said Roger. "You just ate an entire loaf of bread."

"I don't remember any bread," Christine burped.

"I can see that," the lady said without a hint of sarcasm.

"B-b-but s-s-s-she's f-fat," Roger said.

"No," the lady said. "Your sister is so malnourished that her belly is puffing up.

"Yeah," Christine nodded. Roger could tell that she was clapping inside her head. "I am not fat. I don't eat enough." She smacked her ballooning belly.

"Do they keep you from eating and tell you you're fat?"

"All the time," Christine responded.

"B-b-b-but sh-she eats a-all the t-time! Sh-sh-she w-w-weighs l-l-like 200 p-pounds!" Roger stammered.

"No I don't," Christine said. The bed protested as she climbed on it while the lady looked around disapprovingly.

Roger didn't know if the lady saw Lucky Joy's pile, but the smell coming from the litter box obviously disturbed her. Mr. Smith didn't pick a good time to go to the bathroom. Roger's concern grew as the woman looked around the messy house, jotting things down in her notepad.

"And you sleep here in the living room?" the lady asked Christine. One of the peeling tiles in the dining room crashed down in a plume of dust. Lucky Joy howled in surprise.

"Yeah," Christine answered. She wasn't really paying attention to the lady anymore. Wrestling was on. "Doot! Yeah, you got him now." Christine laughed at the screen.

The lady looked up from her writing. "Boys," she said to Tommy and Roger, "do you live here too? Show me where you sleep."

Roger gulped. He always did what authority figures said. He turned toward the basement. But Tommy was smarter than him. "We don't live here," he said. Ignoring Roger's surprised look, Tommy explained, "we're Christine's friends. Just visiting."

The lady looked at them for a moment. "The paperwork says there's two children here, with a third who has the same address. Are you Roger and Tommy?"

"No," Tommy said.

"No," Roger followed Tommy's lead.

"What are your names then?"

"Kurt," said Tommy, pointing at himself. "He's Friedrich," he pointed at Roger. "We're just visiting," he repeated.

"They messed up the paperwork again," the lady exhaled, scribbling something. "Alright Christine, you're coming with me."

"Is there food there?" Christine asked.

"You will be fed," the lady promised.

Tommy choked back tears and hugged his sister before she left with the lady.

Mario came back a few minutes later. "They took Christine! They took Christine!" Tommy cried.

"Right," Mario said. "Now, about Thanksgiving. I bought..." he went on to list all of the ingredients that Tommy had written for him. Edith deposited all of the grocery bags on the porch and drove off to work, run errands for Mario, and to meet with lawyers regarding two lawsuits that a union filed against her. Mario was so excited about Thanksgiving that he didn't pay attention to what Tommy tried to tell him.

Tommy didn't back down, and Roger joined in. Eventually Mario had enough of their interruptions and decided to ignore them. That was what Mario did when he thought people were not listening to him. He pretended that they weren't there. Many parents spanked their kids or grounded them, taking away their privileges or sending them to their rooms. Mario never did that. His ultimate punishment was giving the silent treatment. As it was something Tommy feared most, he always tried to be in his father's good graces. This meant agreeing with everything his father said, and telling him his food was delicious when he cooked, even if it was inedible. Tommy mentioned once that Mario made a soup that looked and smelled so bad, no one wanted to eat it. Christine, Tommy, and Lucian all said they were really full. Edith, the eternal suck up and show off, ate two bowls in front of them, saying something like "see, I can do it. You're all scardey cats." That was probably not an exact quote, but it was Tommy's story. Mario, with good reason, never ate his own food. For the next two days, Tommy told Roger, Edith had horrible diarrhea and stomach cramps. She said it was more painful than giving birth to Christine. But that, in her view, was better than refusing Mario's food and incurring his silent wrath.

"What do we do now?" Tommy asked when they were downstairs.

"What if we tell Lucian?"

"Noppers. He's a big wuss. He won't do anything."

"What if we tell your aunt? Doesn't Christine still have to do some work for her?"

Tommy was skeptical about talking to his aunt about an internal family matter. "She'll just make it worst anyway."

"Worse," Roger corrected. "So we have to wait for your mom then?" He thought for a moment. "Why can't we write your dad a note or something?"

"It won't work," Tommy said. "When he gets this way you just have to wait."

It seemed stupid to Roger. How could a parent refuse to listen? It seemed impossible. But he saw it with his own eyes. "This is so retarded," Roger said.

Tommy started crying again. He hoped they wouldn't experiment on her.

"Like she won't break all their equipment?" Roger joked and Tommy let out a giggle between tears. "Maybe she's better off, you know?"

Tommy punched him. Hard.

CHAPTER SEVENTEEN
Wednesday, November 20, 1991

Tommy and Roger missed Edith in her comings and goings. She either came home late and left early, or hadn't come back at all. The notes they left for her looked slept on, but were probably unread. They didn't know what to do. They had even told Lucian the story. He was now receiving the silent treatment too.

Mario popped into their room after school. "Have you seen Christine?" he asked. "She's supposed to help me with some Ph.D. applications." Mario had trouble filling out forms. That job was usually assigned to Christine. "I can't find her anywhere though."

"They took her!" Tommy yelled.

"Who?"

"Protective Child Services!"

"What? When?"

"Monday."

"Oh my God! Why didn't you tell me?"

"We've been trying for days two!"

"We'll get to why it's your fault you didn't tell me later. For now, tell me everything about what happened."

Tommy repeated what they had tried to tell Mario. He finally listened. When Mario left the house to go find his daughter, Tommy and Roger found a large stack of correspondence under Tigger. It had been Christine's job to sort through all the mail. Among Mario's various publications, catalogs, second, third, and final notices, was a notice from the Child Protective Services. A hearing had been scheduled for that Friday.

* * *

Mario came back in the evening. After complaining about how terrible the subway service was, he told the expectant boys and Lucian about his ordeals. First they said no record of his daughter existed. Then that he was an unfit parent. He eventually found out about the hearing that Friday. Mario was a bit unclear about what happened to him after that point. A scuffle ensued and he was escorted out of the building by police officers. Roger imagined that Mario had tried to give them a lecture, perhaps walking into cubicles and offices, causing a scene.

CHAPTER EIGHTEEN
Friday, November 22, 1991

Mario had trouble at the government building again on Thursday. He was now banned from the premises and couldn't attend the hearing. Roger and Tommy thought this was just as well. Perhaps now Christine had a better chance of coming home.

Edith was sent to the hearing by herself. Mario waited in the car with Tommy, Roger, and Lucian. They had wanted to go in with Edith, but Mario objected because he would be lonely. Edith emerged from the building, wearing her smart business outfit. She attempted to tell them what happened, but Mario kept interrupting her. He tried to give a lecture about how the government was evil. Everyone else waited patiently until Mario took a pause to catch his breath. They were a block from home at that point.

Finally given the chance, Edith said that the hearing went well, and that Christine would be sent home on Monday or Tuesday. Various forms had to be filled out and processed, or something like that. Mario gushed with happiness. He made Edith turn the car around. They went back to Manhattan to celebrate, eating at Christine's favorite restaurant where everything on the menu had deep fried tofu.

They came home in high spirits, with Mario again discussing, mostly with himself, what Tommy would cook next week for Thanksgiving. Mario applauded himself for forcing the government to return his daughter. Assembled in the kitchen, with their sparkling apple cider and Mario preparing to make a toast while Lucky Joy tried to beat him to it, they almost didn't notice Christine as she came in.

"I'm starving," Christine said. "What's for dinner?"

Tommy and Roger were put in charge of making sandwiches after Mario erupted in a paroxysm of joy. Christine then explained her surprise return and told them the story of her incredible ordeal at the hands of the government.

Christine clapped. Everyone gathered in the kitchen. The cats sat around on counter tops. Two were on Edith's belly. Edith had somehow squeezed into Mario's usual interstice on the couch. Galen and Shadow rose up and down with her breathing. Lucian swept the floor with his broom. Mario sat on a bucket in the middle of the room next to his daughter, affectionately punching her shoulder. Roger and Tommy were squeezed to the counter by the stove. Roger sliced tomatoes while Tommy did something with tempeh. Lucky Joy scampered around between everyone's feet. His nails made tiny clicking sounds on the kitchen tiles between his vigorous barks.

Christine was not adept at descriptions. Roger's imagination, as a result, formed only partial images of her adventure. "They took me in the thingy to the thingy," Christine began, clapping excitedly. "They took my fingerprints and a picture, like I was a criminal or a minority."

"Aren't you a minority?" Roger inquired.

"Wharton, stop interrupting," Christine clapped. "Then the lady said there would be food, but all they gave me was two slices of wonder bread with a cheese and baloney." Christine ended up eating a "bite sized" cheese sandwich, depositing the bologna in the fridge when no one saw. Scouring the fridge, she found more sandwiches. She estimated that she ate maybe twenty of them, depositing a lopsided (Roger imagined) stack of bologna on a fridge shelf. They only had milk to drink. As there were just two full cartons, Christine was forced to ration. She finished them both over the course of a dozen minutes. Roger and Tommy praised her restraint. Because of the limited adult supervision, Christine had no one to complain to about the desperate food situation.

One girl tried to play doctor with her, but Christine punched her in the face. Her low blood sugar, she explained, made her more prone to anger. A while later, perhaps in a different room, Christine witnessed a scuffle between two or three girls. She wasn't sure whether the third was trying to join in or stop the fight. At any rate, she took the opportunity to secure for herself some candy that the girls had in their possession. It was terrible candy, but Christine ate it to keep up her strength.

Their supervisor made various dingy dolls and other toys available. Christine wasn't interested in these. The television, which had a cage around it, did not have cable. As a result Christine missed her wrestling program. Some show about how wives cheated on their husbands interested the kids, but Christine thought it boring. Of these sorts of shows she only liked Jerry Springer, which she would watch when she stayed home from school, chanting "Je-rry! Je-rry!" with the studio audience.

At dinner they were served mac and cheese with milk and some kind of green things (bean sprouts, Roger guessed). Christine didn't eat the green things. When she wanted more mac and cheese, she wandered around the rooms, looking for an adult. Christine finally found two. They were playing doctor on the desk, or maybe they were wrestling. At any rate, they were both naked. Most egregious of all, they refused to give Christine additional food and slammed the door in her face. They locked it when she tried again to ask for sustenance.

She could not sleep that night because her bed was less comfortable than the floor, her stomach hurt from hunger, cockroaches tickled her as they climbed over her body, and her roommate, a pale girl named Amanda, screamed the whole night because of the rats. "What that place needs," Christine said, "is a few cats. Isn't that right, Mr. Smith?" She kissed the big white cat on his forehead. He thumped his tail from side to side to show his appreciation. Christine said that she would have slept just fine if they had given her something more to eat. At one point she joined in the screaming, but this didn't get anyone's attention.

The next morning they were given shredded wheat. Amanda wasn't hungry, so Christine ate her portion. A lady warned Christine that her actions were a crime, and if she did that again she would be charged with stealing. It was also announced that someone had eaten all of the bologna and cheese sandwiches, which were their lunch. An investigation was underway. A police officer was supposed to dust the stack of bologna slices for prints. So when no one paid attention, Christine hid the bologna in her pockets. Officials told the twenty girls, by Christine's estimate, that paperwork was being processed to find them new homes. "It was even more boring than at school. With all the fights and stuff, I couldn't get any sleep during the day."

The place was a dump. What upset her most was the lack of late morning and late afternoon snacks. The portion of pizza served at lunch couldn't have been any smaller. Christine was once again denied seconds. Threat of arrest didn't deter her from eating Amanda's portion, because Christine thought it was okay, having traded some of the bologna for the slice.

That day too was spent in boredom, and the next. Christine was despondent about missing her wrestling. She was also afraid she was losing her touch at Nintendo. She believed one had to practice daily or one would forget how to play entirely after a short period. The lack of televised wrestling was partially made up by all the fights that took place: children vs. children, children vs. adults, adults vs. adults, cockroaches vs. rats. Roger imagined that's what prison was like. "No," Christine said. "In prison there's better food."

"And how would you know?"

"I saw a documentary on it before they took me away."

The rest of Christine's time in the City's care was the same. New kids were delivered and processed; others were processed and shipped away. The food was the same everyday: some sort of wheat and milk combination. Christine didn't like that the portions were small.

"You already said that," Roger said. He and Tommy were making Christine a stir fry. The gigantic sandwich didn't tame her appetite. This was partly because Mario ate most of it.

"Yeah so?" Christine cradled Lucky Joy like a baby. "I missed you, you little bastard," she said to the dog. He looked up and licked his nose. As he yawned, Christine continued, "the portions were really small. At least there weren't onions. I hate onions."

"What about onion rings?"

"That's not onions."

"So how did you escape, or did they let you go?" Roger asked.

"That's a good question," Christine put the dog down and started clapping. "I will tell you." She clapped for a while, pacing around the room. She started to do her little exercise where she bowed down, quickly rose up, jumped, and bowed down again. Christine almost hit Mario in the face, but he didn't notice.

"Well?" Roger asked. Tommy looked at Christine expectantly.

"I'll tell you. I'll tell you," she muttered, and continued her clap, bow, rise, jump.

"You're weird," Roger said to her.

Christine laughed and said, "shut up, Wharton. When are you going to get a job?"

"You want this food or not?"

"Yes please."

As Christine finished her meal, a whole 20 seconds after receiving it ("thank you, it was delicious. You really shouldn't have"), she explained that she got bored where they kept her. That morning, when no one was looking, and from what Roger gathered this was most of the time, Christine took all the edible things she could find from the fridge. This consisted of wonder bread and milk. She stuffed some bread in her mouth and washed it down with most of the carton. She didn't want to be a pig or seem ungracious, so she left some of the milk and half a slice of bread in the fridge. From past experience Roger knew that the milk carton Christine put back in the fridge was empty. If you opened it and put it upside down maybe in a few minutes a couple of drops would drizzle out.

Having fortified herself for the journey, Christine went to her room, left the remaining bologna under her bed for the rats, grabbed her coat, and walked out the front door. She stopped at the corner to buy a pretzel with mustard. She spent her remaining money a block away on a bag of potato chips. She wandered around the neighborhood, which she thought was a bit seedy, for quite some time. After discovering she was lost, she flagged down a cab, which drove her home. Incidentally, the cab driver was outside waiting for his fare. "But maybe he got tired of waiting and left already," Christine burped.

Mario instructed Edith to give Tommy money to give to the taxi driver.

Tommy and Roger worked in the kitchen. Mario had told them to take the day off from school so that they could cook for the next day's celebration. Lucian kept getting in their way, sweeping a pile of dirt from the stove to the middle of the room, and back again. Lucky Joy growled and tried to bite the broom. Mario and Edith were out again, getting more ingredients for Tommy and Roger to cook. Christine was in school.

Everyone looked up from what they were doing when the loud knocking started. Roger and Tommy crept through the dining room to the hall. They stuck their heads into the hall, along with all the orange kittens. Through the glass doorway, next to which Lucky Joy prepared to take a dump, and through the small windows of the front door they saw the lady that had taken Christine away the previous week.

She knocked again but didn't appear to see them. What could she want now? A hesitant Lucian was sent to find out. He was instructed to say that no one else was home. Roger and Tommy hid in the kitchen while Lucian went to the door.

The door creaked open. Lucian protested something. "Just sign here," Roger heard the lady say, followed by more muffled talking. Then the door closed and Lucky Joy started barking. In the pauses between barks Roger heard the dog spin.

"What's he barking about?" Roger asked.

Tommy shrugged.

They went back to the hall to see. The first thing Roger registered was a familiar sight. Lucian stooped down with a plastic bag in his hand to pick up the dog's mess. The girl about their age shivering in the corner with her back to the wall was new, however. She stared at Lucky Joy, paralyzed with fear. She was a round Asian girl, rounder and shorter than Tommy, with dark skin. Roger turned to Tommy with wide eyes. Tommy shrugged and made an "I don't know" face, answering Roger's silent question.

"Be careful," Tommy told the girl. "He bites."

The girl was now a pancake against the wall. Lucian left the hall without acknowledging her presence. Lucky Joy stopped barking because he had a sneeze attack. He scampered to the dining room, jumping backwards with each sneeze and spinning.

"Hello! My name is Tommy!"

The girl looked up at him.

"This is Roger."

"H-hi," Roger said.

The girl unstuck herself from the wall. She still looked scared, but Lucky Joy's acrobatics and sneezing put her somewhat at ease.

"Are you hungry?" Tommy asked. He shared his family's belief that food could solve almost any problem.

The girl seemed to nod. Tommy beckoned for her to follow them to the kitchen. "What do you like to eat?"

The girl shrugged and looked down at the floor. Lucky Joy was back, wagging his tail and panting. He rubbed his side on the girl's legs. She froze again.

"He wants you to pet him," Tommy explained.

"He won't bite?" the girl uttered her first words.

"Not when he wants to be petted," Tommy replied. "How does lemony tofu with string beans sound?" Tommy asked. Roger grumbled under his breath. They weren't supposed to make that until tomorrow.

"Okay," said the girl. She had the look of a survivor of some terrible tragedy. Her face reminded Roger of Tigger, Shadow, and Peek-a-boo's mom. He found a spot to put the carrots he had been chopping, went to the fridge to get a package of tofu, and started cutting it into chunks.

Tommy told the girl to sit down in Mario's spot. Roger winced as the two piles framing the small space were shaken by the girl's climbing on the couch. Tigger immediately climbed up and onto the girl's lap. Shadow positioned himself next to her head, sniffing curiously.

Roger looked for his sunglasses. That was Tommy's idea. As Roger seemed to always get shot in the eye with oil when they fried something, he now wore sunglasses. They were heart shaped (the only ones Tommy could find) and Christine made fun of Roger for it, calling him Elton John.

"I-i-it's j-just t-to p-p-p—c-cover my eyes," Roger tried to explain. He changed the subject. "W-w-what's y-your name?"

"That's a good question," Tommy said. "Why didn't I think of that?"

"Amanda," the girl said, patting purring Tigger on the head. Galen tried to play with Tigger's tail from the floor, jumping and clawing at the ripped cushion.

"Oh. W-were you w-with a g-g-girl Christine?"

"Yeah," the girl replied.

"So how come you're here?" Tommy asked.

"I don't know," said Amanda. "How do you know Christine?" She appeared to become more at ease. The cats had a calming quality when they weren't running around like maniacs.

"She's my sister," Tommy said.

Amanda instantly tensed up. Tigger lifted his head to see what was the matter. "She lives here?" Amanda asked nervously.

"Yeah," Tommy said. "Why? How come you're anxietied?"

"A-Anxious," Roger corrected.

"Anxious" Tommy repeated, rolling his eyes at Roger. "Anxieted sounds better."

"What does Anxious mean?" Amanda asked.

"I don't know," said Tommy.

"Nervous," said Roger.

"Yeah, how come you're nervous?" asked Tommy.

"Because your sister is crazy."

Roger nodded while Tommy said, "She's not crazy! She's special."

"Real special," Roger repeated, stretching the words out. Tommy punched him in the shoulder.

"She screamed the whole night for a whole week," Amanda explained. "I couldn't sleep. She's a psycho killer."

There Roger had to disagree. Christine might accidentally kill something with her breath or by leaning her big head on it, but she wasn't a psycho.

According to Amanda, Christine screamed about how she was starving, and how rats were coming to get her. Amanda tried to comfort her by saying there were no rats, but Christine insisted she heard them. Then, during mealtime, Christine ate everyone else's food while the adults weren't looking. In some cases Christine's actions were so fast that those who had their food taken didn't know quite what happened. They looked around and under the table to see where their food had gone. When Amanda was about to complain, Christine thrust a piece of bologna with fuzz stuck on it in Amanda's face. Amanda took it as a threat and remained quiet.

"N-no, sh-sh-she was t-trying to trade y-y-you," Roger explained.

Amanda made a face.

The front door banged open then, and Mario stomped into the house. He never did anything quietly. He came into the kitchen, squinting at the guest in his seat. Edith followed behind, carrying packages of food. Roger saw what looked like ten pounds of cranberries. What were they going to do with that? Before he could whisper to Tommy, he was sent to help unload the car. He was glad to be out of the kitchen. Activity always stirred the animals. Mario's excitement often led to the cats jumping and running around, knocking things over and sending tufts of their hair sailing through the air. Lucky Joy's barking started by the time Roger got to the hallway.

Edith began stacking various items on the porch. These weren't bagged. They hauled pineapples, packages of strawberries, multiple jars of nut butters, large cases of tofu, gallon jugs of oil, numerous boxes of frozen TV dinners that Christine liked to eat, and more cranberries. It seemed like Mario and Edith brought the entire market home with them.

After Roger finished bringing the porch items inside to the chaos of the kitchen, where Tommy sorted things between the ones that were going to the kitchen fridge and those that were going to the downstairs fridge, he helped Edith take things out of the trunk. Even outside Mario could be heard talking loudly and laughing. It was as if he was drunk, but as far as Roger knew Mario had alcohol but once a year, in his glass of sparkling wine on New Year's. He always gave it to Edith after one sip, Tommy had told him while Mario sprinkled the wine at them with the tips of his fingers. Roger turned to the task at hand. This newer used car seemed to have more room than the previous one. On his last trip Roger helped Edith untie and take down a large, flat rectangular box from the station wagon's roof. As they carried it into the house, wobbling from side to side, Roger read that it was a treadmill.

They put the box on its side in the hallway. Lucky Joy came up to it, did his little dance, and left his mark. In the kitchen Mario lectured their guest on the benefits of eating organic food. Tommy was still putting things away. Edith went to the basement, probably to take a nap. Did no one besides Roger think it was weird that Child Protective Services delivered a girl to their house? Apparently not.

They had just finished cooking the tofu when Christine came home. Roger heard the front door slam and Christine say, "Peek-a-boo, did you get a job yet?" The big girl came into the kitchen and grabbed Amanda's bowl from her. "What's she doing here?" Christine asked, pointing at Amanda with the bowl as a clumsily held fork stuffed food into her mouth.

"I dunno," said Tommy.

"Ch-ch-child p-protec-ct-tive s-services b-b-b-brought her I th-think," Roger said.

"Oh my God!" Christine laughed while swallowing. Some of the food went down the wrong pipe. She said between coughs, "Thank you, it was delicious. Is there more?" Her eyes teared.

"J-j-just onion in on-onion s-sauce," Roger joked.

"Oh. I'm full then," Christine said and stormed out. Roger gave Amanda a new bowl. "Wrestling!" Christine clapped on her way to the living room. "Lucky Joy you lazy bum, wrestling is on." Christine captured one of the squeaking animals. The clapping stopped and a series of kisses rang out from the living room.

Tommy and Roger continued cooking until late in the evening. Then, exhausted, they crashed in their bunks. "I'll be right back," said Tommy and fell asleep as soon as his head hit his pillow. Roger did likewise. Not even Christine's pacing back and forth in the kitchen above him prevented sleep for long. Christine had been displaced once again. Amanda had her bed for the night.

"I'm back!" Tommy announced from his bunk.

"Back from what?" Roger asked groggily.

"Sleepsies, silly." Tommy was full of energy. Roger didn't have to open his eyes to know that it was a sunny day. Tommy's tone told him everything. He was like a plant, Tommy. Give him some sunshine and some water, preferably with "bubblies" (carbon dioxide, you know), and he was ready to go. "Come on. It's time to go cook."

"Oh man." Why didn't Tommy know that the morning was the best time to sleep? It was scientifically proven. Well, no, but at some point in the future Roger would prove it. Nothing should start before noon.

The bathrooms were occupied. Of course. Roger noticed this was especially so during the holidays that called for gorging. It was as if they emptied themselves out as thoroughly as possible, to be able to fit more food later on.

Amanda watched Christine play video games in the living room. She occasionally came into the kitchen to watch Roger and Tommy toil. Tommy stood on his little stool, his apron pressing against the counter. He tried their sauces while Roger, wearing his heart shaped sunglasses, dipped tea spoons into the bubbling pots and pans. "Needs more salt," Tommy would say. Or, "needs more pepper." "A little more sugar." "That's perfect."

After two days of almost nonstop cooking they were finally done around six. Junk was cleared off the dining room table with a crash that scattered all the animals into hiding. Roger was surprised to see how nice the table looked with its rosy wood. After furtively coming out from the room's corners, the cats watched as Tommy and Roger put on a table cloth that Mario bought for the occasion. Christine was put in charge of keeping them off the table. A minute or so later Amanda was charged to supervise Christine. Then everything they made was assembled on the table.

Creamy garlic mashed potatoes. Stir fried rice. Tofu in several styles. Tempeh in several styles. Mock meat, made out of some sort of processed soy and wheat protein combination and purchased from a Buddhist shop in China Town, also in several different styles. Roasted vegetables of all sorts. Vegetable tempura. Avocado sushi rolls with a creamy wasabi sauce. Szechuan eggplant. Grilled Portobello mushroom burgers. Pakoras, samosas, paneer. Penne in marinara sauce, gnocchi, eggplant parm. Three kinds of vegetable soups. Roger's favorite was the one with ginger and lemon grass. Vegetarian Siberian dumplings with a dill sauce. Beet salad. Potato salad. Pumpkin pie. Pecan pie.

Cranberry sauce. Cranberry chutney. Cranberry-apple tart. Cranberry-peach crumble. Cranberry infused virgin Mojito. Cranberry compote. Cranberry scones. Chocolate covered cranberries. Cranberry cheesecake. Cranberry sorbet, waiting in the freezer ("See, I told you the ice cream machine would come in handy," Mario said). Cranberry lemonade. Roger never wanted to see another cranberry again.

That evening, with their bellies stretched and protruding out in front of them, Roger and Tommy found a cute little squeaker in the backyard. He was a puffy orange guy with poop on his head. They took him in and called him Hurley. Mario took to head-butting him and calling him Bernie, but the kitten was Hurley to everyone else. Lucky Joy wasn't happy. Even though she didn't know that Hurley pooped in her shoe, Christine shared his opinion. "Not another one Tommy!" Clap. Clap. Clap. But Roger and Tommy knew that it wouldn't be long before Christine was kissing the new guy and telling him to get a job. The cats either hissed or pretended the new kitten wasn't there. It was getting crowded. Christine complained about having to share a bed with Edith again. Roger wondered if that's what it was like when he moved in the prior year.

CHAPTER TWENTY ONE
Wednesday, December 11, 1991

The house felt emptier. Amanda had stayed almost two weeks before her grandmother picked her up. Roger wasn't quite sure how the woman tracked her granddaughter down. The City must have kept some sort of record. They had also received a letter regarding Christine. It said that the City was working diligently on locating her in the system and returning her as soon as possible. Until they received that letter, Roger thought that the City had mixed up Amanda with Christine. Now it appeared that the error was more complicated.

The treadmill, finally assembled, leaned by the window in the dining room in a little crook next to the living room entrance. It had been folded up almost as soon as it was assembled. As far as Roger knew, no one had used it. He had asked Tommy why his parents got one. Tommy explained that his dad wanted to jog. Roger pointed out that one could jog outside for free. Tommy countered that it was getting cold and Mario didn't like jogging in cold weather. Roger inquired whether Mario's gym membership was still active. Tommy was confident that at least two of the three gym memberships Mario had were in good standing. Roger asked why Mario couldn't use the treadmills that the gym had.

Here Tommy was stumped. The cost was $800. As they couldn't afford a lump sum payment, Roger learned, Mario took out a line of credit. He was happy that he could pay off the machine over as long a period as he liked, all at a modest interest rate of 20%. Roger sighed and shook his head, ending that conversation.

Christine was depressed. Despite complaining during most of Amanda's stay, Christine was sad to see her go. "Do you think she'll be okay?" she kept asking last night. Her appetite was unaffected, however. She said through mouthfuls, "But she'll be okay?" Clap, clap, clap. These were not the usual claps. They were sad somehow. "She'll be okay, right?" They were supposed to go to one of Christine's favorite restaurants that evening to make her feel better.

After lunch, Mr. Gorton rolled in the television and VCR. Roger hoped it wasn't another alien movie. He still had the occasional nightmare about aliens coming to get him. Christine believed that magic and wrestling were real, but not aliens. She asked once, "how come in America people are always getting abducted, but just south of the border no one gets abducted and they just see strange lights in the sky?" She implied that aliens wouldn't differentiate between borders and that the whole abduction thing was a cultural phenomenon. "Americans have a complex. They fantasize about being taken and abused," Christine explained. Roger couldn't remember which psychology book she was reading for Mario at the time. Mario's research assistant did seem to have a point, but it offered little comfort in the dark. At those terrifying moments, when every little sound accelerated his already racing heart, Roger didn't think it would so farfetched if the American government signed a treaty allowing abductions while neighboring states did not. They experimented on people and animals all the time, so why not let others do it?

As the opening sequence of *E.T.* started on the screen, a knock came from the door. Mr. Gorton stumbled in the dark, cursed under his breath after crashing into something, and then asked Clyde to open the door. A fifth grader whose name Roger didn't know came into the room. He had a note for Mr. Gorton. The teacher finally got to the door. He raised his glasses above his eyes, reading by the hallway light.

"Roger. Tommy. You are wanted in the Principal's Office. This monitor is to take you there."

Roger gulped. He felt flushed, following Tommy out into the hall. Then they walked slowly with the fifth grader. Tommy looked a bit pale. The butterflies started their party in Roger's stomach. Maybe it was discovered that they lived at the same address. Christine's description of the Child Protective Services purgatory didn't sound like a place where he wanted to stay.

"Ah boys," Mr. Leslie said after the monitor led them to his desk. He seemed in a good mood for once, folding what looked like the sports page of a newspaper. "Sit down, sit down," the Assistant Principal gestured. Roger was still nervous, but less so. Perhaps his butt wouldn't leave a sweat line in the chair when he got up. "You boys did very well," he said. "Candice," he turned to the nearby typist, "can you get me a coffee?" The lady gave him the same look as when Roger sat there with Edith. He wondered if Mr. Leslie tried to do that often. "I'll be right back," he trotted off.

As soon as the Assistant Principal left, Tommy began shuffling through the papers on the desk. He was curious about the weirdest things. Roger shook his head. Candice sighed. "Useless," Roger thought he heard her say. She and Tommy both straightened up when the Assistant Principal returned. They sat too straight, Roger thought—a dead giveaway of wrongdoing. Tommy's cheeks were up and his eyes were naughty as he tried to act nonchalant.

Mr. Leslie sat down in his chair and looked for a spot to put his mug. His once neat stacks now formed a layer of paper, covering the entire desk. "So boys," he said, putting the papers in order. "You've done a remarkable job. Not as good as

Robert, but still deserving of some praise." He clapped. Some of the secretaries looked at him like he was an idiot. "Candice, you want to applaud these boys for a job well done?" The secretary responded with an annoyed sigh and looked back down at her work.

Tommy seemed happy, but Roger didn't know what was going on. "You boys are tied for second place," Mr. Leslie explained.

"Yay!" Tommy clasped his hands.

Second place for what?

The Assistant Principal studied Roger's confused face. "You've both sold the same amount of candy. I don't know how that happened, that the numbers are exactly the same, but I'm very proud of you boys. You did the school some good. With all the funds raised for the school, after administrative costs, we can now replace a few pens and pencils. Very proud, boys. Very proud." Mr. Leslie smiled at them. His yellow teeth glinted in the florescent light reflecting from his coffee mug. He gave first Tommy and then Roger a piece of paper. Typewritten in Old English font on both of them was "Certificate of Achievement." "Now off you go," he shooed them away. "Go learn. Very proud boys. Very proud."

The door closed softly behind them. "Why did I get this?" Roger asked Tommy. "I never sold any candy. And I didn't submit a form."

"Yuppers," Tommy replied happily. "My parents wanted you to have a bike too, so I filled it out for you."

"You spent an extra $800 so I could get a crappy bike?"

"Yeah. What's wrong? Why are you yelling?" Tommy looked worried.

"Because I was specifically against it when you mentioned it! A bike costs one eighth that in the store! At most! Your family can't pay its bills and they spent $1600?"

"No, it was more than that," Tommy muttered, looking down.

"More? How much more?"

"A little bit. I wanted those headphones and radio also."

"$1,700?"

"Noppers. It was a little more."

"$1,800?"

Tommy shook his head.

"How much was it then?"

"Three thousand something."

Roger was speechless.

"Don't be mad. We wanted to make you happy."

* * *

Edith and Mario met them after school. After picking up Christine, they went to Manhattan. Christine was excited. They were going to an all

329

you could eat Indian restaurant. Roger was excited too. He had never been to an all you could eat restaurant with Christine before. How much would she eat? Would they be asked to leave? Roger asked Christine these questions. She just laughed and rubbed her face. All she said was, "She'll be alright, right?"

"Yes, Christine," Tommy groaned. Other people's anxiety gave him stomach aches.

The restaurant's interior looked like a town square in India. Trees planted into ornately patterned gravel cast shadows onto the booths, which hovered along the sides like patios. Roger thought the trees were real. The air seemed fresher inside the restaurant than outside. The walls were painted with blue and white clouds, and sculptures of Indian gods and goddesses similar to the ones Mario had placed all over the house stood next to the exits.

A portly woman wearing an orange sari led them to a booth. Her hair was tied in a bun and she had stringy, dangling gold earrings. The five of them walked on a cobble stone path between various flowers, fountains, and trees. Quiet sitar music swirled all around them from hidden speakers. At the entrance to their booth, they were instructed to take off their shoes. Roger quickly slid out of his sneakers and jumped in. He didn't want Christine to see the holes in his socks. She usually made fun of him for such things.

Tommy sat next to Roger, at his right. Christine, the last to get into the booth sat perpendicular to them. Mario and Edith sat across. Edith, on Mario's left, had some trouble squeezing in, and sat in a sort of slant. It reminded Roger of how the ancients ate, on their sides. The tree next to him was real. Looking up, he spotted a speaker. The ceiling had a sky painted on it. The space appeared much like the outdoors, like some quiet cul de sac on an evening in India.

The portly woman returned with stainless steel cups and a pitcher of water. From a pocket in the wall next to Christine, she retrieved their menus, and passed them around. They had a single laminated page. The menu choices were mild, medium, and hot. Everyone but Christine chose mild. Christine chose hot, and iced tea. Edith had an Indian beer, and Tommy ordered a mango lassi, smacking his lips. Mario and Roger chose to stick with their water in steel cups. The waitress took their menus, set up a foldout table, and disappeared into the town square.

She came back a couple of minutes later with their drinks. Christine downed hers before Tommy was even passed his mango lassi. She immediately asked for a refill. She was off to a good start, Roger thought. He imagined the waitress running back and forth with more food for Christine. Maybe she would shout in the kitchen, "there is a monster out there that won't stop eating!" Roger chuckled to himself. He eyed Tommy's drink curiously. He figured that the boy's "Tommy" would hurt soon.

The waitress came back with a large tray holding their meals. She placed it on the foldout table. She set a bowl of rice in the middle of the table. Then she passed around trays that reminded Roger of the ones they had in school. But these were stainless steel instead of Styrofoam. Christine got her tray last. The waitress pointed at the various things in it, explaining what they were. Her explanation was so quick that Roger didn't understand a single thing.

"What's this?" he asked Tommy, pointing.

"Potatoes," Tommy said. "Cauliflower." "I'm not sure." "I don't know." "Fennel seeds." "Naan bread."

Roger tried a bit of everything, carefully. They had eaten at an Indian takeout before, and he had stomach problems for two weeks. Everything burned his tongue. He chose to stick with the rice, potatoes, and bread. Only the bread wasn't super spicy. Roger tried to get rice, but Mario beat him to it, dumping the entire bowl into his plate. Roger picked at his potatoes. He looked over at Christine, who sweated even more than him. "Too spicy for you?" he teased.

"No," Christine replied.

"Mines is super spicy," said Tommy, sipping his drink. "Yours must be..."

"Hotter than the merchandise in China Town," Christine finished for him.

The waitress came back with more rice, but Mario once again appropriated it for himself. A few minutes later Roger's stomach was on fire. He decided not to eat anymore. He just sipped his water. Christine had finished her portion and leaned back against the wall, rubbing her face.

"Aren't you going to have more?" Roger asked.

"No. I'm full." Christine said.

Roger was confused. The portions weren't large, even by his standards. For Christine, who always complained about small portions even when they were gigantic, not to want more food was exceedingly strange. "But it's all you could eat!"

"I know. I know. I'm a bit full."

What a disappointment. "Oh come on. You eat more than that in your sleep."

"Yeah," Tommy said. "What the hell, sis? It's all you could eat." Tommy had been excited by the prospect too.

"I'm a bit full right now," Christine replied, continuing to rub her head.

"Wuss!" Roger said.

"I'm a bit full right now."

"Did you not like the food or something?"

"No. It was delicious."

"Was it too spicy for you?"

"No." That was true. Roger remembered how he and Tommy once conducted an experiment. Well, how he conducted an experiment. Tommy participated, but he didn't know Christine's tolerance to spices was being tested. Roger neglected to tell him because he would probably object to it. Anyway, one day Roger fed Christine a sandwich filled with habanero peppers and their seeds along with wasabi and Chinese mustard, and lots of black and red ground pepper. Christine sweated profusely, said it was delicious, and asked for more.

"So what's the deal then?"

"I'm just a bit full right now."

After they left the restaurant and packed into the station wagon, Christine asked if they could stop by Curry in a Hurry so she could get something to eat. She was starving now.

"But we were just inside an all you could eat restaurant!" Roger exclaimed.

"Yeah. But I was a bit full. Now I'm hungry."

"But that was a minute ago!"

"So?"

Tommy was strangely quiet as they waited for Christine outside the Indian takeout. After Christine got back in the car, Tommy said, "Can we please go home now? I really have to go!"

Edith started driving.

Tommy repeated, "I have to go have to go have to go," over and over, between trying to calm himself with deep breaths. To Roger it looked like Tommy was turning blue.

Christine laughed and ate her Indian food.

Roger asked, "So how is what you're eating different than what we had at the restaurant just now?"

Christine stopped shoveling for a moment to say, "This isn't as good."

"Then why—" Roger stopped himself, exasperated.

Tommy continued under his breath, "have to go have to go have to go."

Edith tried to drive faster, honking and swerving around slow vehicles.

"You're turning blue!" Christine laughed, shoveling the last of her food into her maw.

"I don't feel so good," said Tommy. Roger was glad he declined to try Tommy's drink at the restaurant. Christine seemed to be getting a kick out of it.

* * *

When they got home, a pale Tommy raced up the stairs. "Have to go, have to go, have to go" trailed behind him. Roger heard Lucian's door open and a pair of footsteps quickly thump in the direction of the bathroom. A door slammed and a lock snapped into place. A few seconds later Tommy

335

appeared on the landing. He whizzed down the stairs. "Have to go have to go have to go," Tommy raced past Roger. He was down the basement stairs before a surprised Lucky Joy could bark at him.

A few seconds later Tommy ran past him in the opposite direction, "stupid Christine...have to go have to go have to go." Tommy bounded up the stairs two at a time. He turned at the landing and disappeared. Roger heard him knock on the bathroom door.

"Lucian! I have to go!" More knocking. "I have to go!"

Tommy shot past Roger again, almost bumping into Christine who had just emerged from the basement. As Tommy ran down the stairs, Christine picked up Shadow and started kissing him. "It's Shadow, the black guy!" Kiss, kiss, kiss. "Did you get a job yet, Shadow?" Kiss, kiss, kiss. "It's tough being a black guy, but keep trying." She kissed the cat some more. It purred.

Tommy was back up the stairs. "Now my dad's in there!" he stomped his feet in frustration. Lucky Joy started barking. Tommy turned bluer. He climbed the stairs slowly this time, clutching his belly.

Roger went to the basement, remembering that it was time to feed the newest member of the household. He found the powdered kitten formula in their room. After putting some in a tiny bottle, he waited for Lucian to finish using the sink in the kitchen. At least that meant that Tommy got access to the bathroom. Lucian seemed to have a talent for getting in everyone's way. Mario was giving him the silent treatment for something relating to that. Tommy had been unclear about whether it had to do with the bathroom, the kitchen, or asking Edith to drive him somewhere when Mario needed a driver.

With a bottle of lukewarm milk in hand, Roger returned to their room. He found the kitten in its shoe box, snuggled between two socks, which contained bottles of warm water. These were Tommy's version of a portable radiator.

The kitten looked up at him and started crying. It tried to get out of the box. Roger thrust the nipple into the kitten's mouth. It drank quickly, its ears pulled back and its eyes squinted. It was still crying somehow. Orange paws scratched at Roger's fingers. He had to readjust several times as the kitten complained. Roger wondered why all the kittens that he'd known so far did that. Was that why they were rejected? Or did all kittens scratch while feeding?

Soon little Hurley would be climbing out of his box. They would introduce him to wet food. As soon as he started walking around on his own they would place him in the litter box when he started squatting. Then he'd run around with his butt awkwardly in the air, as if he were wearing diapers. From that point on, he'd cause trouble like all the other cats. Roger petted Hurley's head as the kitten suckled and scratched. If Tommy were here now he'd probably talk or sing to it. He was especially fond of a Mercedes Sosa song, "Duerme Negrito." Roger never understood the need to talk to animals. He'd never said a word to Lucky Joy and the dog liked him just fine.

Tommy came into the room then. "Oh good. I was worried about him," Tommy said. He stepped around Roger on the carpet and started looking through the garbage bag that contained his clean clothes.

"What are you doing?" Roger asked.

"I'm looking for my underwear."

"How come?"

"I didn't make it."

CHAPTER TWENTY TWO
Friday, March 6, 1992

Roger walked slowly behind Tommy, lugging a gigantic rolled up poster. He hated the science fair. Every year they had to do a project and put it on display in the auditorium. What was the point? Robert always won with his miniature volcano. Roger didn't understand how that was supposed to show anything, either as an outcome of an experiment or to demonstrate some property of volcanoes. What did the reaction caused by baking soda and vinegar have anything to do with lava? He didn't even think Robert built it. The model looked like it was bought in a store.

So, every year Roger brought in the same poster. It had been based on an experiment he did in kindergarten. He had a bunch of plants in the basement. Some he watered with regular tap water. Some he watered with cola. All of the cola fed plants died, as he hypothesized. He concluded that that type of plant grew better with regular water than with that particular brand of cola. On his poster he drew a picture of a couple of dead plants, and a couple of living ones. He attached a sheet of loose leaf paper, where his results were scrawled. All the teachers that looked at the poster commented that they thought the plant watered with cola would do better. Obviously something was wrong with the experiment. Then they moved on to ooh and ahh at Robert's volcano. Roger had been impressed with Clyde's robot, but no one else seemed to be interested in it. Realizing that it was pointless to do any real kind of science, Roger brought the same poster to the science fair in the first and second grades.

He had hastily constructed a replica in the third grade because the original had been left in his house. Something happened to the replica. Lucian probably threw it out, or it was in storage. Roger began to make another copy in February, but Tommy said that was cheating.

"What are you, my conscience?"

"Noppers! I'm not your conscious!"

When Roger said he'd have to go find or buy some plants, Tommy was upset. It was mean to experiment on plants in such a way. Why was everything always mean to Tommy?

"Guess what Sunday is?" Tommy's excited voice interrupted Roger's thoughts.

"I have no idea," he said. Of course he knew. How could he not? Tommy had only been going on about it since the year began.

"It's going to be my birthday! Birthday birthday birthday!" Tommy sang. He carried his own poster. Edith was supposed to help them deliver their science projects, but her trip with Mario to a Yoga retreat in Massachusetts took priority.

Tommy's experiment had to do with the kittens, of course. He sought to answer the question, "are cats happier when you sing to them while petting them or when you don't sing to them while petting them?" Roger had a problem with Tommy's quantification of happiness, but he thought the experiment potentially had important theoretical and practical implications.

For his own experiment, Roger chose to study Christine. In particular, after being admonished by Tommy for designing a B.F. Skinner type experiment, he was interested in the effect of beliefs on her eating behavior. He had been quite puzzled about why Christine ate so little, compared with her usual intake per meal, when they went to the all you could eat restaurant. He hypothesized that Christine wouldn't gorge herself if she thought that food was plentiful. If, on the other hand, she thought only a small amount was available, a finite quantity, she would eat as much as possible, even stealing from the plates of others.

For a month Roger mentioned to Tommy in Christine's presence, or to Christine, something that would make her think that there was plenty of food. He already knew how much she ate normally, when she wasn't in an all you can eat situation. Roger thought it was a good project for a fourth grader. He didn't have to do any extra work, really, except for writing down how much the girl ate.

It turned out he was right, and he made Christine lose almost 10 pounds. His poster bore the results. Roger speculated in his conclusion that the reason for Christine's behavior had to do either with primitive instincts for self preservation: gorge when there is food because the next meal may be a long time in coming, or some sort of behavioral adaptation that Christine had evolved because of her environment. Mario often declared fasts. Sometimes the fridge was as empty as their bellies. So when food was available, Christine had as much as she could. If this were true, Roger speculated, the same principle was involved in Tommy's eating. He, of course, ate as fast as he could to avoid Christine's thievery.

* * *

The class lined up in the gym. It was noisier than usual as many kids shuffled about with their parents, who helped them with their science projects. Tommy gave out invitations to his party. They were handmade. He spent the last two days making them.

"Why are you giving me one?" Roger asked. "You know I'll be there. I only heard that it's going to be your birthday for the past two months. And I kind of live with you."

"I wanted to make sure you'd come," Tommy paused to give Clyde his invitation. Not only were they handmade, Roger observed as he opened his, they were also individualized.

Roger looked around at all the parents, comparing them to their miniatures. Michael's mom looked just like her son, and tapped on people's shoulders while pretending she did nothing. Most of the parents, it sounded like, knew even less of the pledge of allegiance than their children.

After they got upstairs and the parents left, Mr. Gorton led the class down to the auditorium so they could set up their projects. Normally Roger would grumble about such inefficiency, as he did with Mario's incessant back and forth travel between the boroughs, but he was for almost anything that wasted time in the school day.

He and Tommy set up their projects quickly, having only to unroll their posters and tape them to the wall. They were free to wander among the tables, looking at the other projects. The projects would be here a few days, making the kindergarteners, first and second graders eat lunch in their classrooms.

Already a crowd of kids gathered around Robert as he set up his volcano. Roger couldn't understand what the big deal was, but Tommy insisted that they have a look too. It was definitely made out of plastic, and painted brown. Miniature roadways, along with tiny cars, houses, and people encircled the volcano. There were little drainage ditches where Roger imagined the "lava" was to flow. Again he wondered what the model was supposed to show. Nothing would be destroyed. Nothing would be burnt up. The lava would not harden into rock as it cooled. It wasn't even hot!

Roger and Tommy left the gawking crowd behind, surveying the other projects on display. Robert's project was definitely bought. George Cinoptikus, of the other fourth grade class, had the exact same thing. Maybe they would finally see, the judges, that the volcano was nothing special. George's project had no fans, however. Maybe because he wasn't popular, or because his mother wasn't the head of the PTA. Roger wanted to ask Tommy, but the boy had gone ahead of him.

Roger left Tommy at a cage with a hamster in it. Once the boy found an animal, he wasn't interested in anything else. Roger was glad that Tommy didn't read what the project was about, and how it started with seven rodents. Otherwise there might be an uproar, and, at the very least, some crying. Why were kids so cruel? Roger mused. No. Why were people so cruel? This remaining hamster didn't even have food or water. How was it supposed to survive for the next few days? And it didn't have hay or anything. It just stood there shivering on the metal grating. Then he shook his head, as if out of a daze, like a wet dog. Tommy was rubbing off on him.

Clyde was still setting up his project. It was a robot, again. It looked different from last year.

"Is that another robot?"

"Yeah," Clyde replied, adjusting his glasses. His chapped lips flaked onto the display.

"Does it still roll back and forth?" Roger asked.

"Yeah. And I made improvements."

"Oh yeah?" Roger knelt down to study the little metal arm attached to a wheel, probably from a radio controlled car. The box on which the metal wheel sat was attached to a bigger box by a series of wires. "Is that the battery?"

"No. That's over here," Clyde tapped on the robot. "It runs on rechargeable batteries. I'm recharging the batteries over here with the potatoes." Roger nodded. He wondered what the potatoes were for. "This," Clyde pointed to what Roger initially thought was a battery, "is the programming."

"Programming?"

"Yeah. The robot is going to build a wall made out of Legos."

"Oh wow. Hey Tommy! Check this out! Tommy!"

The little boy strolled over. His face was flushed. His puffed cheeks were wet with tears. "Why are people so mean?" he asked.

"I don't know," Roger said. "The other hamsters died of old age," he tried to comfort the boy.

"Really?" Tommy sniffled. "But the thingy said —"

"They were old," Roger said. "They were old. They lived a full and happy life. They died of old age. Natural causes that couldn't be helped."

"But the—"

"They were old. Do you really think a kid's parents would let him feed his hamsters poison to see how long it would take for them to die?" Well, yes. Scientists did that in labs all the time. They did it to animals and people. "The kid just made it up. People are lazy." Well that last part was true. But they were mysteriously efficient and disciplined when it came to cruelty. "It's like when I just made up the plant results. She just made it up."

"Okay." Tommy seemed to feel better. Roger could tell that Tommy thought what he said was a load of crap. The little boy probably thought that Roger would be upset if he knew the truth, so he played along. Roger began thinking about the levels of lying involved here when Tommy interrupted by asking Clyde, "hey, is that a zinc electrode?"

"Yeah," said Clyde.

"That one's copper?"

"Yeah."

"Coolness!" Tommy seemed happy again. "You're coming to my birthday, right?"

"If my parents let me," Clyde clicked something into place.

"You don't have to give me a gift or anything. Just come over. We'll have delicious food and video games!"

Roger continued to stroll around the room. It was getting crowded. The first and second graders came down and began setting up their displays. Soon Mr. Gorton would take them upstairs. At the moment he was chatting with Mr. Bayer, one of the fifth grade teachers, whose class had also come down to set up their projects.

Roger started back toward his class's side of the room. They began to assemble in a line along their projects, although a large portion of them still fawned over the volcano. Roger bumped into Joanna, the fifth grader who did the hamster project. "H-hi." Roger said. The girl ignored him. "Y-you mm-m-ade the h-hamster p-p-pro-thing over th-there?" he pointed.

"Yeah," the girl brightened. "My dad works at a lab where they test things. He got me the poison and the hamsters. I hope I win. I want to be a re-search scientist like my dad."

Roger nodded. "W-what a-are y-you gonna d-do w-with the h-h-ha—"

"Burn it. Dad can't take it back to the lab anymore because it's contaminated."

"C-c-can I h-have it then?"

347

"No."

"W-w-why not?"

"I have to go now," said the girl.

Roger was left standing by himself. A whistle blew and Mr. Gorton called for his class to assemble. Roger thought for a moment. Then he rushed to the hamster cage. He stopped in front of it. "Roger!" Mr. Gorton called. "We're waiting on you."

He had to be quick about it. He knelt down next to the cage. Roger reached to open it. He was so focused on finding the latch, he didn't realize that the hamster wasn't in the cage. Now he discovered that the cage was empty.

"Roger!" Mr. Gorton called again.

Confused, Roger joined the line and followed them out of the auditorium and up the stairs to their classroom.

* * *

After lunch, Mr. Leslie entered their classroom with Joanna in tow. "There he is," she pointed at Roger. "That's him. He did it. I saw him!"

Roger felt the blood drain out of him.

"He asked if he could have the subject. And then it was gone. So he took it."

"N-no," Roger stammered in his defense.

"Oooo! Roger's in trouble!" Michael teased. "Roger the hamster thief!"

"Be quiet, Michael," Mr. Gorton scolded. "What's this all about?" he asked Mr. Leslie.

"We have probable cause to assume Roger here stole a part of Miss Huntington's experiment," the Assistant Principal replied.

"No I d-d-didn't!" Roger felt guilty. He was going to steal the hamster, after all. But he was innocent of the crime charged.

The Assistant Principal checked in Roger's desk. He also sifted through the boy's school bag and jacket. Nothing was found. Flustered, Mr. Leslie said, "Get those books covered," before he left the room with Joanna at his heels. She gave him a nasty look before slamming the door.

* * *

Michael grabbed Roger's schoolbag on the second floor landing, making him stop. "Come on," Theodore said behind them. "I want to go home." It was already past three. They had been watching *Starman*, and it ended at 3:05. Mr. Gorton's schedule had been messed up by Mr. Leslie's inspection.

"Why do you always do this?" Roger asked Michael. "What's wrong with you?" He prepared to defend against Michael's jabs.

"You don't want this then?" Michael, with uncharacteristic gentleness, put a brown paper bag in Roger's hands.

"Come on! Go already!" Theodore sounded like he had an extremely important appointment.

Michael raced down the stairs to catch up with the class. Roger followed. "Finally!" Theodore said behind him.

As Roger exited the building, Mr. Gorton looked at the bag in his hand. "I see Michael gave it to you. Be careful with it. Have a nice weekend, Roger."

"Y-you t-too," Roger managed as the teacher closed the door behind him. Roger looked inside the bag. The hamster sat in the shadows, its eyes glinting up at him. Roger knew what he was giving Tommy for his birthday.

"What's in the bag?" Tommy asked after they crossed Juniper Blvd South.

"Nothing," Roger replied.

"What do you think happened to that cute hamster?"

"I don't know. I think he escaped."

"That would be so awesome."

"Yeah," Roger said.

"Do you think he'll be okay?"

"Yeah. I think he'll find a really good home."

"I hope so toopers." They walked for a couple of minutes in silence. Roger enjoyed the sunshine on his face. Leaves were starting to sprout on some of the trees across the street.

Tommy said then, "Hey, guess what Sunday is?"

"Um, I don't quite remember. I know there was supposed to be something. Is there a basketball game?"

"Noppers."

"Is it that wrestling thing Christine mentioned yesterday?"

"Noppers."

"I give up. What is it?"

"It's my birthday! Birthday birthday birthday. The day I was born because it's my birthday! Birthday birthday birthday!"

CHAPTER TWENTY THREE
Sunday, March 8, 1992

Tommy heard the rustling from the shoe box that sat next to the wall near Roger's pillow. "Who's in there?" he asked.

"What?" Roger opened his eyes to see the top of Tommy's head. The boy jumped up and Roger briefly saw his excited eyes.

"There's noises from the box!" Tommy said. "Is it for me? Is it my present?"

"Present? What present?" Roger feigned ignorance. "Must be my stomach rumbling."

"Oh, okay." Tommy was disappointed.

It was hard to keep the hamster secret from Tommy. The boy was drawn to animals. At one point on Saturday Roger let the hamster walk around to get some fresh air. Tommy came in the room and Roger quickly stuffed the light brown rodent into his pocket. Had he not been wearing sweat pants, he didn't know what he'd do. Roger then had to pretend that nothing was scratching at him as Tommy made him guess what Sunday was.

Roger was also almost caught stealing some of Friedrich Nietzsche's food and hay. "What are you doing with those?" Tommy had asked.

"Nothing," Roger replied, putting the shoe box behind his back and whistling awkwardly while pretending to be interested in something across the room.

Roger had asked Christine to ask Edith to buy a hamster habitat for Tommy's birthday. He had the money all saved up, but was hoping that Edith would pick it up for him, or at least give him a ride. This was on Friday. He found out last night that Christine hadn't done it. "I'll do it soon," she said. "I'll do it soon." Clap, clap, clap.

Tommy looked a bit glum as they drank their breakfast smoothie. His parents left to go to the yoga retreat again. "That sucks," Roger said. "When are they coming back?"

"Tomorrow morning I think," Tommy pouted.

As Roger finished his drink, Christine waltzed into the kitchen. "Happy birthday bro!" she told Tommy, handing him a badly wrapped plastic package. Its edges stuck out.

"For me?" Tommy's face lit up.

"Ahuh. Open it."

"Thanks!" Tommy said.

"Nice wrapping paper choice," Roger said.

"Thanks," Christine was oblivious to his sarcasm.

Tommy took the toilet paper off, revealing a plastic box with a Hulk Hogan action figure inside. "Thanks, sis. Best present ever," Tommy said. His tone had fake excitement in it.

"Sure sure. Enjoy. If you don't like it, you can always give it to me." Christine always gave people presents she intended for herself.

Tommy turned to Roger. "Will you help me cook for the party?"

"Uh, yeah...I'll try. I have to go somewhere, but I'll definitely help when I come back."

"Oh, okay."

"I'll be back in about an hour," Roger said going downstairs to change. It took about 20 minutes to walk to the CheapPets on Grand Avenue, and another 20 back. Another 20 minutes to choose a home for the hamster should be plenty of time.

* * *

A bell rang when he entered the pet store. Glancing at his watch, Roger noted to himself that the journey took five minutes less than anticipated. So far so good. He looked down the aisles, four or five in total, trying to determine which one had the habitat. Fish tanks, mostly containing tropical fish, percolated in the back of the store. Hamsters, gerbils, mice, rats, guinea pigs, snakes, and various lizards also resided there, waiting for a permanent home. Birds squawked from that direction, but were out of sight.

Roger went up and down all the aisles twice, carefully looking at everything on the shelves. He couldn't find anything for a hamster. Normally a sales person pestered him as soon as he ventured into a store. Now that he needed someone, no one was in sight. Roger walked around some more, examining the shelves. His watch told him he was already in the store for 20 minutes. After another ten, Roger's objective changed from finding the hamster house to finding someone that worked there.

He couldn't find anyone but the lady at the cash register. Her name tag said Gina. She had permed reddish-blond hair that to Roger looked dyed. Gina read a magazine with pictures of celebrities on the glossy cover. At least that's who Roger thought the people were, though he never saw them before. All those pictures always looked the same. The fake smiles, full of artificially white teeth. The airbrushed faces, with their tons of makeup, though not as apparent as Gina's. The awkward and surely uncomfortable poses that usually showed some cleavage. Did those breasts have makeup on them too?

"H-hi." Roger began, looking up from the magazine to Gina's face. She didn't seem to hear him. What could possibly be so interesting in that magazine of hers? "Eh-eh-excuse m-me."

The woman looked around her magazine.

"H-hi. I'm l-looking for a h-h-h—. Hamster —"

"In the back on the left," Gina went back to her magazine.

Roger was about to walk away. No, God damn it. He was a customer. He took a deep breath. "Eh-excuse me."

"In the back on the left," the lady repeated in a slightly annoyed tone.

"H-h-hamster h-h-h-house," Roger finally managed as the lady read her magazine. She had long red nails. Roger thought if he had nails that long he'd poke himself in the eye.

"Aisle three," the woman said surlily.

"I-it's not there."

"Fa," the woman let out an exasperated sigh. She put her magazine down, and, acting like she did him the biggest favor in the world, descended from her stool and strolled to aisle three. Roger always wondered about the pace at which store employees walked. He didn't think he could walk that slow if he tried. Gina was oddly shaped. All her fat collected in her backside. It looked like a lifebuoy got stuck in her tan pants. Roger was unsure whether to follow her. What was the protocol for such situations? Wait for the help to retrieve the item for you at their station, or follow them to where they thought the requested item was? Making them carry the thing to you seemed a bit rude. But so did standing next to them while they searched. Roger hated it when a teacher stood behind him as he did school work. Maybe store workers felt the same way?

He decided to wait at the head of the aisle. Roger walked as slowly as he could behind the lady, but he still caught up to her. She scanned the shelves as he had done, a dozen times by now, but much slower. After a few minutes she said she'd go check in the back. It took her forever to reach the doors on the side that said "Employees Only."

After a dozen or so minutes Roger began to wonder if maybe the lady forgot all about him and went on her lunch break or something. He hoped Tommy wasn't too upset. He wanted to help him cook. It was his birthday, after all, but he also wanted to give him a present. It sucked that the hamster couldn't go in the same abode as the gerbil. He had heard from numerous sources that the two species just didn't get along. Hamsters, apparently, were known to eat gerbils. And gerbils were known to attack hamsters. Maybe Tommy would know the nature of their dispute.

Another ten minutes passed. Gina finally emerged, the double doors swinging with her entrance. "We're out of stock," she said.

Oh well. "Th-thanks anyway," Roger said.

He must have sounded upset because just as he was about to exit the store the lady said, "Hold on a sec. Lemme call an see who has it."

"Okay," Roger returned to the register. He marveled at how the lady's nails didn't stab the phone as she dialed.

She popped her gum inside her mouth. "Hey, this is Gina from 113." Roger furrowed his brow slightly. He had thought her name was Geena, but apparently it was G-i-na, like the i sound in China. "Oh hey Billy. How are ya? Oh yeah. Oh well. You know how it goes. Yeah. Yeah. Listen, I got a guy here who needs a hamster house. You got those where you're at?"

Gina twirled the phone cord and popped her gum. Roger imagined a guy at another CheapPets walking slowly toward some shelves to examine their contents. Roger looked at his watch. He'd been there far longer than planned.

"Yeah. Okay. Thanks. Bye. You too. Bye." Gina hung up. "They got one of those hamster houses at the CheapPets on 63rd Drive and Queens Boulevard. You know where that is?"

"Yeah," Roger started to leave, but Gina told him to wait as she wrote down the address. "Thanks," Roger said. He left the store about an hour after he entered, and he had nothing to show for it. He thought about how to get to that other store quickly. Go back to 80th, walk to the park, cut across the small park, walk on Penelope, cross Woodhaven...another place where a street inexplicably changed names. Penelope Avenue became 63rd Drive when it intersected Woodhaven Boulevard. What was the point of that? Anyway, then he had to walk on 63rd Drive until he got to Queens Boulevard.

It was going to take a while. Roger debated whether he should go at all. Tommy would be happy with the hamster by itself. He knew that. But they'd have to go get a house for it anyway, and Roger wanted to surprise him. Tommy loved surprises. So much so that sometimes he tried to surprise himself. When he got to Caldwell Avenue and 80th Street Roger decided to keep going.

It took about 40 minutes to get to the other CheapPets. With his jacket open and droplets of sweat on his brow, Roger entered the pet store. He went straight to the cashier. "H-hamster h-house," he said, slightly out of breath.

"Billy," said the lady at the register, "this boy needs help."

"Hamster h-h-how-house," Roger told Billy. He was in no mood for dillydallying.

"People been askin' about that today," Billy said in front of him, doing the special slow walk. "Lemme see if I can find it."

Roger waited, impatiently rubbing his hands together. It reminded him of Christine and he forced himself to stop. He looked down at Billy's bald head and ponytail and inadvertently caught sight of the upper portion of the man's butt crack. Roger hastily turned away. "I'm gonna check in the back," Billy got up. Roger waited among the hamster wheels.

The husky man came back several minutes later. "We're out of stock," he said, scratching his beard. "I'll tell you what you could do though," scratch, scratch, scratch. "You could go down to the CheapPets they have on Grand Avenue. They should have what you're looking for. I just talked to someone from there maybe an hour ago." Scratch, "can I help you with anything else?" scratch, scratch.

"N-no. Th-thanks anyway," Roger said. Billy walked away. Roger walked down the aisle looking for a substitute. He didn't come all this way to leave empty handed. So he wouldn't get the cool, multi-level hamster house he imagined with its many tunnels and hatches, but maybe something else would do. He spotted a few cages, but they reminded him of Joanna's cage. In the end he settled for a 10 gallon fish tank. Tommy's gerbil seemed happy with his, so maybe it wouldn't be so bad.

All the boxes looked like they had already been opened. Roger tried to pick the least dilapidated one. He brought it to the cashier without difficulty, despite its size. He paid the $10, and, without waiting for his receipt, was almost out the door.

"Hey," said the cashier. "You forgot your tank."

Blushing, Roger retrieved the tank and left the store. Halfway up the block he realized just how heavy it was. His biceps began to burn. Two blocks later Roger tried to carry the tank as he would a regular grocery bag. The thin yellow CheapPets bag the cashier put the tank in ripped almost immediately. Roger prevented the tank from falling by catching it with his foot. Now limping, he tried to carry it first on one shoulder, then on the other. He was glad it wasn't filled with water.

Roger reached the house exhausted and cranky. He was wet with sweat and rain. His foot hurt and his arms throbbed. Roger walked past the cats and a barking Lucky Joy. "Look at Wharton with a big box," Christine clapped.

"Out of my way," Roger snapped.

Tommy had *Nevermind* blaring out of Mario's CD player. He stood on his stool over some pots, and didn't seem to notice as Roger thudded his way down to the basement.

He put the tank down in the middle of the room and began peeling the tape that kept the box closed. Roger cursed as he cut himself on the cardboard. It was turning out to be a crappy day for him. He finally got it open, but encountered more trouble getting it out of the box. In the end, he decided to leave it in the box for the time being.

Roger took some hay out of the gerbil's tank and put it in the new tank, spreading it around.

After he put some food and a water bowl in the tank's corner, he climbed up the ladder to his bunk. He took the shoe box down, placed it on the floor next to the tank, and removed the cover. The hamster wasn't there. A chewed through hole gave him a view of the carpet below. Dumping the shoebox's remaining hay into the tank, Roger became worried.

If the hamster got out, the cats might have eaten it. They were a bit slow, and wouldn't survive on their own outside, but they were capable of catching mice. Tommy had saved two so far from the grip of Shadow's mouth.

He frantically looked around the floor and under Tommy's bed. He saw no sign of it. Roger looked behind the bookcases, but found nothing. It was gone.

The door slid open then and Tommy came in. "Oooo, is that for me?" he said with wide eyes.

"No!" Roger snapped. "Get out of here!"

The wide eyes remained, but the bottom half of Tommy's face changed from an expectant smile to a quivering pout. The boy left his room with a quiet "okay." It seemed like he was holding back tears. Roger breathed out and shook his head. That was Tommy's problem. He was always such a wuss. Always with the this or that is mean, and the feeling bad for and about things.

Roger got his jacket sleeve caught on something. He yanked it angrily, dragging several books to the floor. He picked them up and threw them against the wall. Roger tried to calm down. He felt all wet and sticky. Nothing was going right. His thumb hurt, and now his shoulder throbbed from his awkward throw. And that stupid hamster escaped. If the cats ate him, that served him right.

Roger stripped down to his boxer shorts, threw his clothing to the foot of the bed, and climbed into his bunk. Fuck it. He'd spend the day in bed. Never mind the delicious smells coming from above. He drew the covers over his head. Roger tried not to think about his parents. He started to cry.

* * *

Roger awoke to something furry nestling against his neck. He jumped up in fright, hitting his head on the ceiling. Rubbing it, he looked down at his pillow. In the shadows was the hamster, its cheeks puffy, standing on its hind legs, sniffing up at him. It took Roger a few seconds to realize what he saw.

Roger grabbed the hamster, jumped down to the floor, and put it in the tank. He fumbled with his slippers and bounded up the stairs, two at a time. "Tommy!" he called. "Come downstairs! Sorry I was mean earlier."

The kitchen was dark. Roger turned the corner into the dining room. Tommy and a few of their classmates were playing a board game of some sort. It wasn't until Michael pointed at him and laughed that Roger realized all he had on were his boxers.

* * *

"Sorry I was cranky before," Roger said later that evening after Tommy's guests left.

"It's okay," Tommy replied. "You've had a tough day."

Christine's footsteps sounded above them. She was probably searching for leftovers. Tommy had decided to make Mexican food. Roger thought the enchiladas were the best things he ever ate. That was until he tried the tamales. Clapping and the movement of pans upstairs told them Christine was eating again. Tommy said she had been hiding up-stairs for the duration of the party, so she must have been hungry. From previous experience Roger knew that Christine sneaked down and took hand-fuls of food when no one saw. So she may have been hungry, but she wasn't *that* hungry.

"Happy birthday."

"You remembered my birthday?" Tommy was genuinely delighted and surprised. He sat on the carpet, playing with the hamster. "I name you Little Guy," he told it while Roger filled the tank, now out of its box, with fresh hay. Tommy seemed to

have had a good day, Roger's behavior toward him
notwithstanding.

It was the final day of the science fair. The judges, the school's science teachers and Mr. Leslie, examined the projects for the last three days. They were set to arrive at their decisions. Roger and Tommy looked on while Clyde demonstrated his robot.

"That's so cool!" Tommy said as the robotic arm began assembling a Lego wall.

The teachers made notes on their clipboards. Clyde explained his contraption. The robotic arm rolled back and forth, picking up blocks and depositing them neatly.

"How does it know where the blocks are?" Tommy inquired.

"I programmed that in. I had to put them in specific places. But I'm working on visual recognition. Maybe next year," Clyde dusted dandruff off his shoulders.

The judges gathered in a circle, talking in whispers. Roger thought Clyde would definitely win, if not the entire science fair, then certainly the top prize for the fourth grade. He couldn't imagine Clyde losing to anyone.

The circle broke apart, and the judges moved on to the next, and final, project that required a demonstration. That was Robert's volcano, where a crowd had already gathered. Before joining the other judges, Mrs. Dixon came over to Clyde. "I'm very disappointed in you," she said to the boy. "As you should know, having learned a great deal in my class last year, robots cannot do that," she pointed to the robot building the wall. "Since your robot is doing that and we know robots can't, you are disqualified. I know you tried hard. In the future, try to make your projects more realistic and scientific. Clyde, it's okay. Stop crying. Just because you're Asian it doesn't mean you have to be good at math and science. It is actually racist of you for trying so hard. Now if you'll excuse me, I have to judge some real science. You should come too. You will learn something from Robert's volcano." Mrs. Dixon left. Clyde turned off his robot silently, his head down.

"Don't feel so bad," Tommy said. "We got disqualified too."

"Yeah," Roger said. "They told Tommy that no one has that many cats, and cats aren't happy. And they told me that no one eats that much."

"Are you talking about that big girl that kept coming down the stairs and eating on Sunday?" Clyde asked.

"Yuppers, that's my sister."

Gasps and awed whispers came from the crowd at Robert's display. The foam must have started flowing from the top. Mrs. Dixon looked amazed. "Wow," she marked her clipboard.

"How dumb," Roger said, turning to Tommy for agreement.

But the boy wasn't there. Roger looked back ahead of him, finally spotting Tommy off to the side of the crowd. He was on his toes, trying to glimpse the volcano, unsuccessfully, over the heads of some fifth graders. Tommy looked to Roger like one of the cats, stretching and pawing at something above it.

A few minutes later Mrs. Dixon got up on the stage to announce the science fair winners. She cleared her throat. Roger wasn't sure if it was to get everyone's attention or if she didn't know that the microphone was on. In any event, the room quieted down and everyone turned toward the stage.

After a speech about the importance of science, without which she said there would be no earthquakes or floods, Mrs. Dixon announced the winners. The winner of the third grade ribbon was one Nicolas Miceli. His project involved helium filled balloons, and sought to demonstrate that air was less dense than helium. The judges thought the project was a resounding success, and Nick was also awarded third place in the fair.

Joanna won the top prize for the fifth grade with her experiment entitled "Poisoning

Hamsters." Mrs. Dixon congratulated her on the win, adding that it was "unfortunate that your hamster was stolen. Even now its dead body would show us the power and majesty of science. Majesty means goodness, for those of you who haven't been doing your homework," she told the blank faces. An investigation was underway, she assured the crowd. Roger felt himself turn red. Joanna also took second place in the overall competition.

As expected, Robert won first place for the fourth grade, and the overall fair. Mrs. Dixon, running out of words of praise, called his project "supercalafragalisticexpialadoshus." Roger had been hearing that word in school a lot lately, but he couldn't find it in the dictionary. "I'm highly confident that Robert will be a very important scientist when he grows up," Mrs. Dixon said to cheers and applause. "Remember this moment, children. You are standing next to greatness." Roger wondered why George didn't get a prize, or even a mention.

CHAPTER TWENTY FIVE
April 29, 1992

"I'm so sleepy," Tommy said as he opened the front *door.* School had made him unusually tired that day.

"You're always sleepy," Roger said. "Or sleeping."

Lucian spotted Tommy in the hall as he was turning to go up the stairs. "Something in the mail came for you today. Brown boxes," Tommy's uncle said.

Tommy was excited. "What do you think it is?" He swept aside a few second and final notices. A couple fell on the floor, almost hitting the barking dog. Tommy struggled with the container that was addressed to him. "It's not opening," he said to Roger, his eyes wide. "The duck tape is too strong."

"Get a knife or something," Roger said.

"You're a genius!" Tommy ran off to the kitchen with the packages. Lucky Joy chased him, snapping at his heels with excited barks. There, Tommy punctured the duct tape. Lucky Joy wagged his tail, running in circles and barking. He probably thought the packages were for him and contained food, as sometimes happened during the holidays.

Tommy finally got his open, and handed the knife to Roger. He took out crumpled newspaper pages. "I think it's empty," he said with disappointment in his voice. And then excitement. "I founded something!"

"What is it?" Roger asked.

"I dunno." Tommy took it out of the small box and set it on the counter between the sink and the fridge. Whatever it was, it fit into his hand. They looked at the object. Roger laughed because he remembered. Tommy was perplexed. "I don't get it," he said.

"Remember how you wanted to get that bike from selling that awful candy?"

"Oh...yeah..." Tommy desperately tried to recall.

"Well there it is."

"No!" Tommy's mouth dropped. He had, of course, forgotten all about the bike probably a week, two weeks at most, after he sent in the prize form. But Roger remembered. He didn't think Tommy would get a figurine of a bike, a girl's bike no less. Rather, he thought it was going to be like the cheap bikes he saw in toy stores, or perhaps a bit worse. But a figurine? For all that money?

"No!" Tommy exclaimed again. He took out a pair of miniature headphones and a cardboard box that had the word "radio" printed on it. Roger opened his box. He got the same thing, except his was a boy's bike.

"Turns out that picture they had in the brochure was actual size." Roger held his figurine up to the light. Its underside informed him that it was made in China.

"I don't like it!" Tommy said over Lucky Joy's barks. The dog would soon be disappointed too. Plenty of the premium chocolates were left, but Lucky wasn't allowed to eat those on account of his being a dog (although Roger suspected the bars lacked real chocolate). Not that he would, anyway. That they were still uneaten, having arrived shortly before Christmas to a house where Christine lived, spoke to their quality. The chocolates would be dispensed on Halloween, if they weren't taken to storage before that time.

"Hey, remember I said that you were better off buying a bike from the store?"

"Know it all." Tommy silently mimicked Roger with a mocking face and stuck out his tongue.

CHAPTER TWENTY SIX
Thursday, August 27, 1992

The notice must have been there for several weeks. Roger found Tigger trying to eat it. There was something wrong with that cat. He had all of the sudden developed an appetite for paper and plastic. Wrestling the envelope away from the playful feline, who pounced on his arm, Roger saw that it was from their mortgage creditor. It seemed important. He and Tommy opened it together.

"What's fork plosure?" Tommy asked. They decided to look it up in the dictionary. Flipping through the pages, Tommy said, "it's not in here."

"Let me try," Roger grabbed the dictionary. "Here it is. You were looking in the wrong place." Roger put his finger on the entry.

They read the definition together, "Prevention." That was almost as mysterious as "foreclosure." Looking up "prevention" yielded "foreclosure." "Where did your dad get this dictionary?" Roger asked.

Tommy shrugged.

They read over the rest of the document. "It says your parents are in default and their payments are accelerated," Roger looked up at Tommy, who stared back at him blankly. "It says they have to repay the entire loan in 90 days from August first."

Tommy still didn't understand, but he looked worried. He petted Lucky Joy absentmindedly as the dog swayed like an eel next to his leg.

"I think it means that if your parents don't pay by the end of October, the bank will take away the house."

Tommy's eyes widened. He looked like a deer in headlights. "How much do they have to pay?"

"$141,792 and fees, it says."

"My tummy hurts. I have to lie down."

Mario was apprised of the situation later that night. He, in turn, told Edith. And Edith said that she would take care of it.

Roger, breathing hard, reached the front door first.

"No fairs!" Tommy screamed behind him, also out of breath and with a red face. "My legs are too short."

It had been a good day. Ordinary classes were canceled and instead they watched movies in the auditorium about Halloween safety.

"Stop, drop, and roll," Tommy sang to the barking dog that greeted them in the hall. A fireman had repeated that phrase a number of times in one of the films. On the way home Tommy made it into a song.

"I think we get it," Roger said, wincing at Tommy's excited screeches.

"Well, Lucky Joy likes my song." Tommy turned away from Roger in affected hurt. "Mail's here," he handed Roger the November *Scientific American*. "Uh oh."

"Uh oh what?"

"This isn't good."

"What?"

Tommy gave him the notice. Lucian probably took it off the door and put it with the mail. "Fork plosure," Tommy said worriedly.

Roger looked at the notice, which stated that foreclosure proceedings had been initiated. "I thought your mom said she would take care of it."

"She always messes everything up."

"It's not like your dad does anything to help."

"You always defend my mom."

"She's the only one that works."

Shouting and cursing came from the ceiling that evening as Roger thumbed through his magazine. Christine screamed and stomped her feet, challenging Edith to a fight. Edith stomped back. Mario shouted over everyone, though Roger had trouble understanding what he said. It was something about going to therapy and meditation.

Roger asked Tommy, "why is it that they have enough money to buy all that stuff but they can't pay for the house?" He was a bit angry. "Like how come they still pay the car insurance when they don't even have that car anymore?"

"I dunno," Tommy said. Roger heard him shrug in the bunk below. "They pay for the house most of the time, but their checks always bounce."

They were silent for a while, trying not to listen to the arguing above.

"My tummy hurts," Tommy complained.

"I know," Roger said. His did too. "We'll think of something."

"Really?"

"Yeah. Everything will be alright."

"You promise?"

"Yeah."

sss. Tommy fell asleep. Although he was less than a month older than Tommy, Roger thought the boy was much younger than him sometimes. The stomping and shouting continued upstairs. Selling lemonade wouldn't do it. Roger tried to think of ways to make money quickly.

CHAPTER TWENTY EIGHT
Saturday, October 31, 1992

They had all their supplies: ski masks on their heads, ready to be rolled down once they entered the bank, toy revolvers in their pockets, a deposit slip in hand with clearly written instructions for the teller, and a bag with a dollar sign for the money, flapping against Roger's leg. He began reciting the plan to Tommy, perhaps for the sixth or seventh time that morning, more to lessen his nervousness than to make sure Tommy knew what to do. Roger looked Tommy over, from head to toe. At Tommy's waist he did a double take.

"Did you take a dump while wearing your coat before we left the house?"

Tommy's eyes widened and he opened his mouth in wonder. "How did you know?"

"Your coat is tucked into your pants."

"Oh." Tommy blushed. He concentrated, hoisting the ends of his heavy coat out of the back portion of his pants. "I was wonderling how come my butt felt funny," he said.

Roger began reciting the plan again. "One. We roll our masks down over our faces. Two. We enter the bank. Three. We take out our guns. Four. I proceed to the teller while you find the old security guard and make sure he is sleeping. If he isn't, you point the gun at him and say 'trick or treat.' Keep him distracted as long as you can. Five. —Are you listening?"

"Yuppers. Can we go trick or treating after? It would be so cool if we got the dulce le—"

"Focus! Five. I point my gun at the teller and give her the deposit slip. If the guard—what's the matter?"

"You're yelling at me," Tommy pouted.

"No I'm not!"

"But you are," the red cheeks said solemnly. "Why are you being mean to me?" Tommy blinked.

"I'm not, but I'm sorry," Roger said in what he hoped was a calm tone. "Now where was I? I make the teller give me money. If the guard is sleeping, which he should be from our observations, you come next to me and watch the customers and bank employees for any funny business. If they try to do anything, say 'trick or treat.' Got it?"

"Yeah."

"Good. Six or is it Seven? Six. Once we have the money, you lead the way to the door. I'll follow closely behind you. Seven. When we get out, we run as fast as we can toward 64th Road. We turn right on 64th, take off our masks, then run as fast as we can to Fitchett Street. After we turn the corner onto Fitchett, we stop. Eight. We take off our jackets and turn them right-side out, so they look normal again. Nine. We divide the money amongst our pockets. Ten. I fold the money bag and put it away. Eleven. We walk calmly to 65th Avenue, make a right. Cross Woodhaven Boulevard, get to Furmanville Avenue, and go home. If cops come looking for us, we can hop the fence and hide in the cemetery." That was probably more than eleven steps, but Roger recently developed a strong interest in odd, especially prime, numbers. "You remember all that?" How could he not? It was the seventh time (another prime!) Roger recited the plan to Tommy that day.

"Yuppers." Tommy sounded more cheerful. "I'm thirsty. Can we buy sparklies?"

"We have some at home. You can have your Seltzer then."

"Okay," Tommy replied sorrowfully.

They approached the bank's parking lot. Roger pulled his mask down over his face and motioned to Tommy to do the same. Tommy did so, but the eye and mouth holes were on the back of his head. Roger opened his mouth to warn him, but it was too late. Tommy crashed into a parking meter. "Ow!"

"You okay?" Roger tried to stifle a laugh.

"Yeah," Tommy said. He rubbed his shoulder.

The mishap took Roger's mind off the butterflies in his stomach, but only for a second. "Alright, let's go." He tensed his butt to prevent anything from coming out.

"Thanks," Tommy said after Roger helped him twist his mask around.

"Showtime."

Roger quickened his pace, and Tommy sped up after him, still getting used to how the world looked with the mask on. They entered through the first door where the ATM machines were with no trouble, but experienced difficulty at the second, where Tommy crashed into Roger after Roger confused pulling the door with pushing it.

As expected, they came upon a line. Banks always have lines. Roger ran up to the nearest teller and aimed his gun at her over the counter. Roger chose Maspeth Federal Savings because it didn't have safety glass between the tellers and customers. This provided the bank employee with plenty of room to hand over the cash. A bank with safety glass would require a bigger team, for they would have to get behind the glass.

Roger stood on his toes to give the teller the money bag and the deposit slip. On the slip, he had written in his kid scrawl the following:

Dear Sir or Madam:

Although this is Halloween and we are children, this is a real robbery. The weapon pointed at your person is real and I am prepared to use it. Kindly take the proffered bag and fill it with all of your $100, $50, $20, and $10 bills, in that order, starting with the 100s. Do not be alarmed. If you take no hostile action, harm will not come to you. If we suspect that anything is

not aboveboard, we will take hostages. Thank you for
your help and cooperation in this matter.

The teller, a chubby Italian woman in her late 40s or early 50s with permed brown hair, looked down at Roger and his gun. She read the note again. "One second, hon," she said. Roger noticed her long, pink nails as she took the bag from him. Just then Tommy bumped into him, so he surmised that the guard was asleep or not to be found. The teller spoke with a short, stocky man, probably branch's manager. He wore a white short sleeved shirt, a red tie, and blue pants, over which his large gut protruded. He looked at Roger and Tommy as the clerk talked to him, putting a hand on his comb-over, as if making sure a sudden wind would not blow his remaining wisps of hair out of alignment. The manager said something and the teller nodded. She disappeared from view behind a wall. The manager remained where he was, his left hand still on his head, looking at them with his beady eyes.

Roger surveyed the other bank employees and the customers waiting in line. So far it looked like business as usual. The tellers worked at the customarily slow pace. An old lady was arguing with one of them with a thick Russian accent. Other than this scene of conflict, calm pervaded the bank's interior. Even the customer Roger beat to the teller didn't seem to care. He appeared to be listening to whatever was playing through his headphones, bobbing his head up and down and occasionally turning to the street, as if waiting for someone. His hands were in the pockets of his dirty, gray hooded sweatshirt. Roger couldn't see his face, but the man seemed familiar.

So far everything went according to plan. Tommy comforted himself by sucking on his lower lip. His gun wasn't out, but Roger didn't mind. They were going to receive a large sum of money shortly, and that made him happy.

About a minute later, the teller came back into view. The bag, which had been neatly rolled up by Tommy was now filled. The dollar sign on its side bulged. Roger couldn't believe how easily it went.

As soon as the bag was in his hand, Roger grabbed Tommy and ran for the door. Tommy wobbled after him, trying to keep up. He had trouble opening the door once more, pushing it instead of pulling in his haste. Tommy said "trick or treat," in an effort to be helpful. Someone yelled "put your hands up!" when they finally opened the door. Roger thought maybe the guard woke up. They had trouble at the second door. This one had to be pushed. Who designed these things?

Roger made a mental note to blame Tommy when they deviated from the plan and turned left upon exiting the bank. They ran as fast as they could. They turned right at the light and ran across the boulevard. They walked on Furmanville Avenue opposite the cemetery without talking, gasping for breath. Sirens sounded in the distance.

They made a right at 84th Place, where Roger stopped to look at the spoils of their heist. The source of the crinkling they heard during their escape became evident when Roger opened the bag. "God damn it!" he screamed. "It's all candy!"

"Really?" Tommy sounded excited. He put his small paw inside and took out a Hershey's chocolate bar. "Oh wow! Do they have a dulce leche?"

Roger let Tommy, who now had chocolate smeared around his mouth, rummage through the bag. "At least take the stupid mask off." Roger stripped off his own and threw it to the ground. He began walking home.

"Hey wait up! You dropped this." Tommy ran after Roger.

They got home after a 40 minute trek through Middle Village. Tommy ran to the kitchen to drink his seltzer. Two cats and a barking dog chased after him.

Christine sat on the living room floor, her back against the bed. A Super Nintendo game flashed on the small screen in front of her. Under her controller, spread across her lap, was a copy of the *Financial Times*. "Doof!" Christine clapped as one wrestler slammed another on the larger television screen off to her side.

"Did they get you a new TV and SNES?"

"Yeah."

Roger sighed.

A cat rested on Christine's bulky right leg. She petted him between claps, eliciting sporadic purrs. It was as if Christine conducted an atonal symphony: the percussive crunch of the potato chips in her mouth and her hands clapping, the deep snoring of Edith above her on the bed (who had a large white cat perched atop her wide belly), random noises from the video game, the purring cat, the outbursts from the television audience, and Christine's occasional yelps and mutterings. "Ow!" The kitten playfully bit Christine's finger. "You dirty little Jew," she said, planting a kiss between his eyes.

Roger stood there for a moment, mesmerized by the chaotic yet somehow organized scene. Then he realized that he was thirsty too and turned toward the kitchen. Christine's voice caught him before he took his first step. "So, Wharton, did you find a job yet?"

"You find me a job that will get us out of this hole and I'll take it." Roger meant it.

"Oh come on." She rubbed her palms together excitedly. "Stop being lazy."

Roger walked to the kitchen. He was greeted with noxious odors coming from the litter box, where, as usual, Shadow cleaned his paws. The stink combined with the putrid smell of the spaghetti sauce Mario was cooking. Incredibly, Tommy was still gulping down his seltzer. He drank straight from the bottle, leaving chocolate lip prints on the mouth and bead. Mario's hair was tied back in a ponytail, swaying from side to side with his passionate, off key singing of a Frank Sinatra song that was in the CD player. *This is my QUEST, to follow that STAR, no matter how HOPELESS, no matter how FAR.* He added capers into the bubbling red sauce. He petted Hurley, who sat contentedly on the counter next to the stove, warming himself.

How unsanitary and dangerous, Roger thought. He made a mental note to tell Tommy later not to allow this sort of behavior. The cat might get injured. Vet bills were expensive. Moreover, he detested cat hair in his food. Lucian was in the kitchen too, spreading dirt around with his mop.

Roger went down the creaky steps to the basement where he set the kitten down on Edith's bed. He washed his hands, went to their room, and changed into his inside clothes. He climbed up to his bunk and opened the November issue of *Scientific American*. He flipped through the pages scanning the titles and pictures, deciding to read "Expansion Rate and Size of the Universe."

He reviewed their robbery attempt. It seemed as though everything was going in their favor, but all they got was candy. Candy! The whole Halloween thing backfired, though Tommy was happy enough. Roger made a mental note to tell Tommy not to eat it all. Better to hide it in a safe place to prevent further stomach aches. Roger briefly puzzled over their exit from the bank. Why was there a racket when they left, when clearly the teller thought they were innocent trick or treaters? Why did they hear approaching sirens?

CHAPTER TWENTY NINE
Sunday, November 1, 1992

Roger got his answer the next morning, when Christine laughed and clapped her hands over a copy of a newspaper. She sat on the bucket by the radio. Roger saw the headline between claps: "Robber Robs Masp Fed Savings, 1 Dead, 2 Injured."

"*The Halloween Massacre,*" Christine said in her voice-over voice, rubbing her palms together. "Oh my God," she said, "that's near here, on Woodhaven Boulevard." Clap. Clap. Clap.

Mario glanced over at the paper. "Oh wow."

"Clappy, can I see that when you're done?" Roger had an uncomfortable sensation in his stomach.

"Here you go, Wharton. You want to apply to that job now that there's an opening?" Christine laughed. She grabbed the big white cat that was sauntering toward the water bowl. "Hello Mr. Smith! You're up early today!" After letting out a few cranky meows, Mr. Smith stretched himself out on her, enjoying a belly rub.

Roger took the newspaper. Under and to the right of the headline he saw a picture of the teller. Underneath was a caption that said "Queens muther of 3 gunned down during bank robbery."

On Saturday it was a picturesk Halloween day in the afternoon at the Maspeth Federal Savings when a robber came in and robbed it on Saturday. Gun shots from an unidentified handgun disturbed the bank on Saturday.

He seemed like a nice youg man But the robber's true intentions were soon chillingly evident as he wipped out a threatening note from within his sweatshirt and handed it over to a shocked teller, police said. "Give me all your $100's, 50's!" the note read, but not outloud.

Police are investigating why the robber started shooting with a gun. Penelope Lamonte, resident of Middle Village and mother of three growing children died from 2 fatal gun shot wounds, one of whom missed her. She is survived by her next of kin, including two of her children.

The robber, who struck shortly before 5 a.m., was described as a Hispanic or Afro-American or white man in his early 30s or 50s, about 5-feet-8 with hair. He wore a grey sweet shirt, jeans and white Reebok pumps or air Jordan's.

The gunman also had shot the bank manager at the head. Tony Macentire who is not seriously hurt arrived in the hospital in critical condition. The bank security guard sustaineded heavy injuries when a bullet grazed him in the arm.

"Thank God no one was hurt", Terrence Baker, a witness who did not wish to be named or identified was quoted as saying after the incidence.

Police told the press that the robber escaped

If you have the information to make a call to the NYPD's confidential Crime Stoppers at (800) 577-TIPS.

"Is this the *NY News Herald* or something?" asked Roger. He examined the paper in his hand.

"Why?"

"Oh, no reason."

"Oh, I see."

"Said the blind man!" Tommy yelled happily, coming into the kitchen. Mr. Smith escaped Christine's grasp and jumped down to Tommy, rubbing himself on his legs and making loud complaining meows.

"Chris, why is it that you read papers like the *Financial Times* and then this crap?" Roger pointed at the article. He determined to get his hands on a real newspaper later that day, if he could.

"I don't know. It's funny. And the subscription was free."

"Didn't I see the bill on the floor somewhere the other day?" Roger asked.

"I said it *was* free," Christine reiterated.

"So why don't you cancel it then? You can save money."

"I can't find the bill."

"I like saving monies," Tommy said. "What's going on guys? You're sooo cute!" All the cats were suddenly there, vying for his attention. He tapped the tops of their heads with his flattened palms. "Yes you are! I'm going to brush you so good! Hello Peek-a-boo!"

Roger decided to get breakfast later. He thought he might be developing cat allergies. Maybe it was the stress, but it was better to avoid the cats. Once he started sneezing and his nose got stuffed, it would be a long time before he felt better. He went to the living room to hang out with the dog, who was still sleeping.

"Oh my God. Tomorrow is Monday. I hate Mondays," Christine walked through the dining room and toward the stairs.

"Where are you going?" Roger fiddled with the TV remote, trying to find a local news channel.

"To the temple to pray tomorrow is not Monday." Her clapping trailed off as she ascended the stairs.

"I see..." Roger muttered to himself.

"Said the blind man!" Tommy sat down on the floor at Roger's dangling legs. "Care Bears are on, can we watch that?"

"Okay."

391

"Coolness."

"Can we go to a newsstand later? I want to see something in a paper."

"Roger Roger," Tommy said happily and slurped his cereal. He already had a sugar high. Roger scolded himself for not hiding the candy better.

Roger sneezed, waking Lucky Joy. After belting out a howl and urinating on a nearby table leg, he began demanding food from Tommy in the usual way. Bark, bark, spin. Bark, bark, spin. The two spent half an hour offering their king treats, trying to determine what appeased him that day. When Lucky finally settled himself down on his pillow with an arepa, a sort of corn pancake, Peek-a-boo positioned herself on the table above him. She lazily extended a paw to bump him on his head as it bobbed up and down with his chewing. He seemed not to notice that he was fraternizing with the enemy. Roger took the opportunity to grab his own bowl of cereal. The best time to eat was when Lucky Joy was already eating—less chance of him demanding a piece as tax that way.

* * *

They were about to go out to find a newsstand when Mario announced an outing to Long Island. They had to stock up on groceries. Tommy was sent down to the basement to wake Edith up from her nap. Roger went down too, to find his jacket.

When he expressed his desire to do his homework, Tommy said they'd be home in a couple of hours.

Back on the first floor, they waited for Christine to come down from the temple where she had decided to take her own morning nap. Lucky Joy saw everyone in their jackets and immediately voiced his objections to their impending departure. Angry bark, bark, circle. Angry bark, bark, circle. This pattern was interrupted by his journey to the far reaches of his territory, where he pooped next to the front door. Having relieved himself, he came back to his position near the coffee table and resumed barking. Roger thought he heard a demand for food in those barks as well.

Lucky stopped his barking and hid under the coffee table when he heard the sound of his leash and saw Christine's gigantic feet approaching. He flattened himself on his carpet and snapped at her fingers as she clumsily reached for him. This tricked him every time. In the next instant his eyes bulged with surprise as Christine grabbed his tail with her other hand, and, in a grace that belied her heft, gently whisked him out from under the table and onto her forearm. She cradled him like a baby, kissing the top of his dusty head. "Come here you little bastard!" Lucky Joy looked up at her, licking his nose calmly. Subdued for the moment, the king resigned himself to an excursion outside his domain.

The five of them and Lucky Joy piled into the creaky Caprice station wagon after Edith took out various cleaning solutions and a couple of vacuums from the back seat and put them in the alley to the right of the house, behind the yellowing picket gate. As they drove off, Lucky Joy ran from window to window excitedly. He took breaks occasionally, sitting on Roger, panting with his tongue out.

Roger hoped Lucky's bladder wasn't at capacity. He also thought about the robbery and the dead lady. He didn't know much, thanks to Christine's poor taste, but it looked as though someone robbed the bank after he and Tommy left it. The man in the gray sweatshirt, who had been in line waiting for them, was probably the culprit. A note was evidently recovered. Roger worried over whether it was his note or if the bandit made one of his own. He was almost positive that he didn't leave any prints. That was part of the plan, after all. But he did not want to get caught up in the police investigation. Roger also worried about what the police would think when they saw the security camera footage. Would he and Tommy be considered innocent trick-or-treaters or accomplices?

As if reading his mind, Christine whispered to Lucky Joy, *"The Halloween day massacre."* The dog looked up at her as she massaged him, panting and licking his nose.

When Christine started breathing hard through her nose and rubbing her face, Lucky Joy walked across Tommy and sat down on Roger again. They looked out the window together. Roger petted him unconsciously. He determined not to tell Tommy, as the sensitive boy felt too much sympathy for everyone. Since he felt bad for the woman, he figured Tommy would have a crying fit. To distract himself, Roger zoned in to Mario and Edith's conversation (more a lecture by Mario, really, with Edith nodding and saying "yeah, yeah," as she drove) about charging clients less to generate more business.

Their Caprice hobbled off the Long Island Expressway with a screeching noise, one exit short of the Price Club, their purported destination. During the lecture, it came up that Mario had to get a new yoga mat at one of the department stores or outlet malls. Roger wondered if there might be a newsstand there.

Christine remained in the car with Lucky Joy as the rest of them ventured into the shops. Roger couldn't find a newsstand as he followed on the heels of Tommy into The Gap. Edith wobbled behind him, pulling her pants up to her waist, where they stayed only a moment.

* * *

"Tag! You're it!" Tommy tapped Roger's shoulder and attempted to flee. Roger immediately tagged him back by outstretching his arm, and disappeared into an aisle of clothing. "Hey, no fair!" Tommy laughed and ran after him. They whizzed all around the store. Tommy chased Roger out of The Gap and into Eddie Bauer. Roger ran past a crowd of yuppies, as Christine called them, and Mario, who browsed in the aisles with a couple of Gap bags in one of his hands.

Deciding to head back out, Roger pivoted and ran the opposite way. Tommy, close on his tail, lunged for him, but Roger got past by quickly changing directions. "You can't get me!" he yelled triumphantly and ran toward the exit. He turned the corner and came to a halt. The exit was blocked by several people. Roger tried to get around them, but it seemed that the group moved in whichever direction he tried to go. His brow furrowed. They stood there doing nothing! Just talking, and blocking everyone's way. They couldn't move a few feet? Roger decided they were traffic cops. Their bodies were fat enough and their faces looked dumb enough. Give them a couple of whistles and they could turn any Manhattan street, no matter how smoothly running, into a traffic jam.

Just then he felt a tap on his back and heard a triumphant "got you!" Roger swiveled, stretching out his arm, but Tommy, now red cheeked and sweating, was out of reach. Roger gave chase. Tommy ran, laughing, in a straight line, his short legs pumping frantically. His coat, like a giant parachute behind him, slowed him down enough for Roger to catch up and tag him back. Roger made a quick turn and vanished into some unpleasant looking clothing, on sale for half off. He made a series of turns, glancing back to see if Tommy followed him.

Roger soon realized he lost Tommy. He ambled in the direction of the cash registers, figuring he would meet up with him there. One aisle over, Roger came across a manager with two trainees.

"—no, that's the trick, you see," the manager was saying. He projected an air of wisdom, as if he told them the secret of life. "Nothing is ever on sale. This is how we get them to spend more. Say you want to sell this shirt for $28. You put a price tag for $56, and then put a 50% sale on it."

The trainees nodded and grinned back at the manager.

"You boys label these with the sale prices. I'll be back later to check in." The manager trotted off.

The trainee with blood shot eyes said to his coworker, "hot damn. This shirt's on sale for 28. How they sell them so cheap when the original price is 56? That's like 30% off."

"Yeah," replied the other. "I gotta get my ma and girl in here before the sale runs out. Does the employee discount makes it more cheaper? Like

$50 maybe? That's why I signed up for this. The employee discount."

Future math teachers, Roger thought, and continued walking. (He'd found an Ayn Rand book on Tommy's shelves a few days ago.) Or maybe Keynesian economists. Public school math teachers who became Nobel Prize winning Keynesian economists. What was wrong with the world? The Vice President couldn't even spell potato. He wondered what election day would bring. Another term for the current destroyers of the middle class, or would the other guys get their shot? He doubted the hillbilly billionaire with his charts would win (he made too much sense and had too many charts). Roger didn't have high hopes for Clinton, should he win, as Mr. Bayer clearly favored him. But Christine was the expert to turn to on this subject.

Roger found Tommy and Mario in the checkout line. Mario was applying for a store credit card. Edith was there too. She had ice cream in the corners of her mouth. Roger asked Tommy how much longer they would be clothing shopping. He was delighted to hear it would be only another 15 minutes.

* * *

It was about two hours later, maybe closer to three, when they finally made it back to the parking lot. Trudging toward the station wagon, Edith, Tommy, and Roger carried Mario's bags. Roger didn't see anything that might be a yoga mat sticking out of any of them. As he walked, Mario flipped through a magazine with the words "detox" and "health" on the cover. Roger's curiosity about why that magazine was an impulse item at a clothing outlet was put to rest.

They got to the car and started loading the area behind the back seats. It took a while because Edith had to make room, moving a vacuum and some paint cans from spot to spot. Christine happily played her Gameboy in the backseat. Lucky Joy slept next to her. He got up, stretched, and barked excitedly after they loaded the trunk. His tail, up in a curl, wagged fervently. Not everything fit. Roger and Tommy found themselves holding a few bags in their laps.

When they pulled out of the lot, Mario announced, turning to face them from the passenger seat, that they were going to have veggie burgers at Houston's for lunch.

"There's one around here?" Roger asked Tommy.

"Noppers. We're going to the city."

"I thought we were going to buy groceries at the Price..."

"I think we're going to do that after," Tommy said. "I got sleepy all of the sudden." He yawned.

Roger sighed. Edith merged onto the highway, going west.

"So, Wharton. Did you apply for a job today?" Christine interjected.

"No," Roger said curtly. "Did you?"

Christine laughed and said, "*Lucky Joy for president!*" in a voice-over voice. Then she whispered, "*the architect of the Halloween day massacre.*" She looked intently at Roger. "Wharton, I know what you should be: a hotdog vendor. Come on, stop being lazy. Be a hotdog guy." She looked down at Lucky. "*The evil!*" The dog panted and smiled.

"Where do you come up with this stuff?" Roger asked, annoyed. Four hours of shopping does that to a person.

"Clinton is going to win the election."

"How come?"

"He played a saxophone on TV."

"So?"

"He's going to win." She rubbed her face, making strange noises, back in Christine land.

They rode the rest of the way mostly in silence. Edith occasionally sang along with a tune on the radio, and Mario tried to join in. A small commotion ensued as Edith rummaged through her wallet to find some cash to pay for the Midtown Tunnel. Although cars honked behind them, the mood remained subdued. They were all tired from Mario's shopping spree and it was about time for their afternoon nap. Tommy fell asleep, leaning his head against Roger, who stared out the window, thinking about the nice teller lady who gave them candy before being murdered.

* * *

Roger sat between Tommy and Christine on the padded bench while Mario and Edith sat on chairs. Tommy, refreshed from his nap, cheerfully smacked his lips as he chewed his veggie burger. BBQ sauce squirted out onto his plate. More went on his face. Roger laughed. This momentary distraction left a couple of his fries unguarded, allowing Christine to deftly reach over and grab them. They were swallowed before Roger even knew they were missing.

"Hey!" Roger swept his fries closer to himself, turning his body and leaning forward to block most of the plate. He left his Brussels sprouts undefended. No longer hungry, Christine wasn't interested in them. She attempted to get at the fries again, leaving a greasy print on Roger's shirt. "Hey! Cut it out!"

"Look at Wharton eating," she smiled devilishly, exposing the big gap between her front teeth. Christine folded and rubbed her hands over her empty plate. Roger felt the bench move under him as Christine shook her legs.

"At least I chew," Roger replied. Her wide-eyed stare (the "psycho eyes," as Tommy called them) made him feel self conscious. But that was the least of it. The real discomfort was the periodic

401

gust of warmth and moisture on his neck from Christine's nose, about an inch, maybe less, from him. "You eat like a snake," he said, cringing. "You don't even chew. Just open your mouth, stuff it in, and swallow! You don't even taste anything!"

"Hahaha," Christine laughed, still staring at him, nearly touching. "Can I have a fry please?" She rubbed her hands together.

Everyone was looking at him and he felt uncomfortable saying no. "Okay, I guess." He dropped his defensive stance.

Christine reached over and grabbed a handful of his French fries. She put them in her mouth and swallowed. Before Roger could do anything, Christine reached back and grabbed the remaining fries. A moment later they were in her stomach. Christine started rubbing her face and hair. Just as well, Roger thought. She probably grazed the food with her large paws the first time around, contaminating it. He took his cloth napkin from his thighs and wiped his neck.

Tommy, who watched all this (or attempted to by leaning back and forth), offered Roger some of his food. He had managed to get ketchup or BBQ sauce, maybe both, in his hair while Roger was paying attention to Christine. He looked sympathetically at Roger, smacking his lips as the last of his burger went into his mouth. "It's sooo good!" he said between smacks. "We should make this at home."

Mario, who had ordered a vegetable wrap, ate Edith's burger and fries. He commented, placing his plate next to Edith, that they were going to have to cut down on their spending. Business wasn't as good as it used to be. November would be a month with less food. They had a good attorney looking into the foreclosure.

"It's cool," Roger told Tommy. He worked on his burger, leaving his Brussels sprouts (which were actually really good at Houston's) for last. Being distinctly vegetable-like, they were safe from Christine in her contented state. Roger wasn't so foolish, however, as to think that she was sated. Indeed, as he watched her cautiously, she tried to pick at the food her dad recently liberated from her mom. Mario slapped her hand away without a pause in his lecture on fiscal responsibility. Edith nodded and repeated what she heard, not really listening. She picked at her husband's wrap, which was also safe from Christine, without much enthusiasm.

While they waited for the sweets that Edith, Tommy, and Christine ordered (Roger didn't like dessert much and Mario was on his latest "detox diet, and dessert doesn't fit into the three week plan"), Mario told them about his purchases: sweaters from the Gap, pants from Eddie Bauer, and a

403

whole bunch of other stuff that Roger couldn't keep track of. Mario was happy about the great deals he got. He saved lots of money because most of what he bought was on sale for half off. And by applying for store credit cards, which gave an extra 5% off and only charged 17% interest he saved even more. To save yet more money, he put some items on layaway. It would take some time, but he'd get a coat and some other stuff for half off as well. Mario also explained how he put a new ice cream machine (nothing was wrong with the old one, as far as Roger knew) on layaway because they didn't have room for it at home. Some things would have to be moved from the kitchen to storage. They'd probably have to rent extra storage space for this. Mario wasn't sure yet, as they owed the storage center money. Roger didn't think he heard anything about a yoga mat, the original reason for the detour to the mall.

Dessert came. As was expected, Christine scarfed down her key lime pie before the others picked up their spoons. Edith ate her slice of chocolate cake delicately. She expertly sliced off slice by small slice. On the other side of the dish, Mario broke off large pieces with his fork, heaping them into his mouth. "This cake is really good, isn't it?"

Edith nodded her agreement. "Yeah, yeah."

Meanwhile, Tommy shivered over his ice cream. He ate most of it, giving the rest to his dad and sister.

Roger pondered why it wouldn't make more sense to buy fewer things (Tommy had once told him that his dad usually bought three of the same exact thing) or not to buy anything. He made a mental note to impress upon Tommy to be reasonable with their spending. But did it really matter? Their impending doom seemed certain.

After lunch, they stopped by Viva Pizza to pick up a couple of organic (and too greasy, in Roger's opinion) slices of pizza for Lucky Joy. Christine also got an eggplant Parmesan. When they entered the car Lucky barked and growled furiously. He smelled food on them. How dare they eat without him? The audacity! Christine ate her sandwich as Lucky demanded on her lap. Tommy mentioned that he was cold and that his tummy hurt. Roger tried to cheer him up with a game of 20 questions, but Tommy fell asleep after the second question.

"Is it a car?" Christine asked.

"No. Remember I said 'yes' when Tommy asked if it was a plant?"

"Then I don't know what it is, Wharton." Christine decided to talk to and pet Lucky Joy instead. "You're so evil!"

Tommy slept the rest of the way to the Price Club, despite Mario's animated lecture on tai chi.

Roger spent most of his time looking out the window. Once they were out of the five boroughs, all the highways looked the same. The road was ensconced between rows of dense foliage, with the occasional growth in the middle along the divider. Roger turned to the trees on the other side of the freeway. He wondered what animals lived there, and what they did in their cozy nooks. He imagined what it would be like for him to go there. What would he find in the dense growth? Perhaps mushrooms and deer tracks. Farther from the highway, where the cars couldn't be heard anymore, there might be the sound of birds chirping, and maybe chipmunks scurrying about. Sunbeams would fall in patches on the mossy and plant covered ground. There might be a pond still further in, glistening in the sunlight and enclosed by tall grass, the home of catfish and happy Crappies.

He shook his head. Of course it wasn't really a forest, but a dense patch of trees and various weeds that took root around them. The former had been planted for the specific purpose of occluding the road from what lay beyond. And what lay beyond the road garbage littering the forest floor—soda cans, newspapers, beer bottles, used condoms, burger wrappers, tampons, potato chip bags, flat tires, baggies that once contained illicit drugs, and murder weapons—were roads and people's houses. How unexciting.

406

They arrived at the Price around 2 PM. After Edith parked the Caprice, Roger made himself useful by grabbing a gigantic shopping cart. He ran, pushing it toward the store with his arms at shoulder level. He jumped onto the bar that connected the back wheels together. Tommy jogged after him as he rode the shaking cart through the parking lot. Tommy caught up with him at the entrance, and they waited for Mario and Edith, who had the membership card, to be let inside. Christine was left in the car with Lucky Joy and her Gameboy.

Roger felt smaller than usual in the warehouse store. Everything was larger than he remembered. The carts, the shelves, and most of the products seemed made for giants. Tommy struggled with a bag of potato chips almost as big as he was. Edith said she was going to the bathroom. Roger and Tommy looked at each other and smiled. They knew her real destination was the food court.

The boys stayed with Mario. Roger followed him with the cart, and Tommy walked alongside.

"My head hurts and I feel nauseous. Dad, can we get sparklies?" Tommy smacked his lips and raised his head like a hungry baby bird.

"Sure, sure." Mario wandered through the clothing section. It would be a while before they got to actually loading foodstuffs into the cart. They left the cart with Mario, who examined a pair of jeans, and walked toward the book section. Tommy liked to look at all the covers, and choose the book that had the most appealing one. As he did so now, Roger remembered the well-worn dictum from school: "don't judge a book by its cover." He looked at Tommy and smiled. How stupid was that? How else did one decide take a book off of a library or store shelf? The title, the author's name, summary, quotations by critics about how awesome the book was (Roger never understood the point of these—as if they'd ever put anything but praise there), and other relevant things were all on the cover. A judgment had to be made, after looking at these, whether to put the book back on the shelf or to inspect it further by flipping through its pages.

Roger surveyed the titles of the hardcovers and paperbacks quickly. The selection wasn't that big or of much interest. It was, for the most part, a bunch of bestsellers and a couple of self help books. The closest things that came to literature here were, in Roger's opinion, the works by Stephen King and Dean Koontz. Roger looked at these, but did not find anything new. He had everything King wrote up to that point and was working on Koontz. The Price didn't have a philosophy section.

So Roger walked with Tommy, watching the small round boy pick up and drop books, seemingly at random. Tommy found one he liked. He opened it and looked inside, his mouth slack with excitement. His small chubby hands obscured most of the title and the author's name.

"What's that?" Roger asked him.

"It's about kids in space. They're slaves and space pirates. It looks really good." He giggled. "One of the kids is called TumTum. I'm gonna get this one."

Roger rolled his eyes. "Are you sure you don't want to take it out from the library, or at least wait for the paperback?"

"No," Tommy said in a slightly whiny voice. "I want it now."

"But your dad was talking about how we have to save money."

"It's the weekend."

To argue against such logic was pointless, so Roger shut up. They walked away from the books to find Mario. Tommy announced again that his tummy and head hurt. In the distance they saw Edith eating something, probably a hotdog. They found Mario where they left him. Tommy dunked his book onto a pile of clothing in the massive cart. They set out, finally, to get what they came here for: food.

* * *

Tommy had to help Roger push the overflowing cart toward the car. Once there, they remembered that they had no space in the trunk.

Mario announced that Edith would call Lucian, who would take a cab to them, pick up their purchases, and take the cab back home. They would then wait for Lucian to come back in the cab and Edith would drive them to their favorite pizzeria. No one said anything, so it was agreed. Tommy and Roger helped Edith load the car while Mario and Lucky Joy supervised them. Christine leaned on the car, holding Lucky Joy's leash and laughing. Roger didn't understand why they had to load the car if Lucian was supposed to come for the food. He also thought it was incredibly wasteful, both in time and money, for Lucian to take three trips in a cab. The better solution, which Mario rejected without listening to Tommy relay Roger's idea, was to have Edith drive home, drop off the stuff, and then come to pick them up.

After they finished loading the car, Edith wobbled in the direction of the payphones. Roger hoped that Lucian wouldn't answer the phone and his idea would be implemented. He was disheartened when Edith came back 15 minutes later, informing them that Lucian was on his way.

They shivered by the car, waiting for Lucian for the next hour. To pass the time Christine went through a list of jobs that Roger should do: airplane mechanic, dog catcher, president of the PTA ("that's not a job, Chris. It's what authoritarian housewives with a lot of free time do to maintain their self worth"), blood diamond mining slave ("also not a job"), a clown, a congressman, a thief ("those last three are a bit redundant, Chris"), a horticulturalist ("that's only profitable if you grow drugs"), and a men's room attendant ("I heard that union keeps newbies out"). Christine was excited, but she didn't clap. Just as Lucky Joy with his urinating, Christine clapped only at home. Tommy once mentioned to Roger that the neighbors asked if they had a ping pong table (they did actually, in storage). They had apparently confused Christine's almost constant clapping for a bouncing ping pong ball.

Meanwhile, Tommy had wandered off. He returned as the last rays of the sun slipped below the horizon. Tommy sheltered something in his shirt. Roger knew right away that they had a new addition in the family.

"Oh poor thing," Mario said, looking down at the warbler Tommy now cupped in his palms for all to see.

"His name is Chirpy McChirpy and he has an owwie on his wing," Tommy said.

Roger peeked at the little bird as it snuggled itself in Tommy's gentle hands. Tommy rubbed the top of its head with his index finger until it fell asleep. Edith was then quietly ordered back to the warehouse club to purchase a small dropper to dispense water and wet dog food, because Tommy adjudged the patient, much to his dismay, a carnivore. An insectivore, actually, but the prospect of catching live insects to feed the bird was rejected by everyone on moral grounds. Roger didn't really see what the problem was—he killed mosquitoes all the time—but he respected their wishes.

"Where are you going to keep her?" Roger asked him. The cats would surely find it delicious.

"It's a boy. I don't know."

"Somewhere away from the cats, I imagine..."

"Yeah. They can be evil." They remembered the numerous animals in the backyard when Roger first met them. Birds of various kinds battled against each other and plump squirrels over seeds at the bird feeder. More birds bathed in the fountain that was bought for them, at the Price probably. Then the stray cats came. Tommy's family bought cat food and water bowls. As the cats took up residence in the backyard and grew fatter and more fecund, the bird and squirrel population diminished. On occasion, Tommy wept at the sadness in the world while Christine buried a few unfortunate critters. Roger's attempts to cheer him up ("it's okay; it's evolution") hardly ever worked. Eventually only cats and bugs remained in the backyard. The runts of every litter, of course, ended up inside the house.

Tommy watched the bird, thinking. "I don't know."

"In our room maybe?" The cats were not allowed in there on account of the rodents.

"Yeah!" Tommy brightened.

"What are you going to keep it in?"

"A shoebox for now." All new additions, except Roger, always went into a shoe box first, a sort of airlock.

Tommy's uncle arrived to pick up their purchases just as Tommy got ready to feed the bird. They would have to wait another two hours, at least, in the dark parking lot for Lucian's return. While Roger helped unload the car, he hoped that perhaps there would be a change of plans, on account of the bird.

The plan didn't change. They were to wait for Lucian. At least they could sit inside the car now. It was still a mystery to Roger why they had to load and unload the car in the first place. The food, clothing, and books (plural because Mario got himself a couple of books on saving money and budgeting) were perfectly fine in the cart, as far as Roger could see.

In the back seat, Roger enjoyed the sensation of sitting. He was sore from being on his feet for several hours. Tommy opened the can of dog food, dipped a thin stick into it to scoop some out, and offered it to the bird. "It's so stinky," he said. "Why must animals eat meat? It's so mean."

413

Lucky Joy watched from Christine's lap. His ears pricked forward and he jumped, barking, when he saw the dog food going into the bird's mouth. Tommy put some more on the stick and offered it to Lucky Joy. The dog sniffed at it for a long moment before rejecting it. He sat back down. Tommy shrugged and put the stick next to the bird's beak. Lucky immediately sprang up and started barking again. He refused to touch such low quality fare, but he was damned if he would let someone else eat before him.

After the bird finished eating (Roger wondered what they would do with the remaining 23 and 7/8 cans of dog food), Edith turned off the interior light. The bird, petted by Tommy, fell asleep almost instantly. A few minutes later everyone but Roger was asleep. He looked out the window and listened to the interesting rhythm Edith, Christine, and Lucky Joy made with their snores. He had yet to locate a legitimate newspaper, but his fatigue lessened his earlier pressing need to find one. Roger almost fell asleep himself, but it occurred to him that he hadn't done any of his homework. Friday night was for relaxing. Saturday had been spent robbing the bank, trick or treating, and baking pumpkin pies with Mario. And most of today was spent shopping. The jolt of adrenaline kept him up until Lucian arrived.

Mario decided that, on account of the bird, they shouldn't go to the pizza place after all. They drove home with Lucian, Christine, and Lucky Joy in the back seat. Tommy, Roger, and the bird sat behind them in the storage area. Lucian talked in his loud voice about something Roger did not care to follow. He moved back and forth with the car's motion as every imperfection in the road made itself known to him with painful bumps. Tommy slept happily, cradling the bird, seemingly without a care in the world.

When they finally arrived back at the house, Roger's butt and legs were numb. When he moved them, he felt what he regarded as a Nietzschean sensation. The pins and needles running down his legs, and the pulses, like electric shocks, traveling up from his toes to his trunk with every step, felt at once extremely unpleasant and quite exquisite. Every movement he made, as new blood rushed to awaken his nerve endings, was simultaneously unbearable and yet able to be borne. Tommy, on the other hand, got out of the car without much trouble, save for somehow bumping his head on the door as he tried to close it.

"There is something wrong with the bird," Tommy said worriedly, rubbing his head. It looked the same to Roger as when he first saw it.

"Yeah, its wing is messed up, you said."

"No, I think its Tommy hurts."

After leaving Lucky Joy, Christine, and Lucian at home, Edith drove the rest of them to the emergency vet. Roger yawned and sat down on a plastic chair in the empty waiting room, next to a giant gray cat. It paid him no mind, watching goldfish float lazily in their tank next to the wall. Tommy and Mario were in the examination room with the bird, and Edith waited outside in the car. Roger watched the traffic stream by on Queens Boulevard through the giant front window. He heard noises in his head every time the red lights flickered as the drivers braked. As he started to investigate his propensity for creating sounds in his mind to correspond with flickering lights, Roger found himself staring at a disorganized pile of periodicals on a shelf next to the window. It seemed to ring a faint bell. Roger yawned again and rubbed his eyes.

The cat turned to him when Roger jumped up. Maybe the newspaper he'd been looking for all day could be found there. He had several choices, and time to read them all. He and Tommy weren't mentioned and the police considered the robbery part of the case closed. The security cameras were down for maintenance. As a result, the police had no footage to review.

Adrenaline shot into Roger's bloodstream when a familiar name appeared in the black and white print. Jim Flannery, assistant janitor at the local elementary school almost made off with over

$70,000. Not enough to pay off the mortgage, Roger mused. Jim shot several people during the robbery, including the teller whose picture was published in the *NY News Herald*. The majority of the newspapers Roger flipped through said she was in critical condition at Elmhurst Hospital.

The police caught Jim as he ran down Woodhaven Boulevard, apparently in the same direction Roger wanted to run with Tommy. It was a good thing, then, that they ran the other way. Upon arrest, the distraught assistant janitor confessed to everything. He had robbed the bank to settle his gambling debts. In a twist emphasized in one of the headlines, a Parks Department employee and a police officer from the 104th Precinct were fingered as low level agents in a gambling ring. Roger recognized the photographs instantly. Police were looking for the men as the stories went to print. Roger reread the articles and breathed a sigh of relief.

Edith came into the office just as they were about to leave. Mario finished writing a check for several hundred dollars as Tommy informed Roger and the gray cat that Chirpy McChirpy would be okay. Edith told them in a series of whispers that the car had been repossessed while they were inside.

"What?" Mario exclaimed. The bird, which had been sleeping in Tommy's hands, let out a chirp. No one bothered to ask how it happened. Everyone knew. Edith explained anyway. She had a brief "errand" to run, and so exited the car for a few moments. Everyone turned to the diner's neon sign across the boulevard.

"My lotto ticket's in there!" Mario explained his outrage. He had Edith flag down a cab for him. "I must get that ticket back. It might be a winner."

Aside from Tommy's occasional yawn and announcement that he was sleepy and his tummy hurt, they walked home in silence. Edith, not used to walking such a long distance (for her), suggested that next time they should take a cab too.

"Head of the PTA," Roger challenged with a yawn. Mario came home late at night, causing a big commotion in the kitchen. The lotto ticket turned out not to be a winner. What a surprise.

"Umm. Teachers," Tommy shot back. He'd slept through it all, of course. And he didn't appear anxious about not having his homework done, or his mom's court hearing that day.

Roger paused to think. Playing this game over breakfast allayed his nervousness somewhat. It took his mind off their imminent homelessness. "Investment bankers." That was a good one. He was proud of himself.

"Government workers," Tommy said haughtily. He did a little victory dance.

Roger squinted. He didn't want to bring out the big guns, but Tommy forced his hand. "Psychoanalysts," Roger said.

"No. Lawyers," Tommy replied. But he couldn't decide. "Policemen," he said, and before Roger could respond, "politicians. That's it. Politicians. I win. I win, don't I?"

"I don't know. Seems like cheating somehow —"

"What are you guys playing?" Christine entered the kitchen.

"Most useless professions," Roger said.

"Chevy Chase," Christine said. "Where's my prize?" She reached for her cereal bowl.

"Chevy Chase is not a job, Clappy" Roger said.

"Oh come on. He's Chevy Chase. Look at him. He's so useless," Christine replied between claps, her voice briefly intoning a Bronx-Italian accent. She finished her cereal in one gulp, put her bowl in the sink and asked for the first but not last time that day, "are we gonna lose the house?" Now Tommy looked nervous. He clutched his stomach. Roger had no trouble empathizing. The quest for stability in a world of chaos often led to one kind of pain or another.

* * *

Roger didn't have to wait long. Mr. Bayer checked their homework first thing every morning. He ignored the temptation to pass off a previous assignment as the current one when he noticed that everyone had drawn a pie chart. The stocky bald man would definitely notice him not having a pie chart. Maybe if he drew one? Too late.

"Mr. Wharton, did you do your homework?" Mr. Bayer scowled over him, his glasses reflecting Roger's frightened face.

"N-n-no."

"No what?"

420

"N-n-n-no, s-sir."

This teacher was a stickler for what he thought were appropriate ways of speaking. "Is homework important, Mr. Wharton?"

Roger didn't think so, but he knew the correct response. "Yeah."

"Mr. Wharton?" the teacher admonished.

"Y-yes, s-s-sir," Roger corrected himself.

"That is better." To the class Mr. Bayer said, "when you say 'yeah,' people do not think you are very smart. Say 'yes.' Then people will think you are smart. You're fifth graders. You should know this by now."

Now came the punishment. Tommy, Michael, and Roger, the teacher announced, were to stay upstairs with him during lunch and write a 50 word composition about why they should have done their homework. Tommy groaned next to Roger, "I hate 50 word competitions."

Roger, who never had to write one, didn't think it was such a big deal. Especially because the 50 word one was the minimum punishment Mr. Bayer gave out. A student laboring over and counting the words on a loose leaf paper was a familiar sight when they came up from lunch. Someone had to write 100 words about something they did wrong a couple of times a week. That they were given 50 words spoke to the lack of seriousness of their offense. That didn't stop Michael from complaining either, he who a month ago had to write 500 words about why it was wrong to bring his father's *Playboy* to class. Michael was the principal composition writer in class. If Roger were in his shoes, he would use the same one over and over, instead of struggling over a new one as Michael seemed to every other week.

Roger didn't think Mr. Bayer even read them. He saw him once, counting the words. Feeling brave that day, Roger decided to find out. Putting his lunch tray down on his desk, he debated writing random words. He decided against it, however. Propriety and respect were chief among the things that Mr. Bayer looked for in his students. To be caught violating these would be penalized far more harshly than not doing one's homework. No. He'd test his theory another way.

As Tommy chewed thoughtfully on a pen cap next to him, Roger bent down to write. It was to be a brief argument against compositions as punishment. "School is supposed to encourage writing," Roger began. The argument took considerably more than 50 words. To Tommy's and Michael's amazement, he had to ask for two additional sheets of paper.

Roger sat in anticipation for the rest of the day. A wave of heat went through his body when, during their spelling exercises, he saw Mr. Bayer examining the compositions.

The final bell sounded. Before they left the room, Mr. Bayer handed Roger his papers. A red check marked the top. Little red dots hovered above each word—the first 50 anyway. Everything after that was crossed out. "It was a 50 word composition, Mr. Wharton."

"Lemme see," Michael said to Roger in the schoolyard. "Why'd you write so much?"

Roger shrugged.

"Let's see yours," Tommy said to Michael.

Michael gave him the sheet and Tommy cracked up. Roger looked over Tommy's shoulder. "Fart fart tamatows ham," the composition began.

Edith came home with somewhat good news. Both the federal government and NY State had liens on the house and were blocking the foreclosure. But both governments instituted their own proceedings to evict the family. It would take a couple of months. Mario proclaimed this a reason to celebrate. They were almost out the door when Mario remembered that the car was repossessed. Tommy did his best to discourage his father from calling a cab. He met with success, but the price was silent treatment for the rest of the day.

CHAPTER THIRTY ONE
Wednesday, January 6, 1993

Their mood was as gray as the light from the window. Roger and Tommy packed their boxes in silence. Roger's stomach rumbled and his chest burned. He'd been to the bathroom several times that morning, but that didn't quiet the army of butterflies inside him.

Tommy didn't seem much better. Paler than normal, the boy had none of his usual cheer. Not even the three new kittens, abandoned by their mother and rescued from the cold, could chirk him up. Two orange ones and a gray slept snuggled in their socks, surrounded by blankets and warm bottles. They would be chirping before long, demanding food and affection. Tommy worried about what they would do with them, and all the other animals.

Christine paced over them in the kitchen. Lucky Joy's tiny clicks followed her heavy steps. The dog didn't like the sudden activity in the house and made sure everyone knew it.

That morning Mario announced that a sheriff or marshal could come at any moment to evict them. He instructed everyone to pack while he took a cab to the local nursery to buy a money plant. "It's something I should've done long ago.

Maybe your mother wouldn't even put us in this mess."

Why did they pack? Where would all this stuff go? Where would they go? Roger didn't know. Everything was always a secret with Mario until the last instant. But packing was something to do, though he would have preferred to be in school.

Roger's hands were so cold that the books he packed away into a cardboard box felt warm. Tommy left for upstairs to secure more boxes and tape. Mr. Smith greeted him with a grunt at the threshold. His eye looked worried to Roger. He must have been through something like this before.

Christine stopped pacing. She talked with Tommy about something, their voices high and anxious. A few minutes later Tommy came down paler than he left. Almost as white as the door he slid open, he said, "my mom stopped packing."

"Okay?" Roger wanted to know if plans had changed. He hadn't heard Mario stomping around upstairs. It was unusual for plans to change without Mario's presence.

"She's lying on Christine's bed and can't get up." That didn't sound good. Not at all.

"What do you mean?"

Tommy repeated, "she's lying on Christine's bed and can't get up."

"Is she okay?"

"I dunno." Tommy's white fingers turned purple where he clasped them.

Roger got up off the carpet and lightly slapped Tommy's hands to his sides. They went up the stairs together. Roger didn't notice when Tommy crashed into him as he rounded the corner from the kitchen into the dining room.

Lying on her back, Edith insisted that she was alright. When asked to get up, she said she didn't want to, but that of course she was able. Something about her demeanor said otherwise. Tommy went upstairs to consult with Lucian. His uncle came down with him. Lucian tended to agree with Edith that she was just fine. He went back upstairs after Edith told everyone to leave her be.

Roger went back down with Tommy. The chirping kittens, with the equally loud bird, kept them occupied for over an hour.

Christine came down and announced that Edith had not moved an inch during that time. Roger knew her account could be taken literally, as she was wont to stand closely and watch for hours at a time. Their concern grew until finally they decided to call an ambulance.

Their phone service had been cut off. Too embarrassed to ask the neighbors, they walked two blocks to Caldwell Avenue to use the emergency pole. It took a few tries for the operator to believe them. After threatening to send a squad car, the operator finally agreed to dispatch an ambulance.

An hour later, Edith needed help getting off the bed. She stumbled down the porch stairs and inched her way to the flashing lights. Roger watched through the living room window as Lucky Joy barked at his feet and ran around the boxes and piles of stuff. Lucian and Tommy climbed into the back of the ambulance after Edith, and the flashing lights moved out of view. Roger stood there for a few minutes, watching the wind blow the last of the leaves off the tree next to the road. His throat was tight. He'd seen this before. He didn't want to think about how it might end.

Christine came from the kitchen then, rubbing her face. "Wharton, are we going to lose the house?"

What did she think all the packing was for? She should have known something was up, despite all of Mario's eccentricities. Roger didn't have the heart to tell her. "No," he said.

"Okay," Christine nodded and started clapping. She sat down and opened a newspaper. "That Clinton is a moron," she said.

"Isn't he a Rhodes Scholar?" Just the title sounded smart to Roger. That it meant free graduate study at Oxford sealed the deal.

"So? That just means his education was paid with blood diamonds."

Roger couldn't help smiling at that.

CHAPTER THIRTY TWO
Thursday, January 7, 1993

Tommy and Lucian didn't come home the previous night. Neither did Mario, after Christine told him what happened. The sheriff, thankfully, didn't visit the house either.

After asking Roger to make her a sandwich, Christine took advantage of the situation by taking a nap. Roger went to school because he didn't know what else to do. Although most of his thoughts centered on Edith and the house, he was also worried about how his and Tommy's concurrent absences might look to Mr. Bayer. Appearance interested the man above all. As a result, when that afternoon Mr. Bayer asked Roger whether he lived with Tommy, the question didn't shock him into a mistake. "S-s-same a-a-ap-p-partment b-building," he replied. Mr. Bayer nodded and put away a manila folder, apparently satisfied.

The empty house after school gave Roger an unpleasantly familiar feeling. Only Lucky Joy's and the cats' demands to be petted distracted him from thinking it was all a dream. He made dinner for everyone, hoping they would *all* return soon. After doing his homework, Roger read Nietzsche in his bunk by the decaying light from the window. How right Nietzsche was about the world.

Roger awoke from a fitful sleep to stomping above him. He concentrated on the sounds. That was definitely Mario. The clicking came from Lucky's nails as he ran around. The soft steps probably belonged to Tommy while the thud-thud came from Christine's jumping. There was no gentle tapping, however.

A series of footfalls quickly rolled down the stairs and the door slid open. Roger saw Tommy's silhouette before the lights were switched on and he was momentarily blinded.

"The food was delicious," Tommy said. "My dad said to tell you thank you."

"Where's your mom," Roger asked the pallid looking, sleepy boy.

"She's in the hospital," his voice screeched up in a somewhat complaintive fashion.

"What happened?" Roger sat up and almost hit his head.

Tommy opened the shoe box to check on the kittens while he explained the situation. When they got to the hospital, the EMT workers forgot to unload Edith before going to another call. They realized their mistake halfway to their next destination. At the hospital, the person in charge in the emergency room said that Edith was fine and should go home. He finally relented when Edith couldn't get out of the stretcher. A doctor examined her then, and said that she had diabetes, on account of her weight. He also tried to release her. Another doctor wanted to give her various tests, after which he recommended amputating her legs. Mario raised a big fuss and almost got arrested. In the early morning hours yet another doctor examined Tommy's mom. This one appeared to be more competent. For one thing, he knew how to speak English and didn't look like a used car salesman. That last part was Christine's description. She now stood in the doorway, helping Tommy tell the tale. That she wasn't there didn't seem to affect her knowledge of what transpired. This more competent doctor determined from Edith's symptoms and scans of her head that she had suffered a minor stroke.

"Will she be okay?" Roger asked.

"I think so." Edith was supposed to remain in the hospital for several weeks for tests and observation.

Roger breathed a sigh of relief.

A few minutes later Mario called them up to pack in the living room. He went up to the temple room to find just the right spot for the money plant. The cats had already destroyed most of it where it stood overnight in the living room.

Useless junk everywhere. Roger hated packing and cleaning. It roused the dust, making his nose run. Behind the table where the typewriter once stood, for instance, was an army of dust bunnies. They guarded unopened junk mail and a large number of crumpled lottery tickets. Roger chuckled to himself as he thought, Mario's retirement account.

He asked offhand, more to have something to complain about than to request information, "does your dad even check the lottery tickets to see if he won?"

"I don't think so," Tommy responded with a sneeze.

"So why does he even buy them?" Roger raised his voice.

"I dunno. Stop yelling at me," Tommy said.

"So we might've won something and we don't even know?"

"Yuppers."

"Maybe we should check?"

"Good idea!" Tommy tapped his chin. "How do we check?"

"Christine keeps her old newspapers, doesn't she?"

"Yuppers. You're a genius!"

They summoned Christine from the kitchen. Through a full mouth she informed them of all the places throughout the house where she stored her periodicals. Roger didn't want to do all that work for nothing, but Tommy insisted. Since his dad got the money tree, he had a good feeling about it.

The search lasted well past their bedtime. It sped up, though, once Lucian was enlisted. While the two looked through the clutter, Roger worked on matching the papers with the lotto drawing dates listed on the tickets. Most of the tickets were worthless, but two winnings, one of a dollar and another of ten, spurred them on past midnight.

"Daddy, daddy!" Tommy ran up the stairs shouting. Roger and Lucian followed. "Daddy!" Tommy banged on his dad's door. Peek-a-boo and Shadow ran up the stairs after them to see what all the excitement was about.

Mario opened the door sleepily after a few minutes. He had on a winter hat, coat, gloves, and boxer shorts. Roger thought it a strange set of pajamas.

"Daddy!" Tommy hugged him. "Guess what? Guess what?" He let go and started dancing.

Mario looked at him for a while. "Is it your birthday already?"

"Noppers," Tommy continued his dance.

"What is it then?" Mario said through a long yawn.

"We won the lotto!"

"What? Really?"

"Yuppers!"

"Oh wow!" All the sleepiness left Mario's face. He took a moment to dance with Tommy. Then, "how much?"

"We won a bunch!" Tommy jumped.

Mario looked at him expectantly.

"One ticket won a dollar. And also another won ten dollars!"

Mario's smile dropped into a frown. "We need a lot more than that, little one." He opened his door with a loud push and yawned.

"But daddy! Aren't you excited that we won $40 million?"

"What?" Mario jumped back into the hall.

"Oh, wait. I said that one in my head," Tommy said.

While Mario collected himself, Roger mentioned the details. After taxes, and if they wanted the lump sum, it was more like $10 million. But they had a slight problem. The ticket was a year old. In fact, it expired the next day, or technically that day since it was past midnight.

"I don't know if Edith is well enough to drive us," Mario mused. "The lottery will just have to wait until your mom feels better. Go to bed now. We'll discuss it in the morning."

Roger couldn't sleep. Tommy said he couldn't either, just before he drifted off.

Mario remained hardheaded in the morning. He refused going to the claim center without Edith. Tommy insisted at Roger's urging. His dad responded by giving him the silent treatment.

"But it expires today!" Roger was dumbfounded. "What the hell is wrong with him?"

Tommy rubbed his hands together in his sweater's pouch. "I dunno. He's just crazy that way."

They needed an adult to sign the ticket, but Lucian refused to do so. He didn't want to incur Mario's wrath.

"How freaking retarded are they?"

"A lot, I guess," Tommy replied.

For some undisclosed reason Mario also forbade them from telling Christine about the previous night's events. Roger wondered if Tommy's aunt might accompany them, but Tommy didn't think so. He feared she would abscond with the ticket. Paranoia ran in the family, so Roger didn't bother arguing over the issue. They thought over their remaining options and finally decided on a course of action.

After spending two hours looking for past tax returns to find Edith's social security number, Tommy forged his mother's signature on the back of the ticket. The boxes around them reminded Roger of the precariousness of their situation, so he suggested they write Hernia's address. "You're a genius!" Tommy agreed. His complexion regained some color.

They looked up the lottery claims center in the phone book and then took the train to lower Manhattan. Roger expected to encounter trouble because of their age, but everything went with surprising smoothness. The woman who received them offered her congratulations in a monotone voice and informed them that it would take a few weeks before everything was processed.

Roger and Tommy returned to Queens hungry and tired, but in good spirits. They found Mario and Christine sitting on the curb among the boxes from the living room. Christine had the three newest kittens in her lap. Lucky Joy sat shivering at her side. The rest of the cats sat in a circle around the bird, the hamster, and the gerbil, watching with predatory eyes and moving their tails back and forth.

Mario didn't have to explain that they'd been evicted, but he did so anyway. He lamented how he couldn't find the lottery ticket. The money tree had worked, but they just couldn't take advantage of it. He had gotten it into his head to trade the ticket for keeping the house a while longer. After Roger finished rolling his eyes, he and Tommy exchanged secret smiles. Lucian had gone to Hernia to negotiate for their stay at her house. Their worst fears had been realized, and here Roger was, smiling. He chuckled to himself over the stupidity of having a lottery based savings plan. And yet it had worked. Taking a seat on the porch steps next to Tommy, Roger wondered aloud how many chores Christine would have to do during the summer.

"Shut up, Wharton," Christine grumbled.

"So Wharton," Christine clapped from her lawn chair, *"when are you gonna get a job?"*

"You mean I'm not getting paid for this?" Roger looked up, sweaty, from the grill.

Christine laughed. "Can I have another veggie burger please?" she said with sudden politeness.

"I want one toopers," Tommy descended from the backdoor with a plate of vegetables marinated for grilling.

"I miss the old house sometimes," Christine's burger squirted ketchup on her shirt.

"This one's bigger though," Roger said. They all looked up at their brownstone. "You get to have a room and everything."

"I still miss it though," Christine said over the pops of firecrackers exploding nearby. "Lucky Joy misses it too." Her burger gone already, she picked up the dog to kiss it.

"I don't like Brooklyn," Roger said. Moving there had been Mario's idea. Christine didn't mind the location, as she had a valid excuse for not visiting Hernia. It was simply too far, and Edith, in her condition (she, now snoring in a lawn chair next to the rose bushes with McChirpy roosting on her belly, had recovered almost completely), was prohibited by Mario from driving Christine such a great distance. That she still had to drive Mario around to all his activities didn't seem a contradiction. Roger was glad that they'd picked the annuity option over the lump sum. Turning the sizzling vegetables over and admiring their grill marks, Roger smiled.

AFTERWORD

1

I debated whether to include an afterword. Is there a need for explanation, or will readers get it? Will my explanation take anything away from the book, or will it add to it? A full explanation deserves more space than is available here. In fact, I wrote about 80 pages on the subject in grad school (if you're thinking about going, don't—it's a waste of money and time). So what should I do? Provide a sliver, or say nothing at all? Since you're reading this, you know my decision.

2

Some readers may be offended by the "intolerance" (racism, antisemitism, stereotyping, etc) present throughout the novel. Good. You should be. But I hope you're angry for the right reasons.

Humans have a knack for categorizing and ranking things. It's how we thrive in a chaotic world. Although no two things are exactly alike, we group together the ones that are similar to a certain degree and call them the same. We call the things that have a greater degree of difference opposites. So we have hot and cold, light and dark, and so on. We also rank things in a hierarchical fashion, often with opposites at the ends: top ten lists, leaders and followers, best and worst, and so on. One particularly odious categorization and ranking that we engage in daily is the categorizing and ranking of people by race, ethnicity, religion, and the like.

Racism permeates our society. I have trouble thinking of an aspect of our culture that is not in some way connected to racism. It underlies our attitudes, opinions, and beliefs about ourselves and other people. Our actions are frequently either shaped by racism or are a reaction to it.

There's the not so hidden bigotry. I hear the word Jew used as a verb all the time, as in "that guy Jewed me out of my money." It's also an insult: "stop being such a Jew!" Words appropriated by homosexuals to counter bigotry have been co-opted by bigots and are now standard insults in our vernacular: "that's so gay!" People, particularly the young, say these things without thinking. They're part of their vocabulary. And we all know the overt, "we don't want your kind around here," that people of every color, creed, and orientation face—many of them on a daily basis.

Then there's the hidden racism. Practically no one says the n-word anymore. (It's the word that shall not be spoken aloud, even when we talk about it, unless our skin is a certain color or we're openly racist.) Nor do we say any of the other epithets in public. But neighborhoods are still segregated. Opportunities are still spread disproportionately, and as a result so is the prison population. People are welcomed and turned away because of their race or religion. We do it all the time, usually unintentionally and without knowing. And I would bet tens of dollars that quite a few people say an epithet or two in their head when they're angry with someone who is of a different color or ethnic background. Sometimes it gets the better of them and escapes their mouth, which takes us back to the not so hidden bigotry.

And then there's the openly hidden racism (if ever there was an oxymoron): the self censorship and hyper-correction—all the efforts made to appear tolerant. ("Look at me! I have black friends!" "This African American gentleman from France," etc.) There was a sketch comedy show on FOX called MADtv when I was growing up that addressed this phenomenon perfectly. It had a recurring sketch about a musical group called The Eracists. They were so concerned with eliminating racism and bigotry that they ended up being more bigoted and racist than those they criticized.

The novel isn't meant to be preachy. Nor is its purpose anything other than entertaining you. But to that end, I wanted to make it realistic in certain ways. So some characters act and view the world in a particular manner. Take Christine, for instance. She's not really a racist, but she says racist things. Her various outbursts are merely a reflection of how people talk. Indeed, most of the dialogue in the novel was taken verbatim from what I heard people say in the street.

3

Should we be more tolerant then? Is that the novel's message? No. First, the novel doesn't really have a message. I write about stupidity and injustice, but I do not attempt to do anything other than mock them. Second, tolerance is a bunch of crap.

Tolerance and intolerance come from the same impulse—the impulse to categorize and rank individual, unique things. As a result, intolerance is always right around the corner. We can have an educated, perfectly civil population one moment and in the next they're lynching someone or putting people into ovens. Even in our remarkably tolerant society, by historical standards, if we encounter enough people during the day, we will meet those who are intolerant of something or someone. We might perhaps find ourselves to be intolerant (if we're honest).

When we are tolerant, what we do is tolerate. To tolerate something suggests our disliking it without outward complaint. We tolerate our neighbors' opposing (wrong and stupid) political views, their weird religious rituals, the foul odors coming from their kitchen. We tolerate their way of dressing, their smoking, their loud music, their accent, and so on. We tolerate because we do not like it.

If we did not find it unfamiliar, foreign, repulsive, or offensive, it would not be tolerance. There would be no need for tolerance if we liked it, if instead of bearing it we enjoyed it. We tolerate pain and discomfort. It makes no sense to say that we tolerate something pleasant. Tolerance is concentrating on similarities while actively suppressing, or at least not complaining about, the differences. Being intolerant is acting to reduce or eliminate what we perceive as a threat, the cause of our discomfort. Being tolerant is bearing it. That is, tolerance is conditional acceptance. It is internal suppression of what we dislike whereas intolerance is suppression directed outward.

4

So if tolerance is crap, then what? Consider the concept of hospitality as a better alternative. Hospitality is unconditional openness. When we are hosts, we are open to others. We let them into our domain. Hospitality comes from inner strength. Tolerance (and its mirror image intolerance), on the other hand, comes from weakness and fear.

We need less tolerance and intolerance and more hospitality. When we take each person as an irreducibly unique individual and not as a member of a group, we have no need to say stupid racist stuff like this: "just because x has y characteristics, that doesn't mean group X has y characteristics." This is a prime example of the third kind of racism

I mentioned earlier. When you put a person into a group like that your battle against racism is already lost.

But now I'm preaching. So I'll leave you with this: just because some people are kind, compassionate, smart, and generous, that doesn't mean the human race is.

ABOUT THE AUTHOR

Devin Hobbes is a curmudgeon who lives in New York and worries about the future. He is the author of numerous short stories, a few of which would have won him various accolades and medals had he submitted them to contests. Devin is proud of one story in particular. It won second place in a contest where it was the only entry.

www.ingramcontent.com/pod-product-compliance
Lightning Source LLC
Chambersburg PA
CBHW071635260626
47170CB00001B/106